The Science of Food

AN INTRODUCTION TO FOOD SCIENCE,
NUTRITION AND MICROBIOLOGY

THIRD EDITION

Titles of related interest

BIRCH *et al.*
Food Science, 3rd Edition

KENT & EVERS
Technology of Cereals, 4th Edition

LAWRIE
Meat Science, 5th Edition

STANBURY & WHITAKER
Principles of Fermentation Technology, 2nd Edition

TAMIME
Yoghurt: Science & Technology

The Science of Food

AN INTRODUCTION TO FOOD SCIENCE, NUTRITION AND MICROBIOLOGY

THIRD EDITION

by

P. M. GAMAN

and

K. B. SHERRINGTON

Butterworth-Heinemann
Linacre House, Jordan Hill, Oxford OX2 8DP
A division of Reed Educational and Professional Publishing Ltd

-R A member of the Reed Elsevier plc group

OXFORD LONDON BOSTON
NEW DELHI SINGAPORE SYDNEY
TOKYO TORONTO WELLINGTON

First published 1977
Second edition 1981
Third edition 1990
Reprinted 1994, 1996

British Library Cataloguing in Publication Data
Gaman, P. M.
    The science of food – 3rd ed.
    1. Food. Chemical constituents and properties
    I. Title   II. Sherrington, K. B.
    641.1

Library of Congress Cataloguing in Publication Data
Gaman, P. M.
    The science of food: an introduction to food science,
    nutrition, and microbiology 3rd ed.
    p. cm
    Includes bibliographical references
    1. Food – Composition. 2. Food – Microbiology
    3. Nutrition.   I. Sherrington, K. B.   II. Title
    641.1

ISBN 0 7506 2957 6

Printed and bound in Great Britain by BPC Wheatons Ltd, Exeter

Preface to Third Edition

In the course of teaching applied science to catering students, we came to realise the need for a textbook which dealt with the various scientific aspects of food preparation at an intermediate level.

In this book we have covered three different subject areas; food science, nutrition and microbiology. Microbiology has been given more emphasis than is usual in books on food science and nutrition, since we feel that this is an area which is often overlooked.

This book is intended to fill the gap between elementary books, containing little scientific explanation, and advanced books which examine the subjects in detail but are only suitable for those students who have a comprehensive scientific training. We have assumed little prior scientific knowledge on the part of the reader. An attempt has been made to convey basic scientific facts and principles, necessary for the understanding of food science, nutrition and microbiology, which are dealt with in some depth.

This book is intended primarily for students following BTEC diploma courses in Catering and Hospitality Management. It should also be of value to Home Economics students and students taking diploma courses in Food Science, Food Technology, Dietetics and Nutrition. It will serve as an introduction for undergraduates following degree courses in food related subjects. Science teachers in secondary schools may find it useful for developing courses in applied science. There may also be many other people, wishing to find out more about food and health, who would find this book both informative and interesting.

The third edition contains revised and updated information and figures. Since the second edition was published, there have been many changes in relation to nutrition and health, and in relation to the types and incidence of food poisoning. In this latest edition we have included sections on the NACNE and COMA reports together with practical measures for 'healthy eating'. The chapter on food poisoning and its prevention has been expanded into two chapters to include up-to-date information on food poisoning and an extended section on food legislation. We have also included an expanded section on irradiation of foods and a new chapter on food additives and food labelling.

Acknowledgements

We wish to acknowledge the help and encouragement given to us by many friends and colleagues during the writing of this book. Particular thanks go to Mrs. Valerie Ward for her very valuable assistance with proof reading.

Much of the statistical data in the book has been obtained from H.M.S.O. publications. The figures relating to the nutrient content of foods are taken from *McCance and Widdowson's The Composition of Foods* by A. A. Paul and D. A. T. Southgate and from the *Manual of Nutrition*.

The table in Appendix I which shows the percentage contribution of different foods to the nutrient content of the average household diet is an abridged version of that published in *Household Food Composition and Expenditure: 1984*. Appendix II, the table of recommended nutrient intakes, is a modified version of that published in *Recommended Daily Amounts of Food Energy and Nutrients for Groups of People in the U.K.* (1979). Both of these tables are reproduced with the permission of the Controller of Her Majesty's Stationery Office.

Contents

Introduction

Many people do not associate science with food. Even though they are aware of the rapid development of technology and of the applications of science to many aspects of everyday life, they remain unaware of the importance of science in the preparation of the food on their tables.

Scientific study related to the food we eat can be roughly divided into three broad categories: food science, nutrition and microbiology.

Food science involves the study of all aspects of science related to food. A major part of this book deals with the chemistry of food, since this is an important aspect. An understanding of the chemical nature of food is essential if one is to achieve an understanding of the composition of food and the reactions which take place in food when conditions are changed. A study of food science will explain, for example, why baking powder makes cakes rise or why freshly cut apples go brown when exposed to the air.

Food, like oxygen, is a necessity of life. The human body requires food as a source of energy and for the growth and replacement of tissues. Food also supplies substances which help to regulate the reactions involved in these processes. Nutrition is the study of the composition of food and the utilisation of food by the body. Foods are mixtures of substances known as nutrients. Each nutrient has a particular type of chemical composition and performs at least one specific function in the body.

The six groups of nutrients are:

1. Carbohydrates   provide energy and dietary fibre.
2. Fats and oils   provide energy.
3. Proteins   used for the growth and replacement of tissue, may also provide energy.
4. Vitamins   regulate body processes.
5. Minerals   regulate body processes; some are used for growth and replacement of tissue.
6. Water   essential for body processes.

A well-balanced diet is necessary for the maintenance of good health. This means that the food a person consumes should provide adequate, but not excessive, amounts of essential nutrients and energy. A poor diet leads to malnutrition, which literally means 'bad nutrition'. There are many types of malnutrition. Malnutrition may be caused by a lack of one or more of the essential nutrients in the diet. For example, a prolonged lack of vitamin C will give rise to a deficiency disease known as scurvy.

Not only is malnutrition caused by the consumption of foods with an incorrect nutrient balance but also by the consumption of either too little or too much food.

Insufficient food will lead to starvation, a form of malnutrition which, if prolonged, will lead to death. In some poorer, less developed parts of the world in recent years natural disasters, such as drought and flooding, have caused famines in which many people have died.

In wealthy, industrialised countries malnutrition occurs either as a result of eating too much food, or by the consumption of a diet with an unbalanced nutrient intake. Excesses and deficiencies of some components of the diet are associated with certain 'diseases of affluence'. For example, an excessive intake of fat is linked with heart disease, too little dietary fibre with cancer of the bowel, too much sugar with tooth decay and too much food (energy) with obesity (overweight). Advice is now available on how the diet should be altered in order to make it more healthy. It is recommended that the amounts of fat, sugar and salt in the diet should be reduced, while the amounts of starch and dietary fibre should be increased.

Microbiology is the study of microorganisms; these are very small, simple forms of life, such as bacteria and yeasts. Some species of microorganisms are beneficial and are used extensively in food production. Other types are responsible for many undesirable effects in food. Certain bacteria, if present in food in large enough numbers, will cause food poisoning. Currently there is widespread concern over the rapid increase in cases of food poisoning in England and Wales in recent years. Microorganisms can also cause food spoilage, e.g. the souring of milk, the growth of moulds on foods such as bread and cheese. A knowledge of the nature of microorganisms, their growth requirements and how growth can be prevented, is necessary if one is to understand correct procedures of hygiene and the principles involved in the various methods of food preservation.

In order to obtain adequate food supplies in urbanised societies, we depend very greatly on food technology. It is no longer possible for people to depend on locally grown, fresh foods. Food is now transported, often over very great distances, from rural areas, where it is produced, to urban areas. Unless food is processed or preserved in some way, much of it would be unfit for human consumption by the time it reaches the consumer. Food can be canned, frozen, chilled or dried in order to extend its shelf life. Preservation of food may also reduce the preparation and cooking time and is advantageous from the point of view of convenience. Many foods are 'manufactured' with convenience and acceptability in mind. Food technologists have developed a large variety of products ranging from frozen complete meals, dried soups, pie fillings and cake mixes to breakfast cereals. Food technology is an important part of modern society.

CHAPTER 1

Measurement

All scientific study involves accurate measurement. This applies to food science, nutrition and microbiology as much as to any other scientific discipline. For example, in order to assess the nutritional value of a food it is necessary to be able to state its nutrient content in precise terms.

The metric system has, for a long time, been the universal system of measurement in pure science. Being a decimal system it is logical and easy to use. Many people in Britain may still be more familiar with Imperial units (inches, pints, pounds, etc.) than with metric units (metres, litres, kilograms, etc.) but Imperial units are being phased out.

SI units

SI is an abbreviation for Système International d'Unités (International System of Units). It is an extension and refinement of the traditional metric system and it has been adopted in the United Kingdom for all scientific measurement. There are six basic SI units; each is used for measuring a different physical quantity and each is represented by a different symbol. These basic units are shown in Table 1.1.

TABLE 1.1. *Basic SI units*

Physical quantity	Name of unit	Symbol
Length	metre	m
Mass	kilogram	kg
Time	second	s
Electric current	ampere	A
Thermodynamic temperature	degree Kelvin	K
Luminous intensity	candela	cd

In addition there are other units, derived from these basic quantities, and also some non-SI units, still in common use, which are allowed in conjunction with SI. Units which are relevant to this book are shown in Table 1.2.

It is sometimes more convenient for practical purposes to use a unit considerably larger or smaller than the standard unit. In order to make the units larger or smaller, words can be used in front of the unit. These prefixes increase or decrease the basic units

1

TABLE 1.2. *Other units*

Physical quantity	Name of unit	Symbol	
Energy	joule	J	
Customary temperature	degree Celsius	°C	
Area	square metre	m²	
Volume	cubic metre	m³	derived units
Density	kilogram per cubic metre	kg m⁻³	
Force	newton	N	
Pressure	pascal	Pa	
Volume	litre	l	allowed in conjunction with SI

by multiples or fractions of ten. Each multiple or fraction has a symbol which is placed in front of the symbol of the unit (Table 1.3).

The following examples illustrate the use of prefixes:

$$5 \text{ kJ} = \text{five kilojoules} = \text{five thousand joules}$$
$$12 \text{ mm} = \text{twelve millimetres} = \text{twelve thousandths of a metre}$$
$$8 \text{ } \mu\text{g} = \text{eight micrograms} = \text{eight millionths of a gram}$$

N.B. Symbols never take a plural form; 12 mms would be incorrect.

TABLE 1.3. *Metric prefixes*

Multiple	Prefix	Symbol
10 (ten)	deca-	da
10^2 (hundred)	hecto-	h
10^3 (thousand)	kilo-	k
10^6 (million)	mega-	M

Fraction	Prefix	Symbol
10^{-1} (tenth)	deci-	d
10^{-2} (hundredth)	centi-	c
10^{-3} (thousandth)	milli-	m
10^{-6} (millionth)	micro-	μ
10^{-9} (thousand millionth)	nano-	n

Length

The basic unit for the measurement of length is the metre. Large distances are now measured in kilometres rather than miles, and small distances in centimetres or millimetres. Very short lengths, such as the wavelength of light and the size of micro-organisms, are measured in micrometres or nanometres.

$$1 \text{ kilometre (km)} = 1000 \text{ metres } (10^3 \text{ m})$$
$$1 \text{ centimetre (cm)} = \tfrac{1}{100} \text{ metre } (10^{-2} \text{ m})$$
$$1 \text{ millimetre (mm)} = \tfrac{1}{1000} \text{ metre } (10^{-3} \text{ m})$$

$$1 \text{ micrometre } (\mu m) = \tfrac{1}{1,000,000} \text{ metre } (10^{-6} \text{ m})$$
$$1 \text{ nanometre } (nm) = \tfrac{1}{1,000,000,000} \text{ metre } (10^{-9} \text{ m})$$

Some of the factors used for converting Imperial units to SI units are as follows:

$$1 \text{ inch} = 2.54 \text{ cm (approximately } 2\tfrac{1}{2}\text{)}$$
$$1 \text{ mile} = 1.61 \text{ km (approximately } \tfrac{8}{5}\text{)}$$

Area

Area is a physical quantity derived from the measurement of length.

$$\text{Area} = \text{length} \times \text{breadth}$$

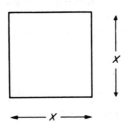

The area of a square of side x is x^2

The SI unit of area is the square metre.

$$1 \text{ square metre } (m^2) = 100 \text{ cm} \times 100 \text{ cm}$$
$$= 10,000 \text{ square centimetres } (10^4 \text{ cm}^2)$$

Volume and capacity

Volume is also derived from the measurement of length.

$$\text{Volume} = \text{length} \times \text{breadth} \times \text{height}$$

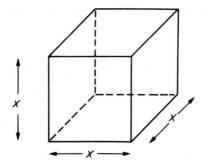

The volume of a cube of side x is x^3

The SI unit of volume is the cubic metre.

$$1 \text{ cubic metre (m}^3) = 100 \text{ cm} \times 100 \text{ cm} \times 100 \text{ cm}$$
$$= 1{,}000{,}000 \text{ cubic centimetres (}10^6 \text{ cm}^3)$$

For liquid measure or capacity the litre is the unit most often used. Quantities of wine are often measured in centilitres. The litre is derived from the measurment of volume, since it was originally defined as the volume occupied by 1 kg of water at its temperature of maximum density and under a pressure of one standard atmosphere.

$$1 \text{ litre (l)} = 1000 \text{ cm}^3$$
$$1 \text{ millilitre (ml)} = \tfrac{1}{1000} \text{ litre (}10^{-3}\text{ l)}$$

It will therefore follow that

$$1 \text{ millilitre (ml)} = 1 \text{ cubic centimetre (cm}^3)$$

Some of the factors used for converting Imperial units to SI units are as follows:

$$1 \text{ fluid ounce} = 28.4 \text{ ml}$$
$$1 \text{ pint} = 568 \text{ ml } (0.568 \text{ l})$$
$$1 \text{ gallon} = 4.55 \text{ l}$$

For some purposes it is convenient to know that

$$1 \text{ litre} = 1.76 \text{ pints (approximately } 1\tfrac{3}{4})$$

Mass and weight

For practical purposes mass and weight are the same and the terms are interchangeable, although the scientific definitions of mass and weight are different.

The basic SI unit of mass is the kilogram, which is now used instead of the pound. It has been suggested that a new name be found for the kilogram, since it is the only basic unit which is a multiple and has a prefix in its name. Quantities formerly measured in ounces are now measured in grams. Very small quantities of substances found in foods, such as vitamins and mineral elements, are measured in milligrams or micrograms. For large weights the tonne is used.

$$1 \text{ tonne (t)} = 1{,}000{,}000 \text{ grams (}10^6 \text{ g)}$$
$$1 \text{ kilogram (kg)} = 1000 \text{ grams (}10^3 \text{ g)}$$
$$1 \text{ milligram (mg)} = \tfrac{1}{1000} \text{ gram (}10^{-3} \text{ g)}$$
$$1 \text{ microgram (}\mu\text{g)} = \tfrac{1}{1{,}000{,}000} \text{ gram (}10^{-6} \text{ g)}$$

Some of the factors used for converting Imperial units to SI units are as follows:

$$1 \text{ ounce} = 28.4 \text{ g (approximately 30)}$$
$$1 \text{ pound} = 454 \text{ g } (0.454 \text{ kg—approximately } \tfrac{1}{2})$$
$$1 \text{ stone} = 6.35 \text{ kg}$$
$$1 \text{ ton} = 1.016 \text{ t (metric tonnes)}$$

For some purposes it is useful to remember that

$$1 \text{ kg} = 2.2 \text{ pounds}$$

Density

Density is derived from volume and weight. The density of a substance is a measure of its 'heaviness'. The popular expressions 'as heavy as lead' and 'as light as a feather' imply correctly that lead has a high density and feathers a very low density. A given weight of feathers will occupy a much greater volume than the same weight of lead.

$$\text{Density} = \frac{\text{Weight}}{\text{Volume}}$$

Since the SI unit of weight is the kilogram and the unit of volume is the cubic metre, the SI unit of density is the kilogram per cubic metre (kg/m^3 or more correctly $kg\ m^{-3}$). Density is also measured in grams per cubic centimetre ($g\ cm^{-3}$). The density of water is $1.0\ g\ cm^{-3}$. The **Relative Density** (RD) of a substance is the number of times a substance is heavier than an equal volume of water, i.e. its density relative to water.

$$\text{Relative Density} = \frac{\text{Density of substance}}{\text{Density of water}}$$

N.B. Relative density is a ratio and therefore has no units.

If a substance is dissolved in water to form a solution, the density is altered. The density varies directly with the concentration of the solution. Most substances, e.g. sugar and salt, cause the density to increase but sometimes the density may be lowered, e.g. by the presence of fat or alcohol.

A quick method of determining the concentration of pure solutions in water is to measure the density of the solution, using an instrument known as a **hydrometer**.

A hydrometer consists of a glass bulb weighted with lead shot; attached to this is a thin glass stem bearing a scale (see Figure 1.1).

The hydrometer is placed in the solution so that it floats freely. The further it sinks into the solution the lower the density. The scale may give the density of the solution or it may be calibrated to give a direct reading of the concentration of a substance. Some examples of hydrometers used to give direct readings of concentration are saccharo-

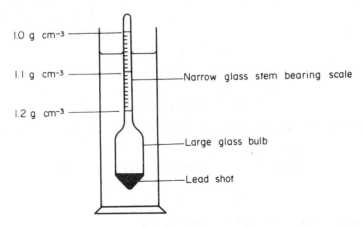

1.0 g cm⁻³

1.1 g cm⁻³

1.2 g cm⁻³

—Narrow glass stem bearing scale

—Large glass bulb

—Lead shot

Fig. 1.1. Diagram of a hydrometer used to measure densities in the range $1.0\ g\ cm^{-3}$ to $1.2\ g\ cm^{-3}$.

meters, used to measure sugar in solution, and salinometers, which measure the concentration of brine (salt solutions). Lactometers are used in dairies to give a rapid measurement of the density of milk, giving an indication of its quality. Normal milk should have a relative density of 1.030. In the wine industry hydrometers are used to show how much alcohol has been produced during fermentation.

Energy

The measurement of the energy released when a nutrient or food is oxidised is of importance in nutrition. The energy value of a food can be assessed by burning the food in oxygen and measuring the amount of heat energy produced.

The SI unit of energy is the joule and this has replaced the calorie. In nutrition the kilojoule has replaced the kilocalorie.

$$1 \text{ kilojoule (kJ)} = 1000 \text{ joules}$$

The factor used for conversion is

$$1 \text{ kilocalorie (kcal)} = 4.18 \text{ kilojoules (kJ)}$$

Kilocalories are often written as Calories (using a capital letter).

$$1 \text{ kilocalorie} = 1 \text{ Calorie (Cal)} = 1000 \text{ calories (cal)}$$

The use of the same word for two units of widely differing magnitudes causes a lot of confusion and term kilocalorie is preferred.

Temperature

The customary unit of temperature is the degree Celsius (°C). The Celsius (or Centigrade) scale is a temperature scale in which the melting point of ice is 0° and the boiling point of water is 100°. On the Fahrenheit scale the melting point of ice is 32° and the boiling point of water is 212°.

Fixed point	Celsius scale	Fahrenheit scale
Melting point of ice	0°	32°
Boiling point of water	100°	212°

On the Celsius scale it can be seen that there are 100 degrees between the two fixed points, whereas on the Fahrenheit scale there are 180 degrees. The ratio 100:180 is equal to 5:9 and therefore 5 Celsius degrees are equal to 9 Fahrenheit degrees.

To convert °C to °F
(a) Multiply by 9 then
(b) Divide by 5 then
(c) Add 32

Example: to convert 10°C to °F
(a) $10 \times 9 = 90$
(b) $90 \div 5 = 18$
(c) $18 + 32 = 50$
10°Celsius = 50°Fahrenheit

To convert $°F$ *to* $°C$
(a) Subtract 32 then
(b) Multiply by 5 then
(c) Divide by 9

Example: to convert $104°F$ *to* $°C$
(a) $104 - 32 = 72$
(b) $72 \times 5 = 360$
(c) $360 \div 9 = 40$

$104°$Fahrenheit $= 40°$Celsius

CHAPTER 2

Basic Chemistry

All foods are either pure chemical compounds or mixtures of chemical compounds. Therefore, in order to understand something of the nature of food substances and the way in which they behave, it is necessary to have a fundamental knowledge of chemistry. Substances, also termed matter, can exist in three states: solid, liquid and gaseous. Chemistry is the study of the composition and behaviour of matter.

Atoms and elements

All substances that exist, either living or non-living, are made up of atoms. Atoms themselves are made up of smaller particles, the three main ones being the proton, the neutron and the electron. The nucleus of an atom consists of protons and neutrons. The proton has a positive electrical charge and the neutron has no charge. The electron orbits the nucleus and has a negative electrical charge, which is equal but opposite to the charge on the proton.

The simplest type of atom is the hydrogen atom. Its nucleus consists of a single proton and it has one electron orbiting the nucleus (see Figure 2.1). The carbon atom, on the other hand, has six protons and six neutrons in the nucleus and six electrons orbiting the nucleus. There are two electrons in the first orbit and four in the second orbit. Simple representations of a hydrogen atom and a carbon atom are shown in Figure 2.1.

It will be noticed that, in each case, the number of protons is equal to the number of electrons. Since the charges on the proton and electron are equal but opposite, the atom is electrically neutral.

So far, 105 different types of atoms have been discovered. This means that matter is made up of 105 fundamental substances called elements. Each element has its own type of atom; the hydrogen atom, for example, is different from the carbon atom.

An element is a simple substance consisting of atoms of only one type. It cannot be broken down into anything simpler by any known chemical process. By including the phrase 'by any known chemical process' in this definition, allowance is made for the fact that, since the discovery of radioactivity, certain elements, e.g. uranium, have been shown to undergo a *physical* process of decay producing other substances, i.e. other elements.

An atom may be defined as the smallest particle of an element which can exist and still show the properties of that element.

Of the 105 elements, 92 occur naturally in the Earth's crust or its atmosphere. The remainder have been made artificially by the use of nuclear processes.

Hydrogen atom   Carbon atom

Fig. 2.1. Diagrammatic representation of a hydrogen atom and a carbon atom.

Elements can be divided into two groups, according to their chemical behaviour. They are either metals or non-metals.

Each element has a chemical symbol, i.e. one or two letters which represent one atom of the element. In many cases this symbol is the first letter of the name written as a capital:

C for carbon

Since many elements start with the same letter, it is often necessary to use the first letter and another:

Ca for calcium   Cl for chlorine

For some elements, the symbol is not derived from the English name but from the name in another language:

Na for sodium   K for potassium

Table 2.1 gives the symbols of elements of importance in food science.

TABLE 2.1. *Elements of importance in food science*

Element	Symbol	
Carbon	C	
Hydrogen	H	
Oxygen	O	Non-metals. The constituents of proteins, fats
Nitrogen	N	and carbohydrates.
Sulphur	S	
Phosphorus	P	
Sodium	Na	
Potassium	K	Reactive metals. Found in foods and essential
Calcium	Ca	for the functioning of the body.
Magnesium	Mg	
Chlorine	Cl	
Iodine	I	Halogens. A group of non-metals with similar
Fluorine	F	chemical properties. Chlorine and iodine
Bromine	Br	are essential in the diet.
Iron	Fe	
Zinc	Zn	
Copper	Cu	Metals. All are essential in the diet.
Cobalt	Co	
Manganese	Mn	
Aluminium	Al	
Lead	Pb	Metals. Not essential in the diet.
Tin	Sn	

Molecules and compounds

In many elements, particularly in the gaseous state, atoms are incapable of existing independently and are found combined with each other. Two or more atoms so combined form a molecule.

$$H \quad + \quad H \quad \longrightarrow \quad H_2$$

| 1 atom of | 1 atom of | 1 molecule of |
| hydrogen | hydrogen | hydrogen |

A small number after the symbol H indicates the presence of two hydrogen atoms in the molecule. The number of atoms contained in each molecule is constant and is termed the atomicity. Most common gases are diatomic (one molecule contains two atoms), e.g. oxygen (O_2), nitrogen (N_2) and chlorine (Cl_2).

A molecule may be defined as the smallest portion of a substance capable of existing independently and retaining the properties of the original substance.

Atoms of different elements may also combine chemically to form molecules, e.g. one molecule of water (H_2O) consists of two atoms of hydrogen combined with one atom of oxygen. In nature elements rarely occur in the pure state. They are usually found in combination with each other as more complex substances. These substances are called compounds.

A compound is a substance containing two or more elements chemically combined.

Water is a substance formed when the elements oxygen and hydrogen combine. Sodium chloride (NaCl) or table salt is another example of a compound; it contains the elements sodium and chlorine. It can be seen that a molecule is the smallest particle of a compound that can exist.

The formation of molecules

Some elements are very reactive and readily form compounds; others are unreactive or stable. The electrons of an atom are arranged in orbits or *shells*. The reactivity of an atom depends on the number of electrons in the outer shell and these are called the valency electrons. Each shell can only contain a certain number of electrons. The first or

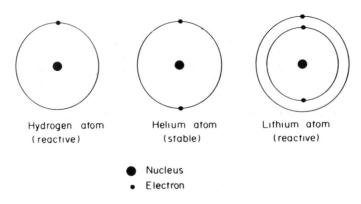

| Hydrogen atom | Helium atom | Lithium atom |
| (reactive) | (stable) | (reactive) |

● Nucleus
• Electron

Fig. 2.2. Atoms of the three lightest elements.

TABLE 2.2. *Electron arrangements in inert gases and halogens*

Inert gases	Electron shells			Halogens	Electron shells				
	1st	2nd	3rd		1st	2nd	3rd	4th	5th
Helium	2			Fluorine	2	7			
Neon	2	8		Chlorine	2	8	7		
Argon	2	8	8	Bromine	2	8	18	7	
				Iodine	2	8	18	18	7

innermost shell can contain two electrons but no more. The second shell is capable of holding eight electrons. The third can also hold eight, though atoms of some elements can hold eighteen, ten being in a sub-shell.

Each shell is filled in turn starting with the innermost shell and moving outwards. If the outer shell is 'full up' with electrons then that atom will be stable and unreactive. If a shell is not 'full up' then the atom is said to be reactive, because it will tend to combine with other atoms to obtain full shells.

Looking at the three lightest elements (shown in Figure 2.2) it can be seen that hydrogen has one electron only and it therefore needs one more electron to become stable. Helium has two electrons; this is a stable number (first shell) and therefore helium is unreactive. Lithium has two electrons in the first shell and one electron in the second shell. It needs to lose one electron to become stable. Lithium is a very reactive metal.

Elements with the same number of electrons in the outer shell of their atoms have similar chemical properties since they will react in a similar way with other elements. The inert gases are a group of elements which all have outer shells which are 'full up'. The halogens are a group of elements which all have seven electrons in the outer shell (see Table 2.2).

Elements combine in one of two ways to form compounds.

1. Ionic compounds

Ionic bonding involves the transfer of electrons. Atoms containing one, two or three electrons in the outer shell, i.e. metallic elements, may lose electrons in order to obtain a

Sodium atom   Chlorine atom   Sodium ion   Chloride ion

Sodium chloride 'molecule'

● Nucleus

• Valency electron

○ Inner shell electron

FIG. 2.3. Formation of a sodium chloride 'molecule'.

stable structure. These electrons are donated to atoms of non-metallic elements containing six or seven electrons in the outer shell, thus filling these shells.

For example, during the formation of sodium chloride each sodium atom loses an electron and this is transferred to the outer shell of a chlorine atom (see Figure 2.3). Since the sodium atom has lost an electron it will have an overall positive charge. A charged atom is called an **ion**. Similarly the chlorine atom becomes a chloride ion.

The positively and negatively charged ions attract each other and are held together by this electrostatic force forming a 'molecule' of sodium chloride. The structure of sodium chloride is three-dimensional but can be represented in two dimensions as illustrated in Figure 2.4.

○ – Sodium ion

● – Chloride ion

FIG. 2.4. The structure of sodium chloride.

An ion is represented by the symbol for an element together with a sign indicating the number and nature of the charges it carries:

Na^+ represents a sodium ion
Cl^- represents a chloride ion

An atom which loses two electrons, e.g. calcium, forms ions with two positive charges:

Ca^{2+} represents a calcium ion

A 'molecule' of sodium chloride contains one sodium and one chloride ion and can be represented as Na^+Cl^-. It is more usual to write Na^+Cl^- simply as NaCl. NaCl is not strictly a molecule, since the ions are not actually joined, but it can be thought of as a molecule for the purposes of studying chemical reactions and writing chemical equations.

2. Covalent compounds

Covalent bonding involves the sharing of electrons. Atoms containing four, five or six electrons in the outer shell can obtain a stable structure by sharing electrons. Hydrogen can also form compounds in this way. The majority of carbon compounds are covalent. Carbon has four valency electrons, i.e. four electrons in the outer shell, and each of these is available for sharing.

In the formation of a molecule of methane one carbon atom combines with four hydrogen atoms as shown in Figure 2.5. It can be seen that the carbon atom will now have a stable number of eight electrons in its outer shell and each hydrogen nucleus will have two electrons orbiting it. This is a stable number for hydrogen since the first shell can only hold two electrons.

Mixtures

A substance may be composed of two or more elements or compounds which are physically mixed together but are not chemically combined. This type of substance is called a mixture. It is important to distinguish between compounds and mixtures. When compounds are formed a **chemical change** takes place. If substances are only mixed

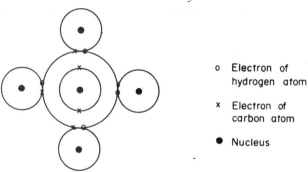

o Electron of
   hydrogen atom

x Electron of
   carbon atom

● Nucleus

FIG. 2.5. A methane molecule.

together it is a **physical change**. Changes of state, e.g. from solid to liquid, are also physical changes. In a physical change no new substances are produced but a chemical reaction always produces new substances.

A compound is a substance which has a fixed composition. For example, water always contains twice as many hydrogen atoms as oxygen atoms. A mixture, on the other hand, has no fixed composition. A mixture of hydrogen and oxygen could contain 50% hydrogen and 50% oxygen, or 90% hydrogen and 10% oxygen or any other proportions. A further difference between compounds and mixtures is that a mixture will always show the same properties as the elements or compounds from which it is made. A compound does not show the properties of its constituent elements. For example, the compound sodium chloride (common salt) is made of the elements sodium and chlorine. Sodium is a dangerous, reactive metal and chlorine is a poisonous gas but the compound sodium chloride is neither dangerous nor poisonous.

A compound can only be separated into its constituent elements by chemical means, whereas a mixture can be separated by physical means. For example, a mixture of salt and water can be separated into its components (salt and water) by a physical process of distillation. The formation of a compound is accompanied by a significant energy change. For example, in the burning of coal, when carbon combines with oxygen to form carbon dioxide, a large amount of heat is produced.

Table 2.3 summarises the main differences between compounds and mixtures.

TABLE 2.3. *The main differences between compounds and mixtures*

Compounds	Mixtures
Have a definite composition	No fixed composition
Do not show properties of constituent elements	Show properties of constituent elements and compounds
Can only be separated into their constituent elements by chemical means	Can be separated into their constituents by physical means
Examples:	Examples:
Water	Air
Salt	Salt solution
Carbon dioxide	Flour
	Milk

Salt is a compound of the elements sodium and chlorine, whereas a salt solution is a mixture of the two compounds salt and water. Air is a mixture of the elements oxygen and nitrogen and the compound carbon dioxide. Milk, flour and most other foods are complex mixtures of many substances.

Chemical formulae and equations

Molecular formulae

Chemical compounds may be represented by molecular formulae, which show the number of atoms of each type of element present in one molecule.

H_2O represents one molecule of water containing two atoms of hydrogen and one atom of oxygen.

$NaCl$ represents one molecule of sodium chloride containing one atom of sodium and one atom of chlorine.

CH_4 represents one molecule of methane containing one atom of carbon and four atoms of hydrogen.

The small number after the symbol indicates how many atoms of that element are present in the molecule. A large number in front of the molecule indicates the number of molecules present, e.g. $2H_2O$ represents two molecules of water.

Equations

All chemical reactions can be represented by using molecular formulae and writing a **chemical equation**. An equation shows the rearrangement of atoms which takes place during a chemical reaction. In a chemical reaction matter is neither created nor destroyed and therefore the same number of atoms of each element must remain after the reaction has taken place.

The following is an example of a chemical equation:

$$2H_2 \quad + \quad O_2 \quad \longrightarrow \quad 2H_2O$$

two molecules of hydrogen	one molecule of oxygen	two molecules of water
(four atoms of hydrogen)	(two atoms of oxygen)	(four atoms of hydrogen and two atoms of oxygen)

Sometimes in a reaction a group of atoms remain joined together and tend to behave as a single ion. These groups of atoms are called **radicals**. They are incapable of an independent existence and always combine with other ions.

Table 2.4 shows some of the common radicals.

TABLE 2.4. *Some common radicals and their symbols*

Radical	Symbol
Ammonium	NH_4^+
Hydrogen carbonate	HCO_3^-
Carbonate	CO_3^{2-}
Hydroxide	OH^-
Nitrate	NO_3^-
Nitrite	NO_2^-
Phosphate	PO_4^{3-}
Sulphate	SO_4^{2-}
Sulphite	SO_3^{2-}

In order to write a chemical formula or equation, it is necessary to know the **valency** of the elements and radicals involved. The valency of an atom or radical is a whole number indicating its combining power. It is related to the atomic structure and more precisely to the number of valency electrons. Valency is equal to the number of electrons needed to be gained or lost in order to obtain a stable number of electrons in the outer shell (2, 8, 8, etc.). The hydrogen atom is the simplest atom and contains one valency electron. This electron can be given to another atom or can be used to form part of a covalent bond. Valency is defined using hydrogen as a standard. **Valency is the number of hydrogen atoms which will combine with or replace an atom or radical.**

One atom of oxygen (which has six valency electrons and requires two more to become stable) combines with two atoms of hydrogen to form water. Therefore, the valency of oxygen is two.

Table 2.5 shows the valencies of common elements and radicals.

Hydrogen is capable of showing both metallic and non-metallic behaviour, when it takes part in chemical reactions. Some elements, e.g. copper and iron, exhibit more than one valency. In compounds, the valency is indicated by a Roman numeral placed in brackets after the name of the element, e.g. copper(I) oxide and copper(II) oxide.

The valency of atoms and radicals may be represented by drawing the atoms and radicals with hooks. If the valency is one, the atom or radical is drawn with one hook; if the valency is two, it is drawn with two hooks, etc. When atoms and radicals combine, all the hooks must link up. For example, when magnesium combines with oxygen:

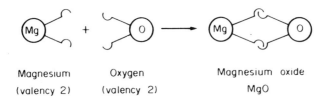

Magnesium	Oxygen	Magnesium oxide
(valency 2)	(valency 2)	MgO

When aluminium ions combine with sulphate radicals:

Aluminium	Sulphate	Aluminium sulphate
(valency 3)	(valency 2)	$Al_2(SO_4)_3$

Three sulphate ions are present in the aluminium sulphate molecule and this is represented by using brackets with a small '3' outside.

Having determined the formulae of the starting materials and products in a chemical

The Science of Food

Table 2.5. *Valencies of common elements and radicals*

Valency	Elements		Radicals
	Metals	Non-metals	
1	Hydrogen (H) Copper (Cu) Potassium (K) Sodium (Na)	Chlorine (Cl) Hydrogen (H) Iodine (I)	Ammonium (NH_4) Hydrogen carbonate (HCO_3) Hydroxide (OH) Nitrate (NO_3) Nitrite (NO_2)
2	Calcium (Ca) Copper (Cu) Iron (Fe) Magnesium (Mg) Zinc (Zn)	Oxygen (O) Sulphur (S)	Carbonate (CO_3) Sulphate (SO_4) Sulphite (SO_3)
3	Aluminium (Al) Iron (Fe)	Nitrogen (N)	Phosphate (PO_4)
4		Carbon (C)	

reaction, an equation can be written. For example:

$$NaHCO_3 \longrightarrow Na_2CO_3 + CO_2 + H_2O$$

sodium hydrogen carbonate   sodium carbonate   carbon dioxide   water

This equation is not correct, since it is not balanced. There are not the same number of atoms of each element on each side of the equation. There are two sodium atoms on the right-hand side and only one on the left-hand side. There must, therefore, be two molecules of sodium hydrogen carbonate taking part in this reaction. It can now be seen that the equation will balance:

$$2NaHCO_3 \longrightarrow Na_2CO_3 + CO_2 + H_2O$$

A more complicated reaction is the oxidation of glucose. Glucose, when oxidised, produces carbon dioxide and water.

$$C_6H_{12}O_6 + O_2 \longrightarrow CO_2 + H_2O$$

glucose   oxygen   carbon dioxide   water

To balance this equation it must be written:

$$C_6H_{12}O_6 + 6O_2 \longrightarrow 6CO_2 + 6H_2O$$

Acids, alkalis and salts

Nearly all foods contain water and the nutrients are dispersed in this water. Therefore, in the study of food science it is necessary to understand something of the nature of water and the way in which it behaves. Nearly all the water is in the form of molecules but a small number of molecules are ionised.

$$H_2O \rightleftharpoons H^+ + OH^-$$

water molecule   hydrogen ion   hydroxyl ion

In pure water the number of hydrogen ions is equal to the number of hydroxyl ions, therefore pure water is neutral, i.e. neither acidic nor alkaline.

When substances are dissolved in water, the ratio of hydrogen to hydroxyl ions may be altered. If the number of hydrogen ions is greater than the number of hydroxyl ions, the solution is said to be acidic. If it is the reverse, the solution is alkaline.

pH

pH is a measure of the acidity or alkalinity of a solution. It is a term derived from the concentration of hydrogen ions in the solution.

$$pH = \log_{10}\frac{1}{[H^+]} \quad \text{where} \quad [H^+] = \text{hydrogen ion concentration}$$

If the concentration of hydrogen ions (i.e. acidity) increases, the pH decreases.
The pH scale extends from 0 to 14, 7 being neutral.

$$0 \longleftarrow 7 \longrightarrow 14$$

increasing $\uparrow$ increasing
acidity | alkalinity
neutral

Alterations in pH of solutions are important and can have dramatic effects, e.g. egg white coagulates when the solution is made very acidic or very alkaline. The growth of microorganisms can be controlled by reducing the pH of food. For example, the pickling of foods in vinegar, which contains acetic acid, is a method of preventing microbial food spoilage.

When foods are pickled, they may change colour, because the vegetable dyes responsible for colour are altered by changes of pH. Red cabbage is red when pickled but purple when fresh and blue if placed in alkali. Vegetable dyes may be used as indicators of pH, e.g. litmus is red in acids and blue in alkalis. Universal indicator is a mixture of several indicators and shows the degree of acidity or alkalinity of a solution.

Acids

Acids are substances which dissolve in water, producing hydrogen ions.
For example:

$$HCl \longrightarrow H^+ + Cl^-$$

hydrochloric   hydrogen   chloride
acid   ion   ion

Hydrochloric acid is a strong acid, since it ionises completely. Weak acids are those which ionise partially in dilute solution, e.g. acetic acid.

$$CH_3COOH \rightleftharpoons CH_3COO^- + H^+$$

acetic   acetate   hydrogen
acid   ion   ion

The terms 'strong' and 'weak' should not be confused with concentration. Concentrated solutions of some weak acids, e.g. acetic acid, are dangerous and should be handled with care.

Properties of acids

1. The pH of acids is in the range 0 to 7. Acids will turn blue litmus paper red.
2. Acids have a sour taste, e.g. citric acid is responsible for the sour taste of lemon juice.
3. Concentrated solutions of strong acids are corrosive and may damage skin and clothing.
4. Acids react with carbonates or hydrogen carbonates producing carbon dioxide. This is the basis of the action of baking powders (see page 20).

INORGANIC ACIDS

Hydrochloric acid	HCl
Sulphuric acid	H_2SO_4
Nitric acid	HNO_3

These are strong acids and are useful as laboratory reagents. Hydrochloric acid is one of the constituents of gastric juice. It is secreted by the stomach wall and assists the action of the enzyme pepsin (see page 133).

ORGANIC ACIDS

These are weak acids and many are found in foods. Some of the more important ones are shown in Table 2.6. The formulae of some of these acids are given in Chapter 3.

TABLE 2.6. *Some acids found in foods*

Common name of acid	Chemical name	Found in/used in
Acetic	Ethanoic acid	Vinegar
Ascorbic (Vitamin C)		Fresh fruits and vegetables
Benzoic		Preservative. Added to fruit drinks
Citric	Hydroxypropane 1,2,3 tricarboxylic acid	Citrus fruits
Lactic	2 hydroxypropanoic acid	Sour milk, yoghurt
Malic	2 hydroxybutanedioic acid	Apples, cherries
Oxalic	Ethanedioic acid	Spinach, rhubarb. Poisonous in large quantities
Tartaric	2,3 dihydroxybutanedioic acid	Grapes. Used in baking powders

Alkalis

Alkalis are substances which dissolve in water, producing hydroxyl ions. Alkalis are usually oxides or hydroxides of metals, e.g. sodium hydroxide.

$$NaOH \longrightarrow Na^+ + OH^-$$

sodium hydroxide	sodium ion	hydroxyl ion

Properties of alkalis

1. The pH of an alkali is in the range 7 to 14. Alkaline solutions turn red litmus paper blue.
2. Alkalis have a bitter taste. Very few foods are alkaline.
3. Solutions of alkalis have a soapy feel. A solution of soap in water is alkaline.
4. Concentrated solutions of alkalis are corrosive.

Some common alkalis are shown in Table 2.7.

TABLE 2.7. *Some common alkalis*

Alkali	Common name	Formula	Uses
Ammonium hydroxide		NH_4OH	Cleaning agents, e.g. non-scratch bath cleaners
Calcium hydroxide	Slaked lime	$Ca(OH)_2$	Water softener. Commercial extraction of gelatin from bones and skin
Potassium hydroxide	Caustic potash	KOH	Manufacture of toilet soap
Sodium hydroxide	Caustic soda	$NaOH$	Manufacture of soap and soap powder. Grease remover

Neutralisation

Neutralisation is the reaction between an acid and an alkali producing a salt and water only.

$$\text{Acid} \ + \ \text{Alkali} \longrightarrow \text{Salt} \ + \ \text{Water}$$

For example:

$$\underset{\substack{\text{hydrochloric} \\ \text{acid}}}{HCl} \ + \ \underset{\substack{\text{sodium} \\ \text{hydroxide}}}{NaOH} \longrightarrow \underset{\substack{\text{sodium} \\ \text{chloride} \\ \text{(a salt)}}}{NaCl} \ + \ \underset{\text{water}}{H_2O}$$

The hydrogen ions produced by the acid combine with the hydroxyl ions produced by the alkali and form water.

$$H^+ \ + \ OH^- \longrightarrow H_2O$$

Vinegar can be used for rinsing woollen garments after they have been washed in soap. This neutralises the alkaline soap solution, which can damage wool.

Salts

Salts are ionic compounds, which can be produced by neutralisation or by the reaction between a metal and an acid.

$$\text{Metal} \ + \ \text{Acid} \longrightarrow \text{Salt} \ + \ \text{Hydrogen}$$

For example:

$$Zn \quad + \quad H_2SO_4 \quad \longrightarrow \quad ZnSO_4 \quad + \quad H_2$$

zinc   sulphuric   zinc   hydrogen
acid   sulphate

If an acid which contains more than one hydrogen ion is not completely neutralised, an acid salt is produced. For example:

$$H_2SO_4 \quad + \quad NaOH \longrightarrow \quad NaHSO_4 \quad + \quad H_2O$$

sulphuric   sodium   sodium   water
acid   hydroxide   hydrogen
sulphate
(sodium bisulphate)

Sodium hydrogen sulphate is an acid salt, since it still contains a replaceable hydrogen atom.

Properties of salts

1. Salts have a high melting-point and can be obtained as crystalline solids.
2. Salts in solution in water usually have a pH of 7, i.e. they are neutral. This is not always the case. If the salt is formed from a strong alkali and a weak acid, the solution will be alkaline. Sodium carbonate is formed from sodium hydroxide, a strong alkali and carbonic acid, a weak acid, and therefore sodium carbonate is alkaline in solution.
3. The solubility of salts varies. Many, but not all, salts are soluble in water. In general, salts of sodium and potassium are soluble and calcium salts are insoluble.

Table 2.8 lists some salts, together with their formulae and uses.

Chemical aeration

Baking powders

Baking powders are mixtures of substances which produce carbon dioxide when water is added and they are heated. The carbon dioxide gas causes baked goods to rise.

The most usual type of baking powder contains sodium hydrogen carbonate (bicarbonate of soda) and an acid ingredient. On the addition of water the acid reacts with the hydrogen carbonate, producing a salt, water and carbon dioxide.

$$NaHCO_3 + \quad HX \quad \longrightarrow \quad NaX \quad + \quad H_2O \quad + \quad CO_2$$

sodium   acid   salt   water   carbon
hydrogen   dioxide
carbonate

One of the most usual acid ingredients is potassium hydrogen tartrate (cream of tartar). This is an acid salt of tartaric acid, since it still retains some replaceable hydrogen.

| Sodium hydrogen carbonate | + | Potassium hydrogen tartrate | $\longrightarrow$ | Sodium potassium tartrate | + | Water | + | Carbon dioxide |

TABLE 2.8. *Some salts of importance in food science*

Salts of inorganic acids	Formula	Use
Ammonium carbonate 'Vol'	$(NH_4)_2CO_3$	Raising agent
Calcium carbonate 'chalk'	$CaCO_3$	Flour additive (increases calcium content)
Potassium bromate	$KBrO_3$	Flour improver
Potassium chloride	KCl	Salt substitute for low sodium diets
Potassium iodide	KI	Iodine constituent of 'iodised' salt
Potassium nitrate 'saltpetre'	KNO_3	Meat preservative
Sodium carbonate 'washing soda'	Na_2CO_3	Water softener
Sodium chloride 'salt'	$NaCl$	Flavouring agent and preservative
Sodium hydrogen carbonate 'baking soda'	$NaHCO_3$	Raising agent
Sodium hypochlorite	$NaOCl$	Bleach and disinfectant
Sodium metabisulphite 'Campden tablets'	$Na_2S_2O_5$	Fruit and vegetable preservative
Sodium nitrate 'Chile saltpetre'	$NaNO_3$	Meat preservative
Sodium sulphite	Na_2SO_3	Fruit and vegetable preservative

Salts of organic acids		Use
Monosodium glutamate 'MSG'		Flavour enhancer
Potassium hydrogen tartrate 'cream of tartar'		Baking powder

Other acid ingredients which are used include tartaric acid, acid calcium phosphate (ACP) and acid sodium pyrophosphate (ASP).

Tartaric acid, cream of tartar and ACP are used in quick-acting baking powders, in which most of the carbon dioxide is produced when water is added. ASP is used in slow-acting baking powders, which produce most of their carbon dioxide during baking. Most commercial baking powders contain both slow-acting and quick-acting ingredients. They also contain a filler, usually corn starch, which helps to keep the ingredients dry and prevents them reacting with each other before baking.

The acid ingredients may be supplied by a food. The best example of this is the use of sour milk, containing lactic acid, in the making of soda bread. Vinegar or lemon juice may also be used to provide acids.

Hydrogen carbonates or carbonates can be used on their own without an acid ingredient; they release carbon dioxide on heating. If sodium hydrogen carbonate is used alone, sodium carbonate, carbon dioxide and water are produced.

$$2NaHCO_3 \longrightarrow Na_2CO_3 + H_2O + CO_2$$

sodium hydrogen carbonate — sodium carbonate — water — carbon dioxide

Sodium carbonate is present in the baked product as an alkaline residue, which is yellow in colour and slightly bitter in taste. In a dark, strongly flavoured product, such as gingerbread, this does not matter.

Ammonium hydrogen carbonate and ammonium carbonate are used commercially in the production of some biscuits. They do not leave an alkaline residue. Ammonia is released as a vapour during baking.

$$NH_4HCO_3 \longrightarrow NH_3 + H_2O + CO_2$$

ammonium   ammonia   water   carbon
hydrogen   dioxide
carbonate

$$(NH_4)_2CO_3 \longrightarrow 2NH_3 + H_2O + CO_2$$

ammonium   ammonia   water   carbon
carbonate   dioxide

Oxidation and reduction

Oxidation is a reaction in which an element or compound combines with oxygen. For example, when iron rusts, the metal combines with oxygen forming the oxide.

$$4Fe + 3O_2 \longrightarrow 2Fe_2O_3$$

iron   oxygen   iron(III) oxide
(rust)

When methane is oxidised, the hydrogen is removed and is combined with oxygen, forming water.

$$CH_4 + 2O_2 \longrightarrow CO_2 + H_2O$$

methane   oxygen   carbon   water
dioxide

The term 'oxidation' can be extended to include the displacement of hydrogen in reactions in which there is no oxygen present. Hydrogen sulphide can be oxidised by chlorine, which combines with the hydrogen, forming hydrochloric acid.

$$H_2S + Cl_2 \longrightarrow 2HCl + S$$

hydrogen   chlorine   hydrochloric   sulphur
sulphide   acid

Examples of oxidation processes:

1. *Combustion,* in which substances combine with oxygen, forming oxides. Heat and light are produced during the reaction, e.g. the burning of coal in air.

$$C + O_2 \longrightarrow CO_2$$

carbon   oxygen   carbon
in coal   in air   dioxide

2. *Aerobic respiration* is the liberation of energy from food by reaction with oxygen, e.g. the oxidation of glucose.

$$C_6H_{12}O_6 + 6O_2 \longrightarrow 6CO_2 + 6H_2O$$

glucose   oxygen   carbon   water
dioxide

3. *Bleaching* involves the addition of oxygen to a coloured compound, converting it into a colourless compound, e.g. chlorine dioxide is used to bleach flour.

4. *Rusting* is a slow process, in which oxygen combines with iron in the presence of water, forming rust (iron (III) oxide).

5. *Rancidity* in fats is partly due to the addition of oxygen to fatty acids and the production of peroxides, which are responsible for 'off' flavours.

6. *Enzymic browning* occurs when oxygen from the air reacts with substances in food, in the presence of enzymes, forming brown compounds, e.g. the browning of freshly cut apples.

7. *Tarnishing* of metals is the slow addition of oxygen to the surface layer of a metal, forming a dull oxide layer. Aluminium is one of the metals which tarnishes in this way.

$$4Al \quad + \quad 3O_2 \quad \longrightarrow \quad 2Al_2O_3$$

aluminium   oxygen   aluminium
                                   oxide

8. *Action of disinfectants.* Chlorine, which is used as a disinfectant, i.e. it kills bacteria, combines with water forming hypochlorous acid.

$$Cl_2 \quad + \quad H_2O \quad \longrightarrow \quad HCl \quad + \quad HOCl$$

chlorine   water   hydrochloric   hypochlorous
                              acid   acid

The hypochlorous acid kills bacteria by oxidation and is converted to hydrochloric acid.

An **oxidising agent** is a substance which brings about oxidation. For example, chlorine and chlorine dioxide are oxidising agents.

Oxidation of foods can be prevented by the use of antioxidants, substances which are oxidised in preference to the food, e.g. butylated hydroxytoluene (BHT) is added to fats to prevent rancidity. Vitamin E, often found in fat, is a naturally occurring antioxidant.

Reduction is the reverse of oxidation, i.e. it is the addition of hydrogen or removal of oxygen. There are fewer common examples of reduction since hydrogen is not present in the air.

1. *Photosynthesis* is a process which occurs in green plants. Glucose is formed from carbon dioxide and water, and oxygen is produced.

$$6CO_2 \quad + \quad 6H_2O \quad \longrightarrow \quad C_6H_{12}O_6 \quad + \quad 6O_2$$

carbon   water   glucose   oxygen
dioxide

It can be seen that this is the reverse of aerobic respiration.

2. *Hydrogenation of oils.* The addition of hydrogen to an oil hardens the oil and converts it into a fat. This process is used in the manufacture of margarine (see page 63).

3. *The cleaning of silver.* Hydrogen, produced by a reaction involving sodium carbonate and aluminium, removes sulphide tarnish from silver.

$$Ag_2S \quad + \quad H_2 \quad \longrightarrow \quad 2Ag \quad + \quad H_2S$$

silver   hydrogen   silver   hydrogen
sulphide   sulphide
(tarnish)

A **reducing agent** is a substance which brings about reduction, e.g. hydrogen.

CHAPTER 3

Organic Chemistry

All the components of food, with the exception of water and the mineral salts, are organic compounds. Therefore, a knowledge of organic chemistry is essential in the study of food science and nutrition.

Organic chemistry is the study of covalent carbon compounds. All forms of life are based on these organic carbon compounds. When the term organic chemistry was first introduced, it was thought that these compounds were found only in living organisms and that they could not be produced synthetically. This is now known to be incorrect and a wide variety of organic compounds are produced commercially. Nowadays, it is possible to synthesise vitamins, some sugars and fats, and some simple proteins. Many synthetic organic compounds are an important part of our life; these include plastics, such as polythene and polystyrene, and man-made fibres, such as nylon and polyester.

Carbon is unique among the elements in that it is capable of forming thousands of different compounds. The reason for this is that carbon atoms join together very easily and, therefore, a large number of different molecules can be obtained. These molecules are sometimes very large and complex. Carbon atoms, as well as forming bonds with other carbon atoms, also form bonds with atoms of other elements. The elements which most often combine with carbon to form organic compounds are hydrogen, oxygen and nitrogen. Sulphur, phosphorus and the halogens (fluorine, chlorine, bromine and iodine) may also be present in organic compounds.

Carbon has a valency of four, since the four electrons in the outer shell readily form covalent bonds. The covalent bonds can be represented by lines. When a carbon atom is present in a molecule the atom and bonds can be represented as follows:

$$\overset{\textstyle |}{\underset{\textstyle |}{-\text{C}-}}$$

Carbon atoms may be joined by single, double or triple bonds. In a single bond, one pair of electrons is shared between the two carbon atoms. Two pairs of shared electrons form a double bond and three pairs a triple bond. The conventional representations of single, double and triple bonds are shown in Figure 3.1.

Table 3.1 shows the valency of some of the other elements which are found in organic compounds.

$$-\overset{\displaystyle |}{\underset{\displaystyle |}{C}}-\overset{\displaystyle |}{\underset{\displaystyle |}{C}}- \qquad -\overset{\displaystyle |}{C}=\overset{\displaystyle |}{C}- \qquad -C\equiv C-$$

single   double   triple
bond   bond   bond

FIG. 3.1. Bonds between carbon atoms.

The simplest organic compounds are the hydrocarbons which contain carbon and hydrogen only. There are basically two types of organic compound: aliphatic and aromatic. The structures of these can be illustrated by considering simple hydrocarbon structures.

TABLE 3.1. *Valency of some of the elements (other than carbon) commonly found in organic compounds*

Elements	Valency	Representation
Hydrogen	1	H—
Oxygen	2	—O—
Nitrogen	3	—N— (with bond below)
Sulphur	2	—S—
Phosphorus	3	—P— (with bond below)
Fluorine	1	F—
Chlorine	1	Cl—
Bromine	1	Br—
Iodine	1	I—

1. Aliphatic compounds

These compounds contain chains of carbon atoms. The length of the chain ranges from two to several thousand carbon atoms. The chains may be either straight or branched.

$$H-\overset{H}{\underset{H}{C}}-\overset{H}{\underset{H}{C}}-\overset{H}{\underset{H}{C}}-\overset{H}{\underset{H}{C}}-\overset{H}{\underset{H}{C}}-\overset{H}{\underset{H}{C}}-\overset{H}{\underset{H}{C}}-\overset{H}{\underset{H}{C}}-\overset{H}{\underset{H}{C}}-\overset{H}{\underset{H}{C}}-H$$

A straight-chain hydrocarbon

$$
\begin{array}{cccccccc}
& H & H & H & H & H & H & H \\
& | & | & | & | & | & | & | \\
H- & C- & C- & C- & C- & C- & C- & C-H \\
& | & | & | & | & | & | & | \\
& H & H & H & | & H & H & H \\
& & & & H-C-H & & & \\
& & & & | & & & \\
& & & & H-C-H & & & \\
& & & & | & & & \\
& & & & H-C-H & & & \\
& & & & | & & & \\
& & & & H & & &
\end{array}
$$

A branched-chain hydrocarbon

2. Aromatic compounds

Aromatic compounds, as their name suggests, often have a distinctive smell. In addition to forming chains, carbon atoms form ring structures. The most stable of these is the six-membered benzene ring, which is the basis of aromatic compounds.

Benzene

The carbon and hydrogen atoms may be omitted, and the formula of benzene may be conveniently written as:

Homologous series

There are several million organic compounds and therefore it is almost impossible to study each compound individually. It is more convenient to place the compounds in groups and to study the properties of these groups. Organic compounds are therefore classified into groups known as homologous series. A homologous series is a group of compounds which have similar structures and therefore similar chemical properties. All members of the group can be represented by the same general formula. The molecular formula of a compound differs from the next in the series by $-CH_2$. The physical properties of the compounds show a gradation throughout the series.

Hydrocarbons

Hydrocarbons are important as fuels and as raw materials for the plastics industry. There are three main types of aliphatic hydrocarbons.

1. Alkanes

Alkanes are saturated hydrocarbons, i.e. all the bonds between the carbon atoms are single bonds. The structures and formulae of the simplest members of this series are shown in Table 3.2.

TABLE 3.2. *The simpler alkanes*

Name	Molecular formula	Structural formula	

| Methane | CH_4 | | |

H
|
H—C—H   or CH_4
|
H

| Ethane | C_2H_6 | | |

H H
| |
H—C—C—H   or $CH_3 \cdot CH_3$
| |
H H

| Propane | C_3H_8 | | |

H H H
| | |
H—C—C—C—H   or $CH_3 \cdot CH_2 \cdot CH_3$
| | |
H H H

| n-Butane | C_4H_{10} | | |

H H H H
| | | |
H—C—C—C—C—H   or $CH_3 \cdot CH_2 \cdot CH_2 \cdot CH_3$
| | | |
H H H H

| iso-Butane | C_4H_{10} | | |

H H H
| | |
H—C—C—C—H   or $CH_3 \cdot CHCH_3 \cdot CH_3$
| | |
H | H
   |
H—C—H
   |
   H

The main use of alkanes is as fuels. They all undergo combustion, i.e. are oxidised by burning in air to produce heat energy. One of the most important members of the series is methane. Over 90% of the gas in 'natural gas' is methane.

When methane is burned in a plentiful supply of air the products are carbon dioxide and water. The complete combustion of methane is shown by the following equation:

$$CH_4 \ + \ 2O_2 \ \longrightarrow \ CO_2 \ + \ 2H_2O$$

methane   oxygen   carbon   water
                        dioxide

If combustion is incomplete carbon monoxide may be formed. Carbon monoxide is poisonous and therefore it is essential to have an adequate air supply for gas water heaters and other gas equipment.

Propane and butane are used in gas cylinders for portable camping stoves and for industry.

The Science of Food

Crude oil is a mixture of hydrocarbons. After the oil is refined a variety of products, including petrol, paraffin, diesel oil and lubricating oils, is produced.

FORMULAE

It can be seen from Table 3.2 that there are three ways of writing the formulae of organic compounds.

The **molecular formula** shows the total number of atoms of each element present in one molecule of the compound. It does not, however, give any indication as to how the atoms are joined to each other. Several or many organic compounds may exist with the same molecular formula. For instance, the formula C_4H_{10} may equally well refer to n-butane and iso-butane. Similarly, the formula $C_2H_4O_2$ may apply to both acetic acid and methyl formate. The **structural formula** indicates the arrangement of atoms within the molecule. This may be written as a *graphic formula*, using lines to represent the bonds between atoms, or as a *condensed structural formula* in which most of the lines are omitted and the way in which the atoms are joined is shown by writing their symbols in conventional groups. The graphic and condensed structural formulae of n-butane and iso-butane are shown in Table 3.2. The structural formulae of acetic acid and methyl formate are shown in Table 3.3.

TABLE 3.3. *Structures of acetic acid and methyl formate*

Compound	Molecular formula	Structural formulae	
		Graphic	Condensed
Acetic acid (ethanoic acid)	$C_2H_4O_2$		$CH_3 \cdot COOH$
Methyl formate (methyl methanoate)	$C_2H_4O_2$		$H \cdot COOCH_3$

ISOMERISM

Isomerism is the occurrence of two or more compounds with the same molecular formula but different structural formulae. There are two isomers of butane. The two isomers contain the same number of atoms of each element but the atoms are joined to each other in a different manner. Normal butane (abbreviated to n-butane) is an isomer of butane in which the chain of carbon atoms is unbranched. Iso-butane is a branched chain isomer. As the number of carbon atoms per molecule increases the number of possible isomers also increases. Pentane, the next alkane in the series after butane, has three isomers.

Acetic acid and methyl formate are isomers since they have the same molecular formula, $C_2H_4O_2$.

2. *Alkenes*

Alkenes are unsaturated hydrocarbons, i.e. they contain carbon–carbon double bonds. The first two members of the series are ethene (ethylene) and propene (propylene), see Table 3.4.

TABLE 3.4. *The simpler alkenes*

Name	Molecular formula	Structural formula	
Ethene (ethylene)	C_2H_4	$\begin{matrix} H & H \\ \| & \| \\ C{=}C \\ \| & \| \\ H & H \end{matrix}$	or $CH_2{=}CH_2$
Propene (propylene)	C_3H_6	$\begin{matrix} H & H & H \\ \| & \| & \| \\ H{-}C{-}C{=}C \\ \| & & \| \\ H & & H \end{matrix}$	or $CH_3 . CH{=}CH_2$

All unsaturated compounds are reactive and will combine with hydrogen or other elements to form saturated compounds. A molecule containing one double bond will react with two atoms, i.e. one molecule, of hydrogen. For example, ethene combines with two atoms of hydrogen to form ethane.

$$\begin{matrix} H & H \\ \| & \| \\ C{=}C \\ \| & \| \\ H & H \end{matrix} \quad + \quad H_2 \quad \longrightarrow \quad \begin{matrix} H & H \\ \| & \| \\ H{-}C{-}C{-}H \\ \| & \| \\ H & H \end{matrix}$$

$$\text{ethene} \qquad \text{hydrogen} \qquad \qquad \text{ethane}$$

This type of reaction is called an **addition reaction**.

POLYMERISATION

Polymerisation is a chemical reaction in which small molecules, known as **monomers**, combine to form long chains, known as **polymers**. Molecules such as ethene and propene, which contain double bonds, undergo **addition polymerisation**. In the formation of the polymer the double bonds are broken.

The following equation shows the formation of the plastic material polyethene (polyethylene), commonly known as polythene, from ethene:

$$n \begin{matrix} H & H \\ \| & \| \\ C{=}C \\ \| & \| \\ H & H \end{matrix} \quad \longrightarrow \quad {-}{-}{-}\begin{matrix} H & H & H & H & H & H & H & H & H & H & H \\ \| & \| & \| & \| & \| & \| & \| & \| & \| & \| & \| \\ C{-}C{-}C{-}C{-}C{-}C{-}C{-}C{-}C{-}C{-}C \\ \| & \| & \| & \| & \| & \| & \| & \| & \| & \| & \| \\ H & H & H & H & H & H & H & H & H & H & H \end{matrix}{-}{-}{-}$$

$$\begin{matrix} \text{ethene} \\ \text{(monomer)} \\ n = \text{a large number} \end{matrix} \qquad \qquad \begin{matrix} \text{polyethene} \\ \text{(polymer)} \end{matrix}$$

Propene polymerises in a similar way to form polypropene (polypropylene).

3. Alkynes

Alkynes are a series of unsaturated hydrocarbons containing a carbon–carbon triple bond. The first member of the series is ethyne (acetylene); its structure is shown in Table 3.5.

TABLE 3.5. *The simplest alkyne*

Name	Molecular formula	Structural formula
Ethyne (Acetylene)	C_2H_2	$H-C\equiv C-H$ or $HC\equiv CH$

Alkynes also undergo addition reactions and ethyne is used as a starting material in the production of many organic compounds.

Halogen derivatives of hydrocarbons

There are several important halogen derivatives of hydrocarbons. These are hydrocarbons in which one or more of the hydrogen atoms is replaced by a halogen atom. One of these is tetrafluoroethene, which is the monomer used in the manufacture of polytetrafluoroethene (PTFE). This polymer is better known by its trade name Teflon and forms the coating on non-stick pans. The following equation shows the polymerisation of tetrafluoroethene:

$$
n \;
\begin{array}{c}
\text{F} \;\; \text{F} \\[-2pt]
| \;\;\;\; | \\[-2pt]
\text{C}=\text{C} \\[-2pt]
| \;\;\;\; | \\[-2pt]
\text{F} \;\; \text{F}
\end{array}
\longrightarrow
- - -
\begin{array}{c}
\text{F F F F F F F F F F F} \\[-2pt]
| \; | \; | \; | \; | \; | \; | \; | \; | \; | \; | \\[-2pt]
-\text{C}-\text{C}-\text{C}-\text{C}-\text{C}-\text{C}-\text{C}-\text{C}-\text{C}-\text{C}-\text{C}- \\[-2pt]
| \; | \; | \; | \; | \; | \; | \; | \; | \; | \; | \\[-2pt]
\text{F F F F F F F F F F F}
\end{array}
- - -
$$

tetrafluoroethene   polytetrafluoroethene (PTFE)

Chloroethene (vinyl chloride) is the monomer used in the manufacture of polychloroethene (polyvinyl chloride or PVC). PVC has many uses as a plastic. It is used as packaging film in the food industry and in the manufacture of cold water pipes. The formation of PVC is shown by the following equation:

$$
n \;
\begin{array}{c}
\text{H} \;\; \text{Cl} \\[-2pt]
| \;\;\;\; | \\[-2pt]
\text{C}=\text{C} \\[-2pt]
| \;\;\;\; | \\[-2pt]
\text{H} \;\; \text{H}
\end{array}
\longrightarrow
- - -
\begin{array}{c}
\text{H Cl H Cl H Cl H Cl H Cl} \\[-2pt]
| \; | \; | \; | \; | \; | \; | \; | \; | \; | \\[-2pt]
-\text{C}-\text{C}-\text{C}-\text{C}-\text{C}-\text{C}-\text{C}-\text{C}-\text{C}-\text{C}- \\[-2pt]
| \; | \; | \; | \; | \; | \; | \; | \; | \; | \\[-2pt]
\text{H H H H H H H H H H}
\end{array}
- - -
$$

chloroethene   polychloroethene
(vinyl chloride)   (polyvinyl chloride, PVC)

Functional groups

Many organic compounds have structures in which one of the hydrogen atoms in a hydrocarbon molecule is replaced by a functional group. A functional group is a group of atoms which, to a large extent, determines the chemical properties of the compound. Compounds containing the same functional group are members of the same homologous series.

Names of simpler organic compounds consist of two parts. The first part indicates the number of carbon atoms present in the molecule. This is shown in Table 3.6.

TABLE 3.6. *Naming of organic compounds according to the number of carbon atoms*

Name of compound	Number of carbon atoms
Meth-	1
Eth-	2
Prop-	3
But-	4
Pent-	5
Hex-	6
Hept-	7
Oct-	8
Non-	9
Dec-	10

The last part of the name of an organic compound indicates the functional group. Table 3.7 lists the names and formulae of functional groups of importance in this book.

TABLE 3.7. *Functional groups and their formulae*

Name of compound	Functional group	Formula	Name of homologous series
-ane		—H	alkanes
-anol	hydroxyl	—OH	alcohols
-anoic acid	carboxyl	—COOH	carboxylic acids
-anal	aldehyde	—CHO	aldehydes
-anone	carbonyl	$>$CO	ketones
-amine	amino	—NH_2	amines

Ethanol is derived from ethane and is composed of a hydrocarbon stem containing two carbon atoms (C_2H_5—) and a hydroxyl group (—OH). The formula of ethanol is C_2H_5OH. Acetic acid (ethanoic acid) contains two carbon atoms and has the formula $CH_3 . COOH$.

Naming organic compounds

Many organic compounds have two names: a systematic name and a trivial name. The systematic names have been derived under the IUPAC system (IUPAC stands for International Union of Pure and Applied Chemistry), which was devised in 1960 by an international convention of scientists. Under this system the names used are based on the structure of the compounds. Using this system it is possible to write the structural formula of any compound from its name. The only disadvantage of the system is that for complicated molecules the name becomes very cumbersome; in such cases it is more sensible to use the trivial or common name. For example, 'glucose' is to be preferred to '2,3,4,5,6-pentahydroxyhexanal'. The trivial name is the common name by which the compound was originally known. Wherever possible systematic names have been used in this book but, for the sake of convenience, trivial names have sometimes been preferred, either because the systematic name is too long or because the trivial name is more meaningful. Where alternative names are given, the preferred name has been used in the main text and the alternative has been given in parentheses.

THE IUPAC SYSTEM

The procedure for naming a compound, given its structural formula, is as follows:

1. Look for the longest unbranched chain in the molecule and select the systematic name for this skeleton.

2. Number the carbon atoms in this skeleton 1, 2, 3, etc., starting at a functional group if there is one present.

3. Look for the side groups attached to the main chain and the numbers of the carbon atoms to which they are attached.

4. The name then consists of the name of the longest unbranched chain, prefixed by the names of the side groups preceded by the numbers of the carbon atoms to which they are attached.

Alcohols

Alcohols are a homologous series of compounds in which one of the hydrogen atoms of a hydrocarbon molecule is replaced by a hydroxyl (—OH) group. The simplest members of the series are methanol and ethanol (see Table 3.8).

TABLE 3.8. *The simplest alcohols*

Name	Structural formula
Methanol	H | H—C—OH or CH_3OH | H
Ethanol	H H | | H—C—C—OH or C_2H_5OH | | H H

Methanol, also called methyl alcohol, is found in methylated spirits and badly distilled liquor. It is harmful and may cause blindness if taken in sufficient quantity. Ethanol, also called ethyl alcohol, is the alcohol found in beers, wines and spirits. It is produced by a fermentation process whereby yeast enzymes break down sugars forming ethanol and carbon dioxide (see page 182).

Methanol and ethanol are monohydric alcohols, i.e. each molecule contains one hydroxyl group. Some compounds contain more than one hydroxyl group per molecule. The most important of these is glycerol (propanetriol), which is a constituent of fats and oils. It is a trihydric alcohol, i.e. each molecule contains three hydroxyl groups.

$$\begin{array}{c} H \\ | \\ H—C—OH \\ | \\ H—C—OH \\ | \\ H—C—OH \\ | \\ H \end{array}$$

glycerol
(propanetriol)

Glycerol, also known as glycerine, is used as a softening and moistening agent in confectionery. It prevents hardening of Royal icing during storage. Sorbitol, a sugar substitute used in diabetic foods, is also an alcohol.

Carboxylic acids

Carboxylic acids, also known as organic acids, contain one or more carboxyl (—COOH) groups. These compounds are weak acids; the molecules partially dissociate to produce hydrogen ions. Organic acids resemble inorganic acids in that they are capable of forming salts.

Monocarboxylic acids contain one —COOH group. The simplest members of the series are shown in Table 3.9.

Monocarboxylic acids from butyric acid upwards combine with glycerol to form fats, and are known as fatty acids.

Vinegar is a dilute solution of acetic acid (ethanoic acid). In the presence of air certain bacteria convert ethanol into acetic acid. This process is used in the commercial

TABLE 3.9. *The simplest monocarboxylic acids*

Name	Structural formula	
Acetic acid (ethanoic acid)	$\begin{array}{cc} H & O \\ | & \| \\ H—C—C—OH \\ | \\ H \end{array}$	or $CH_3 \cdot COOH$
Propionic acid (propanoic acid)	$\begin{array}{ccc} H & H & O \\ | & | & \| \\ H—C—C—C—OH \\ | & | \\ H & H \end{array}$	or $CH_3 \cdot CH_2 \cdot COOH$
Butyric acid (butanoic acid)	$\begin{array}{cccc} H & H & H & O \\ | & | & | & \| \\ H—C—C—C—C—OH \\ | & | & | \\ H & H & H \end{array}$	or $CH_3 \cdot CH_2 \cdot CH_2 \cdot COOH$

production of vinegar. Propionic acid (propanoic acid) and its calcium and sodium salts are widely used as preservatives in flour confectionery. The salts are also used to impregnate wrapping materials to preserve fruits and vegetables.

Some organic acids contain more than one functional group. Lactic acid (2-hydroxy-propanoic acid) contains both a carboxyl group and a hydroxyl group and has the following structure:

$$
\begin{array}{ccccc}
 & H & H & O & \\
 & | & | & \| & \\
H\!-\!&C\!-\!&C\!-\!&C\!-\!&OH \\
 & | & | & & \\
 & H & OH & &
\end{array}
$$

lactic acid
(2-hydroxypropanoic acid)

Lactic acid is found in muscle tissue. It is also formed, during the souring of milk, by the action of certain bacteria on lactose, the sugar in milk. There are two optical isomers of lactic acid. Optical isomerism occurs when a compound has an asymmetric carbon atom, i.e. a carbon atom with four different groups attached to it. The four groups in the lactic acid molecule are —CH$_3$, —H, —COOH and —OH. The isomers cannot be shown in two dimensions and it is necessary to imagine the three-dimensional structure of the molecule. The four covalent bonds of the carbon atom are arranged in space so that they are directed towards the corners of a tetrahedron. If the molecule has four different groups attached to the central carbon atom, two different structures or isomers are possible. The isomers are mirror images of one another, as shown below.

The main difference between the isomers is that they rotate the plane of polarised light in different directions. Light consists of waves vibrating in all directions, at right angles to the direction of the beam. Polarised light consists of waves vibrating in one direction or plane only.

Unpolarised   Polarised
light   light

If a beam of polarised light is passed through a solution of one isomer, it is rotated to the right and this isomer is known as the dextro- (or d-) form of the compound. A solution of the other isomer will rotate the light to the left and is, therefore, called the laevo- (or l-) form of the compound. Substances which show this type of isomerism are described as optically active compounds.

An instrument known as a polarimeter can be used to measure concentrations of optically active substances in solution by measuring the degree of rotation of polarised light.

Pyruvic acid (2-oxopropanoic acid) also contains two functional groups. It contains a carboxyl group and a carbonyl group ($>C=O$) and has the following structure:

$$
\begin{array}{c}
\text{H} \quad \text{O} \quad \text{O} \\
| \quad\; || \quad || \\
\text{H—C—C—C—OH} \\
| \\
\text{H}
\end{array}
$$

pyruvic acid
(2-oxopropanoic acid)

Pyruvic acid is formed in the body as a step in the breakdown of glucose to produce energy (see page 118).

Tartaric acid (2,3-dihydroxybutanedioic acid) is a dicarboxylic acid, i.e. each molecule contains two carboxyl groups. In addition there are two hydroxyl groups in each molecule. It has two asymmetric carbon atoms and is optically active.

$$
\begin{array}{c}
\text{H} \\
| \\
\text{HO—C—COOH} \\
| \\
\text{HO—C—COOH} \\
| \\
\text{H}
\end{array}
$$

tartaric acid
(2,3-dihydroxybutanedioic acid)

It is found in fruits, especially in grapes, and is obtained commercially as a by-product in the production of wines.

Citric acid (2-hydroxypropane tricarboxylic acid) is a tricarboxylic acid, i.e. each molecule contains three carboxyl groups. In addition there is a hydroxyl group attached to the central carbon atom.

$$
\begin{array}{c}
\text{H} \\
| \\
\text{H—C—COOH} \\
| \\
\text{HO—C—COOH} \\
| \\
\text{H—C—COOH} \\
| \\
\text{H}
\end{array}
$$

citric acid
(2-hydroxypropane tricarboxylic acid)

It occurs in citrus fruits and is widely used in the food industry for flavouring fruit drinks and other fruit products.

Esters

Esters are compounds formed when carboxylic acids react with alcohols.

Carboxylic acid   +   Alcohol ⟶ Ester   +   Water

For example:

$$CH_3—\overset{\overset{\displaystyle O}{\|}}{C}—O|H \quad + \quad HO|C_2H_5 \quad \longrightarrow \quad CH_3—\overset{\overset{\displaystyle O}{\|}}{C}—O—C_2H_5 \quad + \quad H_2O$$

Acetic acid   Ethanol   Ethyl acetate   Water
(ethanoic acid)   (ethyl ethanoate)

A large variety of esters are found in food, especially in fruits. They are responsible for some of the characteristic flavours and odours of foods and are particularly important in wines, where they contribute to the bouquet. Esters can be produced synthetically and are used in the production of artificial flavours. For example, ethyl lactate (ethyl hydroxypropanoate) is used in synthetic grape flavouring and amyl acetate (pentyl ethanoate) is responsible for the characteristic flavour of pear drops.

Fats and oils are esters of fatty acids and glycerol (see page 61).

Aldehydes

Aldehydes are a homologous series of compounds in which one of the hydrogen atoms of a hydrocarbon molecule is replaced by an aldehyde (—CHO) group. The names and structural formulae of some aldehydes are shown in Table 3.10.

Formaldehyde (methanal) is used in the manufacture of plastics, such as Melamine, and as a disinfectant. Aldehydes contribute to the flavour of foods. Acetaldehyde (ethanal), for example, is partly responsible for the characteristic flavour of yoghurt. Many aldehydes are used in the production of synthetic flavours. For example, benzaldehyde is used in artificial almond essences.

TABLE 3.10. *Some of the simpler aldehydes*

Name	Structural formula
Formaldehyde (methanal)	$H—\overset{\overset{\displaystyle O}{\|}}{C}—H$ or $H \cdot CHO$
Acetaldehyde (ethanal)	$H—\overset{\overset{\displaystyle H}{\|}}{\underset{\underset{\displaystyle H}{\|}}{C}}—\overset{\overset{\displaystyle O}{\|}}{C}—H$ or $CH_3 \cdot CHO$
Benzaldehyde	$C_6H_5 \cdot CHO$

Ketones

Ketones are a homologous series of compounds containing a carbonyl ($>CO$) group. The simplest member of the series is acetone (propanone) which has the following structure:

$$H_3C - \overset{\overset{\textstyle O}{\|}}{C} - CH_3$$

acetone
(propanone)

Many organic compounds dissolve in acetone and therefore acetone is used as a solvent in many industries.

Amines

Amines are a series of compounds in which a hydrogen atom of a hydrocarbon molecule is replaced by an amino (—NH_2) group. The simplest member of the series, methylamine (methamine), has the following structure:

$$H - \overset{\overset{\textstyle H}{|}}{\underset{\underset{\textstyle H}{|}}{C}} - N \overset{\diagup H}{\diagdown H}$$

methylamine
(methamine)

Amines are produced during the spoilage and decay of protein foods. Trimethylamine, for example, has the characteristic odour of rotting fish. Compounds called diamines, which contain two amino groups per molecule, are used in the manufacture of nylon.

Amino acids

Amino acids are a series of compounds containing two functional groups, an amino group and a carboxylic acid group, attached to the same carbon atom. The simplest amino acid, glycine, has the following structure:

$$\overset{H}{\underset{H}{\diagup}}N - \overset{\overset{\textstyle H}{|}}{\underset{\underset{\textstyle H}{|}}{C}} - \overset{\overset{\textstyle O}{\|}}{C} - OH$$

glycine

Amino acids are the monomers from which the polymers, proteins are made. The formation of proteins is an example of **condensation polymerisation**. In this type of polymerisation, when the monomers join together, a small molecule, usually water, is produced. Unlike addition polymerisation it does not involve the breaking of double bonds.

CHAPTER 4

Food Dispersions

Nearly all foods contain a high percentage of water and the other nutrients present in the food are dispersed in this water. Solids, liquids and gases may be dispersed in water to form either solutions or colloids.

Solutions

If sugar is placed in water it dissolves and produces a solution. A solution is homogeneous, i.e. the composition is uniform throughout.

A solution is made up of two components; the **solute**, which is the substance dissolved, e.g. sugar in the above example, and the **solvent**, the liquid in which the solute is dissolved, e.g. water in the above example. Solutions are not necessarily composed of a solid dissolved in a liquid. Soda water is a solution of a gas (carbon dioxide) dissolved in a liquid (water). Vinegar is a solution of one liquid (acetic acid) dissolved in a second liquid (water).

Dissolved substances cause an increase in the boiling-point and a depression of the freezing-point of solutions. The effect of a solute on the boiling-point and freezing-point of a solution is directly proportional to its concentration. Sugar solutions, used in confectionery, have boiling-points well above 100°C, the boiling-point of water. Salt is used to lower the freezing-point of water and to prevent ice forming on roads in winter.

Solutions are formed by inorganic compounds, in which the particles or ions have an affinity for water. If the particles of a compound have a greater attraction for each other than they have for water, the compound will be insoluble.

Mineral elements found in foods, such as sodium and chlorine, are usually present as ions and form true solutions. Small organic molecules, such as sugars, which have an affinity for water, also form true solutions. Vitamins, depending on their structure, may be either dissolved in the water or in the fat present in foods.

Solubility

The solubility of a substance is the extent to which the substance will dissolve in a given solvent. It is usually expressed as g solute/100 ml solvent. The solubility of most substances increases with an increase in temperature.

A **saturated solution** is one in which no more solute will dissolve in the solvent at a given temperature.

Under certain conditions a **supersaturated solution** may be formed. A super-saturated solution contains more dissolved solute than a saturated solution. (It can be obtained by cooling a saturated solution.) Supersaturated solutions are unstable and the excess dissolved solvent will readily revert to the solid form by the formation of crystals.

Crystallisation

Under normal circumstances, when a saturated solution is cooled, particles of the solute will be deposited from the solution. The particles of the solid solute assume a characteristic geometrical shape and are known as crystals. Crystals may be a variety of different shapes. For example, crystals of salt (sodium chloride) are cubic. Crystallisation is a useful method of purifying solids. It is used to purify many crystalline substances in the food industry, such as sugar, salt and citric acid.

SUGAR BOILING AND CRYSTALLISATION

Pure water boils at 100°C (212°F). A solution of sugar in water boils at a temperature above 100°C. As the solution boils, water is evaporated from the surface of the solution and the sugar concentration will therefore increase. Different concentrations of sugar solutions are used for different purposes. Some examples are given in Table 4.1.

TABLE 4.1. *Boiling points of sugar solutions used in catering*

Boiling point °C	Name	Use
115	Soft ball	Making of marzipan and fondant
121	Hard ball	Making of nougat, petit fours, etc.
138	Soft crack	Making of Italienne meringue
143	Pulled sugar	Making of ornaments for decoration
154	Hard crack	Dipping of fruit and marzipan for petit fours. To make spun sugar for decoration
177	Caramel	Used for flavouring and colouring

When sugar solutions are cooled, the size of the sugar crystals which are formed depends on the rate of cooling. Slow cooling produces large crystals, which tend to give confectionery a gritty texture. Therefore a variety of techniques are used to reduce crystal size or to avoid the formation of crystals.

Sugar products can be divided into two types:

1. **Crystalline**, e.g. fondant, soft toffee, fudge. These are boiled at lower temperatures and, therefore, have a higher water content.

In the manufacture of these products crystallisation has been partly inhibited in order to result in the production of many microcrystals. This is brought about by the following:

(a) beating. For example, in the manufacture of fondant, a saturated sugar solution is cooled from 115°C to 40°C and is beaten steadily throughout. Care is needed, since a sugar or dust particle can trigger premature crystallisation and the production of large crystals;

(b) inversion, the breakdown of sucrose to produce glucose and fructose (see page 52). For example, in the manufacture of fondant, an acid (cream of tartar) may be added to produce a mixture of glucose and fructose, which crystallises more slowly;

(c) adding glucose;

(d) adding fat. For example, in the manufacture of toffee, cream or butter is added and acts by inhibiting crystal growth.

2. **Non-crystalline**, e.g. boiled sweets, butterscotch, spun sugar. If sugar is heated to 150°C–160°C in an acidic solution, i.e. with vinegar or lemon juice, inversion occurs. The resulting syrup is cooled quickly without agitation and it solidifies without crystallising, forming a glass-like solid, which has a hard, amorphous texture. The degree of inversion must be controlled or else the product will be too hygroscopic, i.e. will absorb water and become sticky on exposure to the atmosphere.

Diffusion

If there is a higher concentration of dissolved solute in one part of a solution, diffusion will take place, i.e. solute particles will move from a region of high solute concentration to a region of low solute concentration. This is due to the particles being in constant motion. Therefore if a solution is left to stand the particles will eventually become thoroughly mixed and the concentration will be equal throughout. Diffusion also takes place in mixtures of gases.

Osmosis

Filter paper is a permeable membrane since true solutions will pass through it. There are, however, some membranes which are only semi-permeable. Water molecules are small enough to pass through or 'permeate' the fine pores of these membranes but the larger solute molecules are not.

If a semi-permeable membrane forms a barrier between two solutions of unequal concentration, diffusion cannot take place, since the membrane forms a barrier preventing the free passage of solute molecules. Instead, water passes through the semi-permeable membrane from the dilute to the more concentrated solution, and the solutions tend to become equal in concentration. This process is called osmosis and is shown diagrammatically in Figure 4.1.

FIG. 4.1. Diagram illustrating osmosis.

The force or pressure set up by the movement of the water is called **osmotic pressure**. The rate at which osmosis takes place depends on the difference between the concentrations of the two solutions.

The membranes of both plant and animal cells are semi-permeable. The root hairs of plants take in water by osmosis, since the dissolved mineral salts inside the cells of the root hairs exert an osmotic pressure. Osmosis plays a part in the regulation of the water content of the body tissues of animals. There are many examples of osmosis in food preparation and processing. If sugar is placed on a half grapefruit it will be noticed that, after a time, juice comes out of the grapefruit and dissolves the sugar. The sugar exerts an osmotic pressure. Both salt and sugar are used as food preservatives because of their osmotic effect on the microorganisms responsible for spoilage (see page 193).

Colloids

If a substance such as albumin, the protein in egg white, is mixed with water it does not dissolve but forms a colloidal dispersion. This dispersion is not a solution and is not homogeneous, since the molecules of protein do not dissolve. The molecules are dispersed throughout the water producing a heterogeneous or two-phase system. The substance which is dispersed in known as the **disperse phase** and it is suspended in the **continuous phase**. In the above example protein is the disperse phase and water the continuous phase. The particles of the disperse phase of a colloid are usually between 1 and 100 nm in diameter. They are intermediate in size between the small particles of a true solution and the larger, visible particles of a suspension. After a period of time the particles in a suspension settle out as a sediment, due to the effect of gravity.

There are various types of colloidal system depending on the physical state (solid, liquid or gas) of the two phases. Some of the colloidal systems found in foods are listed in Table 4.2.

TABLE 4.2. *Types of colloidal system*

Common name	Disperse phase	Continuous phase	Examples
Foam	Gas	Liquid	Beaten egg white Whipped cream 'Head' on beer
Solid foam	Gas	Solid	Bread Cake Meringue
Emulsion	Liquid	Liquid	Milk Cream Mayonnaise
Gel	Liquid	Solid	Jelly Baked egg custard
Sol	Solid	Liquid	Egg white

Aerosols, which are also colloidal systems, consist of solids or liquids dispersed in a gas. There are no food examples of aerosols.

Colloids are formed by large organic molecules or by aggregates of smaller organic molecules. Some inorganic materials may also form colloids if they are of a suitable particle size. In foods, proteins, polysaccharides, such as starch, and fats are often present in the form of colloids.

Most colloidal dispersions are fairly stable but the two phases may separate out over a long period of time. The rate of separation is accelerated by an increase in temperature or by mechanical agitation. Many colloids separate out on freezing; this causes problems when foods containing emulsions of fat and water are frozen.

Colloids in which the continuous phase is a liquid are important in food science, since many foods contain water and/or oil. These liquid-based colloids can be broadly categorised into two groups:

1. **Lyophilic colloids**, in which there is an attraction between the colloidal particles (the disperse phase) and the liquid of the continuous phage, e.g. sols and gels. If the continuous phase is water, these colloids are said to be hydrophilic.

2. **Lyophobic colloids**, in which there is no attraction between the particles of the disperse phase and the continuous phase, e.g. emulsions. If the continuous phase is water, these colloids are said to be hydrophobic.

Sols and gels

In the study of foods we are often concerned with colloidal systems in which the continuous phase is water. Water molecules possess the ability to form bonds, known as **hydrogen bonds**, either with other water molecules or with molecules of other substances. Water molecules consist of two hydrogen atoms joined by covalent bonds to an oxygen atom. The pairs of electrons which make up the covalent bonds are not shared equally but are attracted more strongly by the oxygen atom. The oxygen atom has a very slight negative charge, represented by the symbol $\delta-$. The hydrogen atoms consist of an unshielded proton, since there are no electrons other than the one shared with the oxygen atom. Therefore, there will be a very slight positive charge, $\delta+$, on both of the hydrogen atoms. Water molecules, therefore, have regions of localised charge and are attracted to one another by hydrogen bonds which are weak cohesive forces arising from electrostatic attraction (see Figure 4.2).

The proteins and starch in foods may be present in the form of sols or gels. Proteins consist of amino acids joined by peptide links (see page 72). Each amino acid has a side chain which is basically a hydrocarbon chain but which may contain an amino group or a carboxylic acid group. Hydrogen bonding may take place either between the water

Fig. 4.2. Diagram showing hydrogen bonding between water molecules.

molecules and the peptide links (as shown in Figure 4.3) or between the water molecules
and the amino and carboxyl groups on the side chain.

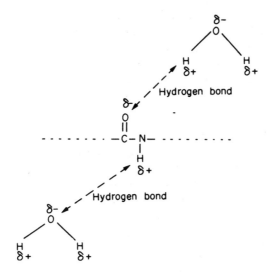

FIG. 4.3. Diagram showing hydrogen bonding between water molecules and atoms in a peptide link.

Because of the attraction between parts of the protein chain and the water, the protein
can be readily dispersed in the form of a colloid.

Starch consists of long chains of glucose units and contains many hydroxyl groups
which can form hydrogen bonds with water molecules. Therefore starch can form
colloids.

When a jelly is made, gelatin (a protein) is dispersed in water and heated forming a
sol. There is little attraction between the protein molecules and the sol behaves like a
liquid, i.e. it is runny and can easily be poured. On cooling, the molecules, which are
compact and coiled in the sol, begin to unwind and cross-links are formed between
adjacent molecules and a mesh or network is formed (see Figure 4.4). The sol has been
converted to a gel and the gel resembles a solid rather than a liquid.

FIG. 4.4. Diagram showing the formation of a gel.

Sometimes gel formation can be reversed. For example, if a jelly is heated it liquefies and forms a sol.

Corn starch (cornflour) and arrowroot are used as thickening agents, since they are both capable of forming sols and gels.

Syneresis is the shrinkage of a gel and the subsequent loss of liquid. This process may take place if a jelly is left to stand for a long time. A pool of liquid surrounding the base of the jelly indicates that syneresis has taken place. Scrambled egg is a gel and if it is overcooked syneresis may occur.

Emulsions

There are two main types of emulsions found in foods:

1. *Oil-in-water* emulsions, where the disperse phase consists of droplets of oil dispersed in the continuous phase, which is mainly water.

2. *Water-in-oil* emulsions, where the disperse phase consists of droplets of water dispersed in the continuous phase, which is mainly oil.

The structures of these two types of dispersions are shown diagrammatically in Figure 4.5.

(i) An oil-in-water emulsion

Water (continuous phase)

Oil (disperse phase)

(ii) A water-in-oil emulsion

Oil (continuous phase)

Water (disperse phase)

Fig. 4.5. Types of emulsions.

Table 4.3 lists some examples of emulsions occurring in foods.

If water and oil are shaken up together and left for a short time the two liquids will separate, with the oil forming a layer on top of the water. Two such liquids which will not normally mix are said to be immiscible. In an emulsion two immiscible liquids are held in a stable colloidal state by means of a third substance, present in small quantities, known as an **emulsifying agent** or **emulsifier**. The mechanisms by which emulsifying

TABLE 4.3. *Emulsions found in foods*

Type of emulsion	Food
Oil-in-water	Milk
	Cream
	Mayonnaise
	Salad cream
	Gravy
	Cream soups
	Ice cream
Water-in-oil	Butter
	Margarine
	Egg yolk

agents assist in the formation of stable emulsions are complex and incompletely understood. However, the following types of action, which can occur either alone or in combination, have been investigated and have been shown to be important.

1. Many emulsifying agents are substances in which one part of the molecule is hydrophilic and has an attraction for water, whereas the other part of the molecule is hydrophobic and has little affinity for water. Examples are lecithin (found in egg yolk), monoglycerides, e.g. glyceryl monostearate (GMS), diglycerides and most detergents. The molecules of the emulsifying agent surround the droplets of the disperse phase so that the hydrophilic part of the molecule is in the water and the hydrophobic part is in the oil. Thus a coating of molecules of emulsifying agent will be formed around the particles of the disperse phase. This can be illustrated by considering the action of a detergent in emulsifying and dispersing grease during washing (see Figure 4.6).

A detergent molecule

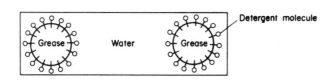

FIG. 4.6. Diagram showing the action of a detergent (an emulsifying agent).

2. Electrostatic forces may increase the stability of some emulsions, since the molecules of some emulsifying agents are readily ionised. For example, soap, which is an

emulsifying agent consists of the sodium salts of fatty acids and has the following structure:

$$
\begin{array}{c}
O \\
\| \\
R\!-\!C\!-\!O^-Na^+
\end{array}
$$

(R is a hydrocarbon chain)

When grease is dispersed during washing, the sodium ions separate from the fatty acid chain and are dispersed throughout the water. The coating which remains around the droplets of grease consists of the fatty acid ions and has a negative charge. Since like charges repel each other, this coating will keep the droplets apart and prevent them from coalescing (see Figure 4.7).

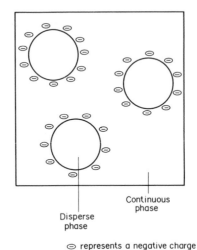

Disperse phase

Continuous phase

⊝ represents a negative charge

FIG. 4.7. Diagram showing coating of electrostatic charge around particles of the disperse phase.

3. Stabilisers help to maintain an emulsion once it has been formed. Stabilisers are long chain molecules, e.g. proteins and starches, which form a network within the continuous phase which separates the droplets of the disperse phase and prevents coalescence (see Figure 4.8).

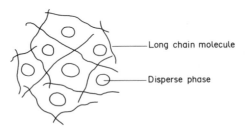

Long chain molecule

Disperse phase

FIG. 4.8. Action of long chain molecules in preventing coalescence.

Stabilisers also increase the stability of the emulsion by increasing the viscosity of the continuous phase. Stabilisers used commercially include proteins, such as gelatin, and carbohydrates, such as pectin, sodium alginate and a variety of gums.

Emulsifying agents, both natural and artificial, are widely used in food preparation. Lecithin is an important naturally-occurring emulsifying agent. It is present in egg yolk and many vegetable oils. Commercially it is extracted from soya bean oil. The most important of the artificial emulsifiers is glyceryl monostearate, which is an ester of glycerol and stearic acid. It is widely used in the manufacture of foods such as margarine, ice cream and salad cream.

BREAKDOWN OF EMULSIONS

There are three ways in which emulsions may break down.

1. Separation into two phases. This may be caused by:
   (a) adding the disperse phase too quickly during preparation;
   (b) the action of heat;
   (c) the action of an acid, i.e. lowering the pH;
   (d) freezing;
   (e) adding too much disperse phase during preparation. (The maximum content of the disperse phase is about 74%.)

2. Separation into two emulsified layers, e.g. the formation of a cream layer in milk.
3. Phase inversion. The disperse phase becomes the continuous phase and vice versa. This occurs during the formation of butter from cream and is caused by mechanical agitation.

Foams

A foam consists of very small bubbles of a gas, usually air, dispersed in a liquid. It is the action of substances dissolved in the liquid which stabilise the foam, since they decrease the surface tension of the liquid and prevent the molecules of the liquid from massing together (see page 221).

EGG WHITE FOAMS

Egg white foams are stabilised in two ways:

1. The protein in egg white, albumin, is a thick, viscous solution. When the egg white is beaten and bubbles of air are incorporated, the albumin drains more slowly out of the bubble walls than a thin liquid would. All of the proteins present in egg white probably act in a similar way. They are large molecules, which get in the way of each other and of the water that surrounds them and therefore contribute to the high viscosity.

2. The various proteins present in egg white confer a mechanical stability on the bubble walls. When egg white is beaten and air is incorporated, one part of the protein molecule is attracted to the water through hydrogen bonds, while other parts of the molecule will align themselves so that they are in contact with the pocket of air, since they have no attraction for the water. This action causes the molecules, which are

normally compact, to unfold. Once unfolded, the protein molecules bond with each other forming a network, which holds the water in place while shielding it from the pockets of air.

Added ingredients affect the stability of egg white foams. Fat, even in small amounts, e.g. a little egg yolk, interferes with foam formation and reduces the volume by as much as two-thirds. Acid, on the other hand, improves stability. Many meringue recipes include a small amount of acid in the form of cream of tartar. Salt increases whipping time and reduces foam stability. Sugar has a mixed effect. It delays foaming and reduces maximum volume but helps to prevent drainage and collapse during cooking. It is, therefore, normally folded into egg white after whipping but before baking.

If an egg white foam is heated, the protein coagulates and a meringue, a solid foam, is formed. Bread is a further example of a solid foam.

ICE CREAM

Ice cream is a complex substance being both an emulsion and a foam. It has four phases:

1. Fat globules. Milk fat is used in dairy ice cream, whereas vegetable fat is used in non-dairy ice cream.
2. Air cells. In order to impart a creamy texture these should be small (less than 0.1 mm diameter).
3. Ice crystals. These consist of pure water. They should be small and well dispersed, otherwise the product will have a gritty texture.
4. Liquid containing dissolved sugar, suspended milk proteins, stabilisers, flavours, colours, etc. The stabilisers, such as alginates or gelatin, give the ice cream body and prevent rapid melting.

CHAPTER 5

Carbohydrates

Carbohydrates are a group of nutrients important in the diet as a source of energy. They contain the elements carbon, hydrogen and oxygen and are produced in plants by the process of **photosynthesis**, which may be represented by the following equation:

$$6CO_2 \quad + \quad 6H_2O \quad \xrightarrow[\text{(solar energy)}]{\text{chlorophyll}} \quad C_6H_{12}O_6 \quad + \quad 6O_2$$

| carbon dioxide (from the air) | water (from the soil) | sunlight (solar energy) | glucose ↓ other carbohydrates | oxygen (released into the air) |

Chlorophyll is a green pigment which absorbs energy from sunlight and enables plants to build up carbohydrates from carbon dioxide and water.

There are various different carbohydrates but they may be divided into three main groups according to the size of their molecules:

| increasing size of molecule | MONOSACCHARIDES DISACCHARIDES POLYSACCHARIDES | SUGARS NON-SUGARS, e.g. starch |

Sugars

1. Monosaccharides

The monosaccharide sugars commonly found in food contain six carbon atoms and have the general formula $C_6H_{12}O_6$. The three most important members of this group are:

(A) GLUCOSE (ALSO KNOWN AS DEXTROSE)

The structure of a molecule of glucose is shown in Figure 5.1. In the conventional representation the carbon atoms in the ring are omitted.

Glucose is found in varying amounts in fruits and vegetables. Large amounts are found in fruits such as grapes and smaller quantities in vegetables such as young peas and carrots. It is also found in the blood of animals.

Glucose syrup or commercial glucose is not pure glucose but a mixture of glucose, other carbohydrates and water (see page 54).

FIG. 5.1. Structure of glucose.

(B) FRUCTOSE (ALSO KNOWN AS LAEVULOSE)

This is chemically similar to glucose except that the arrangement of the atoms within the molecule is slightly different. Fructose is found, together with glucose, in many fruits and in honey.

(C) GALACTOSE

This is also chemically similar to glucose. It does not exist as such in foods but is produced when lactose, a disaccharide, is broken down during digestion.

2. Disaccharides

These sugars have the general formula $C_{12}H_{22}O_{11}$. They are formed when two monosaccharide molecules combine with the elimination of a water molecule.

$$C_6H_{12}O_6 \quad + \quad C_6H_{12}O_6 \quad \longrightarrow \quad C_{12}H_{22}O_{11} \quad + \quad H_2O$$

  monosaccharide   monosaccharide   disaccharide   water

This is an example of a condensation reaction, i.e. a reaction in which two small molecules combine to form one larger molecule with the elimination of a small molecule, usually water, from between them.

(A) SUCROSE

This is ordinary household sugar and is produced in plants by the condensation of glucose and fructose. The structure of sucrose is shown in Figure 5.2.

FIG. 5.2. Structure of sucrose.

Sucrose is found in many fruits and vegetables, some of which, e.g. sugar cane and sugar beet, contain relatively large quantities. It is from cane and beet that sugar is extracted commercially.

PRODUCTION AND REFINING OF SUGAR

Both sugar cane and sugar beet contain about 15% sucrose. Sugar cane is grown in tropical countries. The sugar is extracted by crushing the canes and spraying them with water so that the sucrose diffuses into the water. Impurities in the solution are removed by treatment with lime and carbon dioxide, followed by evaporation. Raw sugar is then separated from the molasses by centrifugal spinning. This raw sugar, which contains about 96% sucrose, is exported to sugar-consuming countries such as Britain to be refined. The refining process involves centrifuging and washing to remove any remaining molasses. This is followed by treatment with lime and carbon dioxide to remove other impurities, treatment with charcoal to decolorise the solution and vacuum evaporation to crystallise the sucrose. At this stage the mixture consists of sugar crystals suspended in syrup. The syrup is removed by spinning in centrifugal separators and the damp sugar is dried in a current of hot air.

Sugar beet, which is produced in countries with a temperate climate such as Britain, is processed to white sugar as one continuous process. The beets are sliced and steeped in hot water to extract the sucrose. The solution is purified with lime and carbon dioxide. This is followed by evaporation and crystallisation. The sugar crystals are centrifugally separated from the remaining syrup and molasses, and finally dried.

Molasses, the main by-product of sugar production, is used as an ingredient by food manufacturers and animal food producers. It can also be fermented and made into rum.

(B) LACTOSE

This sugar is formed by the condensation of glucose and galactose. It is found only in milk, where it is the sole carbohydrate.

(C) MALTOSE

A molecule of maltose is formed by the condensation of two glucose molecules. During the germination or sprouting of barley, starch is broken down into maltose. Malt, a vital ingredient in brewing, is produced by this process.

Formation of disaccharides

$$\text{Glucose} + \text{Fructose} \longrightarrow \text{Sucrose} + \text{Water}$$
$$\text{Glucose} + \text{Galactose} \longrightarrow \text{Lactose} + \text{Water}$$
$$\text{Glucose} + \text{Glucose} \longrightarrow \text{Maltose} + \text{Water}$$

Properties of sugars

1. APPEARANCE AND SOLUBILITY

All sugars are white, crystalline compounds which are soluble in water.

2. SWEETNESS

All sugars are sweet but they do not all have the same degree of sweetness. The sweetness of different sugars may be compared, using a point scale in which the sweetness of sucrose is taken as 100. Table 5.1 shows the relative sweetness of various sugars.

TABLE 5.1. *The relative sweetness of various sugars*

Sugar	Relative sweetness
Fructose	170
*Invert sugar	130*
Sucrose	100
Glucose	75
Maltose	30
Galactose	30
Lactose	15

* A mixture of glucose and fructose (see below).

3. HYDROLYSIS

Disaccharides undergo a process of hydrolysis to form monosaccharides. Hydrolysis is the chemical breakdown of a molecule, by combination with water, producing smaller molecules. This process may be represented by the following equation:

$$AB \quad + \quad H_2O \longrightarrow AOH \quad + \quad BH$$

large molecule   water   small molecule   small molecule

For example:

$$C_{12}H_{22}O_{11} \quad + \quad H_2O \longrightarrow 2C_6H_{12}O_6$$

1 molecule of disaccharide   water   2 molecules of monosaccharide

$$\text{Sucrose} + \text{Water} \longrightarrow \text{Glucose} + \text{Fructose}$$
$$\text{Lactose} + \text{Water} \longrightarrow \text{Glucose} + \text{Galactose}$$
$$\text{Maltose} + \text{Water} \longrightarrow \text{Glucose} + \text{Glucose}$$

It can be seen that these are the reverse of the condensation reactions by which disaccharides are formed.

INVERSION OF SUCROSE

The hydrolysis of sucrose is also known as the inversion of sucrose and the product, a mixture of glucose and fructose, is called 'invert sugar'. Inversion may be brought about either by heating sucrose with an acid or by adding the enzyme invertase. Invert sugar is used in the production of jam, boiled sweets and some other sugar confections. A small quantity of invert sugar, added to a hot sucrose solution will help reduce the likelihood of crystallisation when the solution is cooled.

4. EFFECT OF HEAT

When sugars are heated they caramelise. Although caramelisation occurs most readily in the absence of water, sugar solutions (syrups) will caramelise if heated strongly enough. Caramel is a sweet, brown substance and is a mixture of carbohydrate-like compounds.

5. REDUCING PROPERTIES

All the monosaccharides and disaccharides mentioned, with the exception of sucrose, act as reducing agents (see page 23) and are therefore known as **reducing sugars**. The ability of these sugars to reduce oxidising agents forms the basis of several tests for glucose and other reducing sugars. For example, these sugars reduce the copper(II) ions of Fehling's solution to copper(I) ions on boiling, producing an orange precipitate. Sucrose is a non-reducing sugar and therefore does not reduce Fehling's solution.

Polysaccharides

Polysaccharides are condensation polymers of monosaccharides and are made up of many monosaccharide molecules joined together, with the elimination of one water molecule at each link. They have the general formula $(C_6H_{10}O_5)n$, where 'n' represents a large number.

1. Starch

Starch is the major food reserve of plants. It is in fact a mixture of two different polysaccharides:

(a) *Amylose.* The amylose molecule consists of between 50 and 500 glucose units joined in a straight chain.
(b) *Amylopectin.* This molecule consists of up to 100,000 glucose units joined in a branched-chain structure.

Part of an amylose
molecule

Part of an amylopectin
molecule

O = a glucose unit

FIG. 5.3. Structure of amylose and amylopectin.

The starch in many plants, including wheat, rice, corn and potato, consists of approximately 80% amylopectin and 20% amylose. Microscopic examination shows that the starch in plant cells occurs as small grains or **granules**. The outer layer of each granule consists of closely packed starch molecules which are impervious to cold water. The different plant sources of starch are characterised by the shape of the granules and by the distribution of granule sizes. Typical potato and corn starch granules are shown in Figure 5.4.

Potato starch   Corn starch

Fɪɢ. 5.4. Typical starch granules.

Properties of starch

1. APPEARANCE AND SOLUBILITY

Starch is a white, non-crystalline powder which is insoluble in cold water.

2. SWEETNESS

Unlike monosaccharides and disaccharides, starch and other polysaccharides do not have a sweet taste.

3. HYDROLYSIS

Hydrolysis of starch may be brought about by the action of an acid or an enzyme. If starch is heated with an acid it is broken down into successively smaller molecules, the final product being glucose.

$$(C_6H_{10}O_5)n \ + \ nH_2O \longrightarrow nC_6H_{12}O_6$$

starch   water   glucose

There are various stages in this reaction. The large starch molecules are first broken down into shorter chains of glucose units known as dextrins. The dextrins are further broken down into maltose (two glucose units) and, finally, the maltose is broken down into glucose.

starch $\longrightarrow$ dextrins $\longrightarrow$ maltose $\longrightarrow$ glucose

Hydrolysis of starch may also be brought about by enzymic action. During digestion the enzyme amylase breaks down starch into maltose. Amylase is also present in flour and germinating grain where it is also known as diastase. It is important in breadmaking and brewing since it produces a sugar (maltose) which yeast enzymes are able to break down further to produce carbon dioxide and alcohol. For a more detailed description of the action of enzymes in digestion and breadmaking, see Chapter 11.

Commercial glucose syrups (liquid glucose) are produced by hydrolysing corn (maize) starch with hydrochloric acid and/or the enzyme amylase. Hydrolysis is not complete and the syrups are a mixture of glucose, maltose and longer chains of glucose units. The extent of hydrolysis of a glucose syrup is measured in terms of its dextrose equivalent

(D.E.). A high D.E. syrup contains more dextrose (glucose) and is therefore sweeter than a low D.E. syrup.

4. EFFECT OF HEAT

(a) *Gelatinisation* (with water). If a suspension of starch in water is heated, the water penetrates the outer layers of the granules and the granules begin to swell. This occurs as the temperature rises from 60°C to 80°C. The granules may swell until the volume is as much as five times the original. As the size of the granules increases the mixture becomes viscous. At about 80°C the starch granules break up and the contents become dispersed throughout the water. The long-chain molecules begin to unfold and the starch/water mixture becomes more viscous, i.e. thickens, forming a sol (see page 42). On cooling, if the proportion of starch to water is sufficiently great, the starch molecules form a network with the water enclosed in its meshes so producing a gel. The entire process is known as the **gelatinisation of starch** and is very important in cooking. For example, it is responsible for the thickening of sauces, soups and gravies by the addition of flour or cornflour. It is also important in the baking of bread and other flour goods where it contributes to the desired crumb structure and texture of the product.

The strength of a starch gel depends on a variety of factors including:

  (i) the proportions of starch and water present. The more starch the stronger the gel;
 (ii) the proportion of amylose in the starch. Amylose aids gelling and therefore high amylose starches are used where a rigid gel is needed. High amylopectin starches, i.e. waxy starches, gel only at high concentration;
(iii) the presence of sugar. Sugar competes with the starch for water and therefore reduces gel strength;
 (iv) the presence of acid. Acid hydrolyses starch and reduces gel strength forming a viscous paste. This occurs, for example, in lemon pie filling.

Although amylose-containing starches gel best, they are less stable than high amylopectin starches. The amylose molecules tend to unwind and the gel becomes opaque and like a pulpy sponge. This change is called **retrogradation** and occurs particularly when foods are frozen and then thawed. High amylopectin starches, e.g. waxy corn starch, should be used when preparing foods for a freeze/thaw process. Alternatively, chemically-modified starches are widely used in frozen manufactured foods as they do not retrograde easily.

Pregelatinised starches are used in some manufactured foods. These are cooked in water, i.e. gelatinised, and then dried. They are used, for example, in instant dessert mixes.

(b) *Dextrinisation* (dry heat). Many foods containing starch also contain small amounts of dextrins. On heating, dextrins polymerise to form brown-coloured compounds, called pyrodextrins. Pyrodextrins contribute to the brown colour of many cooked foods including toast and bread crust.

2. *Cellulose*

Cellulose is another polysaccharide consisting of long chains of glucose units. It acts as a structural material in plants, being found in cell walls where it gives rigidity. The basic structure of cellulose is similar to that of starch but the glucose units are linked in a different way. Man does not possess enzymes capable of breaking this type of linkage and therefore is unable to use cellulose as a food. However, cellulose is important for providing fibre or roughage in the diet. Dietary fibre is necessary for the efficient passage of food through the alimentary canal and the regular emptying of the bowel (see page 59). Cows, and other ruminant animals, are able to break down and utilise cellulose for energy due to the presence of cellulose-digesting bacteria in the rumen (the first of the four stomachs of the cow). This explains why cows can utilise grass as food, whereas man cannot.

3. Glycogen

This is a carbohydrate found only in animals. It can be thought of as the carbohydrate reserve in animals in the same way as starch is the carbohydrate reserve in plants. Animals store glycogen in the muscles and liver, and when required it is converted into glucose which is then broken down to provide energy. Glycogen, like amylopectin, is composed of branched chains of glucose units.

4. Pectin

Pectin is a complex mixture of polysaccharides found in many fruits and some root vegetables. Apples and the peel of citrus fruits are particularly rich in pectin. Its main importance is as a gelling agent, especially in jam making. Sugar is needed for gel formation, about 65% giving best results. This is about the amount normally present in jam. pH also affects gel strength, the optimum for gel formation being pH 3.0–3.5. In jams made from fruit with a low pectin content, such as strawberries, the addition of an acid, e.g. lemon juice, lowers pH and aids setting. Pectin is broken down in fruit as the fruit ripens. Jam will not gel satisfactorily if made from overripe fruit.

In some instances the presence of pectin may be undesirable; for example, in wines, pectin produces an unacceptable haze. Unwanted pectin can be removed by the addition of pectolytic enzymes.

5. Gums, alginates and agar

Gums such as tragacanth, arabic and guar are produced by plants and are used in food manufacturing as thickeners, stabilisers and gelling agents in a wide range of foods including ice cream, salad dressings and fruit pie fillings. Certain seaweed extracts are used in a similar manner. These include carageenan (Irish moss), alginates, e.g. sodium alginate, and agar (or agar-agar). Agar is also used in the preparation of microbiological media.

Functions of carbohydrates in the body

Starch and disaccharides are hydrolysed by digestive enzymes and are therefore absorbed as monosaccharides. In the liver, fructose and galactose are converted into glucose. Carbohydrates are used in the body in the following ways.

1. Energy

Glucose is oxidised in the cells. It is broken down in a series of reactions and energy is released when this takes place (see page 118).

1 g of carbohydrate provides 16 kJ (3.76 kcal)

2. Storage

Glucose in excess of energy requirements can be:

(a) converted into glycogen and stored in the liver and muscles as a readily available source of energy;
(b) converted into fat and stored all over the body in the fatty cells of the adipose tissue.

An average adult has about 400 g of stored glycogen and about 12 kg of stored fat. However, an excessive energy intake over a period of time leads to larger fat stores and obesity.

3. Protein sparing

A certain amount of carbohydrate is necessary in the diet since it has a 'protein-sparing' function. If the diet is low in carbohydrate a higher percentage of protein than is usual will be used to provide energy. Since the major function of protein is to provide material for growth and repair of tissues, a moderate carbohydrate intake ensures that most of the dietary protein can be used for growth purposes.

4. Dietary fibre

Unavailable carbohydrates provide dietary fibre (see page 59).

Sources of carbohydrate in the diet

1. Cereals and cereal foods

All cereals contain a high percentage of starch. Wheat is the most important cereal in Britain. However, rice, maize (corn), oats, rye and barley are also included in the diet. Many foods made from cereals, such as bread, cakes, pastry, pasta and breakfast cereals, also contain considerable quanties of starch.

Cereal foods account for 49% of the total carbohydrate content of the average British diet.

2. Refined sugar (sucrose)

Sugar is eaten in large quantities, both in the form of household sugar and in manufactured foods, such as biscuits, sweets, chocolates, ice cream, jams, cakes and soft drinks.

Sugar and preserves account for 18% of the total carbohydrate content of the average British diet.

3. Vegetables

Vegetables contain starch and sugars in varying amounts. The most important vegetable supplying carbohydrate in the diet is the potato. Pulse vegetables also contain a significant amount of carbohydrate but root and green vegetables contain smaller quantities.

Vegetables account for 15% of the total carbohydrate content of the average British diet.

4. Fruits

As fruit ripens starch is turned into sugars. Most fruits contain between 5% and 10% sugars, the sweeter fruits (e.g. grapes) containing the most. Bananas are the only fruit which contain starch as well as sugar when ripe.

Fruit accounts for 5% of the total carbohydrate content of the average British diet.

5. Milk

Milk contains the sugar lactose. Foods such as cheese and butter which are made from milk usually do not contain carbohydrate, though soft cheeses such as cottage cheese contain small amounts.

Milk and related foods account for 8% of the total carbohydrate content of the averagte British diet.

The carbohydrate content of some of these foods is shown in Table 5.2.

TABLE 5.2. *Carbohydrate content of some foods*

Food	% Carbohydrate	% Sugars	% Starch
Sugar	100	100	0
White flour	80	1.7	78
Honey	76	76	0
Biscuits, semi-sweet	75	22	53
Jam	69	69	0
Chocolate, milk	59	57	2.9
White bread	50	1.8	48
Potatoes	21	0.5	20
Apple	12	12	0.1
Peas	11	4.0	6.6
Carrots	5.4	5.4	0
Milk	4.7	4.7	0
Cabbage	3.8	3.7	0.1

Carbohydrates and health

1. Sugars and starch

The main energy-giving foods in the diet are those which contain considerable amounts of sugar, starch or fat. Generally speaking, foods rich in sugar or fat are more expensive than starchy foods. Most countries have a staple food which is a cheap, starchy cereal food. In countries which still have a low standard of living and a poor diet, up to

90% of the energy content of the diet may be provided by one of the staple foods. In most affluent countries the cheap, starch staple is less important, but more sugars and fats are eaten. In Britain, sugar provides 15% of the total energy in the diet and fats 42%. Present sugar consumption is about 100 g (3.5 oz) per person per day but only about one-third of this is sold as packet (household) sugar. The remainder is eaten in the form of manufactured foods, such as sweets, cakes, ice creams and soft drinks. The amount of sugar eaten remains fairly static but the proportion from manufactured foods is increasing.

There is a link between the incidence of tooth decay and a high sugar intake, or more accurately a frequent sugar intake. Tooth decay is caused by acids produced by oral bacteria which break down sugars in the plaque on teeth. As well as contributing to tooth decay, sugar-containing foods being very palatable are often eaten in excess and are, therefore, a contributory factor in the development of obesity (see page 141). Sugar is said to provide 'empty calories'. In other words, it is a soucre of energy but contains no other essential nutrients, such as vitamins and minerals.

Since there are health risks associated with diets containing a lot of sugar and fat, it is recommended that more starchy foods (cereals and potatoes) should be eaten to provide the necessary energy in the diet. Most starchy foods also provide other important nutrients. For example, bread is a good source of protein, calcium, iron, B vitamins and fibre, and potatoes contain vitamin C and B vitamins. Current nutritional guidelines recommend a reduction in sugar intake to 20 kg per person per year (about 55 g per day).

2. Dietary fibre

Dietary fibre is the material in plant foods which is resistant to breakdown by enzymes in the alimentary canal. It consists mainly of cellulose, together with other poly-saccharides such as hemicelluloses, pectin and gums, and the non-carbohydrate lignin.

Fibre acts in the body by binding water and increasing the 'bulk' of the material passing through the large intestine, thus stimulating muscular movements of the intestinal wall (peristalsis) and aiding the voiding of faeces. Research has suggested that the average U.K. diet contains insufficient fibre. In Western, industrialised, countries much of the carbohydrate consumed is in a highly refined form, such as sugar, white flour and white bread. In these countries there is a relatively high incidence of diseases of the alimentary tract such as diverticular disease (small bulges in the wall of the large intestine), cancer of the colon and haemorrhoids (piles). These conditions are associated with constipation and the slow transit of food through the alimentary canal. In rural communities in countries like Africa these diseases are virtually unknown. The diet in these areas contains many coarser unrefined foods and is, therefore, much higher in fibre and the transit time of food through the alimentary canal is much shorter.

There is evidence that fibre binds bile salts derived from cholesterol and therefore lowers blood cholesterol levels and the risk of coronary heart disease. It is also suggested that high fibre diets slow the rate of sugar absorption and reduce the risk of diabetes.

Current intake of dietary fibre in the U.K. is about 20 g per person per day. It is recommended that this is increased to 30 g per day (NACNE report, see page 152). People should be encouraged to eat more wholegrain cereal products, e.g. wholemeal bread, wholegrain breakfast cereals, brown rice, wholemeal pasta, and to increase the

The Science of Food

amount of fruit and vegetables in the diet. Table 5.3 shows the fibre content of a variety of foods.

TABLE 5.3. *Fibre content of some foods*

Food	g fibre per 100 g food
All Bran	27
Weetabix	13
Cornflakes	11
Wholemeal bread	8.5
Peanuts	8.1
Peas	7.8
Baked beans	7.3
Raisins	6.8
Digestive biscuits	5.5
Brown rice	4.2
Bananas	3.4
Carrots	2.9
Cabbage	2.7
White bread	2.7
White rice	2.4
Potatoes	2.1
Apples	2.0

CHAPTER 6

Fats and Oils (Lipids)

Fats and oils, also known as **lipids**, are like carbohydrates in that they contain the elements carbon, hydrogen and oxygen. They are esters of glycerol and fatty acids (see Chapter 3). Glycerol is a trihydric alcohol, i.e. it has three —OH groups. The general formula of a fatty acid (alkanoic acid) is R.COOH where R represents a hydrocarbon chain. Each —OH group of the glycerol reacts with the —COOH of a fatty acid to form a molecule of fat or oil. This is an example of a condensation reaction (see page 50).

$$
\begin{array}{ccc}
& & O \\
& & \parallel \\
CH_2OH & H\!-\!O\!-\!C\!-\!R & \\
| & O & \\
& \parallel & \\
CHOH & +\ H\!-\!O\!-\!C\!-\!R & \longrightarrow \\
| & O & \\
& \parallel & \\
CH_2OH & H\!-\!O\!-\!C\!-\!R & \\
\end{array}
\qquad
\begin{array}{cc}
& O \\
& \parallel \\
CH_2\!-\!O\!-\!C\!-\!R & \\
| & O \\
& \parallel \\
CH\!-\!O\!-\!C\!-\!R & +\ 3H_2O \\
| & O \\
& \parallel \\
CH_2\!-\!O\!-\!C\!-\!R & \\
\end{array}
$$

1 molecule of glycerol	3 molecules of fatty acid	1 molecule of fat or 'triglyceride'	3 molecules of water

Fats and oils are mixtures of **triglycerides**. A triglyceride consists of one molecule of glycerol combined with three fatty acid molecules, as shown in the above equation. Diglycerides consist of glycerol combined with two molecules of fatty acid, and in monoglycerides only one fatty acid molecule is present. Diglycerides and monoglycerides are used as emulsifiers (see page 45).

The simplest type of triglyceride is one in which all three fatty acids are the same. However, triglycerides usually contain two or three different fatty acids and are known as mixed triglycerides. Naturally occurring fats and oils are mixtures of different mixed triglycerides and therefore may contain a number of different fatty acids. There are about 40 different fatty acids found in foods.

There are basically two types:

1. *Saturated fatty acids* in which the hydrocarbon chain is saturated with hydrogen.

$$
\begin{array}{ccccccccc}
& H & H & H & H & H & H & H & H \\
& | & | & | & | & | & | & | & | \\
-C & -C & -C & -C & -C & -C & -C & -C & - \\
& | & | & | & | & | & | & | & | \\
& H & H & H & H & H & H & H & H \\
\end{array}
$$

part of the hydrocarbon chain
of a saturated fatty acid

2. *Unsaturated fatty acids* in which the hydrocarbon chain is not saturated with hydrogen and therefore has one or more double bonds.

$$\begin{array}{ccccccccccccc}
\text{H} & & \text{H} & & \text{H} & & \text{H} & & \text{H} & & \text{H} & & \text{H} \\
| & & | & & | & & | & & | & & | & & | \\
-\text{C} & - & \text{C} & = & \text{C} & - & \text{C} & - & \text{C} & = & \text{C} & - & \text{C}- \\
| & & & & & & | & & & & & & | \\
\text{H} & & & & & & \text{H} & & & & & & \text{H}
\end{array}$$

part of the hydrocarbon chain
of an unsaturated fatty acid

Unsaturated fatty acids may be either:

(a) monounsaturated—containing one double bond, e.g. oleic acid; or
(b) polyunsaturated—containing more than one double bond, e.g. linoleic acid.

In addition, the arrangement of atoms at the double bond may vary and both monounsaturated and polyunsaturated fatty acids can be either:

(a) cis fatty acids—with the two hydrogen atoms on the same side of the double bond; or
(b) trans fatty acids—with the hydrogen atoms on geometrically opposite sides of the double bond.

$$\begin{array}{cc}
\text{H} \quad \text{H} & \text{H} \\
| \quad | & | \\
-\text{C}=\text{C}- & -\text{C}=\text{C}- \\
& | \\
& \text{H}
\end{array}$$

cis   trans

Some of the more important fatty acids are listed in Table 6.1.

Fats and oils have the same general chemical structure. In common use the word 'fat' is used to refer to mixtures of triglycerides which are solid at normal air temperature, whereas the word 'oil' refers to those which are liquid at the same temperature. The difference between a fat and an oil may be explained by the presence of different fatty acids. Fats contain a large proportion of saturated fatty acids distributed among the triglycerides, and oils a large proportion of unsaturated fatty acids. The presence of unsaturated fatty acids lowers the slip point, i.e. the temperature at which the fat or oil

TABLE 6.1. *Some common fatty acids*

Type	Name	Formula	Number of double bonds	Occurrence
Saturated	Butyric acid	C_3H_7COOH	0	Milk fat and butter
	Palmitic acid	$C_{13}H_{31}COOH$	0	Occur widely, particularly
	Stearic acid	$C_{17}H_{35}COOH$	0	in solid fats
Monounsaturated	Oleic acid	$C_{17}H_{33}COOH$	1	Occur in fats and oils
Polyunsaturated	Linoleic acid	$C_{17}H_{31}COOH$	2	
	Linolenic acid	$C_{17}H_{29}COOH$	3	Found mainly in vegetable and fish oils

starts to melt. In general, fats are obtained from animal sources and oils from vegetable sources. Both fats and oils contain small amounts of non-triglyceride; in particular, fatty acid complexes containing phosphate, called phospholipids.

The degree of unsaturation, i.e. the number of double bonds, of a fat or oil may be measured in terms of its **iodine value**. A molecule of iodine (I_2) will react with each double bond, and thus unsaturated oils and have higher iodine values than saturated fats.

Vegetable oils should not be confused with either mineral oils or essential oils. Mineral oils are obtained from crude oil and are mixtures of hydrocarbons (see page 27). Essential oils are found in plants but are not triglycerides. They are volatile organic compounds, i.e. they evaporate easily, and are responsible for the flavour of many spices and other foods. Eugenol, for example, is responsible for the flavour of cloves.

In countries where bread is the staple food there is a greater demand for spreadable fats than for liquid oils. Since vegetable oils are more readily available than animal fats much of the vegetable oil produced in the world is converted into fat by a process of **hydrogenation**. Hydrogenation is the addition of hydrogen across a double bond. Thus an unsaturated fatty acid is turned into a saturated fatty acid. In this way vegetable oils can be used in the manufacture of margarine and cooking fats.

Properties of fats and oils

1. Solubility

Fats and oils are insoluble in water. However, in the presence of a suitable substance known as an emulsifying agent, it is possible to form a stable mixture of fat and water. This mixture is termed an emulsion. The emulsion may be a fat-in-water emulsion, e.g. milk, or a water-in-fat emulsion, e.g. butter. Emulsions are explained in more detail in Chapter 4.

Fats and oils are soluble in organic solvents such as petrol, ether and carbon tetrachloride. Solvents of this type can be used to remove grease stains from clothing.

2. Effect of heat

As fats are heated there are three temperatures at which noticeable changes take place.

(A) MELTING-POINT

Fats melt when heated. Since fats are mixtures of triglycerides they do not have a distinct melting-point but melt over a range of temperature. The temperature at which melting starts is called the slip point. Most fats melt at a temperature between 30°C and 40°C. The melting-point for oils is below normal air temperature. The more double bonds the lower the melting point.

(B) SMOKE-POINT

When a fat or oil is heated to a certain temperature it starts to decompose, producing a blue haze or smoke and a characteristic acrid smell. Most fats and oils start to smoke at a temperature around 200°C. The smoke-point for lard is 185°C and for corn oil is 232°C. In general, vegetable oils have a higher smoke-point than animal fats. Decomposition of the triglycerides produces small quantities of glycerol and fatty acids. The glycerol decomposes further producing a compound called acrolein. This decomposition is irreversible and, when using a fat or oil for deep frying, the frying temperature should be kept below the smoke-point. Smoke-point is a useful measure when assessing the suitability of a fat or oil for frying purposes. Repeated heating of a fat or oil or the presence of burnt food particles will reduce the smoke-point. Repeated heating will also produce oxidative and hydrolytic changes in the fat and result in the accumulation of substances giving undesirable flavours to the foods cooked in the fat.

(C) FLASH-POINT

When a fat is heated to a high enough temperature, the vapours given off will spontaneously ignite. This temperature is known as the flash-point. For corn oil the flash-point is 360°C. A fat fire should **never** be put out with water; this will only spread the fire. The heat should be turned off and the oxygen supply cut off by covering the container of burning fat with a lid or blanket.

3. Plasticity

Substances which possess the property of plasticity will change their shape, when pressure is applied to them, but will remain in their final shape when the pressure is removed. They do not return to their original shape. Fats are plastic at certain temperatures, i.e. they are soft and can be spread. The plasticity of a fat is due to the fact that fats are mixtures of triglycerides and that each triglyceride has its own melting-point; this means that at a given temperature some of the fat will be liquid and some will be in the form of a crystalline solid. Fats containing small crystals, which are produced by rapid cooling of the fat during manufacture, will be more plastic.

The range of temperature over which a fat shows plastic behaviour is known as the plastic range of the fat. A mixture of triglycerides with a large range of melting-points will form a fat with a wide plastic range. This type of fat is better for certain purposes; for example, for creaming and spreading. Margarines are manufactured to have a wide plastic range and will therefore spread straight from the refrigerator. Most animal fats have a narrow plastic range and are hard and difficult to spread.

4. Rancidity

Rancidity is the term used to describe the spoilage of fats and oils. There are basically two types.

(A) OXIDATIVE RANCIDITY

This occurs as a result of the reaction between unsaturated triglycerides and oxygen from the air. Oxygen molecules join across the double bond of the triglyceride molecule and a variety of compounds are formed including aldehydes and ketones, which give rise to an unpleasant rancid taste. The reaction is accelerated by heat, light and traces of metals, such as copper and iron.

(B) HYDROLYTIC RANCIDITY

Enzymes known as lipases hydrolyse fats, breaking them down into glycerol and fatty acids.

$$\text{Fat } + \text{ Water } \xrightarrow{\text{lipase}} \text{ Glycerol } + \text{ Fatty acids}$$

Lipases may occur naturally in fats and oils, but they can be inactivated by heat treatment. They may also be produed by microorganisms present in fatty foods. The free fatty acids, especially the short-chain ones, which are produced by this reaction can give fats an unpleasant taste and smell. For example, the unpleasant taste of rancid butter is mainly due to the fatty acid butyric (butanoic) acid.

Rancidity can be reduced by storing fats and oils in a cool, dark place in a non-metal container and by keeping fats well wrapped. Antioxidants, such as BHT (butylated hydroxytoluene), are added commercially to many fats and fatty foods to reduce oxidative rancidity. Vegetable oils contain natural antioxidants such as vitamin E, though this is destroyed by heat treatment.

5. Saponification

Triglycerides react with alkalis forming a soap and glycerol. This process is known as saponification. Sodium hydroxide (caustic soda) is the alkali most commonly used in soap manufacture but potassium hydroxide (caustic potash) may also be used. The reaction may be represented by the following equation:

triglyceride   caustic soda   glycerol   soap (sodium salt of fatty acid)

R represents a hydrocarbon chain which varies in structure depending on the nature of the fatty acids contained in the fat used. Soap is a mixture of sodium salts of different fatty acids.

Some uses of fats and oils in food preparation

1. Frying

Frying is a rapid method of cooking because high temperatures, usually about 180°C, are employed and heat transfer from the fat or oil to the food is rapid. Fried food has a characteristic colour and flavour found very acceptable by most people.

2. Shortening effect of fats

Fats have a shortening effect in baked goods, i.e. they make products, such as pastry and biscuits, more crumbly and palatable. The fat coats the starch and gluten molecules and so breaks up the structure. In order for fats to have the desired shortening effect they must be fairly soft and of the correct plasticity.

3. Creaming and aerating effect

When making rich cakes, fat and sugar are beaten or creamed together. This process incorporates small air bubbles into the mixture and so lightens the product.

The production of oils and fats

1. Vegetable oils

About 70% of all oils and fats produced in the world are of vegetable origin. Oils are obtained from nuts and seeds of plants such as corn (maize), groundnut (peanut), soya bean, olive, sunflower, cottonseed, palm, coconut and rapeseed. The composition of these oils varies considerably. Soya, sunflower and corn oils are particularly high in poly-unsaturated fatty acids (PUFA), olive oil in monounsaturates and coconut and palm oils are higher in saturates (see Figure 6.1). Rapeseed is now grown in some quantity in Europe. Bright yellow fields of rape in flower in early summer are a common sight in Britain. The original varieties used contained erucic acid, a fatty acid which has been associated with heart disease. However, present varieties contain little or no erucic acid.

Oils are extracted from the nuts or seeds by crushing and by the use of solvent extraction, which involves dissolving the oil in an organic solvent with a low boiling-point and then removing the solvent by evaporation. The oils at this stage are impure and have to be refined. Neutralisation with sodium hydroxide removes the free fatty acids. The soap formed by this process is present as an insoluble solid and can be easily removed. The oil is then bleached with Fuller's earth, which absorbs the coloured matter. Finally, the oil is deodorised by heating under vacuum and injecting steam. This process removes the volatile substances responsible for odour.

2. Margarine

Margarine is an emulsion of water in fat. The fat phase is a blend of refined vegetable oils, a portion of which has been hardened by hydrogenation to produce the desired plasticity in the final product. Fish oils and animal fats may also be incorporated in the blend. The hydrogenation is carried out by heating the oil in large sealed vessels under pressure. Hydrogen is bubbled into the oil and finely divided nickel, which is sub-sequently removed by filtration, is required as a catalyst. The oil blend is mixed with the water phase, which is skimmed milk, soured under controlled conditions to give the desired flavour to the product. Artificial colouring, salt and vitamins A and D are then added. In Britain these vitamins must be added by law. This law is necessary because margarine often replaces butter in the diet and butter is an important source of vitamins A and D. The emulsion is formed in a machine called a votator, in which mixing and cooling occur together, and a fat of the desired consistency is produced.

Hard margarines are more hydrogenated, i.e. saturated, than soft tub margarines. Sunflower margarines are high in PUFA.

3. Low fat spreads

These are not margarines but they are made in a similar way. Their fat content is much lower (about 40%) and their water content higher (about 60%). Since they contain less fat their energy value is a lot lower. Margarine must by law contain at least 80% fat.

4. Cooking fats and shortenings

These were first produced in the U.S.A. as a substitute for lard. They are pure fat products rather than emulsions. The fat is a blend of vegetable and fish oils and animal fats. The oils are partially hydrogenated. The fat blend is cooled to give the desired consistency and air is usually incorporated into the product to improve the texture.

Some fats have an emulsifying agent added. These fats, known as high ratio fats, are specifically designed for high ratio cakes, i.e. cakes made from a batter with a high moisture content.

5. Lard

Lard is fat extracted from pigs. The extraction is carried out by heating or 'rendering'. Lard is almost 100% pure fat.

6. Butter

Butter is made by churning pasteurised cream. During churning the cream becomes more viscous and finally a mass of solid butter is produced. The liquid by-product, known as buttermilk, is removed and the butter is mixed to give the desired consistency. Salt and colouring matter may be added at this stage, although some butter is sold unsalted.

The churning or agitation process reverses the emulsion. Cream is an emulsion of fat globules dispersed in a water phase. During churning the fat globules aggregate and form a solid phase which is interspersed by small water droplets. Butter is therefore a water-in-fat emulsion.

The composition of some of these fats is shown in Figure 6.1.

Functions of fats in the diet

1. Energy

Fat is broken down in the body by a process of oxidation and energy is released. A description of this process is given in Chapter 10.

1 g of fat provides 38 kJ (9 kcal)

Fat has more than twice the calorific value of carbohydrates and is therefore a more concentrated source of energy. For people whose energy requirements are high it is useful

The Science of Food

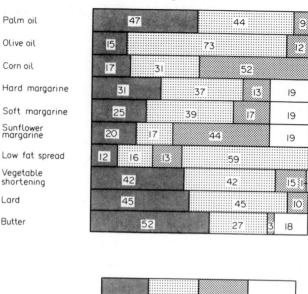

Palm oil	47	44	9
Olive oil	15	73	12
Corn oil	17	31	52
Hard margarine	31	37	13	19
Soft margarine	25	39	17	19
Sunflower margarine	20	17	44	19
Low fat spread	12	16	13	59
Vegetable shortening	42	42	15 1
Lard	45	45	10
Butter	52	27	3	18

Saturates   Monounsat-   Poly-   Water
urates   unsaturates

Fig. 6.1. Percentage composition of various fats and oils.

to include a reasonable quantity of fat in the diet, as it reduces the bulk of food which must be eaten.

2. Formation of adipose tissue

Excess fat, which is not immediately required for energy, is stored in the adipose tissue (see page 121) where it has three functions:

(a) fat stored in this way constitutes an energy reserve;
(b) the fat in the adipose tissue under the skin forms an insulating layer and helps to prevent excessive heat loss from the body. It therefore assists in the maintenance of a constant body temperature;
(c) fat is stored in adipose tissue around delicate organs, such as the kidneys, and protects these organs from physical damage.

3. Essential fatty acids

Some fatty acids are essential in small amounts for the functioning of the body. They must be supplied by fat in the diet since they cannot be synthesised in the body. These essential fatty acids, namely linoleic, linolenic and arachidonic acids, were at one time referred to as vitamin F. The reason for this was that their role in the diet had been discovered by dietary experiments but the exact nature of the substances had not been determined. Linoleic acid is probably the only truly essential fatty acid since linolenic and arachidonic acids can be formed in the body from linoleic acid. Linoleic acid is needed for the formation of cell membranes. Arachidonic acid is used to form prostaglandins, a group of hormone-like substances which help to regulate many bodily functions.

4. Fat-soluble vitamins

Certain fats included in the diet help to ensure an adequate intake of the fat-soluble vitamins A, D and E. However, in countries where fat intake is low, these vitamins can be obtained in other ways.

Sources of fat in the diet

Fats and oils are obtained from both animals and plants. They are formed from carbohydrate and represent a concentrated store of energy.

1. Meat and fish

All meat contains fat, though the percentage of fat varies from animal to animal and from one part of an animal to another. Meat provides 25% of the total fat content of the average British diet. Oily or fatty fish, such as herring and sardines, contain up to 20% oil but they contribute very little to the total intake because they are eaten infrequently.

2. Butter and margarine

These are both important sources of fat in the British diet. Butter contributes 10% and margarine 14% of the total fat content of the average diet.

3. Milk, cream and cheese

Milk contains between 3% and 4% fat; some products made from milk, such as cream and cheese, contain much larger amounts. Milk and cream account for 15% of the total fat content of the average British diet, and cheese contributes a further 5%.

4. Baked goods

Fat is used in the manufacture of cakes, pastry, biscuits and bread. These foods provide 9% of the total fat content of the average British diet.

5. Cooking fats and oils

Vegetable oils, shortenings and lard are used in the preparation of a large number of goods, particularly fried foods. They account for 12% of the total fat content of the average British diet.

6. Eggs

Eggs contain fat in an emulsified form in the yolk. They contribute 3% to the total fat content of the average British diet.

7. Other foods

Many other foods contain a considerable amount of fat. These include ice cream, chocolates and some sweets, nuts and salad dressings.

Vegetables and fruits contain insignificant amounts of fat. Notable exceptions are the soya bean which contains 24% fat and the avocado pear which is 8% fat.

Table 6.2 shows the fat content of a variety of foods.

TABLE 6.2. *Fat content of some foods*

Food	% Fat
Cooking oils	100
Lard	99
Butter	82
Margarine	81
Peanuts, roasted	49
Cream, double	48
Cheese, Cheddar	34
Chocolate, milk	30
Beef, average	24
Cream, single	21
Herring	14
Eggs	11
Chicken	4.3
Milk, full cream	3.8
Milk, semi-skimmed	1.7
Cod	0.7

Fats and health

A small amount of fat is necessary in the diet in order to supply the essential fatty acids. About 2% of the total energy supplied as fat is sufficient to meet this need. Normal fat intake is far greater than this. For example, in the U.K. in 1987, 42% of food energy was derived from fat.

There is much concern about the link between a high fat intake and the incidence of coronary heart disease (CHD). Coronary heart disease is caused by narrowing of the arteries of the heart due to the build up of fatty deposits on their inside walls. A blockage or blood clot in these arteries leads to a heart attack. It has been shown that a high level of cholesterol (a fat-like substance) in the blood increases the risk of the person developing CHD. The type of fat eaten affects the amount of cholesterol in the blood. Saturated fatty acids increase blood cholesterol levels, while PUFA tend to lower the level.

There is some evidence that monounsaturated fats are also cholesterol-lowering. However, other factors affect cholesterol levels including family history; some people have a naturally high level.

The COMA and NACNE reports (see page 152) recommend reducing fat intake, particularly the intake of saturated fats, i.e. animal fats and hardened vegetable fats, and partly compensating by increasing the intake of polyunsaturated products. The polyunsaturated : saturated fatty acid ratio (P/S ratio) should be greater than 1.0. There are many practical ways this may be achieved without drastically altering the diet, e.g.:

1. Eating less red meat but more chicken and fish.
2. Replacing butter by polyunsaturated margarine or low-fat spreads.
3. Using skimmed or semi-skimmed milk in place of full-cream milk.
4. Grilling, boiling, steaming or microwaving foods rather than frying them.
5. Using polyunsaturated oils (e.g. corn, soya) for cooking rather than lard or hardened cooking fats.

CHAPTER 7

Proteins

Proteins are a very important group of nutrients. They are found in the cytoplasm of all living cells, both animal and plant. Proteins are organic substances and they resemble fats and carbohydrates in that they contain the elements carbon, hydrogen and oxygen. However, all proteins also contain nitrogen and most contain sulphur and some contain phosphorus. Proteins show a greater variety and complexity of structure than either fats or carbohydrates. Plants are able to synthesise protein from inorganic materials. Carbon dioxide from the air and water from the soil provide the carbon, hydrogen and oxygen necessary for protein synthesis. Nitrogen is obtained from the soil in the form of inorganic compounds, usually nitrates and nitrites. Some plants, such as the legumes, are able to utilise nitrogen from the air, with the aid of bacteria. Animals, unlike plants, cannot synthesise protein from inorganic compounds, therefore protein is an essential nutrient in the diet of all animals.

The structure of proteins

Protein molecules are extremely large and consist of long chains of amino acids chemically combined. About 20 different amino acids occur in the proteins found in foods (see Table 7.1). Each amino acid molecule contains at least one amino group ($-NH_2$) and at least one acidic group ($-COOH$). Therefore, amino acids show both basic and acidic properties and are said to be **amphoteric**. It is incorrect to think that because they are described as acids they all have a pH below 7.

R = a variable group, basically a hydrocarbon chain, different in each amino acid.

Generalised formula of an amino acid

A typical protein molecule contains about 500 amino acids, joined together by **peptide links**. A peptide link is formed when the amino ($-NH_2$) group of one amino acid reacts with the acidic ($-COOH$) group of an adjacent amino acid. A molecule of water is eliminated during the formation of the peptide link (see Figure 7.1). This type of reaction is an example of condensation polymerisation. Two amino acids joined together form a **dipeptide**, with the $-CONH-$ atoms forming the peptide link. Longer chains of amino acids are called **polypeptides**. A protein molecule consists of a single polypeptide chain or a number of polypeptide chains joined by cross-linkages.

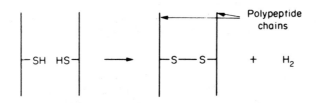

Fig. 7.1. Formation of a peptide link.

Protein molecules have a complex nature since they can contain all 20 amino acids in any arrangement. If a polypeptide was made up of only 10 amino acid units, the possible number of amino acid arrangements would be 20^{10} or well over a billion. Since even the simplest protein contains more than 50 amino acid units, it can be seen that it is possible to have an almost infinite number of different protein molecules. The order or 'pattern' of amino acids in the protein molecule is known as the *primary* protein structure.

Cross-links may be formed between the side groups of amino acids. These links may form between different polypeptide chains or between side groups on the same polypeptide chain. One of the most important types of cross-linkage is the disulphide bridge. The amino acid cysteine contains an —SH group. When two cysteine units are adjacent, a disulphide bridge, —S—S—, may be formed by the oxidation of the —SH groups, as shown in Figure 7.2.

Fig. 7.2. Formation of a disulphide bridge.

Cross-links may also be produced by the formation of hydrogen bonds. These are weak bonds arising from the tendency of hydrogen atoms, when attached to oxygen or nitrogen atoms, to share the electrons of a neighbouring oxygen atom (see page 42). Cross-linking determines the *secondary* structure of the protein, i.e. the shape and the three-dimensional configuration of the protein molecule.

Proteins vary a great deal in structure but they can be classified into two main groups, according to the shape of the molecules.

1. Globular proteins

Molecules of globular proteins are rounded in shape but are not necessarily spherical. The amino acid chain is folded and the molecule is kept in shape by cross-linkages within the amino acid chain. The structure is three-dimensional but it can be represented in two dimensions as shown in Figure 7.3.

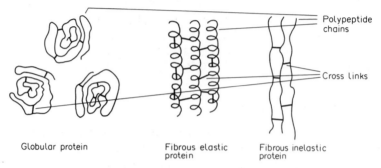

Fig. 7.3. Types of proteins.

The molecules are not closely packed, nor is there any organised arrangement. It is easy for water molecules to penetrate the empty spaces within the protein molecules. Globular proteins are easily dispersed in either water or salt solutions to form colloids (see Chapter 4). Some examples of globular proteins found in foods are ovalbumin, found in egg white and caseinogen, found in milk. Most of the proteins found in body cells are globular, e.g. haemoglobin and myoglobin.

2. Fibrous proteins

Molecules of fibrous proteins are straighter. They may be almost completely straight (inelastic or extended proteins) or coiled in a spiral (elastic proteins) as shown in Figure 7.3.

In fibrous proteins there is usually an organised arrangement and the molecules are closely packed together. There are cross-links between adjacent amino acid chains and it is difficult for water molecules to penetrate the structure. Therefore fibrous proteins are not usually soluble in water.

Gluten, the insoluble protein found in wheat, is an example of an elastic protein. When pulled, gluten will stretch but it tends to return to its original shape when the force is removed. This is because molecules of gluten are coiled and behave like a spring. They return to their original position due to the cross-links holding the chains together. This is shown diagrammatically in Figure 7.4. Elastin, a constituent of connective tissue which is

Fig. 7.4. Stretching of gluten molecules.

found in meat and known as 'gristle', and keratin, the protein found in hair and wool, behave in a similar fashion. Collagen, one of the other proteins found in connective tissue, is an example of an extended protein.

The properties of proteins

The properties of a substance are determined by its structure and since there is a wide variation in the structure of proteins the properties also vary a great deal.

Fibrous proteins are relatively insoluble and are not greatly affected by acids, alkalis and moderate heat. Globular proteins form colloidal solutions and are affected by acids, alkalis and heat.

Denaturation and coagulation

Proteins undergo a process known as **denaturation** when their secondary structure is altered but their primary structure is unchanged. The molecule unfolds and changes shape but the sequence of amino acids remains the same. Denaturation is brought about by various physical and chemical means and involves the breaking of the cross-linkages which maintain the shape of the molecule. It is usually irreversible, it being impossible to regain the original structure of the molecule. As a result of denaturation the properties of the proteins alter; they become less soluble and more viscous. The unfolded molecules tend to bond with each other forming clumps. This results in the hardening or 'setting' of the protein food and is known as **coagulation**. Coagulation can be brought about by various means such as:

1. ACTION OF HEAT

Many proteins coagulate when heated. For example, when an egg is cooked the proteins in the white and the yolk coagulate. Egg-white proteins coagulate first at 60°C and the yolk at approximately 66°C. This coagulation is used extensively in the preparation of many dishes, e.g. egg custard and sponge cake. The muscle fibre proteins in meat coagulate when heated resulting in the shrinkage of meat during cooking.

Denatured proteins are more readily attacked by digestive enzymes and therefore most protein foods (e.g. eggs, meat) are more digestible when cooked.

2. PRESENCE OF ACID

When milk sours, bacteria present in the milk ferment lactose, producing lactic acid. The pH of the milk is lowered and this causes the milk protein, caseinogen, to coagulate. The starter culture, used in the manufacture of some milk products, such as yoghurt and cheese, consists of lactose-fermenting bacteria. The lactic acid, produced by the bacteria, is responsible for the coagulation or 'setting' of the milk and the formation of a curd.

3. ADDITION OF SALT

Certain salts, such as sodium chloride, coagulate some proteins. If salt is added to the cooking water used for boiling eggs, the white will not escape as readily if the shell is cracked. During cheesemaking, salt is often added to the curd to increase firmness and also to suppress the growth of microoganisms.

4. ADDITION OF RENNIN

Rennin, known commercially as rennet, is an enzyme which coagulates protein. Rennet is used to make junket, which is clotted or coagulated milk. Rennin is also used, together with a bacterial starter, to form the curd in cheese manufacture (see page 166).

5. MECHANICAL ACTION

Mechanical action during the whisking of egg white causes a partial coagulation of the protein. The protein molecules unfold and form a reinforcing network round the air bubbles, thus stabilising the foam. This is used in food preparation, e.g. the making of meringues and soufflés.

Maillard reaction (non-enzymic browning)

This is a browning reaction which occurs during the roasting, baking, grilling and frying of many foods. A chemical reaction takes place between the amino group of a free amino acid or a free amino group on a protein chain and the carbonyl group of a reducing sugar, e.g. glucose. Brown-coloured compounds are formed which are responsible for the attractive colour of products such as bread crust, roasted meat, fried potatoes and baked cakes and biscuits. The compounds also confer an appetising flavour to the foods.

Although the reaction is generally considered desirable during cooking, there are two undesirable effects. Firstly, there is some loss of nutritional value of proteins. Amino acids containing an extra amino group, e.g. the essential amino acid lysine, are most likely to be involved. Secondly, the reaction can cause discoloration of foods during storage, for example the gradual browning of dried milk powder.

Functions of proteins in the body

1. Growth and maintenance

Proteins are the main constituents of the cells of the body. The membranes surrounding the cells contain protein and also protein is found within the cell. The number of cells in the body increases during periods of growth, therefore during childhood and adolescence protein requirements are particularly high. In addition, protein in the tissues is constantly being broken down and must be replaced from the amino acids supplied in the diet. This replacement of tissue occurs in all people at all stages of their life. An account of the process by which amino acids in body cells combine to form protein in included in Chapter 10.

Protein is necessary for the formation of enzymes, antibodies and some hormones. These substances are produced within cells and in some cases are released either into the blood-stream (antibodies and hormones) or into the intestine (digestive enzymes). For a description of enzymes see Chapter 11 and for hormones see page 127.

2. Energy

Not all of the protein supplied by food can be used for growth and repair. The amount of protein which is available for use in this way depends on the Biological Values (see page 78) of the various proteins in the diet. In addition, the diet may supply more protein than is required for growth and maintenance. Any excess protein may be used for energy. Amino acids which are not required for protein synthesis are deaminated in the liver, i.e. the nitrogen containing parts of the amino acid molecules are removed to form urea. Urea is a waste product, which is of no value to the body, and it is carried by the blood to the kidneys and from there it is excreted in the urine. The deaminated molecules contain carbon, hydrogen and oxygen. They enter the chain of reactions in which glucose is oxidised in the cells to supply energy (see page 118).

1 g of protein provides 17 kJ (4 kcal)

Essential amino acids and protein quality

Of the 20 amino acids commonly found in proteins, eight are essential in the diet. These essential amino acids must be supplied by the protein in the diet, since they cannot be synthesised in the body. Eight amino acids are essential for all people and one additional one must be supplied in the diets of rapidly growing infants. The non-essential amino acids can be synthesised in the body by converting one amino acid into another within the body cells. Table 7.1 indicates which of the 20 commonly occurring amino acids are essential.

TABLE 7.1. *Essential and non-essential amino acids*

Essential	Non-essential
Isoleucine	Alanine
Leucine	Arginine
Lysine	Aspargine
Methionine	Aspartic acid
Phenylalanine	Cysteine (may occur in the form
Threonine	of Cystine)
Tryptophan	Glutamic acid
Valine	Glycine
Histidine (essential for	Ornithine
infants)	Proline (may occur in the form of
	Hydroxyproline)
	Serine
	Tyrosine

Methionine and cysteine are sulphur-containing amino acids and some of the requirement of methionine can be met by cysteine or cystine.

When protein foods are eaten, the proteins are hydrolysed during digestion to produce amino acids. After absorption the amino acids are transported by the blood to the cells. In the cells the amino acids recombine and new proteins are formed. The distribution of the various essential amino acids in the food we eat is not necessarily the same as is required to synthesise protein in the cells. A protein which has a similar distribution of essential amino acids to the protein in the human body is therefore of more use, or of better quality, than one which does not supply the essential amino acids in the necessary quantities. The **Biological Value** of a protein is used as a measure of protein quality. **Biological Value (BV) is the percentage of absorbed protein which is converted into body protein.** The protein content of a food is difficult to determine by experiment. It is usual to determine the nitrogen derived from protein rather than the total protein content.

$$\textbf{BV} = \frac{\textbf{Retained nitrogen}}{\textbf{Absorbed nitrogen}} \times \textbf{100}$$

The Biological Values of a variety of proteins are given in Table 7.2. Egg protein, which has an amino acid pattern similar to human protein, has a BV of 97. Gelatin has a BV of 0, because it is completely lacking in the essential amino acid tryptophan.

Some years ago the F.A.O. (Food and Agriculture Oganisation of the United Nations) published a reference standard representing a protein having a BV of 100. The amino acid pattern of this protein is shown in histogram form in Figure 7.5.

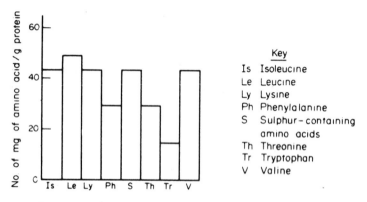

FIG. 7.5. Amino acid histogram for a perfect protein.

Similar histograms showing the amino acid pattern of cheese protein and bread protein (see Figure 7.6) show that cheese is deficient in methionine and the other sulphur-containing amino acids and that bread has a significant deficiency of lysine, sulphur-containing amino acids and tryptophan. Sulphur-containing amino acids are limiting in cheese protein, since only 78% of the required amount is present. All other essential amino acids are present in sufficient quantity. In bread protein, lysine is the limiting amino acid; only 47% of the required amount is present.

Biological Value is a measure of protein quality when the protein concerned is the sole source of protein in the diet. However, people normally eat a mixed diet containing a variety of proteins. When two different proteins are mixed, the resulting mixture has a higher BV than the average BV of the components. One protein may have a surplus of the amino acid which is the limiting amino acid in the other protein. A good example of this complementation is bread and cheese; the lysine deficiency in the bread is made good by the excess in the cheese. This is illustrated in Figure 7.7, which shows the BV of a mixture of three parts of cheese protein to one part of bread protein.

FIG. 7.6. Amino acid histograms for cheese and bread protein.

Other examples of dishes in which the proteins complement each other include breakfast cereals and milk, baked beans on toast, pasta and cheese (e.g. macaroni cheese) and milk and rice (e.g. rice pudding).

Commercially, the BV of plant proteins can be increased by the addition of small quantities of the limiting amino acid. For example, yeast protein has a BV of 67 but the addition of 0.3% methionine (the limiting amino acid in yeast) increases the BV to 91.

Biological Value does not take into account the digestibility of the protein food. Not all the protein taken into the body is absorbed from the intestine. The digestibility of protein present in food will depend on several factors. The method of cooking is important; mild

FIG. 7.7. Amino acid histogram for a mixture of cheese and bread protein.

heat treatment increases digestibility but overcooking causes a decrease. It will also vary with the individual, since some people have more difficulty in digesting certain foods. **Net Protein Utilisation**, another term used to measure protein quality, takes into account the digestibility of the protein (see page 135). **Net Protein Utilisation (NPU) is the percentage of dietary protein which is converted into body protein.**

$$\textbf{NPU} = \frac{\textbf{Retained nitrogen}}{\textbf{Intake of nitrogen}} \times \textbf{100}$$

$$\text{NPU} = \text{BV} \times \text{Digestibility}$$

Table 7.2 lists the NPU for proteins from a variety of sources.

When considering the value of a protein food in the diet, it is not only the BV or NPU of the protein which must be considered, but also the percentage of protein in a food and the amount of the food eaten.

TABLE 7.2. *BV and NPU of proteins from a variety of sources*

Protein source	BV %	NPU %
Egg	97	96
Meat	82	78
Fish	79	77
Milk	77	71
Soya bean	73	61
Rice	67	63
Peas	64	47
Peanuts	55	43
Corn	50	45
Wheat	49	48
Gelatin	0	0

Sources of protein in the diet

Protein can be obtained from both animal and plant sources. In general, foods obtained from animals contain more protein than foods obtained from plants, although some vegetable materials, such as soya beans, have a high protein content. Vegetable proteins usually have a lower BV than animal proteins and in the past much emphasis was placed on this. However, in a mixed diet, this is not serious (see page 79), and vegetable proteins have the advantage of being cheaper than animal proteins. It is no longer usual to differentiate between 'first-class' animal proteins and 'second-class' vegetable proteins.

1. Meat and fish

The term 'meat' usually refers to the muscle tissue of animals but it may be extended to include other parts of the animal, such as liver, kidney and sweetbreads. The contribution of all forms of meat to the protein content of the average British diet is 31%. Fish is eaten less frequently and contributes 5% of the total protein intake.

2. Bread and cereals

Bread contains a significant amount of protein and is one of the most important and one of the cheapest sources in the British diet. However, it is not as important as a protein source as it has been in the past since bread consumption has decreased in recent years. Nevertheless, bread and flour together account for 15% of the total protein intake. Other cereal foods, such as rice, pasta, breakfast cereals, cakes and biscuits, also contain protein and contribute a further 8%.

3. Milk and cheese

Milk is a valuable source of good-quality protein. Protein is present in some foods made from milk, the most important of these being cheese. Milk accounts for 17% of the protein content of the average British diet, while cheese contributes a further 6%.

4. Eggs

Eggs are an excellent source of high-quality protein. However, they are not eaten as much as some other protein foods, therefore their contribution to the protein content of the average British diet is only 4%.

5. Vegetables

The amount of protein in the cells of root and green vegetables is small, although potatoes, mainly because of the quantity in which they are eaten, do contribute 4% to the total protein content of the average British diet. Seeds of plants contain significantly more protein. Pulse vegetables such as peas and lentils contain moderate amounts of protein, though when dried, they have a much higher protein content.

6. Nuts

Although not an important source of protein in the average British diet, nuts are a major source of protein in the diets of many vegans and vegetarians (see page 148).

The protein content of some of these foods is shown in Table 7.3.

TABLE 7.3. *Protein content of some foods*

Food	Protein %
Soya beans	40
Cheese, Cheddar	26
Peanuts, roasted	24
Lentils	24
Chicken	21
Stewing beef	17
Cod and haddock	17
Brazil nuts	12
Eggs	12
White bread	7.8
Rice	6.5
Peas	5.8
Baked beans	5.1
Milk	3.3
Potatoes	2.1
Cabbage	1.9

Protein requirements

The former Department of Health and Social Security (D.H.S.S.) published recommended daily intakes of protein for various groups. Some of these figures are shown in Table 7.4.

TABLE 7.4. *Recommended daily amounts of protein*

Age range	Body-weight (kg)	Protein (g)
Boys, 5–6 years	20.5	43
Boys, 15–17 years	61.0	72
Girls, 15–17 years	56.1	53
Men, 18–34 years		
moderately active	65.0	72
Women, 18–54 years		
most occupations	55.0	54
Pregnancy (last 6 months)		60
Lactation		69

These protein intakes are approximately 10% of the recommended energy intakes in the United Kingdom. This is greater than the minimum amount of protein necessary for health. It has been shown that people can remain in good health on considerably lower intakes, but a safety margin has been included to allow for variations in the NPU of the protein. Also, higher levels of protein intake are more in keeping with the character of the British diet.

The protein requirement of an individual depends on rate of growth and body-weight. An adult requires approximately 1 g of protein for every kg of body-weight. During periods of growth proportionately more protein is required, e.g. for a child aged five to six years, approximately 2 g of protein per kg body-weight are needed.

During pregnancy and lactation (breast feeding), women need more protein in their diet, since they must satisfy the protein requirements of the baby as well as their own.

As a result of illness or an operation, the body loses considerable quantities of protein. For example, as a result of a fracture of the femur (thigh bone) the body loses about 800 g of protein. Therefore, during convalescence the protein content of the diet should be increased to 14% of the total energy intake.

Protein deficiency

In Western, industrialised countries protein intake is normally more than adequate and deficiency is rare. In the less developed countries of the world, particularly in parts of Africa and the Far East, the diet is composed mainly of one staple food (a plant food) and in areas where this food is a low-protein food, such as cassava or yams, protein deficiency is common. Severe protein deficiency causes a disease known as **kwashiorkor**. This condition is caused by a diet low in protein and high in carbohydrate and is most common in young children after weaning. The disease is serious and has many symptoms. The main symptoms are wasting of the muscles, retarded growth and a distended abdomen caused by oedema (fluid in the tissues). The lack of protein also causes anaemia, since protein is necessary for the formation of red blood cells.

The treatment of the disease involves the provision of a diet adequate in energy, vitamins and minerals, containing a good quantity of easily digested protein of high biological value. Dried, skimmed milk is one of the most useful foods for the treatment of kwashiorkor. However, this is only a short-term measure and in the long term the disease must be prevented by improving the normal diet of the people.

The technical means for increasing food production are already available. These means include the development of disease-resistant and high-yielding crops, the use of chemical fertilisers and pesticides, irrigation of infertile land and the further development of fish farming. However, the main causes of food shortage and malnutrition are economic, political and social, rather than technical. The richer, industrialised countries have the purchasing power to take more than their share, whilst the poorer countries do not have the money to invest in their own agriculture or to import sufficient food.

Production of animal protein is not an efficient method of obtaining protein since animals are not efficient at converting dietary protein into body protein. As little as 15% of the protein fed to an animal is actually converted into consumable protein such as meat, milk and eggs. It is therefore more economic to eat plant protein, rather than feed animals with cereals and protein concentrates and eat the animal products. One hectare of land used to graze cattle will provide enough beef to meet the protein requirement of one man for 300 days. If this hectare of land is used for the production of wheat, 3500 days' protein supply can be produced, and if it is used for the cultivation of soya beans, 8000 days' protein requirement can be supplied by the same area of land.

Another factor in food production which is now being given much consideration is the energy output : energy input ratio. The energy output is a measure of the energy value of the food obtained. The energy input is the energy required to grow crops or rear animals. Mechanical energy is necessary for ploughing, sowing and harvesting. Energy is consumed in the manufacture of fertilisers and insecticides. Animals require energy in the form of the food they eat. Intensive methods used for livestock farming necessitate the use of heat and light in animal buildings.

The energy output : energy input ratio of various foods is listed below:

Food	Energy output : input ratio
Wheat	2.3
Bread	1.3
Eggs	0.16
Chickens	0.13

If the ratio is less than one, more energy is used in producing the food than is obtained by its consumption. It can be seen from the figures that the production of animal foods is very energy-intensive and it is therefore preferable to concentrate on producing more vegetable foods.

Novel sources of protein

In recent years attention has been focused on the problem of developing low-cost, protein-rich foods, either by making fuller use of local protein resources or by investigating new types, such as single-cell protein produced by microorganisms. The following are some of these developments.

1. Textured vegetable proteins

The protein from certain oilseeds can be used to make textured products which can be used to replace, or partly replace, meat in a wide variety of dishes. The seeds most frequently used are soya beans. Defatted soya-bean meal contains about 50% protein, but it is not suitable as a human food because it contains substances which inhibit growth. Some of these substances are heat-sensitive and are easily destroyed by cooking or roasting. Others are water-soluble and can be removed by soaking and extraction.

Soya-bean meal can be used to manufacture a product with a meat-like texture, known as textured vegetable protein (TVP). The protein is extracted by adding an alkali and fibres are formed by extruding the protein through fine nozzles or spinerettes. The fibres are combined with fat, a protein binder, colours and flavours. The product is similar to cooked meat and can be frozen, canned or dehydrated. TVP is used in this country, particularly in industrial canteens and the school meals service. It is also sold on the retail market.

2. Single-cell protein

Microorganisms have a high protein content and contain useful quantities of vitamins. Their rate of growth is very rapid and the rate of protein synthesis in microorganisms has been compared favourably with the rate in animals. A 500 kg bullock produces an extra 500 g of protein per day, whereas 500 kg of yeast grown in suitable conditions can produce 50 tonnes of protein in one day. It can be seen that microorganisms are potentially a very valuable source of protein, especially if they can be produced economically by the use of a cheap food. Many foods (or substrates) have been investigated, for example, yeast can be grown on various products obtainable for crude oil; a fungus has been developed which can be grown on waste vegetable matter and work has been carried out on bacteria which utilise methanol obtained by the oxidation of natural gas.

3. Protein-rich preparations

There are a number of protein-rich concentrates which have been developed by various research units, government departments and international agencies, for use as protein supplements in areas where kwashiorkor is common. These usually consist of vegetable protein meal and cereal flours, combined with other nutrients. Many are designed for use as weaning foods.

Incaparina, which has been used successfully in Central America, contains cottonseed flour together with cereal flours made from maize and sorghum; it is fortified with calcium and vitamins. In India use has been made of local groundnuts to produce a product known as Indian Multipurpose Food (IMF), which is 75% groundnut meal and 25% Bengal gram (a pulse vegetable). Having more than one protein in the mixture results in a protein of higher biological value. Pulse vegetables contain an excess of lysine, which is the limiting amino acid in cereal proteins.

CHAPTER 8

Vitamins

The vitamins are a group of complex organic compounds required in small quantities by the body for the maintenance of health. They are not usually synthesised in the body and are therefore essential in the diet. They are present in foods in small amounts.

In the nineteenth century it was assumed that a diet containing carbohydrate, fat, protein and minerals was sufficient to maintain health. However, in 1888, a scientist called Lunin carried out experiments showing that mice could not survive on such a diet although they thrived on the same diet if they were also given milk. It was apparent that milk contained substances other than carbohydrates, fats, proteins and minerals, which were essential for health.

The effects of vitamin deficiencies had been recognised for centuries but the cause of these diseases was unknown. Scurvy, a disease caused by a dietary lack of vitamin C, was common amongst sailors on long sea voyages in the sixteenth and seventeenth centuries. In his voyage round the world from 1772 to 1775, Captain Cook demonstrated that scurvy could be prevented by the consumption of fresh fruits and vegetables.

In 1912 Hopkins published the results of his experiments on rats which showed conclusively the existence of a vitamin, or as he called it an 'accessory food factor' in milk. Since that time over 20 different vitamins have been isolated from food, identified and also synthesised in the laboratory. When the early vitamins were discovered they were named according to the letters of the alphabet. Each vitamin was also given a chemical name when its chemical composition was identified. Letters are still used for naming vitamins but they are gradually being replaced by the chemical names.

Unlike other groups of nutrients, the vitamins are not chemically similar to each other. Each vitamin has a specific chemical structure and a specific function or set of functions in the body. Many of the vitamins are involved in enzyme systems in the body (see Chapter 11).

For most people a sensible and varied diet will supply all the necessary vitamins. It is unnecessary to waste money on vitamin tablets. With few exceptions, most notably babies, young children and pregnant women, people do not require vitamin supplements.

Vitamins can be divided into two main groups.

1. Fat-soluble vitamins

Vitamin A and vitamin D are the two most important vitamins in this group. They will dissolve in fats and oils but not in water. Both of these vitamins can be stored in the body, in the liver. In extreme circumstances it is possible to have an excessive intake of these vitamins leading to high levels in the body and a condition known as 'hyper-vitaminosis'. Quantities of vitamins A and D are measured in micrograms (μg) (see page 4).

2. Water-soluble vitamins

The vitamins of the B group and vitamin C will dissolve in water but not in fats. Since they are water soluble they are not stored in the body, any excess being excreted in the urine. Quantities of the three main B vitamins (thiamin, riboflavin and nicotinic acid) and vitamin C are measured in millgrams (mg).

Vitamin A (retinol)

Retinol is a pale yellow solid which dissolves in fats and oils but not in water. It is found only in animal foods, but many fruits and vegetables contain carotenes, a group of orange pigments, which can be converted into retinol in the body. The most important of these pigments is beta (β)-carotene.

Vitamin A is measured in retinol equivalents.

$$1 \ \mu g \text{ retinol equivalent} = 1 \ \mu g \text{ retinol}$$
$$= 6 \ \mu g \ \beta\text{-carotene}$$

Only a proportion of the β-carotene present in food is converted into retinol.

Sources of retinol

Retinol is found in some fatty animal foods. Since animals and fish can store retinol in the liver, liver and fish liver oils have a high retinol content. Fish liver oils are not foods but are dietary supplements. They are so rich in vitamins A and D that they are potentially dangerous and should be taken only in the recommended doses. Retinol is also found in butter, milk, cheese, eggs and oily fish. It is not present in vegetable oils but since 1954, vitamin A has been added to margarine by law to make margarine nutritionally equivalent to butter. Although liver, kidney and heart are good sources,

TABLE 8.1. *Retinol content of some foods*

Food	μg retinol equivalents per 100 g
Halibut liver oil	900,000
Cod liver oil	18,000
Liver, ox	16,500
*Margarine	900
*Butter	825
Cheese, Cheddar	350
*Eggs	140
Herring	45
*Milk	30

* May include a contribution from carotene.

carcase meat contains only a trace of retinol. Table 8.1 shows the retinol content of some foods.

Sources of carotene

Carotene is found in a variety of vegetables, particularly in carrots and dark green vegetables, and in some yellow-coloured fruits such as peaches and apricots. The carotene content of some foods is shown in Table 8.2.

TABLE 8.2. *Carotene content of some foods*

Food	µg retinol equivalents per 100 g
Carrots	2000
Spinach	1000
Watercress	500
Apricots	250
Tomatoes	100
Cabbage	50
Peas	50

(1 µg retinol equivalent = 6 µg β-carotene.)

In the British diet, approximately two-thirds of the vitamin A is consumed as retinol and one-third as carotene. The most important sources of vitamin A are liver, carrots, milk, margarine and butter (see Table 8.3).

TABLE 8.3. *Contributions made by different foods to the total vitamin A content of the average British diet*

Food	Contribution to total vitamin A intake
Liver	33%
Carrots	14%
Milk and cream	14%
Margarine	10%
Butter	7%

Functions

1. Retinol is essential for growth and metabolism of all body cells.
2. It is also required for the formation of rhodopsin (visual purple), a complex substance formed from retinol and protein. Rhodopsin is a pigment found in the retina, a membrane at the back of the eye, and is necessary for vision in reduced light.
3. Vitamin A is also essential for the maintenance of healthy skin and surface tissues, particularly the moist mucous membranes such as the cornea at the front of the eye and the lining of the respiratory tract.

Deficiency

Since retinol is stored in the body it is possible to exist for a certain period of time on a diet containing little vitamin A. However, if this period is prolonged, signs of deficiency will become apparent.

1. Lack of vitamin A in the diet of children reduces the rate of growth.

2. Since without retinol the body is unable to synthesise rhodopsin, vision in reduced light is impaired, causing a condition known as **night blindness**. If the deficiency is only slight the condition is easily reversed by increasing the intake of vitamin A. The popular fallacy that 'eating carrots helps you to see in the dark' contains an element of truth since carrots contain a significant amount of vitamin A. However, since the average British diet contains sufficient vitamin A, increasing the intake above the required level will cause no improvement in eyesight.

3. Vitamin A deficiency affects the health of the skin and resistance to infection is lowered due to the poor condition of the mucous lining of the respiratory tract. In extreme cases the tear glands become blocked and the membranes at the front of the eye become dry and inflamed. This condition is known as **xerophthalmia**. Severe and prolonged deficiency can lead to ulceration of the cornea causing blindness. Vitamin A deficiency is a common cause of blindness in developing countries where the diet is composed mainly of a staple cereal food and where fruits and vegetables containing carotene are not available. It usually develops in children after weaning when vitamin A is no longer supplied by breast milk.

Vitamin A deficiency is virtually unknown in Britain.

Excess

Very large doses of vitamin A are harmful. Excessive intakes are unlikely to occur with a normal diet, but there have been cases of illness when people have taken large amounts of vitamin preparations over a period of time. Hypervitaminosis A causes drowsiness, irritability, skin and bone disorders and an enlarged liver. Sometimes mothers have been unaware of the harmful effects and have given their children excessive doses of vitamin drops or fish liver oils. In 1957 a maximum level of vitamin A in baby foods was stipulated by law.

Recommended intake

The Department of Health and Social Security (D.H.S.S.) recommended a daily intake of **750 μg** retinol equivalents for adults. During lactation, when a woman must produce milk containing sufficient vitamin A to satisfy the needs of her baby, the recommended daily intake is 1200 μg retinol equivalents.

Losses on cooking and storage

Both retinol and carotene are unaffected by most cooking methods but small amounts may be lost during frying. Some carotene is lost during slow drying of fruit and vegetables, but in modern, quick drying the losses are very much reduced. During storage, retinol in fatty foods may be lost by oxidation. This may be prevented by the use of antioxidants, by refrigeration and by the exclusion of light, e.g. wrapping fats in foil and storing fish liver oils in dark glass bottles.

None of these losses is sufficiently large to be of practical significance. In all cases the majority of the vitamin A value of the food is retained.

The B vitamins

The B vitamins are a group of vitamins which, although chemically different from each other, are all water soluble and tend to occur in similar foods.

Thiamin (vitamin B₁)

Thiamin is a white solid which is soluble in water.

Sources

Thiamin is found in all cereal grains. Most of the thiamin is found in the germ and bran of the grain (see page 169) and therefore white flour contains considerably less thiamin than wholewheat flour. To overcome this deficiency thiamin is added by law to white flour in Britain. Many breakfast cereal manufacturers add thiamin to their products. Brown rice is a good source of thiamin but polished white rice, which is used more extensively, contains very little.

Other sources of thiamin include meat (especially bacon, ham and pork), potatoes, peas, beans, nuts and milk. Brewers' yeast is a particularly rich source since, during the production of beer, the yeast absorbs thiamin from the cereal grain. However, it is not considered to be a food, although it is used by some people as a dietary supplement. Products made from yeast, such as yeast extract, are eaten in such small quantities that they make an almost negligible contribution to the diet. The thiamin content of some foods is shown in Table 8.4.

TABLE 8.4. *Thiamin content of some foods*

Food	mg thiamin per 100 g
Dried brewers' yeast	15.6
Cornflakes	1.8
Pork	0.58
Peas	0.32
Wholemeal bread	0.26
White bread	0.18
Potatoes	0.11
Lamb	0.09
Beef	0.05
Milk	0.04

The most important sources of thiamin in the British diet are bread and other cereal foods, meat, milk and potatoes (see Table 8.5).

TABLE 8.5. *Contributions made by different foods to the total thiamin content of the average British diet*

Food	Contribution to total thiamin intake
Bread	25% ⎫ 50%
Other cereal foods	25% ⎭
Meat	14%
Milk	10%
Potatoes	8%

Function

Thiamin is involved in the oxidation of nutrients and the release of energy in the body. In the cells of the body, glucose is gradually broken down in a series of reactions which release energy in a controlled manner (see page 118). Each reaction in the series requires a specific enzyme. A complex compound containing thiamin acts as a co-enzyme for two of the reactions in the sequence.

Deficiency

If thiamin is deficient in the diet glucose is only partially oxidised. The breakdown stops at a substance called pyruvic acid. A build up of pyruvic acid in the blood causes muscular weakness, palpitations of the heart and degeneration of the nerves. These are the main symptoms of a disease called **beriberi** which is common in parts of Asia where the staple food is polished rice. Beriberi develops more readily with carbohydrate-rich diets. There are two main types of beriberi. In wet beriberi the patient suffers from oedema (fluid in the tissues) and in dry beriberi there is severe emaciation and wastage of the tissues. It has been said that a person suffering from the extreme weakness of beriberi will sum up how he feels by the following statements: 'It is better to sit than to stand. It is better to lie down than to sit. It is better to die than to live.'

Beriberi can, to some extent, be prevented by parboiling unpolished rice. If rice grains are parboiled before the bran and germ are removed much of the thiamin is absorbed by the inner part of the grain.

Beriberi rarely occurs with Western diets, though it has been found in anorexics and alcoholics.

Recommended intake

Since thiamin is necessary for the oxidation of glucose the amount required by the body is related to the amount of carbohydrate in the diet; 0.6 mg thiamin is recommended for every 4200 kJ (1000 kcal) derived from carbohydrate. For practical purposes it is more convenient to relate thiamin requirements to total energy intake and the figure 0.4 mg thiamin per 4200 kJ (1000 kcal) is used. For an adult man whose energy requirement is 12,000 kJ (2900 kcal) per day the recommended daily intake of thiamin is **1.2 mg**.

Losses on cooking and processing

Thiamin, like all other B vitamins, is soluble in water. About 25% of the thiamin is lost when potatoes are boiled. Thiamin decomposes at high temperatures, particularly in alkaline conditions. Meat loses about 40% of its thiamin when roasted and when bread is baked about 25% of the thiamin is destroyed. The loss on baking is greater if an alkaline substance, such as sodium bicarbonate, is used as a raising agent.

Some preservatives have an adverse effect on thiamin. For example, sodium sulphite which is used to prevent the browning of prepeeled potatoes and which is added to many other processed foods including dried fruits and vegetables destroys thiamin.

Riboflavin (vitamin B$_2$)

Riboflavin is a yellow, water-soluble compound.

Sources

Good sources of riboflavin include cheese, liver, kidney and eggs. It is also found in milk, meat, potatoes and green vegetables. Liver is a particularly rich source. Riboflavin is found in bread and cereals but to a lesser extent than thiamin, although, like thiamin, it is added to some breakfast cereals. Table 8.6 shows the riboflavin content of some of these foods.

TABLE 8.6. *Riboflavin content of some foods*

Food	mg riboflavin per 100 g
Dried brewers' yeast	3.68
Liver	3.10
Kidney	2.10
Cornflakes	1.60
Cheese, Cheddar	0.50
Eggs	0.47
Beef	0.20
Milk	0.19
Cabbage	0.05
Potatoes	0.04
White bread	0.03

The main sources of riboflavin in the British diet are milk, cereal foods, meat, vegetables and eggs (see Table 8.7).

TABLE 8.7. *Contributions made by different foods to the total riboflavin content of the average British diet*

Food	Contribution to total riboflavin intake
Milk	33%
Cereal foods	20%
Meat	18%
Vegetables	8%
Eggs	6%

Function

The function of riboflavin is similar to that of thiamin. It forms part of the enzyme system concerned in the oxidation of glucose and the release of energy in body cells.

Deficiency

A deficiency of riboflavin affects the eyes, lips and tongue. Cracks appear at the corners of the mouth and the tongue becomes red and swollen. These symptoms, however, are not specific to riboflavin deficiency; they may be caused by a lack of other B vitamins or by other means. A diet deficient in riboflavin will almost certainly be deficient in other nutrients as well.

Recommended intake

Riboflavin requirements are related more closely to body-weight than to energy intake. The D.H.S.S. recommended daily intake of riboflavin is **1.6 mg** for adult men and **1.3 mg** for adult women.

Cooking losses

Riboflavin is only slightly soluble in water and is fairly stable to heat. The overall loss during cooking is small and very much less than the corresponding loss of thiamin.

Effects of sunlight

Riboflavin is sensitive to light. Milk, the most important source of riboflavin in the diet, loses riboflavin at the rate of about 10% per hour if left in direct sunlight. It is best, therefore, not to leave milk in glass bottles on doorsteps for long periods.

Nicotinic acid (niacin)

Nicotinic acid, also known as niacin, is a white, crystalline, water-soluble solid.

Nicotinic acid is converted into its amide, nicotinamide, in the body. Nicotinamide can also be formed in the body from the amino acid, tryptophan.

$$1 \text{ mg nicotinic acid equivalent} = 1 \text{ mg available nicotinic acid}$$
$$= 60 \text{ mg tryptophan}$$

Sources

Nicotinic acid is widely distributed in plant and animal foods. Foods with a good nicotinic acid activity include yeast, meat (particularly offal), fish, cheese, pulse vegetables and cereals. Much of the nicotinic acid in wheat is lost during the milling process and therefore, in Britain, nicotinic acid is added by law to white flour. Milk, eggs, potatoes and beer are moderately good sources. Table 8.8 shows the nicotinic activity of a variety of foods.

TABLE 8.8. *Nicotinic acid activity of some foods*

Food	mg nicotinic acid equivalents per 100 g
Dried brewers' yeast	62.9
Peanuts, roasted	21.3
Liver	17.9
Beef	7.2
Cheese, Cheddar	6.2
Wholemeal bread	5.6
Cod	4.9
Eggs	3.7
Peas	3.4
White bread	3.0
Potatoes	1.7
Milk	0.9
Beer	0.6

The most important sources in the British diet are meat, milk, bread and other cereals, and potatoes (see Table 8.9).

TABLE 8.9. *Contributions made by different foods to the total nicotinic acid content of the average British diet*

Food	Contribution to total nicotinic acid equivalents
Meat	34%
Milk	11%
Bread	10% ⎫
Other cereal foods	11% ⎬ 21%
Potatoes	8% ⎭

Function

Nicotinic acid, like thiamin and riboflavin, forms part of an enzyme system concerned in the oxidation of glucose and the release of energy in body cells.

Deficiency

A prolonged deficiency of nicotinic acid gives rise to a disease known as **pellagra**. The symptoms of the disease include diarrhoea, dermatitis (scaling and discoloration of the parts of the skin exposed to the sun) and dementia (mental disorders). Pellagra has, therefore, been called the disease of the three Ds. It exists amongst communities of people who live mainly on a diet of maize. There are two reasons for this. Firstly, the nicotinic acid present in maize is bound in a complex form and is unavailable to the body. Secondly, unlike other cereals, maize is deficient in tryptophan. At one time pellagra was responsible for thousands of deaths every year in the southern states of America. Nowadays, the diet in this part of the world is more varied and pellagra is rare.

In Mexico, maize is still widely eaten in the form of tortillas, but the preparation involves treating the maize with lime and this releases the nicotinic acid from its bound form.

Recommended intake

The D.H.S.S. recommended daily intake of nicotinic acid is **18 mg** equivalents for adult men and **15 mg** equivalents for women (18 mg equivalents during pregnancy).

Losses on cooking

Nicotinic acid is soluble in water but is much more resistant to heat than either thiamin or riboflavin. Small amounts are lost during cooking by leaching into cooking water and by the loss of juices from cooked meats.

Folic acid (folate)

Folic acid is a name used to cover several related compounds.

Sources

Folic acid is found in liver, green leafy vegetables and, to a lesser extent, in some other foods such as kidney, nuts, pulse vegetables, flour and cereal foods.

Function

Folic acid has several functions. It is concerned with the synthesis of nucleic acids and the formation of red blood cells.

Deficiency

Folic acid is one of the few nutrients likely to be deficient in the British diet. A dietary deficiency causes a characteristic type of **anaemia**. This may result from a poor diet as occurs with some old people or from increased needs, e.g. during pregnancy. Iron tablets normally taken during pregnancy are supplemented with folic acid.

Recommended intake

The recommended intake of folic acid is **300 μg** per day for adults. During pregnancy the recommended daily intake is 500 mg.

Cooking losses

Folic acid is readily lost during some cooking processes. It leaches into cooking water and is also destroyed by heat, particularly in the presence of oxygen and alkalis. Large losses (up to 90%) occur when green vegetables are boiled.

Other B vitamins

Cyanocobalamin (vitamin B₁₂)

Cyanocobalamin is involved in more than one enzyme system in the body and is needed, together with folic acid, for red blood cell formation. It has a complex structure and contains, as the name indicates, the element cobalt. It occurs naturally only in foods of animal origin and in yeasts. Liver is the richest source but it is also found in milk, meat, fish and eggs. It is now added to some manufactured foods such as breakfast cereals. In herbivorous animals the vitamin is synthesised by bacteria present in the gut. A deficiency of cyanocobalamin causes **pernicious anaemia**. This disease is nearly always caused by a failure to absorb the vitamin rather than by a dietary deficiency. A protein, formed in the stomach, and known as the intrinsic factor, must combine with the vitamin before the vitamin can be absorbed. A lack of intrinsic factor is the usual cause of pernicious anaemia. Vegans, very strict vegetarians who eat no animal produce of any kind, are the only people in whom a dietary deficiency of vitamin B₁₂ has been observed.

Pyridoxine (vitamin B₆)

Pyridoxine is the name given to three related compounds found in many foods, particularly in meat, liver, fish and some vegetables. It functions in many enzyme systems, especially those concerned in protein synthesis. Deficiency is rare. In America infants fed on a pyridoxine-deficient baby food developed convulsions but responded rapidly to treatment with the vitamin. Recently, vitamin B₆ has been prescribed for various conditions and it is thought to be of benefit to some women who are pregnant, taking oral contraceptives, or suffering from premenstrual syndrome. However, there is evidence that large doses can be harmful.

Biotin

Biotin is needed by the body for the release of energy from fats. It is found in a wide variety of foods, particularly egg yolk, liver and yeast. It can be synthesised by bacteria in the intestine and may not be necessary in the diet. Avidin, a substance present in raw egg white, inhibits the absorption of biotin. One of the few recorded cases of biotin deficiency was an eccentric man whose daily diet consisted of ten raw eggs and six bottles of red wine.

Pantothenic acid

This vitamin is also widely distributed in plant and animal foods and there is no danger of deficiency. It is an essential constituent of enzyme systems involved in the release of energy from carbohydrates and fats.

Choline, PABA (para aminobenzoic acid) and inositol

These compounds are also members of the B complex but appear to be of minor nutritional significance.

Vitamin C (ascorbic acid)

Ascorbic acid is a white, crystalline substance which is very soluble in water.

Sources

Vitamin C is not as widely distributed in foods as most other vitamins. It is found almost entirely in vegetable foods, in fresh fruits and vegetables but not in cereals or dried pulse vegetables. Very small amounts may be found in animal foods such as raw liver and kidney. Raw milk contains a little vitamin C and some of this is still retained after pasteurisation.

The amount of ascorbic acid in fruits and vegetables is very variable, even within the same variety. Table 8.10 shows the average ascorbic acid content of some foods.

TABLE 8.10. *Ascorbic acid content of some fruits and vegetables*

Fruits	mg ascorbic acid per 100 g	Vegetables	mg ascorbid acid per 100 g
Blackcurrants	200	Parsley	150
Lemons	80	Peppers, green	128
Strawberries	60	Brussels sprouts	90
Oranges	50	Cauliflower	60
Grapefruit	40	Spinach	60
Gooseberries	40	Cabbage	55
Raspberries	25	Peas	25
Melons	25	Tomatoes	20
Blackberries	20	Carrots	6
Bananas	10	Potatoes:	
Apples	5	New	30
Pears	3	October, November	20
Plums	3	December	15
		January, February	10
		March onwards	8

N.B. All figures are for raw fruits and vegetables.

Pasteurised milk contains 1.5 mg ascorbic acid per 100 g. After 24 hours storage the ascorbic acid content is only 0.5 mg per 100 g. It can be seen from Table 8.10 that the vitamin C content of potatoes also drops considerably during storage. Although the vitamin C content of potatoes is not very high, potatoes are a very important source of vitamin C in the average British diet. This is because of the quantity in which they are eaten; the average consumption of potatoes in Britain is 155 g (5.5 oz) per day.

Blackcurrants are potentially a very good source of ascorbic acid but they are eaten in insufficient quantity to make a significant contribution to vitamin C intake. Similarly, some other foods, such as parsley, rose hips and green (unripe) walnuts, have a high or very high content but are unimportant sources. The most important sources are shown in Table 8.11.

TABLE 8.11. *Contributions made by different foods to the total vitamin C content of the average British diet*

Food	Contribution to total vitamin C intake	
Potatoes	22%	
Green vegetables	11%	} 50%
Other vegetables	17%	
Oranges	7%	
Other fresh fruit	13%	} 40%
Fruit juices and other fruit products	20%	
Milk	5%	

Functions

1. Ascorbic acid is necessary for the formation of collagen, the main protein of connective tissue. Connective tissue is the 'packaging material' which separates, protects and supports the various organs (see page 121).

2. Ascorbic acid aids the absorption of iron from the intestine.

Man, monkeys and guinea-pigs are among the relatively few species which require a dietary source of vitamin C. Other animals synthesise ascorbic acid from glucose in their body cells.

Deficiency

A person existing on a diet containing insufficient ascorbic acid will eventually develop the condition known as **scurvy**. The main symptoms of scurvy are bruising and spontaneous haemorrhaging under the skin. The gums become black and spongy, and wounds and fractures fail to heal in the normal length of time. These symptoms are caused by a failure to form connective tissue. Another common feature of scurvy is anaemia which is due to a failure to absorb iron and an inability to form red blood cells.

Until the eighteenth century, when potatoes became a common food, scurvy was common in the late winter and early spring months due to the scarcity of fresh fruits and vegetables. Nowadays, fresh foods are available all the year round and scurvy is rare. There have been some reports of old people who live on a poor diet with very little fresh fruit or vegetables developing signs of vitamin C deficiency. Also, some long-stay geriatric patients suffering from delayed wound healing and pressure sores may have mild scurvy as a result of eating institutional food in which there is little vitamin C left after cooking (see page 98).

Vitamin C supplements, e.g. vitamin drops, for children under five years have helped to reduce the likelihood of infantile scurvy in the U.K.

Recommended intake

Since vitamin C cannot be stored in the body a regular intake is essential. However, there are many different opinions as to the amount of vitamin C necessary to maintain health. It has been shown that 10 mg per day is sufficient to both cure and prevent scurvy. The D.H.S.S. recommended daily intake is **30 mg** (60 mg for pregnant women).

As a result of major surgery, severe accident or illness, the vitamin C content of the body is reduced and recovery is aided by larger than normal intakes. There is evidence to suggest that massive doses of ascorbic acid, 1000 mg or more, may alleviate some of the symptoms of respiratory infections such as the common cold. Large doses such as this can only be obtained by taking ascorbic acid tablets.

Losses on cooking and storage

Ascorbic acid is readily destroyed during cooking. It is very soluble in water and therefore leaches out into cooking water. It is also readily oxidised. Oxidation is most rapid in alkaline conditions, at high temperatures and on exposure to light and traces of metals such as zinc, iron and particularly copper.

Ascorbic acid oxidase is an enzyme, present in plant cells, which increases the rate of oxidation. In intact cells the enzyme is separated from the vitamin but when fruits and vegetables are bruised, cut or chopped the enzyme comes into contact with the ascorbic acid and the ascorbic acid is destroyed. However, the enzyme is inactivated at

TABLE 8.12. *Recommended methods of minimising vitamin C losses in vegetables and fruits*

Recommendation	Reason
Storage	
1. Store in a cool, dark place.	The rate of oxidation is increased by heat and light.
2. Avoid bruising or damaging fruits and vegetables.	Bruising damages the cells and releases the enzyme.
Preparation	
1. Prepare just before cooking.	The enzyme is released when the cells are cut.
2. Do not soak in cold water.	Ascorbic acid is very water soluble.
3. Do not cut or chop more than necessary.	The enzyme is released when the cells are cut.
4. Tear rather than cut green leaves.	Tearing causes the leaves to break around the cells.
5. Avoid the use of iron (non-stainless) knives, graters, etc.	Iron increases the rate of oxidation.
Cooking	
1. Place in boiling water.	The enzyme is destroyed by heat.
2. Use a minimum quantity of water and a covered pan.	Ascorbic acid leaches into cooking water; the greater the volume of water, the greater the ascorbic acid loss.
3. Do not overcook.	Prolonged heating increases the amount of oxidation.
4. Do not add sodium bicarbonate to green vegetables.	Alkalis increase the rate of oxidation.
Service	
1. Serve immediately; do not keep in hot cabinets for long periods of time.	Keeping hot for 45 minutes reduces ascorbic acid by 50% or more.
2. Avoid mashing and puréeing unless there is some other ascorbic acid source to balance the menu.	Mashing and puréeing increase the rate of oxidation.

temperatures above 60°C and is therefore destroyed during cooking. In the absence of the enzyme, oxidation can still take place but the rate is reduced.

The amount of ascorbic acid lost during the preparation and cooking of fruits and vegetables depends very much on the methods used. Unless care is taken losses of ascorbic acid may be very large. Table 8.12 shows a list of recommendations which, if followed, will minimise the losses during the storage, preparation, cooking and service of vegetables and fruits.

It should be pointed out that in practice, especially in large-scale catering, it is sometimes necessary, as a matter of convenience, to disregard some of the recommendations made in Table 8.12. As long as *reasonable* care is taken, the amount of ascorbic acid lost when green vegetables are cooked will not exceed 70%. This means that 30% will be retained. For example, raw cabbage contains 60 mg of ascorbic acid per 100 g; if 30% is retained, 100 g of cooked cabbage will contain $30/100 \times 60 = 18$ mg of ascorbic acid, i.e. nearly two-thirds of the 30 mg recommended daily intake. In other words, cabbage, even after it is cooked, is still a good source of vitamin C.

Since ascorbic acid is water soluble losses can be reduced by avoiding the use of water during cooking. The average loss of vitamin C when potatoes are boiled is 40%. If potatoes are baked in their skins the loss is only 30% and with fried, chipped potatoes it is only 25%.

The method of peeling potatoes also affects the amount of ascorbic acid lost. Thin hand peeling is preferable to thick hand peeling. Machine peeling damages a large number of cells and causes considerable losses.

Fruits lose less vitamin C when cooked than vegetables because they are more acidic and the rate of oxidation is reduced. The average loss of vitamin C due to cooking fruits is only 10%.

Preserved foods

There is about a 50% loss of vitamin C during the canning of fruits and vegetables but a greater loss during drying. Frozen foods retain most of their ascorbic acid. Frozen vegetables may have more vitamin C than 'fresh' vegetables, since vegetables used for freezing are frozen within a few hours of harvest, whereas so-called fresh vegetables, unless they are home grown, are probably two or three days old when bought. There is a gradual loss of vitamin C in frozen vegetables during storage. For example, peas stored at $-18°C$ for eight months lose about 15% of their vitamin C content.

Vitamin D (cholecalciferol)

Cholecalciferol is a white, crystalline compound which is soluble in oils and fats but is insoluble in water.

There are two distinct forms of vitamin D:

1. Cholecalciferol (vitamin D_3) is the natural form of the vitamin occurring in foods. It can be formed under the skin by the influence of sunlight (ultra-violet radiation).

2. Ergocalciferol (vitamin D_2) is a synthetic form of the vitamin which has the same activity as the natural vitamin. It is produced by the ultra-violet irradiation of ergosterol, a compound which can be extracted from yeast.

Sources

1. *Food.* Vitamin D is found in relatively few foods. It occurs naturally in foods of animal origin. Fish liver oils are very rich sources but are dietary supplements rather than foods. Oily fish, eggs, butter, liver and cheese are good sources of vitamin D. It is important to realise that meats, apart from liver and some other offal, contain only a trace of vitamin D. The vitamin D content of milk varies with the time of year but even summer milk is a relatively poor source. For babies whose diet is largely based on cow's milk, a vitamin D supplement is essential and for children up to the age of five years a supplement is advisable. The vitamin D content of some foods is shown in Table 8.13.

TABLE 8.13. *Vitamin D content of some foods*

Food	μg cholecalciferol per 100 g
Cod liver oil	210.0
Herring	22.5
Margarine	7.9
Sardines, canned	7.5
Eggs	1.8
Butter	0.76
Liver	0.50
Cheese, Cheddar	0.26
Milk, summer	0.03
winter	0.01

It can be seen from Table 8.13 that the vitamin D content of margarine is approximately ten times that of butter. In Britain margarine for retail sale is enriched with vitamin D. This law does not apply to margarine sold for catering purposes.

The main sources of vitamin D in the British diet are margarine, oily fish, eggs, milk and milk products (see Table 8.14).

TABLE 8.14. *Contributions made by different foods to the total vitamin D content of the average British diet*

Food	Contribution to total vitamin D intake
Margarine	45%
Oily fish	14%
Eggs	12%
Milk and cream	8%

2. *Sunlight.* Vitamin D is formed in the skin on exposure to sunlight. The amount formed in this way varies with latitude and the amount of time the person spends outside in the sun. The quantity of vitamin D synthesised also depends on the degree of pigmentation of the skin. In darker-skinned people less synthesis occurs.

Functions

Vitamin D is necessary for the growth and maintenance of bones and teeth. It is required for the absorption of calcium from the intestine and for the uptake of calcium and phosphorus by the bones and teeth.

Deficiency

Children receiving an inadequate supply of vitamin D develop **rickets**, a disease which was at one time very common in England. A lack of vitamin D results in a failure to absorb calcium and softening of the bones. The long bones bend under the weight of the body; knock-knees and bow legs are typical symptoms of rickets. Before 1900 about 75% of the children living in the poorer, industrialised regions of Britain had rickets. The main causes were a cheap diet composed mainly of cereal foods devoid of vitamin D and a lack of sunshine in the smoky, urban areas. In this century the improvement in living conditions, the development of smokeless zones, the use of cod liver oil as a supplement for babies and the fortification of margarine with vitamin D have all helped to ensure that rickets is no longer a major problem in this country. There are, however, still cases in large cities, particularly among the Asian population. Some traditional Asian diets are low in vitamin D and this, together with the facts that darker-skinned people synthesise less vitamin D and Asian cultures do not encourage exposure to sunlight, accounts for the occurrence of rickets in this group of people.

In adults an inadequate supply of vitamin D causes **osteomalacia**, a condition in which the bones become soft, weak and painful. Some cases have occurred in this country, especially among elderly, housebound women.

Excess

Too high an intake of vitamin D is harmful as it leads to excessive amounts of calcium being deposited in the soft tissues such as the kidneys. Hypervitaminosis D can result in kidney damage. Vitamin D intakes should be controlled, particularly in young children, and supplements such as vitamin drops used only in recommended amounts.

Recommended intake

It is not possible to make firm recommendations for the dietary intake of vitamin D since the amount of vitamin D produced in the body by the action of sunlight varies from person to person. Many people may obtain all they need from sunlight. It is, however, certain that babies and growing children require more vitamin D than adults, due to bone growth.

The D.H.S.S. recommended a daily intake of 10 μg cholecalciferol for children under five years and for women during pregnancy and lactation. This amount can only be achieved by supplementation. Adults with inadequate exposure to sunlight, e.g. those who are housebound, may also need a supplement of 10 μg daily.

Effect of cooking

Vitamin D is stable to heat and is insoluble in water. It is therefore unaffected by cooking.

Vitamin E (tocopherols)

A number of related compounds called tocopherols show vitamin E activity, the main one being alpha (α)-tocopherol. Vitamin E is found in many foods, but wheat germ, vegetable oils, margarine and egg yolk are particularly good sources.

Vitamin E is a natural antioxidant. In vegetable oils it helps to reduce rancidity by preventing the oxidation of unsaturated fatty acids. It may also play a part in protecting ascorbic acid against oxidation in fruits and vegetables.

In the body vitamin E, together with selenium (see page 103), has an important role as an anti-oxidant. Substances known as free radicals, which are produced as a result of normal chemical reactions in the body, can damage the lipids (fatty compounds) found in cell membranes. The free radicals oxidise the lipids forming peroxides. This lipid peroxidation can cause damage to the cell membrane and leaking of the cell contents which in turn is thought to increase the risk of cancer and inflammatory diseases such as rheumatoid arthritis. Vitamin E and selenium function together in protecting lipids (especially polyunsaturated fatty acids) against free radical damage.

Deficiency of vitamin E does not normally occur in humans, though there have been some cases of premature babies with a certain type of anaemia benefiting from vitamin E supplements. Male rats deprived of vitamin E become sterile and female rats, although they conceive normally, do not give birth to live young. There is no evidence, however, that vitamin E influences human fertility.

Vitamin K

Vitamin K is found in green vegetables and a variety of other foods. It has been shown to be essential for the normal clotting of blood. A deficiency of vitamin K is rarely seen because the vitamin is synthesised by bacteria present in the intestine as well as being present in a normal diet.

Babies, particularly if they are premature, have low levels of the vitamin in their bodies. Vitamin K is now given routinely to newborn babies in this country.

CHAPTER 9

Mineral Elements and Water

Mineral elements

The mineral elements are those chemical elements, other than carbon, hydrogen, oxygen and nitrogen, which are required by the body. They are present in food, mostly in the form of inorganic salts, e.g. sodium chloride, but some are present in organic compounds, e.g. sulphur and phosphorus are constituents of many proteins.

Mineral elements account for approximately 4% of body-weight. Some, such as calcium and phosphorus, are present in the body in relatively large amounts and are known as major minerals or macrominerals, whereas others occur in very small quantities and are known as trace elements (see Table 9.1).

TABLE 9.1. *Mineral elements required by the body*

Major minerals (macrominerals)	Trace elements
Calcium	Chromium
Chlorine	Cobalt
Iron	Copper
Magnesium	Fluorine
Phosphorus	Iodine
Potassium	Manganese
Sodium	Molybdenum
Sulphur	Selenium
	Zinc

Minerals have three main functions in the body:

1. Calcium, phosphorus and magnesium are constituents of bones and teeth.
2. Some elements are present as soluble salts which help to control the composition of body fluids. These include potassium and magnesium present inside body cells and sodium and chlorine in the fluid outside the cells.
3. Many of the trace elements are concerned in enzyme systems in the body.

103

Calcium

Sources

Milk and some milk products, such as cheese and yoghurt, are good sources of calcium. In Britain, calcium, in the form of calcium carbonate (chalk), is added by law to all flour except true wholemeal. Small fish, such as sardines, sprats and whitebait, which are eaten with the bones, contain very useful quantities of calcium. Fruits and vegetables contain variable but usually quite small amounts of calcium. Table 9.2 shows the calcium content of some of these foods. People living in hard water areas obtain a certain amount of calcium from drinking water.

TABLE 9.2. *Calcium content of some foods*

Food	mg calcium per 100 g
Cheese, Cheddar	800
Sardines	550
Soya beans	200
White flour	150
Milk	120
White bread	100
Cabbage	57
Carrots	48

The most important sources of calcium in the British diet are milk, bread and other cereals, and cheese, as shown in Table 9.3.

TABLE 9.3. *Contributions made by different foods to the total calcium content of the average British diet*

Food	Contribution to total calcium intake
Milk	43%
Bread	14% ⎱ 25%
Other cereal foods	11% ⎰
Cheese	13%

Functions

1. Calcium is necessary for the formation and development of bones and teeth. Bone is a composite material of cartilage and calcium phosphate. The protein fibres of the cartilage form a network on which the calcium phosphate is deposited. Teeth are similar in composition to bone.

2. Calcium is one of the essential factors required for the clotting of blood.

3. Calcium is necessary for the normal functioning of muscles and nerves in the body.

Absorption

Only about one-third of the calcium in the diet is absorbed from the intestine; the rest passes through the alimentary canal and is lost from the body in the faeces. There are several factors which determine the actual amount of calcium absorbed. Vitamin D assists absorption and without it little or no calcium would be absorbed. Absorption increases when the diet is low in calcium, though this adaption does not occur as readily with old people. There is a sharp fall in absorption in women at the time of the menopause. This is thought to be caused by reduction in the level of the hormone oestrogen and is one of the possible causes of osteoporosis (see below). The calcium from milk and milk products is more readily absorbed than from plant sources. It is thought that lactose increases absorption. Dicarboxylic acids such as phytic and oxalic acids interfere with absorption. Phytic acid is found in the bran of cereals. It reacts with calcium in the intestine making it unavailable to the body. Oxalic acid, found in small amounts in many vegetable foods, e.g. rhubarb and spinach, behaves in a similar way.

Deficiency

Since vitamin D is essential for calcium absorption the effects of a dietary deficiency of calcium are the same as a deficiency of vitamin D. Severe calcium deficiency causes **rickets** in children and **osteomalacia** in adults. These diseases have been described in the previous chapter. They are more likely to be caused by a shortage of vitamin D than by a lack of calcium in the diet.

Recently, there has been considerable concern over the condition known as **osteoporosis** which occurs in old people, particularly women. Calcium is gradually lost from the bones, the bones become porous and fracture more readily. Osteoporosis is *not* caused by a lack of calcium or vitamin D, but plenty of dietary calcium together with regular exercise are recommended as preventative measures.

Recommended intake

Since it is required for bone development, calcium is a particularly important nutrient for children and for women during pregnancy and lactation.

Table 9.4 shows the D.H.S.S. recommended daily intakes of calcium for different age groups.

TABLE 9.4. *Recommended daily amounts of calcium*

	mg calcium per day
Children	
0–8 years	600
9–14 years	700
15–17 years	600
Adults	500
Women, last 3 months of	
pregnancy and lactation	1200

Effect of cooking

Cooking has little effect on the calcium content of foods, though small amounts may be lost by leaching into cooking water.

Iron

Sources

Liver and kidney are two of the best sources of iron. Other meats, although not containing quite as much iron, are nevertheless good sources. Egg yolks have a high iron content but there is very little iron in the white. Iron is found in cereals but about half of this is lost in milling if the bran and germ are discarded. Iron is added to white flour in this country; flour must by law contain at least 1.65 mg iron per 100 g. Potatoes and other vegetables, particularly pulses, are moderately good sources. Dried fruits have quite a high iron content but the main reason for this is that the removal of water results in a concentration of all other constituents. Milk is a relatively poor source of iron. After weaning, a baby's diet must include foods which contain a reasonable quantity of iron, e.g. eggs, minced meat and sieved green vegetables.

Certain foods such as black pudding, cocoa, black treacle, shell fish and curry powder have a high iron content. They are not, however, important sources in the average diet since they are not eaten very often in any quantity.

Table 9.5 shows the iron content of a variety of foods.

TABLE 9.5. *Iron content of some foods*

Food	mg iron per 100 g
Cocoa powder	10.5
Liver	7.0
Kidney	5.7
Spinach	4.0
Wholemeal bread	3.0
Eggs	2.5
Beef	2.1
Peas	1.9
White bread	1.8
Baked beans	1.4
Cabbage	0.6
Potatoes	0.5
Milk	0.1

The most important sources of iron in the British diet are meat, bread and other cereal foods, potatoes and other vegetables (see Table 9.6).

Functions

The human body contains about 4 g of iron. The majority of this occurs in haemoglobin, a red pigment present in the red blood corpuscles. Haemoglobin is responsible for transporting oxygen from the lungs to the cells of all body tissues. All cells require oxygen in order to break down nutrients and obtain energy. The life of a red blood corpuscle is

TABLE 9.6. *Contributions made by different foods to the total iron content of the average British diet*

Food	Contribution to total iron intake
Meat	21%
Bread	21% ⎱ 42%
Other cereal foods	21% ⎰
Potatoes	6%
Other vegetables	12%

about 120 days. When the corpuscles break up the iron is not lost from the body; it is used again to make new red corpuscles in the bone marrow.

Iron is also found in myoglobin, a protein which acts as an oxygen carrier in the muscles. It is also present, in small amounts, in all body cells where it is involved in various enzyme systems. Some iron is also stored in the body, in the bone marrow, liver and spleen, as a complex with protein known as ferritin.

Absorption

Only between 5% and 20% of the iron a person eats is absorbed. The absorption of iron is a complex process. The amount of iron absorbed appears to depend very much on the need of the body for iron. A person deficient in iron will be able to absorb more than a person who has adequate stores of ferritin. Absorption increases when requirements are high, e.g. during growth, pregnancy and lactation.

Another factor affecting absorption is the form of the iron. Iron is absorbed most readily from meat which contains haem iron and to a lesser extent from foods containing non-haem iron, e.g. eggs, vegetables and cereals. Non-haem iron is present mostly as trivalent (ferric) Fe^{3+} iron but it is absorbed most readily in the divalent (ferrous) Fe^{2+} form and therefore reduction of the ferric form is necessary. Ascorbic acid (vitamin C) aids the reduction and therefore aids iron absorption. Eating iron-rich foods with a source of vitamin C is therefore sensible, e.g. a glass of orange juice with an iron-fortified breakfast cereal.

Phytic acid, found in wholemeal cereals and pulses, interferes with iron, as well as calcium, absorption. Spinach is often quoted as being an important source of iron. However, it is eaten infrequently and also contains oxalic acid which interferes with iron absorption. Tannins, present in tea, also reduce iron absorption.

Deficiency

A deficiency of iron causes **anaemia**. In an anaemic person the number of red blood corpuscles is reduced and the amount of oxygen carried to the tissues is also reduced. This results in a lack of energy and a feeling of lethargy. Other symptoms of anaemia include headaches and dizziness. Anaemia is the most common deficiency disease in Britain but a dietary deficiency of iron is seldom the sole cause. It has been shown in some large surveys that about one-sixth of the women in Britain are anaemic. Anaemia is much more common in women than in men due to blood loss during menstruation. It is usually not possible to treat anaemia merely by increasing the iron content of the diet. Normally, iron tablets are prescribed together with advice on dietary sources of iron.

Anaemia may also be caused by a deficiency of nutrients other than iron, e.g. by folic acid deficiency (see page 94).

Recommended intake

The DoH figures take into account the fact that women of child-bearing age require more iron due to menstruation. Children and adolescents require relatively large amounts of iron since during periods of growth the blood volume increases. Women during pregnancy and lactation need more iron in order to meet the baby's iron requirement. Table 9.7 shows the DoH recommended daily intakes of iron for some age groups. The full table is shown in Appendix II.

TABLE 9.7. *Recommended daily amounts of iron*

	mg iron per day
Boys and girls, 9–17 years	12
Men	10
Women	
18–54 years	12
55 years and over	10
pregnancy	13
lactation	15

Effect of cooking

Iron is not destroyed by heat but small amounts may be lost in cooking water or discarded meat juices. The use of iron utensils (knives, graters, mincers, etc.) can increase the iron content of food. Some members of the Bantu tribe in South Africa suffer from a condition known as siderosis, in which iron is deposited in the soft tissues of the body. They cook maize and other cereals in iron pots and their iron intake is very high.

Sodium (and chlorine)

Sources

Sodium is eaten mainly in the form of common salt (sodium chloride). Most natural foods contain relatively little sodium, but considerable quantities of salt are added during cooking and during the processing and preservation of many foods. For example, salt is added during the production of bacon, smoked fish, bread, butter, cheese, breakfast cereals and canned vegetables. Sodium is also supplied by other chemicals used in processing, for example, sodium hydrogen carbonate is used as a raising agent, mono-sodium glutamate as a flavour enhancer and sodium nitrate as a meat preservative. About 70% of salt in the diet comes from foods (mostly manufactured foods) and about 30% is added during cooking and at the table. Table 9.8 shows the sodium content of some foods.

TABLE 9.8. *Sodium content of some foods*

Food	mg sodium per 100 g
Yeast extract 'Marmite'	4500
Bacon	1400
Cornflakes	1160
Kippers	990
Corned beef	950
Butter, salted	870
Cheese, Cheddar	610
Potato crisps	550
White bread	540
Peas, canned garden	230
Eggs	140
Beef	69
Milk	50
Peas, fresh	1

Function

Sodium and chlorine are present as ions in the fluid surrounding body cells and are essential in the regulation of the water content of the body. In a temperate climate most people require about 3 g of salt per day but the average intake is between 5 g and 20 g per day. Excess salt is excreted in the urine. The kidneys regulate the loss and so control the level of sodium and chlorine ions in the tissue fluids.

Deficiency

Salt is also lost from the body in sweat, but there is no means of regulating the amount of salt lost in this way. In hot climates or during strenuous work or exercise, large amounts of salt may be lost through sweating. This will cause a lowering of the salt concentration of the tissue fluids resulting in weariness and muscular cramps. It may be necessary, therefore, for athletes and people working in hot, heavy industries to take extra salt.

Excess

In certain diseases, e.g. some types of kidney disease, too much salt is retained in the body. The correct concentration of salt is maintained by retaining an equivalent excess of water. This results in oedema (excess fluid in the tissues).

High salt intakes are associated with raised blood pressure. It is thought that for people likely to develop high blood pressure eating a lot of salt is a contributory factor. Current nutritional ideas (NACNE, see page 152) recommend reducing salt intake by 3 g per day (about 25%). This may be done as follows:

1. use less salt in cooking. Provide flavour from other products, e.g. herbs;
2. do not add salt at the table. Use a salt substitute if necessary, e.g. potassium chloride;
3. avoid very salty snacks, e.g. salted peanuts, crisps;

4. avoid large amounts of high-sodium processed foods, e.g. cured and canned meats, canned vegetables.

Babies cannot tolerate high sodium intakes because their kidneys cannot excrete the excess. They, therefore, should not be given salty foods, e.g. meat and yeast extracts. It is also important that bottle feeds are made up with the correct amount of water. If there is too little water, the sodium concentration could be too high.

Potassium

Potassium is found in an ionised form inside the body cells, whereas sodium occurs in the fluid surrounding the cells. Potassium is concerned in the regulation of the fluid content of cells. It is found in a wide variety of foods, particularly some fruits and vegetables, and sufficient is obtained from a normal diet.

Phosphorus

Phosphorus, together with calcium, is an essential constituent of bones and teeth. It is also present in all living cells where it is involved in the release of energy. Energy produced by the oxidation of glucose is 'stored' in cells in high-energy phosphate compounds. The breaking down of these compounds releases energy when required (see page 119). Phosphorus is also needed for the formation of the nucleic acids, DNA and RNA (see page 119).

Since phosphorus occurs in all living cells it is found in most foods and a dietary deficiency has never been recorded.

Iodine

Sources

The main sources of iodine in the diet are cereals, vegetables and milk. The amount of iodine in these foods varies considerably and depends on the amount of iodine in the soil of the area where the foods are produced. Iodine occurs in very low concentrations in sea-water but organisms living in the sea have the ability to concentrate these small amounts. Sea fish is a good source of iodine and seaweed is a particularly rich source.

Functions

Iodine is a trace element, needed by the body in very small amounts. It is required by the thyroid gland for the formation of hormones involved in the regulation of the rate of oxidation of nutrients in body cells (see page 139).

Deficiency

An insufficient intake of iodine results in **goitre**, an enlargement of the thyroid gland. This condition is common in certain parts of the world, in areas a long way from the sea where the soil contains little iodine. At one time goitre was common in Derbyshire and was known as 'Derbyshire neck'. Nowadays, goitre caused by a lack of iodine is rare in this country since a large proportion of foods is imported. If there is any chance of the diet being deficient in iodine, 'iodised salt' may be used to increase the intake of iodine. This is ordinary table salt with a small quantity of potassium iodide added.

Cabbages and some other vegetables, e.g. turnips, contain substances known as goitrogens which reduce the absorption of iodine. An excessive consumption of these vegetables over a period of time can also cause goitre.

Fluorine

Drinking water is the main source of fluorine. Foods, with the exception of sea fish and tea, contain insignificant quantities. By combining with calcium phosphate, fluorine hardens tooth enamel and so helps to guard against tooth decay. Experiments carried out in Britain and the United States have shown that the addition of fluorine to drinking water reduces the incidence of tooth decay, especially in young children. Certain local authorities add fluoride (a compound containing fluorine) to bring the level of fluorine up to 1 ppm (part per million). An excess of fluorine in water (levels above 3 ppm) causes mottling of teeth.

Zinc

Zinc has become the focus of more attention recently. It has been suggested that mild deficiency may be quite widespread. Zinc is present in a wide variety of foods but the main sources in the diet are meat, milk, bread and other cereals. There is little zinc in fruits and vegetables. Only about 40% of the zinc in the diet is absorbed. Absorption is reduced by phytic acid, present in wholegrain cereals, and by the presence of calcium. Iron tablets also interfere with zinc absorption.

Zinc is involved in a large number of enzyme systems in the body and is essential for normal growth and development. Deficiency causes stunted growth and delayed sexual maturity.

Water

Water is essential to life. All living organisms contain water; the human body is about 65% water. The body of an adult man contains about 40 litres of water. About 15 litres are present in the extracellular fluid (3 litres in the blood plasma and 12 litres in the tissue fluid). The remaining 25 litres make up the intracellular fluid, i.e. the fluid found within the cells.

Water is essential since it provides a medium in which nutrients, enzymes and other chemical substances can be dispersed and in which the chemical reactions necessary for maintaining life can take place. It is also necessary as a means of transport within the body. Nutrients are carried to cells and waste products are transported from the cells by blood plasma which is 90% water. Waste products are removed from the blood by the kidneys and excreted in the urine.

Water balance

It is possible to exist for several weeks without food but the body can only survive a few days without water. The normal functioning of the body involves a continual loss of water. Water cannot be stored in the body and therefore a regular intake is essential. Water is taken into the body in foods and drinks. Many foods contain a high percentage of water. Some foods which, because of their cellular structure, appear fairly solid contain large quantities of water, e.g. fruits and vegetables. Some colloids, e.g. jellies, are solid but have a high water content. Table 9.9 shows the water content of a variety of foods.

TABLE 9.9. *Water content of some foods*

Food	% Water
Melon	94
Beer	93
Cabbage	88
Milk	88
Apples	84
Jelly	84
Potatoes	76
Eggs	75
Beef steak	67
White bread	39
Cheese, Cheddar	37
Butter	15
White flour	13
Cornflakes	7
Sugar	0

Water from food and drinks is mostly absorbed into the body from the large intestine. Some absorption takes place in the stomach and small intestine.

Water is formed within the body by chemical reactions. When nutrients are oxidised in the cells in order to release energy, carbon dioxide and water are formed. For example, the oxidation of 100 g of glucose produces 60 ml of water.

The body inevitably loses about 1.5 litres of water daily. The kidneys must form at least 600 ml of urine in order to get rid of toxic waste products. Water is also lost by evaporation from the surface of the body and as water vapour in expired air. A small quantity of water is lost in the faeces. Table 9.10 shows a typical water balance for an adult man in a temperate climate.

The amount of water taken into the body is determined mainly by habit and social custom. It is also regulated by thirst. The sensation of thirst arises as a result of the

TABLE 9.10. *Typical water balance for an adult man*

Intake		Output	
	ml per day		ml per day
Drink	1300	Urine	1500
Food	900	Skin	550
Oxidation of		Expired air	350
nutrients	300	Faeces	100
Total	2500	Total	2500

concentration of sodium in the blood, caused by a depletion of water. The kidneys control the output of water from the body (see page 124). The body cannot store water and any excess passes into the urine.

Hard water

In many areas of Britain the water from the tap is hard, i.e. it fails to give a lather with soap but tends to form a scum. Hard water is water which contains dissolved mineral salts. There are two types of hardness:

1. Temporary hardness

Temporarily hard water, so called because the hardness can be removed by boiling, contains calcium and magnesium hydrogen carbonates. This type of water is found in chalk and limestone regions. Small amounts of carbon dioxide dissolve in rain water forming carbonic acid, a weak acid.

$$H_2O \ + \ CO_2 \longrightarrow H_2CO_3$$

water   carbon   carbonic
          dioxide   acid

Carbonic acid slowly dissolves calcium carbonate (chalk and limestone) forming soluble calcium hydrogen carbonate.

$$H_2CO_3 \ + \ CaCO_3 \longrightarrow Ca(HCO_3)_2$$

carbonic   calcium   calcium
acid   carbonate   hydrogen
                             carbonate

Small quantities of magnesium hydrogen carbonate are formed in a similar way, from magnesium carbonate in the rocks.

2. Permanent hardness

Permanently hard water contains calcium and magnesium sulphates dissolved as rain water percolates through rocks containing these salts. This type of hardness cannot be removed by boiling.

Water in different parts of the country varies in hardness depending on the composition of soil and rocks. Water supplies are classified according to the amount of dissolved calcium ions; hardness is expressed as parts per million (ppm) of calcium carbonate. Soft water has less than 50 ppm. 100 ppm is described as moderately hard, and over 200 ppm as very hard.

Disadvantages of hard water

1. When soap is used in hard water it will not lather easily; instead, it forms a scum. Soap is composed of the sodium salts of fatty acids. When soap is placed in hard water some of it reacts with the calcium and magnesium salts in the water forming insoluble calcium and magnesium salts of the fatty acids. These insoluble salts cling to the fibres of

textiles and form a scum on the surface of the water. Scum formation and the wastage of soap can be overcome by the use of a synthetic detergent. The calcium and magnesium salts of soapless detergents are soluble.

2. When water containing calcium and magnesium hydrogen carbonates is heated or boiled, insoluble calcium and magnesium carbonates are formed. For example:

$$Ca(HCO_3)_2 \longrightarrow CaCO_3\downarrow + H_2O + CO_2$$

calcium   calcium water carbon
hydrogen   carbonate   dioxide
carbonate

The insoluble carbonates can be seen as scale or 'fur' inside kettles. Scale can build up inside hot-water pipes and boilers reducing their efficiency and in extreme cases scale can cause a complete blockage which could result in an explosion. Scale or fur can be removed by using an acid. Phosphoric and formic acids are used in descaling agents.

3. Used during food preparation, hard water can have an adverse effect on the colour and texture of vegetables, and on the consistency of bread dough.

Advantages of hard water

1. The dissolved calcium salts in hard water increase the dietary intake of calcium.

2. Hard water is more suitable in certain industries, e.g. the steel and brewing industries. It produces better beer.

3. Hard water is safer in conjunction with lead water pipes. Lead poisoning can result from the consumption of soft water which has passed through lead pipes.

Some methods of removing hardness in water

1. ADDITION OF WASHING SODA

Washing soda (sodium carbonate) reacts with the calcium and magnesium salts in hard water forming soluble sodium salts and insoluble calcium and magnesium salts which remain as a precipitate. For example:

$$CaSO_4 + Na_2CO_3 \longrightarrow CaCO_3\downarrow + Na_2SO_4$$

calcium   sodium   calcium   sodium
sulphate   carbonate   carbonate   sulphate
(hard water) (washing soda)   (insoluble)   (soluble)

Sodium carbonate is used in washing powders and bath salts.

2. ION-EXCHANGE PROCESS

This method is used in domestic and industrial installations for removing both types of hardness. It involves the use of natural or synthetic resins such as 'permutit' and zeolite. The hard water is passed through a column packed with resin and the calcium and magnesium ions in the water are exchanged for sodium ions in the resin. The resin is regenerated from time to time by flushing the column with a concentrated salt (sodium chloride) solution. This replenishes the sodium ions.

3. USE OF SEQUESTERING AGENTS, e.g. 'CALGON'

A sequestering agent such as 'Calgon' (sodium hexametaphosphate), when added to hard water, encloses the calcium and magnesium ions in stable complexes which are soluble but which do not react with soap. 'Calgon' is used extensively for domestic purposes but is expensive and is therefore of limited industrial use.

Mineral waters

There has been a sharp increase in the consumption of bottled mineral waters in recent years. Mineral waters come from a spring or well. As rain water percolates through rocks, it picks up mineral salts and then collects when it reaches a layer of impermeable rock. The water may emerge as a spring at a fault in the rock or be brought to the surface through a bore hole or well. The mineral content varies according to the source but is never very high. Mineral waters may be still (labelled 'Natural Mineral Water') or sparkling. If carbon dioxide is added to make it sparkling it is labelled 'Carbonated Natural Mineral Water'.

CHAPTER 10

Basic Physiology

Anatomy is the study of the structure of living organisms; physiology is the study of how organisms work or function. The functioning of an organism involves various changes which maintain the stability of the internal environment and keep the organism alive. Physiology is concerned with the changes that take place, where in the organism these changes occur and how they are regulated. An understanding of basic physiology is a necessary part of the understanding of nutrition.

Cells

All organisms, whether plant or animal, are made up of small units called cells. The human body is composed of thousands of millions of cells which are organised into tissues with specialised functions. For example, muscle is a tissue composed of long, spindle-shaped cells which by contraction and relaxation enable the body to move.

Since food is of either plant or animal origin most natural, unprocessed foods have a cellular structure. Cells themselves, although very small, have a complex structure, as shown in Figure 10.1.

Cell membrane

Surrounding every cell is a non-rigid, selectively permeable membrane which allows small molecules to pass in and out of the cell. The membrane consists of two layers of protein with a lipid (fatty) layer in between.

Cell wall (plant cells)

This is a more rigid structure which surrounds the cell membranes of plant cells. Plant cells tend to have a more definite shape than animal cells. Cellulose is the main component of the cell wall, together with pectins and hemicelluloses.

Nucleus

The nucleus controls the activity of the rest of the cell. It contains nucleic acids which form the chromosomes, the particles which carry the genetically inherited information required for the maintenance of the whole cell.

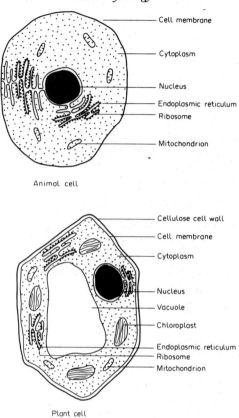

FIG. 10.1. Diagrammatic representations of typical animal and plant cells.

Cytoplasm

Cytoplasm is a colloidal solution of protein and other substances dispersed in water.

Endoplasmic reticulum and ribosomes

The endoplasmic reticulum is a complex network of tubular cavities which, together with the ribosomes, is responsible for the building up of protein molecules from amino acids (see page 119).

Mitochondria

The mitochondria are sometimes called the 'power houses' of the cell. It is in these structures that nutrients are oxidised and energy is released, i.e. respiration takes place.

Chloroplasts

Chloroplasts occur only in the cells of green plants. They contain the green pigment chlorophyll which can convert light energy into a form that can be used for forming complex organic compounds. Chloroplasts are therefore involved in the process of photosynthesis (see page 49).

Vacuoles

Vacuoles are found only in plant cells. They are spaces filled with a solution of sugars and salts, known as cell sap. They help to maintain the shape of plant cells.

Metabolism

The term metabolism is used to include all the chemical processes involved in maintaining life. It is the total of all chemical reactions by which nutrients are used by the body to produce energy and material for growth and maintenance. Metabolism involves two types of reaction. **Catabolism** is the breakdown of large molecules into smaller molecules and **anabolism** is the synthesis, or building up, of large molecules from smaller molecules. In any one cell of the body catabolic and anabolic processes are carried out simultaneously. Each chemical reaction requires a catalyst. Enzymes are protein substances, produced in cells, which act as biological catalysts. They are studied in more detail in Chapter 11. Two of the most important metabolic processes which take place in cells are energy production and protein synthesis.

Energy production (respiration)

Carbohydrates, fats and proteins contain chemical energy 'locked up' in the molecules. Respiration is the breakdown of these substances and the subsequent release of energy. In order to remain alive, both animals and plants must respire. Respiration normally involves the uptake of oxygen and the release of carbon dioxide and it has become synonymous with breathing. For clarity, therefore, the external signs of respiration (breathing) are termed **external respiration** and the breakdown processes within the cells **internal respiration**.

ENERGY FROM CARBOHYDRATES

Glucose and glycogen are broken down in the cells of the body into carbon dioxide and water. The breakdown is a complex process which takes place as a series of reactions involving many intermediate products. One of the main intermediate products is pyruvic acid. The following equation represents the breakdown of glucose into pyruvic acid:

$$C_6H_{12}O_6 \xrightarrow{\text{energy}} 2CH_3COCOOH + 4[H]$$

$$\text{glucose} \qquad\qquad \text{pyruvic acid} \qquad \text{hydrogen}$$

This part of the respiratory process is **anaerobic**, i.e. oxygen is not involved. The hydrogen atoms are not released as free hydrogen but are transferred to co-enzymes which act as hydrogen acceptors. (Eventually the hydrogen atoms combine with oxygen to form water.)

The breakdown of pyruvic acid is **aerobic**, i.e. oxygen is required.

$$2CH_3 \cdot CO \cdot COOH \ + \ 5O_2 \ \xrightarrow{\text{energy}} \ 6CO_2 \ + \ 4H_2O$$

pyruvic acid   oxygen   carbon   water
                                                     dioxide

This stage releases more energy than the first stage.

During periods of strenuous exercise there is insufficient oxygen reaching muscle cells and as a result pyruvic acid is broken down in the anaerobic conditions into lactic acid. A build up of lactic acid causes muscle fatigue. This reaction also occurs during the hanging of meat (see page 157).

A large number of different enzymes are involved in internal respiration since each reaction in the series requires a specific enzyme. Some of the B vitamins are involved in these enzyme systems.

The energy produced by the oxidation of glucose and other nutrients is not released immediately. Certain organic phosphate compounds are able to store energy until it is required. Two of these compounds of particular importance are:

Adenosine diphosphate (ADP), a compound with two phosphate groups

Adenosine triphosphate (ATP), a compound with three phosphate groups

The addition of one more phosphate group to ADP, to convert it into ATP, requires a relatively large amount of energy. Conversely, the removal of a phosphate group from ATP releases a large amount of energy.

The energy released during the oxidation of nutrients is used to produce ATP from ADP. When energy is needed by the cell ATP is converted into ADP.

ENERGY FROM FATS

Fat is first of all transferred from the adipose tissue to the liver. In the liver it is hydrolysed to glycerol and fatty acids. The glycerol is converted into pyruvic acid and oxidised by the method already described. The fatty acids are broken down into acetic (ethanoic) acid $(CH_3 \cdot COOH)$ which joins in with the series of reactions involving the oxidation of pyruvic acid.

ENERGY FROM PROTEINS

Proteins in the diet also yield energy, although their main function is growth and maintenance of cells. Amino acids not required for protein synthesis are deaminated in the liver, i.e. the nitrogen-containing part of the molecule is removed. The deaminated molecules are converted into pyruvic acid and other intermediate products which are oxidised and energy is released (see Figure 10.2).

Protein synthesis

The structure of proteins has been described in some detail in Chapter 7. Proteins are produced in the ribosomes (see page 117) from amino acids. The ribosomes contain ribonucleic acid, RNA. The nucleus of the cell which contains deoxyribonucleic acid, DNA, controls protein synthesis. DNA molecules consist of two long chains twined

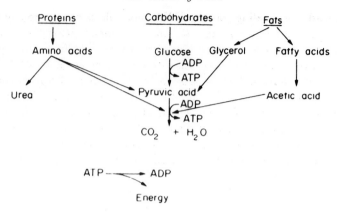

FIG. 10.2. Summary of energy production.

around each other to form a double helix (a spiral-like structure). Cross-links between the chains join sub-units of the molecule called bases. There are four different bases and the order of the bases on the chain determines which proteins are formed in the cell. A sequence of three bases on the chain specifies one individual amino acid. With four different bases available it is possible to produce enough different sequences to cover all the 20 or so amino acids. The DNA molecule does not take part directly in protein

FIG. 10.3. Diagram showing the main stages in protein synthesis.

synthesis. Instead, the 'coding' on the DNA molecule is transferred to shorter single chains of RNA. These RNA molecules are known as messenger RNA since they transfer the code from the nucleus to the ribosomes. Amino acid molecules present in the cytoplasm of the cell join up with another, even shorter, form of RNA called transfer RNA. There is a different kind of transfer RNA for each type of amino acid. The transfer RNA/amino acid complex is conveyed to the ribosome. Here the amino acids are released from the transfer RNA and arranged in a specific order determined by the sequence of bases on the messenger RNA molecule. The adjacent amino acids combine by forming peptide links and so a polypeptide (protein molecule) is produced.

The main stages in protein synthesis are shown diagrammatically in Figure 10.3.

Tissues

The millions of cells which make up the human body are not alike. They differ in size, shape and function. Cells are grouped together into tissues, a tissue being composed of a number of cells identical in function and held together by a ground substance or matrix.

There are five basic tissues in the body:

1. Epithelial	4. Nervous
2. Connective	5. Fluid
3. Muscle	

Epithelial tissue

This tissue covers the surface of the body and lines internal cavities such as the lungs, mouth and stomach. Epithelial cells touch one another and there is little or no intercellular matrix. The functions of epithelial tissue include protection, e.g. the skin, and secretion and absorption, e.g. the internal lining of the intestines.

Connective tissue

Connective tissue connects and supports other tissues of the body. It consists of relatively few cells within an extracellular matrix. Protein fibres are suspended in the matrix; there are three main types:

(a) white collagen fibres—the most common; made of the protein collagen;
(b) reticular fibres—made of a protein called reticulin;
(c) yellow elastic fibres—composed of the protein elastin. These fibres will stretch but recoil to resume their original length.

The relative proportions of these fibres vary in the different types of connective tissue.

1. *Areolar tissue.* This type of tissue is found under the skin and surrounding internal organs, keeping them in place. It contains many loosely packed collagen fibres.

2. *Adipose tissue.* This is the fatty tissue of the body. It is similar to areolar tissue but the cells are swollen with droplets of fat. This fat represents the main energy reserve of the body. Adipose tissue is also found under the skin and around certain organs. It helps to reduce heat loss from the surface of the body and protects organs such as the kidney.

3. *Fibrous tissue.* This is a form of connective tissue in which collagen fibres are closely packed in bundles or sheets. It is tough and inelastic and forms ligaments and tendons. (Ligaments hold bones together at the joints and tendons attach muscles to bones.) Fibrous tissue also surrounds muscle fibres and bundles of muscle fibres.

4. *Cartilage.* This contains a tough, rubbery organic matrix. Some types contain white collagen fibres and some yellow fibres. Cartilage is found at the ends of the long bones and in the wall of the trachea (windpipe). The discs between the bones of the backbone are cartilage.

5. *Bone.* In bone the matrix is hard due to the deposition of calcium salts, mainly calcium phosphate. These mineral salts constitute about two-thirds of the weight of bone. When bone is examined under a microscope it can be seen that the bony matrix is present in concentric layers surrounding small central canals which carry blood-vessels. Bone cells are situated in between the layers of bony material.

Muscle tissue

Muscle tissue is composed of elongated cells or fibres. The fibres are surrounded by thin layers of connective tissue. Muscle fibres contract, i.e. become shorter and thicker, in response to stimulation. Contraction of muscle fibres involves the bonding or overlapping of filaments of two proteins, actin and myosin. Energy for this reaction is obtained from the breakdown of ATP into ADP (see page 119).

Nervous tissue

Nervous tissue consists of nerve cells or neurones which have the ability to respond to stimuli (changes in the environment) and to transmit impulses. A neurone has a cell body with many thread-like projections or processes. There is usually a large number of branched processes called dendrites which conduct impulses to the cell body and a single, long process, the axon, which conducts the impulse away. The axon may be a metre or more in length.

Fluid tissue

Blood and lymph may be classified as fluid tissue. They consist of cells which move in a liquid intercellular matrix. See page 123 for further details.

Organs

The various tissues are grouped together to form the organs of the body. There are numerous organs, e.g. heart, lungs, kidneys, brain and spleen. An organ is composed of at least two tissues. For instance, the heart contains epithelial, connective, muscle, nervous and fluid tissue.

Systems of the body

A system is a group of organs which are closely allied to one another and are concerned with carrying out a particular bodily function.

Circulatory system

The circulatory or vascular system consists of the heart, the blood-vessels and the blood. Its function is to transport oxygen, nutrients, hormones and waste products and to maintain a constant composition of tissue fluid, i.e. the fluid surrounding the cells. Blood is contained in an enclosed system of vessels (arteries, veins and capillaries) and is pumped round the body by the heart. The arteries and veins have impervious walls but the capillaries, the very narrow vessels which bridge the arteries and veins, allow water and other small molecules to pass in and out of the blood.

Blood is composed of:

1. red corpuscles—which contain haemoglobin and convey oxygen from the lungs to the rest of the body;
2. white corpuscles—which are concerned with resistance to infection;
3. platelets—which assist in the clotting of blood;
4. plasma—a pale yellow fluid composed of water together with the blood proteins (albumin and globulin), nutrients, salts and other substances.

The lymphatic system is also considered part of the circulatory system. It drains excess fluid from tissue spaces. Lymph is similar in composition to plasma and tissue fluid. The lymphatic system is a one-way system which connects to the blood system. Lymph enters small lymph capillaries which unite to form larger lymph vessels. The vessels then empty their lymph into veins at the base of the neck. Lymph vessels are interrupted by lymph nodes which remove bacteria and other foreign matter from lymph on its return to the blood system. Lymph nodes are grouped in clumps and can be felt as 'glands' in the armpit, groin and neck. They also produce antibodies.

Respiratory system

The function of the respiratory system is to supply the body with oxygen and to get rid of carbon dioxide. During breathing (external respiration) air containing oxygen is brought into close proximity with the blood capillaries in the lungs, and oxygen passes from the lungs into the blood. At the same time carbon dioxide is released from the blood and is eliminated from the body in the air which is breathed out. This exchange of gases takes place at the necessary rate due to the large surface area of the lungs. Air enters through the nose and passes down the trachea or windpipe. The trachea divides into two pipes (bronchi), one leading to each lung. Each bronchus divides repeatedly until, finally, each branch leads into an air sac which has a large number of very small pouches called alveoli. It is through the thin walls of the alveoli that the exchange of gases takes place.

Internal respiration, the release of energy from nutrients in the cells, has been discussed earlier in the chapter.

Digestive system

The digestive system consists of the alimentary canal and its associated glands (salivary glands, pancreas, etc.). Its function is to break down food into a form which can be absorbed into the blood-stream. Digestion is covered in some detail in Chapter 11.

Excretory system

The urinary system consists of the kidneys, ureters, bladder and urethra. Its function is to eliminate the waste products that result from metabolic activity and to keep the body fluid composition constant. The kidneys form urine by filtering materials from the blood. They are situated in the abdominal cavity, one on each side of the backbone. Each kidney contains about one million small tubules or filtering units called **nephrons** (see Figure 10.4).

FIG. 10.4. Diagrammatic representation of a nephron.

The blood-pressure in the capillaries supplying the capsule is high and blood plasma, minus the proteins, is forced through the wall of the capsule into the cavity of the tubule. The main components of the filtrate, i.e. the solution in the tubule, are water, urea, glucose and mineral salts. As the filtrate passes along the tubule many of its constituents are selectively reabsorbed into the blood capillaries surrounding the tubule. All of the glucose and most of the water and mineral salts are reabsorbed. By the time the filtrate reaches the collecting duct it is urine and consists of about 96% water, 2% mineral salts and 2% urea with traces of other nitrogen-containing substances. A constant flow of urine passes from the collecting ducts down the ureters into the bladder. Urine collects in the bladder and is periodically forced along the urethra and eliminated from the body.

The amount of water lost from the body in urine is controlled by a hormone, ADH or antidiuretic hormone, which is produced by the pituitary gland. ADH regulates the quantity of water reabsorbed into the blood-stream from the filtrate in the tubules.

The kidneys are not the only organs of excretion. The lungs excrete carbon dioxide and water. Water and salts are lost from the skin in sweat and some other excretory products are passed into the alimentary canal and expelled from the body in the faeces.

Nervous system

The function of the nervous system is to control and co-ordinate the activities of the body by enabling the body to perceive changes in the environment (stimuli) and to respond accordingly. The nervous system consists of the sense organs, the nerves, the brain and the spinal cord. The spinal cord is a column of nervous tissue which is continuous with the brain and is enclosed in a channel inside the backbone. The sense organs (eyes, ears, skin, etc.) perceive stimuli and electrical impulses pass along sensory nerve fibres to the brain and spinal cord. In the brain and spinal cord action is determined and impulses are sent along motor nerve fibres to the organs which make the required response. Most nerves are made up of both sensory and motor fibres.

The brain and spinal cord constitute the central nervous system. There is a second system, outside conscious control, called the autonomic nervous system. This system regulates the organs of blood circulation, breathing, digestion, excretion and reproduction entirely by reflex action, i.e. by involuntary responses to stimuli.

The senses of sight, taste and smell play an important role in the appreciation of food and in stimulating the secretion of digestive juices.

THE EYE

The eye consists of a more or less spherical capsule, the main structures of which are illustrated in Figure 10.5. The outer layer consists of a tough, opaque membrane called the sclera which is replaced in the front of the eye by the transparent cornea. The cornea is covered by a thin moist membrane known as the conjunctiva. Behind the cornea is the lens which is held in position by ligaments. Lining the sclera is the choroid layer and inside this is the retina. The retina is pigmented and consists of many nerve endings which combine to form the optic nerve, the link between the eye and the brain. In front of the lens the choroid layer is modified to form a thin muscular sheet, the iris, which has a hole in the centre, the pupil. The iris is the coloured part of the eye. The space between the cornea and the lens contains a watery, colourless fluid, whereas the part of the eyeball behind the lens is filled with a thick, colourless fluid.

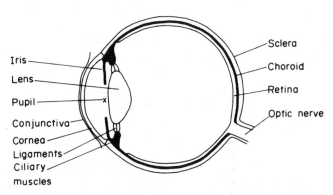

Fig. 10.5. Diagram of the eye.

Light rays enter the eye through the cornea and pupil and are focused by the lens so that they converge on the retina, where an image is formed. When the eye is at rest distant objects are in focus. In order to focus closer objects the shape of the lens is altered by means of the ciliary muscles. This process is known as accommodation. The amount of light entering the eye is controlled by the iris diaphragm. In dim light the pupil is large; in bright light the pupil constricts.

The retina has two types of nerve ending: rods and cones. These are both sensitive to light and impulses are conveyed from them, along the optic nerve, to the brain. The rods contain the pigment rhodopsin (visual purple) and are concerned with black and white vision in dim light. A deficiency of vitamin A depletes the supply of rhodopsin and night blindness results. The cones contain other pigments and are concerned with colour vision in daylight.

THE SENSE OF TASTE

The receptors of taste are the taste buds which are situated on the tongue and soft palate, the back part of the roof of the mouth. Each taste bud is a round cluster of spindle-shaped cells from which nerve fibres lead to the brain, as shown in Figure 10.6.

Fɪɢ. 10.6. Diagrammatic representation of a taste bud.

The sensation of taste depends on water, either from food or from saliva, to carry the stimulating substances to the taste buds. The taste buds are capable of recognising four basic or fundamental tastes, namely, sweet, sour, salt and bitter. These different tastes are transmitted along the nerves by different patterns of impulse. Some parts of the tongue are more sensitive than others to particular tastes, see Table 10.1.

Tᴀʙʟᴇ 10.1. *The four basic tastes*

Basic taste	Substances responsible	Area of tongue where detected
Sweet	Sugars, saccharin, aspartame	Tip
Sour	Acids, e.g. citric, malic, tartaric	Tip and sides
Salt	Chlorides, especially sodium chloride (common salt)	Sides
Bitter	Alkaloids, e.g. quinine (tonic water), caffeine (coffee)	Back

The **threshold** of taste is the minimum concentration of a substance which can be detected. People are more responsive to bitter tastes than to sweet tastes, i.e. the threshold for bitterness is lower than for sweetness. The sense of taste tires or shows adaption. For example, if a sucrose solution is held in the mouth for two minutes the threshold for sucrose may be increased by as much as ten times. This explains why sweet drinks seem less sweet the more you drink. Interactions between different tastes can change threshold values. Sour substances will increase the threshold for sweetness, e.g. lemon juice can mask the presence of sugar.

Taste is a very crude sensation. The subtlety of the flavour of food depends on a combination of the four basic tastes, with a variety of odour or smell sensations. The texture and temperature of food also affect its flavour.

THE SENSE OF SMELL (OLFACTION)

The olfactory organs, the organs responsible for the sense of smell, are found in the upper part of the nose and are somewhat similar in structure to the taste buds. The actual mechanism of olfaction is not clearly understood, but it appears that the hair-like, sensory processes of the olfactory cells are stimulated by molecules of volatile (easily evaporated) substances dissolved in the fluid bathing the cells and that the size and shape of the molecule determines the type of impulse which passes along the nerve to the brain. Sniffing directs air to the olfactory area. There are about 4000 different odours recognised by man.

The sense of smell is very acute. The threshold for smell being much lower than for taste. For example, alcohol can be detected by smell at a concentration of over 20,000 times less than can be detected by taste. Vanillin, the volatile compound responsible for the smell of vanilla, can be detected at a concentration of only 2×10^{-10} grams per cubic metre of air.

Smell receptors adapt to prolonged contact with volatile substances. This may sometimes be of benefit, for example, for people working in an unpleasant-smelling environment.

The pleasant smells produced by food during cooking (baking bread, roasting meat, etc.) occur as a result of volatile substances being formed by chemical reactions. These smells tempt the appetite and stimulate the release of digestive juices.

Endocrine system

There are two systems concerned with the control and co-ordination of the activities of the body. They are the nervous system and the endocrine system. The endocrine system is made up of various glands which release secretions, known as **hormones**, into the blood-stream. Endocrine glands are ductless and are distinct from exocrine glands which release their secretions (e.g. sweat, digestive juices) into a duct to be used locally.

Hormones are sometimes called 'chemical messengers' since they are substances produced in one organ or region of the body, but they control or regulate the function of another organ or region of the body.

Some of the more important endocrine glands together with some of their hormones and functions are shown in Table 10.2.

There are many interactions between hormones and a disturbance in one gland can interfere with other hormones and upset the whole balance of the endocrine system.

TABLE 10.2. *Endocrine glands and their functions*

Gland	Position	Hormone	Function
Pituitary	Base of skull	**ADH** (vasopressin)	Controls water reabsorption in kidney tubules
		Growth hormone	Stimulates growth
Thyroid	Neck	Thyroid hormones	Control basal metabolic rate. Regulate growth
Parathyroids (4 glands)	Embedded in thyroid	Parathyrin	Regulates blood calcium level
Adrenals (2 glands)	Above each kidney	Adrenalin	Increases heart rate and output of glucose from liver in response to fear and stress
		Corticosteroids	Regulate water balance and influence metabolism
Pancreas	Behind the stomach	Insulin	Converts glucose from blood into glycogen (stored in liver and muscles)
Ovaries (female)	Each side of uterus	Oestrogens	Regulate sexual development and functions
Testes (male)	Groin	Androgens	

Reproductive system

The function of the reproductive system is to procreate or reproduce the species. Human life begins as a single-celled embryo formed by the fusion of a sperm from the testes of a male and an ovum (egg) from the ovaries of a female.

CHAPTER 11

Enzymes and Digestion

Enzymes

Enzymes are substances which control all the chemical reactions in living organisms. They are proteins, produced by living cells, and are often called **organic catalysts** because they speed up (catalyse) reactions which otherwise would occur only very slowly, if at all, but are themselves unchanged at the end of the reaction.

Some enzymes have the effect of changing a single-stage reaction requiring a large amount of energy into a multi-stage process involving only small amounts of energy. All cells produce a large number of enzymes (a typical cell contains about 3000 different enzymes); the function of a cell is determined by the nature of the enzymes present in it. Some cells release enzymes which act outside the cell, e.g. the cells lining parts of the alimentary canal produce enzymes which digest food.

Names of enzymes

Most enzymes are named by adding the suffix **-ase** either to a word indicating the nature of the substrate (i.e. the substance affected by the enzyme) or to the name of the type of chemical reaction which the enzyme catalyses.

Hydrol**ases** catalyse hydrolytic reactions. For example:

> carbohydr**ases** break down carbohydrates
> lip**ases** break down lipids (fats and oils)
> prote**ases** break down proteins

Oxid**ases** bring about oxidation reactions. For example, ascorbic acid oxid**ase** is responsible for the oxidation of ascorbic acid (vitamin C).

Some enzymes, e.g. pepsin and rennin, still retain their original or trivial names.

Mode of action

It appears that enzymes function as catalysts by providing within their molecules 'active sites' which receive molecules of the reacting compounds and at which reactions readily take place.

The action of enzymes is highly specific. In general, a given enzyme will catalyse only one reaction. For example, maltase hydrolyses the sugar maltose (to produce two glucose molecules), but it has no effect on other disaccharides. Maltose is the only molecule

129

Fig. 11.1. The action of maltase.

which will 'slot into' the active site on the maltase molecule. The reaction between an enzyme and its substrate has been likened to a lock and key action. Figure 11.1 shows diagrammatically the action of the enzyme maltase.

Factors affecting enzyme action

The activity of enzymes is affected by temperature and pH. Some enzymes are affected by the presence of other substances known as co-factors.

1. EFFECT OF TEMPERATURE

The activity of enzymes is greatly affected by temperature. For animal enzymes the optimum temperature is between 35°C and 40°C, i.e. body temperature. At temperatures above and below the optimum, enzyme activity is reduced. Above 50°C enzymes are gradually inactivated since being proteins they are denatured. At 100°C all enzymes are destroyed. At very low temperatures they are not actually destroyed but their activity is very greatly reduced.

2. EFFECT OF pH

For each enzyme there is an optimum pH. Most enzymes function in a range of pH 5–9, being most active at pH 7 (neutral). If the medium becomes strongly acid or alkaline the enzyme is inactivated. Some enzymes, however, only operate in acid or alkaline conditions. For example, pepsin, an enzyme released into the stomach, can only function in acid conditions; its optimum pH is 2.

3. PRESENCE OF CO-FACTORS

Enzymes often require the help of another substance in order to function effectively. **Co-enzymes** are non-protein compounds which aid enzyme activity. Many co-enzymes are vitamins or vitamin derivatives. Certain mineral ions, e.g. zinc, iron and magnesium, are **enzyme activators**. They must be mixed with the reacting substances before some enzymes will work.

Other substances act as **enzyme inhibitors**. For example, cyanide is a poison because it inhibits respiratory enzymes, resulting in death.

Some enzymes of importance in food production

1. ENZYMES IN BREADMAKING

Enzymes play a very important role in breadmaking. Flour contains **amylases** (diastase) which, in the presence of water, convert starch into maltose. The enzyme

maltase which is secreted by yeast continues the breakdown by splitting maltose into glucose. Glucose is subsequently fermented by a number of enzymes in yeast, known collectively as **zymase**. The products of the fermentation process are carbon dioxide which aerates the dough and ethanol (alcohol) which is driven off during baking.

$$\text{Starch} \xrightarrow[\text{in flour}]{\text{amylases}} \text{maltose} \xrightarrow[\text{in yeast}]{\text{maltase}} \text{glucose} \xrightarrow[\text{in yeast}]{\text{zymase}} \text{carbon dioxide and ethanol}$$

Proteases, present in flour and yeast, are also important in breadmaking. They act on the protein in flour, gluten, making it more extensible and capable of retaining the carbon dioxide produced by the fermentation.

2. PRODUCTION OF ALCOHOLIC DRINKS

The fermentation of glucose by yeast enzymes is also the essential process in the production of beers and wines. In this case the alcohol is retained and the carbon dioxide is allowed to escape or is only partly retained.

Enzymes are used to remove cloudiness in wines and fruit juices. For example, hazes brought about by the presence of pectin in the product can be removed by the addition of small quantities of **pectinase**, an enzyme which breaks down pectin.

3. CHEESE PRODUCTION

Rennet, the essential constituent of which is the enzyme **rennin**, is used in cheese manufacture to coagulate the protein in milk and so form the curd.

4. MEAT TENDERISING ENZYMES

During the hanging of meat, proteases, naturally present in meat, break down the connective tissue thus making the meat more tender. Meat is sometimes treated before cooking with artificial tenderisers. These tenderisers contain protein-splitting enzymes such as **papain**, which is obtained from the papaya plant and **bromelin**, extracted from pineapple juice.

5. TEA PRODUCTION

During the drying of tea leaves important chemical changes take place. Colourless phenolic compounds are oxidised and brown-coloured compounds (including tannins) are formed. The oxidation is brought about by naturally occurring **oxidases**, e.g. polyphenoloxidase.

Some undesirable effects of enzymes in foods

1. AUTOLYSIS

Enzymes naturally present in the tissues of plants and animals continue to act after the harvesting of plants and the slaughter of animals and may bring about undesirable chemical changes in food during storage. This destruction of plant and animal cells by their own enzymes is known as **autolysis** and is one cause of food spoilage.

2. MICROBIAL SPOILAGE

Spoilage of food also results from the activities of microorganisms such as bacteria and moulds. Enzymes contained within the microorganisms break down the constituents of food and produce unpleasant end products. For example, the smell of stale fish is due to a nitrogen-containing compound called trimethylamine which is produced by the enzymic breakdown of protein.

3. ENZYMIC BROWNING

When the cells of apples, potatoes and some other fruits and vegetables are cut and exposed to the air, enzymes present in the cells bring about an oxidation reaction; colourless compounds are converted into brown-coloured compounds. This is similar to the changes which occur during the drying of tea leaves, but in this case the changes are undesirable. Browning does not occur in cooked fruits and vegetables since the enzymes are destroyed by heat.

4. OXIDATION OF ASCORBIC ACID (VITAMIN C)

The enzyme **ascorbic acid oxidase** is responsible for oxidation of vitamin C (see page 98).

Digestion

Food taken into the mouth is of no use to the body until it has been absorbed through the lining of the alimentary canal (digestive tract) and carried by the blood to the cells. Digestion is the breakdown of complex nutrient molecules into molecules small enough to be absorbed through the lining of the intestine. Certain components of food, monosaccharides, salts, vitamins, water and alcohol, do not need to be digested since they are composed of small soluble molecules. Digestion is mainly a chemical process of hydrolysis. Hydrolytic enzymes are produced in various organs and are released into the alimentary canal in digestive juices. The nutrients hydrolysed by digestive enzymes are shown below:

Digestion is also, in part, a physical process. Food particles are reduced in size by the grinding and chewing action of the teeth and by the muscular action of the alimentary canal, e.g. stomach contractions.

Alimentary canal

The alimentary canal can be thought of as a continuous tube, about 8 metres long, open at both ends, the upper opening being the mouth and the lower opening the anus. The various parts of the alimentary canal are shown in Figure 11.2.

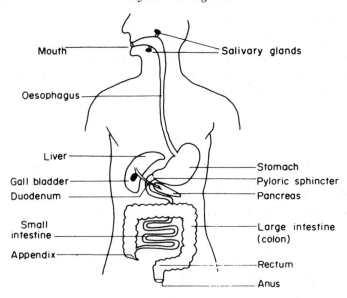

Mouth

Salivary glands

Oesophagus

Liver

Stomach

Gall bladder

Pyloric sphincter

Duodenum

Pancreas

Small
intestine

Large intestine
(colon)

Appendix

Rectum

Anus

Fig. 11.2. Diagram of the alimentary canal and associated organs.

MOUTH

Food is broken into smaller pieces by the grinding and chewing action of the teeth, a process known as mastication. At the sight and smell of food the salivary glands are stimulated and a steady flow of saliva enters the mouth. Saliva is composed of water together with:

1. **mucin**—a slimy, protein substance which lubricates food and makes it easier to swallow;
2. **salivary amylase**—an enzyme which initates the breakdown of starch into maltose.

Food is mixed with saliva and reduced to a soft mass or bolus by the action of the tongue and jaws before it is swallowed. After being swallowed it is carried down the oesophagus by **peristalsis**, rhythmic contractions of the muscles in the wall of the oesophagus.

STOMACH

The stomach acts as a reservoir, so that, rather than eating continually, food need only be consumed at intervals. It is also the site of some digestion. The cells lining the stomach produce gastric juice. Secretion of gastric juice is stimulated by the sight, smell and taste of food and also by the presence of food in the stomach. Gastric juice contains:

1. **pepsin**—an enzyme which breaks down some proteins into smaller molecules called polypeptides;
2. **hydrochloric acid**—which activates pepsin and kills bacteria;
3. **rennin**—an enzyme which coagulates milk protein, important only in babies;
4. **intrinsic factor**—a substance needed for the absorption of vitamin B_{12}.

Waves of muscular contractions in the stomach walls mix the food with the gastric juice producing a mixture known as **chyme**. At intervals small portions of chyme pass through a valve called the pyloric sphincter into the small intestine.

SMALL INTESTINE

The majority of digestive processes take place in the small intestine. As chyme enters the duodenum, the first part of the small intestine, it is acted on by three digestive juices:

1. *Pancreatic juice* which, as its name suggests, is produced in the pancreas and which contains:

(a) **trypsin and chymotrypsin**—enzymes which continue the digestion of proteins;
(b) **pancreatic amylase**—an enzyme which breaks down starch into maltose. It is more effective than salivary amylase;
(c) **lipase**—an enzyme which hydrolyses lipids (fats and oils) into fatty acids and glycerol. Some fats are only partially hydrolysed to diglycerides and mono-glycerides.

2. *Bile* which is a yellow-brown fluid produced in the liver and stored in the gall bladder. The presence of fat and other foods in the duodenum brings about contraction of the gall bladder and the flow of bile into the duodenum. Bile does not contain an enzyme but contains **bile salts** which aid pancreatic lipase by emulsifying fats and oils.

Both pancreatic juice and bile are alkaline and they neutralise the acidic chyme entering the duodenum from the stomach.

3. *Intestinal juice* which is secreted by the cells lining the small intestine and which contains:

(a) **peptidases**—a group of enzymes which complete the breakdown of proteins by splitting polypeptides into their constituent amino acids;
(b) **disaccharide-splitting enzymes**—maltase, sucrase (invertase) and lactase which hydrolyse maltose, sucrose and lactose into their respective mono-saccharides.

Digestion takes place not only in the duodenum but also in the jejunum and ileum, the remaining sections of the small intestine. Some of the final stages of digestion occur in the cells of the intestinal wall. Absorption of nutrients takes place along the whole length of the small intestine. Any food which is not digested and absorbed passes from the ileum into the large intestine.

LARGE INTESTINE (COLON)

The main function of the large intestine is to remove water from the fluid mixture which enters from the small intestine. Water is absorbed through the lining of the colon so that undigested food leaves the body in a semi-solid state. The large intestine contains a very large number of bacteria which break down some of the cellulose and other components of undigested food by their own enzymes and which synthesise certain vitamins, e.g. some B vitamins and vitamin K. The vitamins can be absorbed into the bloodstream.

Undigested food materials, residues from digestive juices, dead cells from the lining of the alimentary canal, bacteria and water form the faeces which are passed out of the body through the anus.

Table 11.1 gives a summary of the digestive processes.

TABLE 11.1. *A summary of the digestive processes*

Part of alimentary canal into which juice is released	Digestive juice	Main components	Action
Mouth	saliva	mucin	aids mastication and swallowing
		amylase	starch → maltose
Stomach	gastric juice	pepsin	protein → polypeptides
		HCl	activates pepsin, kills bacteria
Small intestine	pancreatic juice	trypsin and chymotrypsin	split polypeptides and proteins
		amylase	starch → maltose
		lipase	lipids → fatty acids and glycerol
	bile	bile salts	emulsify fats and oils
	intestinal juice	peptidases	polypeptides → amino acids
		maltase	maltose → glucose
		sucrase	sucrose → glucose and fructose
		lactase	lactose → glucose and galactose

Absorption

Some nutrients are absorbed from the stomach, but most absorption takes place in the small intestine. The small intestine is very long, about 6 metres, and its inner lining is folded into finger-like projections called villi. These two factors mean that the surface area over which absorption can take place is very large, about 20 m² (square metres).

Each villus is supplied with a network of blood capillaries and a lymph vessel, and nutrients are absorbed into the blood- or lymph-system. Non-fatty nutrients, which include monosaccharides, amino acids, water-soluble vitamins and mineral salts, are absorbed directly into the blood-system. Fatty nutrients, such as fatty acids and fat-soluble vitamins, pass into the lymph-vessels and enter the bloodstream at veins in the base of the neck.

Digestibility

The terms 'digestible' and 'indigestible' are normally used subjectively to describe the effect foods have on the digestive system. Indigestible foods are those which cause digestive discomfort. The ease of digestion of a food is of practical importance only in the cases of people with weak or defective digestive systems.

In the stricter scientific sense, the digestibility of a food or nutrient is a measure of the amount which is digested and absorbed. It is normally expressed as a percentage.

Digestibility of a food or nutrient

$$= \frac{\text{weight of food/nutrient digested and absorbed}}{\text{weight of food/nutrient eaten}} \times 100$$

Normally, the digestibility of carbohydrates is about 95% and of proteins and fats about 90%.

CHAPTER 12

Food and Energy

All living organisms require a source of energy. The earth's primary source of energy is the sun, without which there could be no life. Plants, by the process of photosynthesis (see page 49), are able to convert the sun's energy into chemical energy. Animals are unable to utilise the sun's energy directly and so they eat plants or other animals in order to obtain energy. The chemical energy in food is released in the cells of animals by oxidation; this process is known as internal respiration and is explained in some detail in Chapter 10. Some of the energy released is used to maintain metabolic processes in the cells; some is converted into heat to maintain body temperature and some is converted into mechanical energy which is used for physical activity.

Units of energy

As described in Chapter 1, the unit of energy is the **joule**. Since the joule is too small for practical nutrition the kilojoule (kJ) is used. The kilojoule has replaced the kilocalorie (kcal), sometimes written 'Calorie'.

$$\textbf{1 kcal} = \textbf{4.18 kJ}$$

An even larger unit, the megajoule (MJ) is also used.

$$1 \text{ MJ} = 1,000,000 \text{ joules } (10^6 \text{ J})$$
$$= 1000 \text{ kJ}$$

Energy value of nutrients

The three groups of nutrients which provide the body with energy are carbohydrates, fats and proteins.

1 g of carbohydrate provides 16 kJ (3.75 kcal)
1 g of fat provides 38 kJ (9 kcal)
1 g of protein provides 17 kJ (4 kcal)

Alcohol makes a significant contribution to the energy value of beers, wines and spirits.

1 g of alcohol provides 29 kJ (7 kcal)

Energy value of foods

The energy value of a food depends on the quantities of carbohydrate, fat and protein in the food. Since 1 g of fat provides 38 kJ, approximately twice the number of kJ from 1 g of carbohydrate or protein, it follows that fatty foods supply the most energy. Foods containing a high percentage of water, and therefore a smaller proportion of energy giving nutrients, provide the least energy.

Table 12.1 shows the energy value of a selection of foods.

TABLE 12.1. *Energy value of some foods*

Food	kJ per 100 g	kcal per 100 g
Cooking fat	3746	894
Butter	3041	740
Cheese, Cheddar	1682	406
Sugar	1660	394
Cornflakes	1567	368
White flour	1493	356
Bacon	1473	352
Beef	1168	282
White bread	991	233
Eggs	612	147
Canned peaches	373	87
Potatoes	372	87
Bananas	337	79
Cod	322	76
Peas	283	67
Milk	272	65
Apples	196	46
Beer	105	25
Melon	102	24
Cabbage	92	22
Lettuce	51	12

It must be pointed out that the figures in this table are for 100 g of food, not for portions of the foods. To compare the energy values of, say, an egg and a glass of milk the weights of the foods must be taken into account. An egg weighs approximately 50 g and therefore one egg provides 306 kJ ($50/100 \times 612$); a glass of milk weighs about 200 g and provides 554 kJ ($200/100 \times 272$).

There are two methods by which the energy value of foods can be determined. Firstly, if the composition of the food is known its energy value can be calculated as shown in the following example.

100 g of milk contains:

$$4.7 \text{ g carbohydrate which provides } 4.7 \times 16 \text{ kJ} = \quad 75.2 \text{ kJ}$$
$$3.8 \text{ g fat which provides } 3.8 \times 38 \text{ kJ} \qquad = 144.4 \text{ kJ}$$
$$3.3 \text{ g protein which provides } 3.3 \times 17 \text{ kJ} \qquad = \quad 56.1 \text{ kJ}$$
$$\overline{\qquad\qquad\qquad\qquad\qquad\qquad\qquad\qquad 275.7 \text{ kJ}}$$

Secondly, if a weighed portion of food is placed in oxygen and ignited the heat produced by the combustion of the food is a measure of its energy value. This process is carried out in a calorimeter.

Main sources of energy in the British diet

The most important sources of energy in the average British diet are bread and other cereal foods, meat, fats, dairy produce and sugar (see Table 12.2).

TABLE 12.2. *Contribution made by different foods to the total energy content of the average British diet*

Food	Contribution to total energy intake
Bread	14% ⎱ 30%
Other cereal foods	16% ⎰
Meat	16%
Butter, margarine and other fats	15%
Milk, cream and cheese	14%
Sugar	8%

Use of energy by the body

Energy is required by the body for basal metabolism, i.e. for maintaining basic body processes, and for physical activity.

1. BASIC METABOLISM

Basal metabolism is the term used to describe the basic metabolic processes which keep the body alive. Energy is needed to keep the heart beating and the lungs functioning, to maintain body temperature and muscle tone and for the numerous chemical reactions taking place in body cells. The rate at which energy is used up in maintaining basal metabolism is called **basal metabolic rate** (BMR).

BMR varies from person to person and is measured when a person is lying down, relaxed, still and warm and at least 12 hours after a meal. It can be measured by determining the amount of heat given out by the body. This is done by enclosing the person in an insulated chamber and measuring heat output. Another simpler method used for measuring BMR is for the person to breathe into specially designed apparatus which monitors either oxygen uptake or carbon dioxide output. Since oxygen is used up and carbon dioxide is released during the oxidation of nutrients in the body, a measure of either oxygen uptake or carbon dioxide output can be used to determine the rate of energy production in the body.

There are various factors which affect the BMR of an individual.

(a) *Body size.* It is obvious that a large person uses up more energy in maintaining basic body processes than a smaller person. The most critical factor is not total body-weight but lean body mass, i.e. the weight of the body excluding fat. Women have lower metabolic rates than men, partly because they are lighter but also because they have proportionally less lean body tissue and proportionally more body fat.

BMR of an average 70 kg man is 293 kJ per hour (70 kcal per hour)
BMR of an average 55 kg woman is 251 kJ per hour (60 kcal per hour)

In conditions of undernutrition or starvation lean body mass is reduced and this therefore reduces BMR. This partly explains why people are able to exist on diets considerably lower in energy than is normally recognised as adequate.

(b) *Age.* Children have a lower BMR than adults because their body size is smaller but proportionally their BMR is higher, i.e. their BMR per kilogram of body weight is greater. In adults the BMR of both men and women falls with increasing age. The average fall in BMR for a 70 kg man is from 293 kJ per hour at the age of 20 years to 259 kJ (62 kcal) per hour at 70 years of age.

(c) *Activity of the thyroid gland.* The thyroid gland secretes into the bloodstream iodine-containing hormones which control metabolic rate. Thyroxin is the major one of these hormones. In normal healthy people there can be a considerable difference in thyroid gland activity between one person and another. However, in certain cases the thyroid gland may be abnormally active or inactive. An overactive thyroid gland increases BMR by 20% or sometimes more. The person tends to be underweight, very active and excitable, and usually has protruding eyeballs. This condition can be treated by removal, by surgery, of part of the thyroid gland. A person with an abnormally underactive thyroid has a very low BMR and tends to be overweight and slow moving. Administration of thyroxin will help to alleviate this condition.

(d) *Thermogenic effect of food.* The intake of food stimulates metabolism and after a meal metabolic rate increases. The extra energy appears in the form of heat. This stimulation of BMR is known as the thermogenic effect of food.

2. PHYSICAL ACTIVITY

In addition to basal metabolism, energy is used by the body for muscular activity. The energy requirements for various activities have been determined by measuring oxygen uptake during different activities. Average values of some of these figures are shown in Table 12.3.

TABLE 12.3. *Energy consumption of various activities*

Activity	kJ per minute	kcal per minute
Sitting	6	1.4
Writing	7	1.7
Standing	7	1.7
Typing	8	1.9
Washing up	10	2.4
Domestic work	12	2.9
Walking	14–21	3.3–5.0
Running	25–65	6.0–15.6
Swimming	20–50	4.8–12.0
Tennis	20–35	4.8–8.4
Football	20–35	4.8–8.4
Agricultural work	15–30	3.6–7.2
Coalmining	30–40	7.2–9.6

Activities which involve moving the body about, particularly those involved in moving the body upwards, e.g. walking upstairs, require a large amount of energy.

A woman working as a typist might in one day use up energy in the following manner:

		kJ
8 hours sleeping (BMR)	$8 \times 250 =$	2000
1 hour walking	$60 \times 15 \ =$	900
1 hour standing	$60 \times 7 \ \ =$	420
1 hour domestic work	$60 \times 12 \ =$	720
6 hours sitting	$6 \times 60 \times 6 \ =$	2160
6 hours typing	$6 \times 60 \times 8 \ =$	2880
1 hour light exercise	$60 \times 15 \ =$	900
		9980

The body is unable to completely convert chemical energy from food into mechanical energy; the efficiency of conversion is only 15–20%. The energy which cannot be used for physical activity is converted into heat and is used to maintain body temperature. Any excess heat is lost from the body in sweating and this explains why hard work or exercise makes a person hot.

Energy requirements

The amount of energy a person requires depends on age, body size and activity. In adults the degree of activity is largely determined by occupation. For example, a coalminer will need more energy than a typist. However, energy requirements are also affected by leisure activities; playing football or tennis uses more energy than reading or watching television.

The D.H.S.S. figures for recommended daily energy intakes divide men into three occupational categories:

1. **sedentary**—office and shop workers, most professional people;
2. **moderately active**—people engaged in light industry, postmen, plumbers, bus conductors, most farm workers and builders' labourers;
3. **very active**—coalminers, steelworkers, dockers, army recruits, some farm workers and builders' labourers.

Some of the D.H.S.S. figures for men and women are shown in Table 12.4.

In women during pregnancy and lactation, recommended energy intakes are higher in order to meet the energy requirements of the growing baby.

TABLE 12.4. *Recommended daily amounts of food energy*

	Occupational category	kJ	kcal
Men, 18–34 years	sedentary	10,500	2510
	moderately active	12,000	2900
	very active	14,000	3350
Women, 18–54 years	most occupations	9000	2150
	very active	10,500	2500

Energy requirements for children, when related to body-weight, are higher than in adults since BMR when related to body size is higher in children than in adults. Also, children tend to be more active than adults. Babies and young children have proportionally higher energy needs than older children due to rapid growth in the first years of life and to proportionally greater heat losses from the surface of the body (the younger the child the greater the ratio of surface area to body-weight).

The complete table of recommended daily intakes published by the D.H.S.S. is shown in Appendix II.

Obesity

If energy input (food intake) is equal to energy output (energy used for basal metabolism and physical activity), body-weight remains constant. If energy input is greater than output, the excess food is converted into fat and obesity results. It is normally accepted that obesity exists when body-weight is 20% or more above ideal or standard weight; 10–20% above ideal weight is described as 'overweight'. A recent survey showed that 39% of men and 32% of women in Britain are overweight and that 6% of men and 8% of women are obese.

Obesity is one of the major nutritional problems of Western countries and results in various dangers to health. It reduces life expectancy and is related to coronary heart disease and various other conditions including high blood pressure and varicose veins. It also increases the chances of developing diabetes in middle life.

CAUSES

It is difficult to determine the precise causes of obesity. The main sensations regulating food intake are hunger, appetite and satiety. Hunger is the physiological need to eat and is controlled mainly by the hypothalamus, a region at the base of the brain. Appetite is the psychological desire to eat and is triggered by the sight and smell of palatable food. Satiety is the feeling of fullness at the end of a meal which prompts a person to stop eating. These regulating mechanisms may be influenced by a number of factors with the effect that energy input is greater than energy output. Some of the factors involved include:

1. *Heredity*. Body type and structure tend to be inherited. Overweight parents often have overweight children, but it can be argued that this is as much due to family eating habits as to inherited characteristics.

2. *Reduced physical activity*. Obesity is seldom found in people who lead active lives and have jobs involving hard physical work. It is thought that the control of food intake by hunger and appetite works well in active people, but that it fails when activity falls below a certain level so that the normal balance between energy input and output is no longer maintained. This results in a food intake greater than is needed.

Also, people tend to adopt patterns of eating when young and as they get older they continue to eat the same amount, but their physical activity and energy output are reduced. As a result they put on weight.

3. *Eating habits*. People often eat more than they need. This applies particularly to highly palatable, sugar-containing foods such as chocolates and ice creams which have a

high energy value. Eating habits in early life have an effect on body-weight in adult life. If the food intake of babies and young children is in excess of requirements the number of adipose tissue cells increases to store the surplus fat. Once a larger number of cells exists there will always be a tendency to put on weight rather easily. Also, people with a substantial layer of fat under the skin will have a lower energy output since heat loss from the surface of the body is reduced.

4. *Psychological factors.* People with psychological or emotional problems tend to find solace in food and often overeat.

5. *Endocrine factors.* Many overweight people tend to blame their glands. However, endocrine disorders rarely cause obesity. Very occasionally obesity may be the result of defective hormone production by the thyroid, pituitary or sex glands. Obesity is more likely to be due to a disorder of the hypothalamus, which in turn may affect the functioning of the endocrine glands.

TREATMENT

In order to lose weight it is essential to reduce energy intake below the level of energy output so that body fat is used as an energy source. This can be done either by reducing intake, i.e. going on a slimming diet, or by increasing output, i.e. increasing physical activity.

1. *Diet.* The contributions made by the three major nutrients to the total energy intake of the average British diet are as follows:

	Contribution to total energy intake
Carbohydrate	44%
Fat	43%
Protein	13%

In order to reduce energy intake it is not advisable to cut down on protein since it is an essential nutrient and intake must be maintained even on a reducing diet. It is sensible to restrict fat intake by cutting down on the intake of fried foods, butter, cream, full-cream milk, fatty meat, etc. Carbohydrate intake should also be reduced but by restricting sugar rather than starch. Sugar, being 100% carbohydrate, contains no vitamins or minerals, i.e. provides 'empty calories' (see page 59). Foods such as sugar itself, sweets, soft drinks and jams should therefore be reduced as much as possible. Many highly palatable manufactured foods are rich in both fat and sugar, e.g. cakes, biscuits, chocolates, ice cream and other desserts, and should be severely restricted. Alcoholic drinks in excess can lead to obesity and it is sensible to restrict drinking to lose weight.

2. *Activity.* An increase in activity by a sedentary overweight person should have quite a marked effect since increased activity will not only use up more energy but will also help the appetite control function more efficiently. For a moderately active overweight person exercise alone is not sufficient to bring about a significant loss of weight. For example, taking a walk which lasts three-quarters of an hour is only equivalent to using up the energy produced by a packet of potato crisps. Also increased activity stimulates

the appetite and therefore with increased exercise there is a tendency to increase food intake to balance the extra energy output. The best method of weight reduction is to combine a reduced food intake with regular daily exercise.

A further argument in favour of exercise is that if a person loses weight by restricting intake alone they tend to lose both lean body tissue and body fat, but if they exercise as well they lose fatty tissue only.

CHAPTER 13

Nutrition in Practice

Nutritional considerations of groups of people

Nutrient and energy requirements vary according to the age, sex, activity and type of work of the person concerned. There are certain groups of people within the community, for example old people and immigrants, who may have particular nutritional problems and whose diets need particular attention.

Infants and young children

The energy and nutrient requirements of infants and young children are shown in Table 13.1. For the first few months of life these requirements are met by a single food, milk. Babies may be either breast-fed or bottle-fed. There are various dried products on the market available for infant feeding; these are based on modified cow's milk. However, there are several advantages of breast feeding. Human milk is the natural food for babies and it contains nutrients in the correct proportions. Cow's milk contains more protein but less fat, lactose and vitamins A and C. There is the possibility that dried milk

TABLE 13.1. *Recommended daily amounts of food energy and nutrients for children aged up to five years*

	Age range (years)			
	Under 1	1	2	3–4
Energy (kJ)*	2200†	5000	5750	6500
(kcal)*	530†	1200	1400	1560
Protein (g)*	13†	30	35	39
Vitamin A (µg retinol equivalents)	450	300	300	300
Thiamin (mg)*	0.3	0.5	0.6	0.6
Riboflavin (mg)	0.4	0.6	0.7	0.8
Nicotinic acid (mg equivalents)	5	7	8	9
Vitamin C (mg)	20	20	20	20
Vitamin D (µg)	7.5	10	10	10
Calcium (mg)	600	600	600	600
Iron (mg)	6	7	7	8

* These figures are for boys only; figures for girls are slightly lower.
† For 0–3 months of age only. For 3–12 months, see Appendix II.

144

products may be unhygienically prepared or made up to incorrect concentrations with water.

Milk is a satisfactory food for the first few months of life but from about four months, solid foods, such as infant cereal products, should be introduced into the diet. Babies are born with a store of iron which lasts for four to six months. Milk is a poor source of iron, and iron-containing foods, such as puréed fruit and vegetables, egg yolk and minced meat, should be included in the diet at this age. The recommended daily intake of vitamin D for children up to five years is very high and a vitamin D supplement is strongly advised, especially since milk is also a poor source of vitamin D. Supplements of vitamins A and C are also recommended.

Cow's milk may be introduced into the diet from the age of about six months, but this should be whole milk and not skimmed or semi-skimmed, which are both too low in energy and vitamin A for infants and young children. Young children have high energy needs in relation to their small size since they are active and growing fast. Food should, therefore, be of fairly high energy density, i.e. in the region of 10 kJ per gram of food.

Important foods in the diet of children include lean meat, fish, eggs, fruits, vegetables, bread and cereal products. Cereals need not be all wholegrain. A mix of 'white' and wholegrain is best since excessive intakes of fibre can cause toddler diarrhoea.

School children

Recommended energy and nutrient intakes for boys and girls aged seven to eight years and 15 to 17 years are shown in Table 13.2. The full table, for all age groups, is given in Appendix II.

TABLE 13.2. *Recommended daily amounts of food energy and nutrients for boys and girls aged seven to eight years and 15 to 17 years*

	Age range (years)			
	Boys 7–8	Girls 7–8	Boys 15–17	Girls 15–17
Energy (kJ)	8250	8000	12,000	9000
(kcal)	1980	1900	2800	2150
Protein (g)	49	47	72	53
Vitamin A (μg retinol equivalents)	400	400	750	750
Thiamin (mg)	0.8	0.8	1.2	0.9
Riboflavin (mg)	1.0	1.0	1.7	1.7
Nicotinic acid (mg equivalents)	11	11	19	19
Vitamin C (mg)	20	20	30	30
Calcium (mg)	600	600	600	600
Iron (mg)	10	10	12	12

Energy requirements are high in relation to body-weight since children are normally very active and are growing fast. The rate of growth accelerates before and during adolescence, but growth usually stops at 14 to 16 years in girls and 16 to 19 years in boys. Although energy requirements are high, meals should not be too bulky since children have smaller stomachs than adults. Also, obesity among school children and adolescents is becoming more of a problem in Western countries and therefore overeating should be discouraged.

Children should be taught to eat sensibly from an early age. Foods such as meat, liver, fish, cheese, bread, potatoes and other vegetables, fruits and milk are good sources of many nutrients. Encouragement should be given to eat proper meals and not to exist on snack foods. Many of the foods eaten as snacks are not nutritious and displace other more nutrient-rich foods from the diet. These include sweets, crisps, sweet biscuits and soft drinks.

Girls during adolescence should be encouraged to eat plenty of iron-rich foods since iron losses occur due to menstruation.

SCHOOL MEALS

School dinners are the main meal of the day for many children. Until 1980, nutritional standards for school meals were laid down by law, but since the 1980 Education Act local authorities have been given a free rein in the provision of school meals. It is suggested that the NACNE and COMA guidelines (see page 152) should be used as a base for the nutrient content of school meals and that school caterers should spread the 'healthy eating' message and guide children towards a healthy choice.

Adults

The energy requirements of men depend mainly on the type of work they do, as shown in Table 13.3.

TABLE 13.3. *Recommended daily energy intakes for men aged 18 to 35 years of varying occupations*

Occupational category	Recommended energy intakes	
	kJ	kcal
Sedentary (e.g. office workers, teachers, drivers)	10,500	2500
Moderately active (e.g. postmen, plumbers, bus conductors)	12,000	2900
Very active (e.g. coalminers, dockers, forestry workers)	14,000	3350

For most women the recommended daily energy intake is 9000 kJ (2150 kcal). For those whose work requires a lot more physical activity 10,500 kJ (2500 kcal) is recommended. In addition to a person's occupation, their leisure time and recreational activities may make very varied demands on their energy needs. For example, a man spending his evening watching television is obviously using less energy than one playing football or squash. It is important that energy intake does not exceed energy needs since this will lead to obesity. People with sedentary occupations are probably most likely to overeat. Meals and portion sizes should be varied according to energy needs. For example, the diet of a female secretary could include plenty of salads and fruit with moderate amounts of potatoes, cereal products, meat and fish, whereas a man doing heavy manual work will need to fill up with plenty of potatoes, bread and other cereal products and have larger portions of meat, fish, etc.

Women during pregnancy and lactation

Energy and nutrient requirements are increased during pregnancy and lactation (breast feeding), as shown in Table 13.4.

TABLE 13.4. *Recommended daily amounts of food energy and nutrients for non-pregnant, pregnant and lactating women*

	Non-pregnant women	Pregnant women	Lactating women
Energy (kJ)	9000	10,000	11,500
(kcal)	2150	2400	2750
Protein (g)	54	60	69
Vitamin A (μg retinol equivalents)	750	750	1200
Thiamin (mg)	0.9	1.0	1.1
Riboflavin (mg)	1.3	1.6	1.8
Nicotinic acid (mg equivalents)	15	18	21
Vitamin C (mg)	30	60	60
Vitamin D (μg)	—	10	10
Calcium (mg)	500	1200	1200
Iron (mg)	12	13	15

The mother's diet must provide for the laying down of extra tissue in her body and the growth and development of the foetus during pregnancy, and the provision of milk during lactation. Nutrients of particular importance during this period are vitamins C, D and folic acid, together with iron and calcium. The intake of foods rich in these nutrients such as milk, cheese, eggs, fruits and vegetables should be increased to meet these higher requirements. Energy intakes should not be excessive, but should be such as to ensure optimum weight gain during pregnancy (about 12.5 kg). During the last three months of pregnancy, when a large transfer of iron from the mother to the foetus occurs, an iron supplement (e.g. iron tablets) is advisable. Iron tablets prescribed during pregnancy normally contain folic acid as well. Constipation is common during pregnancy and increased amounts of fibre together with adequate fluid intake are recommended.

Old people

The recommended energy and nutrient intakes for elderly men and women are shown in Table 13.5. Elderly people do not need as much energy as younger people since they are less active and since basal metabolic rate declines with age. However, nutrient requirements are similar to, or only slightly less than, those for younger people. This means that they need less food but that the food they do eat must be rich in nutrients.

Some old people, particularly those living on their own, do not obtain an adequate diet. There are a variety of reasons for this, one of the major ones being financial. Other reasons include apathy, poor appetite, ignorance of nutritional values, difficulty in chewing foods and physical disabilities which make shopping and cooking a problem. Storage of fresh foods may also be a problem since some old people do not have a refrigerator and they may find it difficult to buy small portions of foods.

Nutritious foods are not necessarily the most expensive or those which need elaborate cooking. Relatively cheap foods which need little preparation include milk (fresh or

TABLE 13.5. *Recommended daily amounts of food energy and nutrients for elderly men and women*

	Age range (years)			
	Men		Women	
	65–74	75+	55–74	75+
Energy (kJ)	10,000	9000	8000	7000
(kcal)	2400	2150	1900	1680
Protein (g)	60	54	47	42
Vitamin A (μg retinol equivalents)	750	750	750	750
Thiamin (mg)	1.0	0.9	0.8	0.7
Riboflavin (mg)	1.6	1.6	1.3	1.3
Nicotinic acid (mg equivalents)	18	18	15	15
Vitamin C (mg)	30	30	30	30
Calcium (mg)	500	500	500	500
Iron (mg)	10	10	10	10

dried), eggs, cheese, canned fish (e.g. sardines), fruit juices, potatoes (fresh or dried), bread and margarine.

Maintaining an interest in food is important for old people. Luncheon clubs and eating with friends are ways of increasing morale and stimulating the appetite of those who live alone. Many old people receive 'Meals on Wheels' once or sometimes twice a week. The 'Meals on Wheels' scheme aims to supply old people with a nutritionally balanced, hot midday meal. This is organised locally by the Women's Royal Voluntary Service.

Convalescents

Diet is of utmost importance when a person is recovering after an illness or operation. Very often appetite is reduced but a person should be encouraged to eat by being presented with small, attractively served meals. A considerable quantity of protein may be lost as a result of an illness or operation. For example, the breaking of a leg can result in the loss of up to 800 grams of protein. This protein must be replaced during convalescence and, therefore, meals must be high in protein and high enough in energy to enable the body to utilise the protein efficiently. Another nutrient of particular importance during convalescence is vitamin C, which is lost from the body as a result of burns, fractures and surgery.

Vegetarians and vegans

Vegetarians, for a variety of reasons, do not eat meat but many do consume other animal products such as milk, cheese and eggs. The term 'lactovegetarian' is used to describe a person whose diet includes milk and cheese but not meat, poulty, fish or eggs. A 'lacto-ova-vegetarian' consumes milk, cheese and eggs but not meat, poultry or fish. Generally speaking, there are few nutritional problems with these types of diets. The nutrient most likely to be deficient is iron. This can be supplied by eggs (if eaten), cereals, pulses and green vegetables.

The term 'vegan' is used to describe a person who chooses, usually for humanitarian or health reasons, a very much stricter diet that contains no foods of animal origin. Nutrient requirements, with the exception of vitamin B_{12}, can be met by a diet composed only of plant foods, but this requires careful planning and the inclusion of a wide variety of foods. In the average British diet the nutrients provided largely by foods of animal origin include protein, riboflavin, vitamin D and iron. For vegans protein needs can be met by cereals, pulses, nuts and TVP (textured vegetable protein); riboflavin requirements can be met by nuts, cereals, potatoes and soya; vitamin D requirements by margarine and exposure to sunlight; and iron requirements by pulses, green vegetables, cereals and cocoa. There are proprietary yeast extract products available which contain vitamin B_{12}.

Sometimes vegan diets have a low energy density, particularly if they contain a lot of watery fruit and vegetables. Energy density can be kept at a satisfactory level by eating plenty of cereals, nuts and pulses. If well planned, a vegan diet is healthy and adheres to many of the current nutritional guidelines (see page 153). Obesity and coronary heart disease are less common among vegans than the rest of the population.

Immigrants

Nutritional problems occur among some immigrant groups in Britain who keep to their traditional diets and customs. There is increasing concern about low vitamin D intakes and the incidence of rickets in Asian communities. In addition, there is evidence that the iron content of the diet of some immigrant groups is low. The enrichment of chappatti flour with vitamin D has been tried as a means of overcoming the problem of rickets in Asian children. (Chappattis are a type of unleavened bread.)

Meal planning

Meals

It is traditional in Britain to have three meals a day, together with one or more snacks between the main meals.

BREAKFAST

This is an important meal of the day but one that is sometimes missed. The body needs food first thing in the morning since it is generally about 12 hours since the last meal. Research has shown that people who eat breakfast are more efficient, alert and less accident-prone during the morning than those who do not. It is not essential though to have a full, cooked 'English' breakfast. Cereals and milk, toast and marmalade with tea or coffee to drink is sufficient for the majority of people.

MIDDAY MEAL

For many people this is a cooked 'meat and two veg.' type of meal eaten in an industrial canteen or at school. However, it is not essential to have a hot midday meal. Cold meals or packed lunches, if carefully planned, can be equally or more nutritious. Sandwiches with fillings of meat, eggs, fish or cheese together with fruit or salad provide the basis of a well-balanced meal.

EVENING MEAL

Depending in part on what is eaten in the middle of the day, this may be a full cooked meal (i.e. dinner) or a simpler meal. In certain parts of the country 'high tea', which usually consists of a cooked dish or salad with bread and butter and cakes, is still very popular. Many older people prefer their main meal at midday and a lighter meal in the evening.

SNACKS

Between-meal snacks may consist simply of a cup of tea or coffee perhaps with biscuits, mid-morning, mid-afternoon and bedtime, or they may be something more substantial. Many of the foods commonly eaten as between-meal snacks, e.g. sweets, chocolates, cakes, potato crisps and soft drinks, are low in essential nutrients but high in energy. They tend to reduce the appetite for the more nutritious main meals. Foods high in sugar are also harmful to teeth, particularly if eaten frequently. If snacks are eaten between meals more nutritious foods, such as fresh and dried fruit, unsalted nuts, raw vegetables, yoghurt and fruit juices, should be encouraged.

Selection of foods

It is obviously impractical to calculate in detail the nutrient and energy contents of normal menus. It is important, however, that meals are nutritionally balanced, or at least that the food consumed over the period of a day and certainly over a week should be balanced nutritionally.

One of the simplest ways of ensuring a balanced diet is to consider foods as being divided into five groups, each group providing certain essential nutrients. If foods from all five groups are included in reasonable quantities each day the diet should be nutritionally adequate.

1. **Protein foods** (meat, fish, eggs and cheese) which provide protein, energy, B vitamins and iron (meat and eggs).
2. **Milk** which provides calcium, protein, B vitamins, vitamin A and energy.
3. **Fruits and vegetables** which provide vitamin C, vitamin A, minerals and fibre.
4. **Bread and cereals** which provide energy, protein, B vitamins, iron, calcium and fibre.
5. **Butter and margarine** which provide vitamin D, vitamin A and energy.

It will be noticed that sugar and foods containing a high percentage of sugar, e.g. sweets, jams and soft drinks are not included. These types of foods should be kept to a minimum and included only to make the diet more palatable. Their inclusion in the diet should not be at the expense of other more nutritious foods.

In addition to nutritional value there are a number of other factors which should be considered when planning meals and menus. The factors include:

1. *Cost and availability.* Both overall food costs and costs in relation to nutritional value should be considered. In institutional catering (hospitals, schools, etc.), for example, food costs must be kept to a minimum while nutritional standards are maintained. Cheaper

cuts of meat have practically the same nutritional value as more expensive cuts, though they may take longer to cook. Margarine is more nutritious than butter and considerably cheaper. Bread and potatoes are relatively cheap in relation to the nutrients they contain. Seasonal foods such as fruits and vegetables are obviously cheaper when bought in season. Table 13.6 shows some of the cheaper sources of energy and nutrients.

TABLE 13.6. *Cheaper sources of energy and nutrients (in order of cheapness)*

	Foods
Energy	Margarine, vegetable oil, sugar, white bread, butter, wholemeal bread
Protein	White bread, wholemeal bread, pasta, liver, eggs, baked beans, cheese
Vitamin A	Liver, carrots, margarine, butter, eggs, milk, cheese
Thiamin	Fortified breakfast cereals, potatoes, wholemeal bread, white bread, frozen peas, pork, liver
Riboflavin	Liver, fortified breakfast cereals, milk, cheese, wholemeal bread, potatoes
Nicotinic acid	Liver, fortified breakfast cereals, white bread, potatoes, chicken, sausages, frozen peas
Vitamin C	Fruit juices, oranges, old potatoes, new potatoes, tomatoes, fresh green vegetables, frozen peas
Vitamin D	Margarine, oily fish, eggs, fortified breakfast cereals, liver, butter
Calcium	Milk, cheese, white bread, wholemeal bread, carrots , ice cream, biscuits
Iron	Liver, fortified breakfast cereals, wholemeal bread, white bread, baked beans, potatoes, eggs
Fibre	Dried beans, All Bran, wholemeal bread, baked beans, white bread, potatoes, wholegrain breakfast cereals

Food choice is limited by availability, though in Britain wholesalers and retailers stock a wide variety of foods.

2. *Time and labour for food preparation.* A caterer must consider preparation times and the amount of labour required when planning menus. Labour costs must be included in the overall costs of food preparation. On the domestic side, people such as working mothers will aim to keep food preparation time to a minimum. This may necessitate the use of more expensive 'convenience' foods.

3. *Variety and appearance.* Meals should be varied and appetising. There should be variation in the colour, texture, flavour and types of foods. For example, a meal consisting entirely of white foods (such as baked cod, boiled cauliflower, mashed potatoes and rice pudding) is not attractive.

4. *Consumer preferences.* The likes and dislikes of the consumer must be taken into account. There is little point in preparing meals which, although they may be cheap, nutritious and attractive, contain foods disliked by the consumer.

5. *Religious and cultural food habits.* Food choice may be limited by cultural or religious food habits. For example, Orthodox Jews do not eat pork and strict Hindus are vegetarian.

Portion sizes

Portion sizes vary according to the energy needs of the consumer. Table 13.7 shows average portion sizes of a variety of foods.

TABLE 13.7. *Average portion sizes of a variety of foods*

Food	Quantity	Weight
		g
Roast beef	average serving	100
Fish, cooked	average serving	100
Sausage, cooked	1 large	40
Bacon, cooked	1 large rasher	20
Cheese	2.5 cm^3 (1 inch cube)	25
Eggs	1	50
Milk	for 1 cup of tea	25
Milk	1 glass	200
Peas	average serving	80
Tomato	1	50
Potatoes, boiled	average serving	150
Potato chips	average serving	120
Boiled rice	average serving	150
Spaghetti, boiled	average serving	150
Apple, orange	1	125
Bread	1 slice (large loaf)	30
Biscuits	1	10–15
Fruit cake	average portion	60
Butter, margarine	for 1 slice of bread	7
Jam	for 1 slice of bread	10
Breakfast cereals	average serving	25
Soup	average serving	200
Shepherd's pie	average serving	250
Yoghurt	1 carton	125
Ice cream	average serving	100
Apple pie	average serving	125
Sugar	1 teaspoon	5
Coffee, instant	for 1 cup	2

Diet and health

Nutritional knowledge has increased and ideas about what constitutes a healthy diet have changed considerably in recent years. Scientific investigations and research have shown relationships between certain diseases and various factors in the diet. The typical 'Western' diet is high in fat and refined carbohydrate (white flour and sugar) and low in fibre. There are strong links between this type of diet and coronary heart disease, obesity, bowel disorders and tooth decay. It is now realised that by modifying the diet we can reduce the risk of developing these conditions. Various reports have been published over the last few years which recommend changes to our dietary pattern in order to reduce the risk of developing these diseases. The two main reports are:

1. **The NACNE Report.** Proposals for Nutritional Guidelines for Health Education in Britain by the National Advisory Committee on Nutrition Education. 1983.

2. **THE COMA Report.** A report on Diet and Cardiovascular Disease by the Committee of Medical Aspects of Food Policy. 1984.

The main proposals in the NACNE Report involve reducing fat intake, particularly saturated fats, and sugar (sucrose) intake and increasing fibre intake. Recommendations are also made for reducing the intakes of salt and alcohol. These proposals are summarised in Table 13.8 together with present intakes and associated risk factors.

TABLE 13.8. *NACNE recommended dietary intakes*

Dietary constituent	Present intake	Risk factors	Recommended intake (NACNE)
Energy		High intake → obesity	Sufficient to maintain optimum body weight
Fat	40% of total energy	High intake (especially saturated fat) → coronary heart disease	Reduce to 30% of total energy (with saturated fat 10% of total energy)
Sucrose (sugar)	38 kg/person/year	Frequent and/or high intake → tooth decay, obesity	Reduce to 20 kg/person/year
Fibre	20 g/person/day	Low intake → constipation, diverticular disease, cancer of the colon	Increase to 30 g/person/day
Salt	12 g/person/day	High intake → high blood pressure?	Reduce to 9 g/person/day
Alcohol	6% of total energy	High intake → liver damage, obesity, alcoholism, malnutrition	Reduce to 4% of total energy
Protein	12% of total energy		Unchanged but greater proportion of vegetable protein

The COMA Report states that coronary heart disease and cerebrovascular disease (stroke) account for more than one-third of deaths in the U.K. and that dietary changes could reduce this figure. The main recommendations of the report are:

1. to decrease total fat intake to 35% of energy intake with saturated fatty acids 15% of energy intake. The ratio of polyunsaturated fatty acids to saturated fatty acids (see page 70) should be increased to 0.45;
2. not to increase sugar intake;
3. not to increase salt intake but find ways of reducing it;
4. to avoid an excessive intake of alcohol;
5. to compensate for a reduced fat intake by increasing the intake of fibre-rich carbohydrates (bread, cereals, fruit and vegetables);
6. to avoid obesity by a combination of appropriate food intake and regular exercise;
7. people should not smoke cigarettes.

More details on the effects of fat, sugar, fibre and salt on health are given in earlier chapters.

So that individuals may choose a healthier diet, or caterers provide healthier meals, or food manufacturers produce healthier products, the recommendations need to be converted into practical measures. It is important, however, that meals and foods are attractive and appetising as well as healthy. The major changes needed involve reducing the amounts of fatty, animal foods eaten, such as meat, butter, whole milk and cream, and eating more cereal foods and starchy vegetables, e.g. bread, breakfast cereals, pasta, rice and potatoes (particularly wholegrain cereals). Table 13.9 lists items we should be aiming to eat more of or less of, and some of the more healthy alternatives.

TABLE 13.9. *Healthy eating in practice*

EAT MORE:
Poultry and fish
Bread ⎫
Breakfast cereals ⎬ especially wholegrain
Pasta and rice ⎭
Fresh and dried fruit
Pulse vegetables, e.g. baked beans
Potatoes and other vegetables

EAT LESS:	HEALTHIER ALTERNATIVE:
Meat, especially fatty meats, pies, sausages, etc.	Poultry, fish
Whole milk	Skimmed or semi-skimmed milk
Butter ⎫ Hard margarine ⎬	⎰ Polyunsaturated margarine ⎱ Low fat spread
Fried foods	Grilled foods
Cream	Yoghurt
High fat cheeses, e.g. Cheddar	Low fat cheeses
Chips, roast potatoes	Jacket, boiled potatoes
Salt	Herbs, spices
Soft drinks ⎫ Alcoholic drinks ⎬	⎰ Fruit juices ⎱ Low alcohol drinks
Crisps, salted nuts	Unsalted nuts
Sugar	Artificial sweeteners
Cakes, biscuits Sweets, chocolates Ice cream and other desserts ⎬	Fresh and dried fruit

CHAPTER 14

Commodities

Meat

Structure

Meat is the flesh or muscle of animals. It is composed of microscopic fibres, each fibre being an elongated cell. The fibres are held together by connective tissue to form bundles, which are clearly visible in most meats. The whole muscle is also surrounded by connective tissue (see Figure 14.1). Fatty deposits, known as 'marbling', and blood vessels are found between bundles of fibres. The fibrous nature of muscle gives rise to what is known as the 'grain' of meat. It is easier to cut or chew meat with the grain, i.e. in the direction of the fibres, rather than across the fibres.

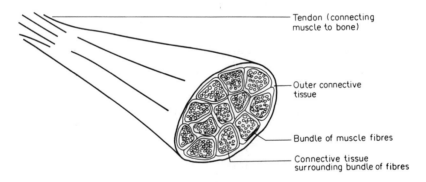

Fig. 14.1. Diagram showing the structure of meat.

Composition

The composition of meat is very variable. The fat content varies from 10% to 50%, depending on the animal and the part of the animal from which the meat has come. Water content is inversely proportional to fat content, i.e. a meat with a high fat content has a low water content and vice versa. Table 14.1 shows the average percentage composition of raw beef, pork and lamb.

155

TABLE 14.1. *Composition of raw beef, pork and lamb*

	Beef %	Pork %	Lamb %
Protein	16	14	15
Fat	24	33	30
Carbohydrate	0	0	0
Water	59	52	54
Vitamins and minerals	1	1	1

MEAT PROTEINS

The cells of the muscle fibres contain two soluble proteins, **actin** and **myosin**, which are responsible for the contraction of muscles. Connective tissue contains the proteins **collagen**, **elastin** and **reticulin** (see page 121). Collagen is found in skin and tendons as well as around muscle fibres. During cooking it is gradually converted into gelatin. Elastin is a tough, insoluble protein and is found in blood vessel walls and ligaments. Reticulin is fibrous and is found between muscle fibres. Neither elastin nor reticulin is affected by cooking. Elastin is very tough and is commonly known as 'gristle'.

FAT

Deposits of fat, marbling, are found in the connective tissue between bundles of fibres. Fat is also stored in the bodies of animals under the skin and around certain organs, e.g. suet around the kidneys. A certain amount of fat in meat is desirable since it keeps meat moist during cooking. Yellow fat normally indicates that the meat has come from an old animal. The yellowness is due to the deposition of carotene (see page 86).

Food value

Meat is a valuable protein food and an important source of B vitamins (especially nicotinic acid) and iron. It is a poor source of calcium. Although liver and kidney contain vitamins A and D, meat does not. Table 14.2 shows the contribution made by meat to the total intake of certain nutrients in the average British diet.

There is no significant difference in nutritional value between expensive and cheaper cuts of meat, or between fresh and frozen meat. Canned meats contain less thiamin than cooked, fresh meat.

TABLE 14.2. *Contribution made by meat to the total content of certain nutrients in the average British diet*

Nutrient	Contribution made by meat to total intake
Nicotinic acid equivalents	34%
Protein	31%
Iron	21%
Riboflavin	18%
Thiamin	14%

Tenderness

The tenderness of meat depends on:

1. *Size of muscle fibres.* Meat composed of small, narrow fibres is more tender than meat made up of larger fibres.

2. *Amount of connective tissue.* Tough meat contains more connective tissue than tender meat. The older the animal and the greater its activity during life, the greater the amount of connective tissue.

3. *Activity of the animal before death.* Animals must be rested before slaughter. If they are not, the supplies of glycogen in the muscle tissues are reduced and less lactic acid is produced during hanging (see point 4).

4. *Length of hanging.* After slaughter meat is hung for several days in order to make it more tender. During hanging glycogen, present in muscle tissue, is converted into lactic acid and the pH of the meat falls from about 7.4 to 5.5. The reduction in pH brings about partial denaturation of the fibre proteins. Also during hanging, enzyme action causes a partial breakdown of the proteins which increases tenderness and contributes to the flavour of meat.

Meat may be further tenderised before cooking in the following ways:

1. Physically, e.g. pounding with a steak hammer, cutting or mincing. This helps to break up fibres and connective tissue.

2. Chemically, by using:

(a) acid marinades, e.g. lemon juice, vinegar, wine. These help to coagulate proteins;
(b) enzymes, which break down proteins, e.g. meat tenderising powders contain papain, a protein-splitting enzyme extracted from the papaya plant.

Colour

The red colour of fresh meat is mainly due to **myoglobin**, a purplish-red pigment somewhat similar in chemical structure to haemoglobin. This pigment reacts under various conditions to form other compounds. When meat is cut and the surface layer exposed to air, bright red oxymyoglobin is formed. During the storage or ageing of meat myoglobin is converted into brownish-red metmyoglobin. When meat is cooked

FIG. 14.2. Meat pigments.

myoglobin is converted, at temperatures above 60°C, into a brown compound called hemichrome. Nitrites which are used in the curing and processing of many meat products, convert myoglobin into pink-coloured nitrosomyoglobin. This accounts for the pink colour of products such as ham, bacon and luncheon meat. These reactions are summarised in Figure 14.2.

Effect of cooking

Meat is cooked in order to increase palatability and tenderness. Also, normal, thorough cooking kills most, if not all, food poisoning organisms that might be present. Various changes occur in meat during cooking.

1. Muscle fibre proteins coagulate and the meat shrinks.
2. Shrinkage results in a loss of juices from the meat. The juices contain water, water soluble salts and vitamins, and peptides (short chains of amino acids). Meat juices, together with fat, are largely responsible for the flavour of meat.
3. Collagen in the connective tissue is converted into gelatin. This makes meat more tender. Moist cooking methods, e.g. stewing and braising, result in a greater breakdown of connective tissue than dry methods, such as roasting, and are therefore more suitable for cheaper cuts which contain greater quantities of connective tissue.
4. Certain nutrients are lost or destroyed during the cooking of meat. B vitamins, being water soluble, are lost in the juices. Thiamin is destroyed by heat and losses during cooking vary from 30% to 50%. Riboflavin and nicotinic acid are more heat stable and losses are smaller.

Offal

Certain organs of animals, such as the liver, kidney and heart, can be eaten and are known collectively as offal. Other types of offal include tripe (the tissues of the stomach) and sweetbreads (the pancreas). Most offal has a high nutritional value. Liver, for example, is a very good source of iron, riboflavin, nicotinic acid, folic acid and vitamin A. Although it is eaten relatively infrequently it provides one-third of the vitamin A in the average British diet. Liver is also a good source of protein, thiamin and vitamin D.

Poultry and game

The term poultry is used for birds reared for their meat and/or eggs and includes chickens, turkeys, ducks and geese. Poultry meat is similar in structure and composition to that of beef, lamb and pork except that chicken and turkey meat is much lower in fat. 'Game' is used to describe wild animals and birds killed for food by hunting or shooting. This includes deer (venison), hare, pheasant, partridge and grouse. The meat is darker and tougher than in domesticated animals and birds and is normally hung for some time to develop flavour and tenderness.

Fish

There are many species of both freshwater and sea-water fish used for human consumption. One of the main differences between meat and fish is that fish deteriorates rapidly and should be eaten as soon as possible after being caught.

Structure

The typically flaky texture of fish is due to the fact that fish muscle consists of blocks of short fibres, called myotomes, rather than the long fibres of animals. The myotomes are separated by thin sheets of connective tissue. Fish has less connective tissue than meat and no elastin, and is, therefore, much more tender.

Composition

There are two main types of fish. Oily fish, such as herring, mackerel, salmon and sardines, contain between 10% and 20% unsaturated oil. White fish, which includes cod, haddock and plaice, contains less than 2% oil. The compositions of raw cod and herring are shown in Table 14.3.

TABLE 14.3. *Composition of raw cod and herring*

	Cod %	Herring %
Protein	17	17
Fat	1	19
Carbohydrate	0	0
Water	82	64
Vitamins and minerals	1	1

Food value

Fish is a good source of protein but it does not make a significant contribution to total protein intake in Britian since fish consumption is low. Oily fish contains vitamins A and D, and all fish provides B vitamins. Small fish, such as sardines, which are eaten with the bones are a good source of calcium. Fish is therefore a nutritious food and its consumption should be encouraged.

Eggs

Structure

A hen's egg weighs about 60 g and is made up of three major parts: shell, white and yolk. The porous shell is composed mainly of calcium carbonate. The colour of the shell does not indicate the quality of the egg but depends on the breed of hen. Inside the shell two thin membranes separate the shell from the white. The white is divided into regions of thick and thin white and accounts for about 60%, of the total weight of the egg. The yolk is suspended in the white and is held in position by strands of protein called chalazae (see Figure 14.3).

The Science of Food

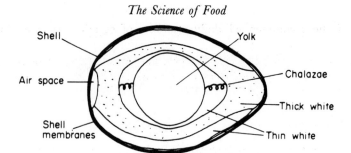

FIG. 14.3. The structure of a hen's egg.

Composition

The white of an egg is basically a colloidal solution of protein (mainly **albumin**) in water, together with small quantities of vitamins and mineral salts. The yolk is a fat-in-water emulsion and is approximately one-third fat, one-half water and one-sixth protein. The main protein is **vitellin**. The yolk also contains vitamins and mineral salts. Table 14.4 shows the approximate percentage composition of the whole egg, the white and the yolk.

TABLE 14.4. *Composition of egg*

	Whole egg (excluding shell) %	White %	Yolk %
Protein	12	9	16
Fat	11	trace	31
Carbohydrate	0	0	0
Water	75	88	51
Vitamins and minerals	1	1	1

Food value

Since an egg supplies a developing chick with all its essential nutrients its food value is high, but it is not a complete food for humans. Eggs are normally considered as protein foods but they also provide substantial quantities of iron, vitamins A and D, and riboflavin. They provide smaller amounts of other B vitamins. Table 14.5 shows the

TABLE 14.5. *Percentage of recommended daily amounts of certain nutrients provided by one egg*

Nutrient	Percentage of recommended daily amount
Riboflavin	18
Vitamin A	15
Protein	12
Iron	10

percentage of the recommended daily amounts of certain nutrients (for an adult) provided by one 60 g egg.

Eggs contain saturated fat and cholesterol and are, therefore, not recommended in large numbers for people at risk from coronary heart disease.

Changes during storage

Various physical and chemical changes take place in an egg during storage:

1. The air space increases in size. This is due to the loss of water through the porous shell and its replacement by air.
2. Water passes from the white to the yolk due to the osmotic pressure exerted by the yolk. The yolk becomes enlarged and the membrane surrounding it weakens.
3. Thick white is gradually converted into thin white.
4. The pH of both the white and yolk increases. This is due to a loss of carbon dioxide through the shell. A solution of carbon dioxide in water is weakly acid and, therefore, a loss of carbon dioxide increases alkalinity.
5. If eggs are stored for a long time bacterial spoilage occurs. Bacteria enter the egg though the porous shell. One of the most noticeable effects is the presence of hydrogen sulphide produced by bacterial breakdown of protein; this gives rise to the typical 'bad egg' smell.

When comparing a fresh egg and a stale egg it will be noticed that the stale egg, when cracked open and placed on a plate, is much flatter and spreads much further than the fresh egg. The stale egg is flatter due to the weakened yolk membrane and it spreads further because it contains more thin white.

Effect of cooking

When eggs are heated the proteins in the white and yolk coagulate. Egg white proteins coagulate first at about 60°C and the white becomes opaque and forms a gel. The yolk proteins coagulate at 66°C and the yolk thickens. The rate of coagulation is increased by the presence of salts and acid. Salt and vinegar can be added to the water used for poaching eggs to bring about rapid coagulation of the white. When eggs are boiled, salt or vinegar in the water coagulates any white which escapes if the shells are cracked.

Iron sulphide is formed in eggs during cooking and sometimes causes a black discoloration around the yolk of hard-boiled eggs. The sulphur is derived from sulphur amino acids in egg white proteins and the iron from the yolk. The reaction occurs more readily in stale eggs than fresh ones. Discoloration can be reduced by placing eggs in cold water immediately after cooking.

There is a small loss of between 5% and 15% of the thiamin and riboflavin in eggs as a result of cooking.

Uses of eggs in cooking

In addition to increasing the nutritional value of dishes, eggs are important in cookery because they have several useful physical properties.

1. *Thickening and binding.* Since egg proteins coagulate when heated, eggs are very useful thickening and binding agents. Egg is used as a thickening agent in dishes such as egg custard and as a binding agent in such products as rissoles.

2. *Emulsifying.* Egg yolk contains lecithin, an emulsifying agent (see page 44), and is used in the preparation of mayonnaise and other emulsions.

3. *Foaming.* When egg white is beaten, air is incorporated and the protein partially coagulates, forming a foam. This is the basis of meringue (see page 48).

Milk

Since, in this country, 'milk' normally implies cow's milk, the following section covers the composition and food value of cow's milk only. In other countries, milk from other animals, such as ewes, goats and even camels and buffalo, is often an important constituent of the diet.

Composition

Milk is composed of a variety of nutrients either dissolved in water or dispersed in the form of a colloid. The colloidal system is complex but is basically a fat-in-water emulsion (see page 44). Table 14.6 shows the average percentage composition of whole milk with skimmed and semi-skimmed (half fat) for comparison.

TABLE 14.6. *Composition of milk*

	Whole %	Semi-skimmed %	Skimmed %
Protein	3.3	3.3	3.4
Fat	3.8	1.7	0.1
Carbohydrate	4.7	4.8	4.9
Water	87.6	89.5	90.9
Vitamins and minerals	0.7	0.7	0.7

The composition of milk varies depending on the age and breed of the cow, the type of food fed to the cow and the time of year. Milk leaving the farm must reach legal standards of quality; it must contain a minimum of 3.0% butterfat and 8.5% solids-not-fat (SNF).

PROTEINS

The proteins in milk are colloidally dispersed in the water phase. The most important proteins are **caseinogen** and the whey proteins, **lactalbumin** and **lactoglobulin**. During digestion caseinogen is converted by the action of rennin into a coagulated form called casein.

FAT

The fat in milk is in an easily digestible, emulsified form. In milk fresh from the cow the fat droplets are uniformly dispersed, but when milk is allowed to stand the droplets rise to the top of the milk and form a layer of cream. Milk can be treated to prevent the formation of a cream layer. This type of milk is known as homogenised milk and is prepared by forcing milk under pressure through very small holes. The fat is broken down into smaller droplets which remain evenly dispersed and the milk has the same composition throughout.

CARBOHYDRATE

The carbohydrate in milk is the disaccharide, **lactose**, which is less sweet than other sugars.

Food value

Milk, being a complete food for young calves, is of high nutritional value. It is a valuable source of protein, riboflavin and calcium and provides important quantities of other B vitamins and vitamin A. It is not, however, a complete food for humans as it is relatively deficient in iron, vitamin C and vitamin D. Table 14.7 shows the contribution made by milk to the total intake of certain nutrients in the average British diet.

TABLE 14.7. *Contribution made by milk to the total content of certain nutrients in the average British diet*

Nutrient	Contribution made by milk to total intake
Calcium	43%
Riboflavin	33%
Protein	17%
Vitamin A (retinol equivalents)	14%
Nicotinic acid equivalents	11%
Thiamin	10%

568 ml (1 pint) of milk provides 680 mg of calcium, i.e. more than the recommended daily intake of calcium for an adult. It also provides one-half of the riboflavin and one-quarter of the protein and vitamin A requirements.

Average milk consumption in Britain is 340 g (more than half a pint) per person per day. An increasing proportion of this is low fat milk, i.e. skimmed or semi-skimmed. Low fat milks are a useful way of reducing saturated fat intake while maintaining intake of protein, calcium and B vitamins. However, they are not suitable for babies and children under five years due to their lower energy and vitamin A contents.

Effect of cooking

When milk is heated, the whey proteins coagulate and a skin forms on the surface. The skin holds steam and is responsible for the ease with which milk 'boils over'. During prolonged cooking caramelisation of the lactose may occur; this contributes to the characteristic flavour of sterilised milk and oven-cooked milk puddings. Some of the thiamin and vitamin C in milk is destroyed by cooking.

Effect of processing

Milk is an ideal medium for bacterial growth and, therefore, in order to make it safe and to improve its keeping quality, it is normally processed before being sold. In Great Britain about 60% of the milk produced is sold as liquid milk; 95% of this is heat treated. (Heat treatment is described in Chapter 18.) The remaining 40% is used to manufacture milk products such as evaporated milk, dried milk, cheese and butter. During processing there is a loss of heat-sensitive vitamins (thiamin and vitamin C). Table 14.8 shows the percentage loss of these two vitamins resulting from the production of various types of milk.

TABLE 14.8. *Percentages of thiamin and vitamin C lost during the processing of milk*

Type of milk	% loss of thiamin	% loss of vitamin C
Pasteurised	10	20
Sterilised	30	50
Spray dried	10	20
Evaporated	20	60
Sweetened, condensed	10	15

The greater the severity of heat treatment the greater the loss of vitamins. Pasteurisation is a mild heat treatment compared with sterilisation. Condensed milk does not require the same degree of heat treatment as evaporated milk because of its high sugar content.

Dried skimmed milk contains only a trace of fat and, therefore, lacks vitamins A and D. It should not, therefore, be used for feeding babies. However, it is a useful protein supplement since it is approximately 37% protein. It also has a high calcium and riboflavin content.

Cream

Cream is a fat-in-water emulsion. It is separated from milk by centrifugation, a process which involves spinning milk in a centrifuge so that the heavier particles are forced to the outside and the lighter particles, which make up the cream, remain nearer the centre.

Composition

Cream contains all of the fat and a proportion of the protein and lactose in milk. Table 14.9 shows the approximate compositions of single and double cream.

By law single cream must have a minimum fat content of 18% and double cream of 48%. Single cream will not whip since only cream with a fat content greater than 30% will whip. Cream which is sold as 'whipping cream' generally contains 35% to 40% fat.

Clotted cream has a very high fat content (at least 55% and often as much as 70%) and is produced by heating milk in special pans and skimming off the cream.

TABLE 14.9. *Composition of single and double cream*

	Single cream %	Double cream %
Protein	2.5	1.5
Fat	21.0	48.0
Carbohydrate	3.0	2.0
Water	72.0	49.0
Vitamins and minerals	0.5	0.5

Food value

All types of cream contain useful quantities of vitamins A and D. Double cream has a higher energy value than single cream since it has a higher fat content.

Butter

Butter is made by churning cream. The conversion of cream into butter is described in Chapter 6. Butter is a water-in-fat emulsion.

Composition

The precise composition of butter is variable, though it must, by law, contain at least 80% milk fat. Table 14.10 shows the composition of an average butter. The composition of margarine is included for comparison.

TABLE 14.10. *Compositions of butter and margarine*

	Butter %	Margarine %
Protein	0.5	0.1
Fat	82.0	81.0
Carbohydrate	0.0	0.1
Water	15.0	16.0
Vitamins and minerals	2.0	2.0

Food value

Both butter and margarine are valuable sources of vitamins A and D, though the actual vitamin content of butter varies considerably, being lower in the winter months when there is a shortage of fresh foods for the cows. Butter provides 7% of the vitamin A and 3% of the vitamin D in the average British diet. Margarine is fortified with these two vitamins by law and contains approximately ten times as much vitamin D as butter. It provides 10% of the vitamin A and 45% of the vitamin D in the average diet.

Butter and margarine both have a high fat content and therefore a very high energy value; 100 g (3.5 oz) butter provides 3041 kJ (740 kcal).

Low fat spreads are a healthier alternative to butter, containing only about 40% fat (see page 67).

Yoghurt

Yoghurt is made by souring milk, using a pure culture of bacteria. The two species of bacteria normally used are *Lactobacillus bulgaricus* and *Streptococcus thermophilus*. They convert the lactose in milk into lactic acid which together with a variety of minor products is responsible for the characteristic flavour of yoghurt. The acid also brings about coagulation of the milk proteins and helps to preserve the product.

Since it is made from milk the composition and food value of yoghurt are similar to milk. Low fat yoghurt is produced from skimmed milk. Fruit yoghurts are normally higher in carbohydrate since, as well as fruit, they usually contain added sugar.

Cheese

Cheesemaking is a traditional method of preserving surplus summer milk. There are more than 400 different varieties of cheese but the basic principles of manufacture are the same for all of them.

Principles of cheesemaking

1. Milk is pasteurised and cooled to about 20°C.
2. A 'starter' culture of souring bacteria is added which converts lactose into lactic acid.
3. Rennet is added and in the acid conditions it rapidly coagulates the protein, forming a curd or 'coagulum' which, as well as casein, contains fat, fat-soluble vitamins, calcium and most of the water-soluble vitamins.
4. The curd is left to harden and is then cut into small pieces to promote the drainage of whey (the fluid which remains when the curd forms). Whey contains only 2% solids which includes the whey proteins (lactalbumin and lactoglobulin) together with lactose and some of the water-soluble vitamins from the milk.
5. The curd is pressed to give a firmer texture and salt is added.
6. The salted cheese is packed into moulds, pressed and left to ripen or mature. During this stage microorganisms grow in the cheese and the flavour develops.

English cheeses such as Cheddar and Cheshire are ripened by the activity of bacteria already present in the cheese. Other cheeses, such as Camembert and Brie, are allowed to develop mould on their outer surfaces. Cheeses such as Stilton and Danish Blue are mould ripened but are pierced with copper wires to encourage mould growth throughout the cheese.

The holes or 'eyes' in cheeses such as Gruyère are a result of the production of carbon dioxide by certain species of bacteria. Cream cheese is prepared from cream rather than whole milk, while cottage cheese is made from skimmed milk and is, therefore, very low in fat. Low fat soft cheese is also made from skimmed milk but with a small amount of cream added.

Vegetarian cheeses are made without rennet (an animal product) but with other enzymes, e.g. a fungal enzyme.

Composition

In some respects cheese can be thought of as a concentrated form of milk (1 litre of milk produces approximately 100 grams of cheese). However, unlike milk, cheese does not contain carbohydrate; the lactose is partly converted into lactic acid and the remainder is lost in the whey.

Table 14.11 shows the composition of Cheddar cheese (a high fat hard cheese), Brie (a medium fat soft cheese) and low fat soft cheese.

TABLE 14.11. *Composition of Cheddar, Brie and low fat soft cheeses*

	Cheddar %	Brie %	Low fat soft %
Protein	26.0	23.0	14.0
Fat	33.0	23.0	4.0
Carbohydrate	0.0	0.0	0.0
Water	37.0	48.0	79.0
Vitamins and minerals	2.5	4.5	2.5

Food value

Since cheese has a lower water content than milk it is a more concentrated source of nutrients. Cheese is particularly rich in calcium and is a good source of protein, vitamin A and riboflavin. It also provides useful quantities of other B vitamins and vitamin D but contains no vitamin C and is a relatively poor source of iron.

Effect of cooking

When cheese is subjected to mild heat the fat melts but there is no significant effect on the nutritive value. Prolonged cooking causes 'stringiness' which is due to over-coagulation of the protein and its separation from the fat and water.

Cereals

Cereal grains are the seeds of cultivated grasses. Cereals are the most important source of food for man and they form the staple food in most countries. In some countries they provide 70% or more of the total energy intake. Cereals may be used as the whole grain, e.g. rice, or they can be ground into a flour, e.g. wheat flour. The most important cereals are wheat, rice, maize (corn), barley, oats and rye.

Wheat

Wheat is grown in Europe, North America and parts of Asia and Australasia where the climate is temperate.

Structure of a wheat grain

A grain of wheat is covered by tough, fibrous layers of pericarp and seed coat which are called the **bran** or husk. Inside is the **germ** which is the actual seed or embryo and which is situated at the base of the grain (see Figure 14.4). By far the largest component of the grain is the **endosperm**, a starchy food reserve for the germ. The outer layer of the endosperm is called the aleurone layer. The germ is separated from the endosperm by the scutellum.

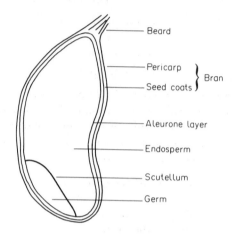

Fɪɢ. 14.4. Vertical section through a grain of wheat.

Composition

The composition of wheat varies depending on the variety. For example, hard Canadian wheats have a high **gluten** (protein) content, whereas the gluten content of soft English wheats is considerably less. The terms 'hard' and 'soft' refer to milling properties of the wheats and should not be confused with 'strong' and 'weak' which refer to the baking properties of a flour. The strength of a flour depends on the quality rather than the quantity of gluten. A strong flour is one which produces a dough that is difficult to stretch and has good gas-retaining properties. Strong flours are suitable for bread-making, whereas weak flours make better cakes and biscuits. In general, hard wheats produce strong flours and soft wheats produce weak flours.

Table 14.12 shows the average composition of a Canadian wheat (Manitoba) and English wheat.

Tᴀʙʟᴇ 14.12. *Compositions of Manitoba and English wheats*

	Manitoba %	English %
Protein	13.5	9.0
Fat	2.5	2.0
Carbohydrate	69.0	74.0
Water	13.5	13.5
Vitamins and minerals	1.5	1.5

Distribution of nutrients within the grain

Nutrients are not uniformly distributed within a grain of wheat.

The endosperm forms about 83% of the total weight of the grain. It is mainly composed of starch but also contains protein, some B vitamins and mineral elements. Of the nutrients in the grain as a whole the endosperm contains:

70–75% of the protein
32% of the riboflavin
12% of the nicotinic acid
3% of the thiamin

The bran and aleurone layer account for 14.5% of the weight of the grain. The bran is largely composed of indigestible cellulose (fibre) but also contains B vitamins and mineral elements. The aleurone layer (which is normally removed with the bran during milling) is rich in protein and B vitamins, especially nicotinic acid. Of the nutrients in the whole grain the bran and aleurone layer contain:

86% of the nicotinic acid
42% of the riboflavin
33% of the thiamin
19% of the protein

The germ (including the scutellum) accounts for only 2.5% of the weight of the grain. The germ is rich in fat, protein, iron and B vitamins (the scutellum is particularly rich in thiamin). Of the nutrients in the whole grain the germ contains:

64% of the thiamin
26% of the riboflavin
8% of the protein
2% of the nicotinic acid

Milling of wheat

In order to turn wheat into a more digestible form it is milled into flour. The bran and germ are removed as flakes and the endosperm is ground into a fine powder. In the 1870s steel roller mills were introduced; they replaced revolving flat stones.

There are three main stages in flour milling.

1. CLEANING AND CONDITIONING

The wheat is first passed through a series of machines which remove dirt, chaff and other impurities. It is then 'conditioned', i.e. brought to the optimum moisture level for milling, by a process involving moistening and drying of the grain. Conditioning toughens the bran so that it is more easily removed during milling and makes the endosperm more friable (easily crumbled) so that it is more easily ground into flour.

2. BREAKING

The cleaned and conditioned wheat is passed through five pairs of corrugated steel rollers known as break rolls. One roller of each pair rotates at two and a half times the speed of the other so that the grain is sheared open and the endosperm is separated from the bran. After passing through each set of rolls the product is sieved and separated into three fractions:

1. Coarse particles of bran with attached endosperm. This is passed on to the next set of break rolls.

2. Coarse endosperm particles known as semolina. Bran particles mixed with the semolina are separated by a current of air, bran being less dense than semolina.

3. A small quantity of fine endosperm particles or flour.

The gap between the break rolls is made progressively narrower so that at each stage a little more endosperm is removed from the bran.

3. REDUCTION

The semolina obtained from the break rolls is passed through ten or more reduction rolls. These are smooth rollers and one roller of each pair rotates one and a half times as fast as the other. The endosperm particles are gradually reduced in size by the crushing action of the rolls and damage to the starch granules is minimised. After passing through each set of rolls the product is sieved and separated into fine particles of flour, larger particles which are passed to the next set of reduction rolls and coarse particles which are returned to a previous set of rolls. As with the break rolls, the reduction rolls are set progressively closer together and at the end of the process fine white flour is obtained. The germ is flattened rather than ground by the reduction system and is removed by sieving.

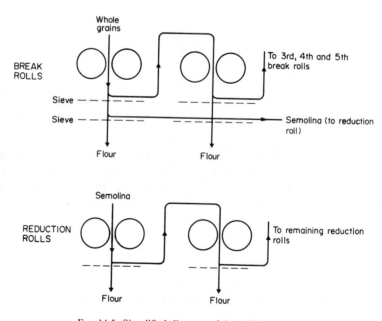

FIG. 14.5. Simplified diagram of the milling process.

Extraction rate

The extraction rate is the percentage of the whole grain which is converted into flour:

Wholemeal flour	100%
Brown flour (wheatmeal)	85–90%
White flour	70–72%

Wholemeal flour consists of the whole grain including the bran and germ, wheatmeal contains the endosperm and germ but only the inner layers of bran, and white flour contains only the endosperm.

Enrichment of low extraction rate flours

Since low extraction rate flours contain little or no bran or germ they have a reduced quantity of protein, fat, B vitamins and fibre. Since 1956 white flour produced in Britain has been enriched with thiamin, nicotinic acid, iron and calcium. By law all flour must contain at least:

0.24 mg thiamin per 100 g
1.60 mg nicotinic acid per 100 g
1.65 mg iron per 100 g

These quantities occur naturally in flour with an extraction rate of 80% or more.

A further legal requirement involves the addition of calcium carbonate (creta praeparata) at the rate of 125 mg calcium per 100 g flour, to all flours except true wholemeal flour (100% extraction).

Bread

Bread is made from a dough of wheat flour, water, salt and yeast. When water is added to flour the wheat proteins, glutenin and gliadin, form gluten which is elastic. Kneading develops a network of gluten in the dough. Before being baked the dough is left to rise. During this stage the dough increases in size due to production of carbon dioxide, a result of the fermentation of sugars by the yeast present in the dough (see page 182). The gluten network traps the gas and during baking the gluten coagulates, thus fixing the size and shape of the loaf.

Much of the bread now made in Britain is produced using the Chorleywood Bread Process in which the initial fermentation stage is replaced by a short period of intense mechanical agitation using special high-speed mixers. Another modern method of breadmaking is the Activated Dough Development (ADD) process. In this method the dough is chemically developed with ascorbic acid and the amino acid cysteine and the fermentation period is reduced.

COMPOSITION

The composition of bread is similar to that of flour except that it contains considerably more water. Table 14.13 shows the percentage composition of white, brown (wheatmeal) and wholemeal bread.

TABLE 14.13. *Composition of white, brown and wholemeal bread*

	White %	Brown %	Wholemeal %
Protein	8.0	8.5	9.0
Fat	1.5	2.0	2.5
Available carbohydrate (starch and sugars)	49.0	44.0	42.0
Dietary fibre	2.5	5.0	8.5
Water	38.0	39.0	38.0
Vitamins and minerals	1.5	1.5	1.5

FOOD VALUE

Bread is one of the most important foods in the British diet. It provides important quantities of protein, B vitamins, iron and calcium. Table 14.14 shows the contribution made by bread to the total intake of certain nutrients in the average diet.

TABLE 14.14. *Contribution made by bread to the total content of certain nutrients in the average British diet*

Nutrient	Contribution made by bread to total intake
Thiamin	25%
Carbohydrate	24%
Iron	21%
Protein	15%
Calcium	14%
Nicotinic acid equivalents	10%

Although consumption of brown and wholemeal bread is increasing, white bread is still more popular. The main reason for this is that white flour has better baking properties and produces a loaf with a more open texture which many people prefer. Also, white flour is more acceptable with millers and bakers since, due to its lower fat content, it is less prone to rancidity during storage, i.e. it has better keeping qualities.

In recent years, though, particularly since the recommendations by the NACNE and COMA Reports to eat more fibre, the consumption of wholemeal bread has increased, as is shown in Table 14.15. The fibre content of wholemeal bread is more than three times that of white bread. Wholemeal bread also contains more B vitamins and minerals,

TABLE 14.15. *Average bread consumption in Britain in 1979 and 1986*

	1979 g/person/day	1986 g/person/day
White bread	93	67
Brown bread	15	15
Wholemeal bread	4.5	22

though white flour does have some of these nutrients 'added back' after milling. Some minerals, although present in larger amounts in wholemeal bread, may not be as readily absorbed due to the presence of phytic acid in the fibre.

There are now various 'soft grain' and 'bran-enriched' breads on the market. These are basically white bread with added cereal grains (wheat, rye and maize) or added bran (sometimes pea bran). The advantage of this type of bread is that it has the texture of white bread but with a fibre content equivalent to wholemeal bread.

Pasta

Pasta is made from hard, durum wheat which is milled into semolina, mixed with water and dried. It may be enriched with egg yolk. It is produced in a variety of shapes and sizes, e.g. spaghetti (thin rods), macaroni (tubes), lasagne (sheets) and farfallette (butterfly-shaped). Pasta provides a good basis for a meal by supplying starch, protein, B vitamins and minerals. When mixed with meat and vegetable sauces it forms a nutritionally well-balanced meal. Wholemeal pasta is also available; this is a good source of dietary fibre.

Rice

Rice grows best in damp tropical climates and is the staple food in many parts of Asia. A grain of rice has approximately the same structure as a grain of wheat. Mechanical milling or 'polishing' removes the bran and germ leaving only the white endosperm. The endosperm represents over 90% of the grain but contains only 9% of the thiamin. In many parts of the East where the staple food is polished rice, thiamin deficiency is common. A deficiency of thiamin causes the disease beriberi which is described in Chapter 8. In some mills the rice is parboiled prior to polishing. If this process is carried out the majority of the thiamin, instead of being lost in the bran, remains in the polished grains. If all rice was parboiled in this way beriberi could be almost completely eradicated.

Brown rice is not polished but contains the whole grain. It takes longer to cook than white rice but is higher in fibre as well as thiamin.

Vegetables

Vegetables have no common biological structure. They are obtained from different parts of many plants. Some vegetables, like cabbage and lettuce, are leaves; others, such as carrots and radishes, are roots; cucumbers and tomatoes are fruits; celery is a stalk; cauliflower is a flower and peas and broad beans are seeds. However, all vegetables possess some similar nutritional properties. They usually have a high water content and, therefore, their contribution to the total energy intake of the diet is low. They are important in the diet because of their content of indigestible carbohydrate (mostly cellulose) which provides fibre. Also many vegetables are good sources of vitamin C, carotene and mineral elements, particularly iron.

Table 14.16 shows the composition of potatoes, cabbage, peas, tomatoes and carrots, the vegetables consumed in the largest quantities in Britain.

TABLE 14.16. *Compositions of some vegetables*

	Potatoes %	Cabbage %	Peas %	Tomatoes %	Carrots %
Protein	2.0	2.5	6.0	1.0	1.0
Fat	0.0	0.0	0.0	0.0	0.0
Available carbohydrate (starch and sugars)	19.0	3.0	10.0	3.0	5.5
Dietary fibre	2.0	3.5	5.0	1.5	3.0
Water	76.0	90.5	78.5	94.0	90.0
Vitamins and minerals	1.0	0.5	0.5	0.5	0.5

Potatoes

The potato is a cheap and popular food in Britain. The average intake is 155 g (5.5 oz) per day. A potato is a swollen underground stem or tuber which acts as a food reserve for the plant. Potatoes have a higher starch content than most other vegetables and provide 372 kJ (87 kcal) per 100 g. They yield more kilojoules per hectare than cereal crops.

Potatoes are the single most important source of vitamin C in the British diet. Their ascorbic acid content is variable since vitamin C is lost during storage; old potatoes may have only one-quarter the vitamin C content of new potatoes. Small but useful quantities of thiamin, nicotinic acid and iron are found in potatoes. The protein content of potatoes is low but the total amount of protein provided by potatoes is not insignificant. Table 14.17 shows the contribution made by potatoes to the total intake of certain nutrients in the average diet.

TABLE 14.17. *Contribution made by potatoes to total content of certain nutrients in the average British diet*

Nutrient	Contribution made by potatoes to total intake
Vitamin C	22%
Thiamin	8%
Nicotinic acid equivalents	8%
Iron	6%
Protein	4%

Green vegetables

These are of particular value in the diet because of their content of vitamin C, iron, β-carotene (the precursor of vitamin A), folic acid and fibre. Green vegetables are best as a source of vitamin C when eaten raw in salads, etc., since their ascorbic acid is readily lost during cooking (see page 98). The β-carotene content varies in different vegetables but increases in proportion to the greenness of the vegetable. Spinach is often quoted as being a good source of iron but, although it has a high iron content, the availability of the iron to the body is reduced by the presence of oxalic acid (see page 107).

Pulse vegetables

Pulse vegetables are the seeds of leguminous plants and include peas, beans and lentils. The crops can be harvested, as they are in Britain, before the seeds are fully mature and dry or, as in the tropics, the seeds can be allowed to mature and can be stored dry, like a cereal crop. In the East, pulses make a larger contribution to the diet than in the West. Soya beans, lentils and dhals (split peas) are important foods in countries such as China and India.

In Britain, green peas and baked beans in tomato sauce are eaten in considerable quantities, though various dried beans, e.g. kidney, borlotti and haricot beans, are becoming more popular, particularly in vegetarian cooking. All pulses contain significant quantities of protein and some, e.g. peas, contain useful amounts of thiamin. Vitamin C and β-carotene are found in fresh pulse vegetables.

Soya beans are particularly rich in protein; dried soya beans are about 40% protein. The importance of soya beans as a meat substitute has been considered in Chapter 7.

Root vegetables

Root vegetables, like all vegetables, provide dietary fibre and a variety of minerals. Carrots are an important source of β-carotene and account for 14% of the total vitamin A content of the average British diet. All root vegetables contain vitamin C but generally not in such large quantities as are found in green vegetables.

Effect of cooking on vegetables

When vegetables are cooked they become more tender and more digestible. This is due to the softening or partial breakdown of the cellulose cell walls and the gelatinisation of the starch. During cooking the green colour of leafy vegetables is intensified, although overcooking results in yellowness.

The major effect of cooking on the nutritive value of vegetables is the loss or destruction of vitamin C; this is considered in Chapter 8.

Fruits

Fruits, like vegetables, contain a high percentage of water and are therefore low in energy value. Also, like vegetables, they are an important source of dietary fibre. One of the main differences between fruits and vegetables is in the nature of the carbohydrates present. In general, fruits have a higher sugar content than vegetables and ripe fruits contain little or no starch. Grapes, for example, contain up to 15% sugar and oranges about 7%; neither fruit contains any starch. The sugar in fruit is usually a mixture of glucose and fructose. Fruits also contain a variety of organic acids, in particular citric, malic and tartaric acids. These acids are responsible for the sourness of unripe fruit. During ripening the concentration of these acids falls and that of sugar rises.

The main importance of fruit in the diet is as a source of vitamin C. Fruits and fruit products provide about 40% of the vitamin C in the average British diet. However, only certain fruits, e.g. blackcurrants, citrus fruits and strawberries, contain valuable quantities. The vitamin C content of many fruits does not compare very favourably with that of vegetables. Apples, pears, plums and peaches are among the fruits with a relatively low vitamin C content.

Commercial fruit juices are now one of the major sources of vitamin C in the diet. They are usually made from concentrated juices which are diluted and preserved by the UHT (ultra heat treatment) process (see page 233).

Dried fruits have a high energy value due to the removal of water but they do not contain any vitamin C.

CHAPTER 15

An Introduction to Microbiology

Microbiology is the study of microorganisms (microbes). Microorganisms are very small, usually single-celled, organisms which are not individually visible to the naked eye. They can only be seen with the aid of a microscope. They are widely distributed in the environment and are found in foods. Certain of them, if present in food in large enough numbers, can cause food poisoning. Microorganisms are the main cause of food 'going off', i.e. food spoilage. However, not all microorganisms are undesirable. In fact, they are essential to all forms of life since they break down complex organic matter and return nutrients to the soil. Microorganisms are used by man in the production of certain foods, e.g. bread and yoghurt.

Although some of the effects of microorganisms have been known and utilised for thousands of years, these microscopic organisms were first seen and studied only 300 years ago. In 1675 a Dutch lens grinder, van Leewenhoek, made a microscope with lenses of sufficiently good quality that he was able to observe microorganisms in a variety of materials such as teeth scrapings and pond water. The significance of his findings was not appreciated at the time. It was nearly 200 years later that a Frenchman, Louis Pasteur, studied fermentation processes and demonstrated that it was microorganisms which caused an undesirable sour taste in some wines. He developed a process of heating wine to kill the microorganisms which caused the souring. This process is still used today to kill undesirable organisms in many food products and is known as pasteurisation. While Pasteur was working in France, Robert Koch, in Germany, demonstrated that anthrax, a fatal disease of sheep and cattle, was caused by a bacterium. From this time onwards great advances were made in the field of microbiology. The organisms responsible for a large number of diseases were identified. In Scotland, Joseph Lister introduced the idea of antiseptic surgery and greatly reduced the incidence of infection in patients during and after surgery.

Classification of microorganisms

Microorganisms can be classified into five biological types:

1. Protozoa	4. Microscopic fungi—
2. Algae	moulds and yeasts
3. Viruses	5. Bacteria

(Each group is described under the appropriate heading later in the chapter.)

This list classifies microorganisms according to their structure. It is sometimes more convenient to classify them according to their role in relation to human beings. In this functional classification there are four groups:

1. Pathogens

These are microorganisms which cause disease. All viruses are pathogenic but only some are pathogenic to man. Certain bacteria also cause disease in man. Some of these diseases can be transmitted by food, e.g. food poisoning, cholera and typhoid (see Chapter 16).

2. Spoilage organisms

These microorganisms do not cause disease but they spoil food by growing in the food and producing substances which alter the colour, texture and odour of the food, making it unfit for human consumption. Examples of food spoilage include the souring of milk, the growth of mould on bread and the rotting of fruits and vegetables. Food spoilage and the methods of preventing it (i.e. food preservation) are covered in Chapter 18.

3. Beneficial organisms

Many microorganisms have a beneficial effect and can be used in the service of man. Few people realise the important part they play in everyday life.

(a) Microorganisms are essential to life since they are responsible for the rotting or decay of organic matter. The complex organic components of dead plants and animals are broken down by microbial activity into simpler, inorganic compounds which are made available for new plant growth, and the whole cycle of life is able to continue.

In the treatment of sewage, microorganisms are used to break down complex organic compounds.

(b) Microorganisms are used at various stages during the manufacture of certain foods. Their activities are essential in the production of foods such as bread, beer, wine, cheese and yoghurt.

(c) Antibiotics, such as penicillin, are substances used to destroy pathogens in the body. Many are produced as a result of microbial activity. For example, penicillin is obtained from a mould called *Penicillium*.

4. Inert organisms

This group includes those organisms which are neither harmful nor beneficial to man. **Commensals** are organisms which live in humans but which do not cause disease in the part of the body where they are normally present. For example, *Streptococcus faecalis* is a bacterium which is harmless in its normal habitat, the large intestine. However, some commensals can be pathogenic if they spread to areas of the body where they are not normally found. *Streptococcus faecalis*, for example, causes disease if it infects the kidneys.

Although it is convenient to use a functional classification, it must be emphasised that this is not a hard and fast division. An individual organism may, in differing circumstances, fall into each of the four groups. For example, the bacterium *Escherichia coli* is generally considered to be inert. However, in some cases it may be pathogenic since it can cause food poisoning. Certain strains can cause food spoilage without causing illness. It has been used for removing glucose from egg white prior to drying, so may therefore be considered useful.

Protozoa

Protozoa are small single-celled animals. They are motile, i.e. capable of independent movement. They mostly live in water, for example in ponds, rivers and the sea and in the water in soil. A common example is *Amoeba*, see Figure 15.1.

Fig. 15.1. Amoeba.

They feed by engulfing tiny food particles and reproduce by binary fission, i.e. dividing into two halves.

The majority of protozoa are non-pathogenic but there are a few pathogenic species of some importance. For example, *Entamoeba histolytica* causes amoebic dysentry, a type of dysentry common in the tropics. Malaria is caused by the protozoan *Plasmodium* which is transmitted by mosquitoes. *Toxoplasma gondii* is an organism sometimes found in animals which may be transmitted to man during the handling of raw meat (particularly pork and mutton). It is estimated that there are one million people in the world infected with the organism and the disease (known as toxoplasmosis) has recently become of more concern in this country.

Algae

Algae are simple plants. Some are macroscopic (large), e.g. seaweeds, but many are microscopic. They contain chlorophyll or a similar pigment which enables them to photosynthesise (see page 49). This means that they do not require complex organic substances as food but can utilise carbon dioxide and water. Microscopic algae usually live in water. Although each cell is capable of an independent existence they tend to grow in a mass and are often visible as green slime on the surface of ponds. Some types of algae, such as *Chlorella*, can be grown on the surface of water, harvested and used as a source of protein.

Viruses

These are the smallest of all microorganisms, varying in size from 10 to 300 nm
(1 nm = 10^{-9} metre). Most viruses are not visible under the light microscope but can be
observed and photographed with the aid of an electron microscope. Viruses are acellular,
i.e. they do not have a cellular structure. They are made up of a central core of nucleic
acid (see page 119) surrounded by a protein coat. They cannot feed, grow or multiply in
isolation; they must always live as parasites in larger living cells. A virus particle attaches
itself to a cell and the core of the virus penetrates and directs the life of the cell so that
many more virus particles are formed. These new particles are then set free to attack
other cells. The host cell is injured or even destroyed by the invading virus. Therefore,
viruses are always pathogenic; they cause disease in man, animals, plants and other
microorganisms. Table 15.1 gives some examples of virus diseases.

TABLE 15.1. *Some examples of virus diseases*

Host	Virus disease
Man	Common cold, Influenza, Measles, Mumps, Chickenpox, Smallpox, Poliomyelitis, AIDS
Animals	Foot-and-mouth disease, Rabies, Distemper, Myxomatosis, Psittacosis, Bovine spongiform encephalopathy (BSE)
Plants	Mosaic diseases

Most virus diseases in man are transmitted by contact, but some are known to be
transmitted by contaminated food or water, e.g. infectious hepatitis and poliomyelitis.
Some diseases may be transmitted to man from animals, for example rabies from dogs
and psittacosis from parrots.

Most virus diseases of man confer immunity, i.e. an attack of the disease confers
resistance to a subsequent attack. This is due to the production of antibodies, substances
formed in the body in response to infection. Artificial immunity may be conferred by
means of vaccination. A vaccine consists of a weakened or dead form of a pathogen and
when it is injected into the body it is practically harmless yet it induces antibody
production.

Many virus diseases of animals and plants are of economic importance. Thousands of
pounds are lost annually due to destruction of crops and livestock by virus diseases.

Microscopic fungi

Fungi are plants but, unlike green plants, they do not possess any chlorophyll. They
are therefore unable to photosynthesise and require complex organic compounds as food.
Those that grow and feed on dead organic material are termed **saprophytes**, while
those feeding on living plants and animals are **parasites**.

1. Moulds

Moulds are usually multicellular, i.e. each mould growth consists of more than one
cell. However, each cell is capable of independent growth and therefore moulds may be

classified as microorganisms. Moulds consist of thin thread-like strands called **hyphae** (sing. hypha). The hyphae grow in a mass on or through the medium on which the mould is growing. This mass of hyphae is known as the mycelium. There are basically two types of mould:

(a) **non-septate moulds**—these do not possess cross walls (septae). The hyphae are continuous tubes containing many nuclei dispersed throughout the cytoplasm and are therefore considered to be multicellular;

(b) **septate moulds**—these possess septae or cross walls (see Figure 15.2) which divide the hyphae into separate cells, each cell containing a nucleus.

REPRODUCTION

Reproduction in moulds is chiefly by means of asexual spores. In non-septate moulds the spores are normally formed within a spore case, or sporangium, at the tip of a fertile hypha. Most septate moulds reproduce by forming unprotected spores known as conidia. Conidia are cut off, either singly or in chains, from the tip of a fertile hypha. Both types of sporing bodies are shown in Figure 15.2.

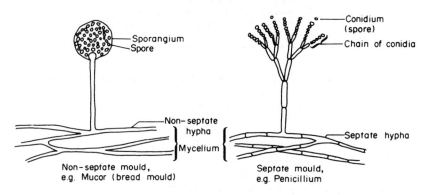

Fig. 15.2. Asexual reproduction in moulds.

When ripe the spores are released into the air. If they find their way to a suitable substrate (food) they germinate and produce a new growth of mould. Some moulds also produce sexual spores, by the fusion of two hyphae.

Many moulds cause food spoilage. Spoilage may occur even in refrigerated foods. However, certain moulds are used in food production, particularly in cheesemaking; Danish blue, Roquefort and Camembert are mould-ripened. Moulds are also used in the manufacture of soy sauce and some products used in the food industry, e.g. citric acid.

Although most moulds are harmless, a few are pathogenic and cause diseases in plants, such as potato blight, and skin infections in man, such as 'athlete's foot' and ringworm. Certain moulds are capable of causing illness by producing toxins in foods known as **mycotoxins**. (Mycology is the study of fungi.) The mould *Aspergillus flavus* produces aflatoxin. This has been found in groundnuts (peanuts), figs, cereals and some other foods. There is considerable concern over levels of aflatoxin in some of these foods and in animal feeds. High levels of aflatoxin are associated with cancer of the liver. Ergot is a fungus which attacks rye and it can cause a serious illness (known as ergotism) in people who eat bread made from infected grain.

One of the most spectacular developments in medicine in this century was the discovery of penicillin and other antibiotics produced by moulds.

2. Yeasts

Yeasts are simple single-celled fungi. They are mainly saprophytic and usually grow on plant foods. Yeast cells may be oval, rod-shaped or spherical. They are larger than bacteria and under a high-power microscope a distinct nucleus is visible.

REPRODUCTION

Most yeasts reproduce asexually by a simple process known as 'budding'. In one part of the cell the cytoplasm bulges out of the cell wall. The bulge or 'bud' grows in size and finally separates as a new yeast cell. This process is shown in Figure 15.3.

FIG. 15.3. Budding in yeast.

Yeasts may cause spoilage in certain foods, e.g. fruit juices, jams and meat. These yeasts are normally referred to as 'wild yeasts' in order to distinguish them from those used commercially in the production of alcoholic drinks and bread.

The economic importance of yeast lies in its ability to break down carbohydrate foods into alcohol and carbon dioxide. This process, known as **alcoholic fermentation**, is anaerobic, i.e. takes place in the absence of oxygen. Yeast contains a collection of enzymes known as zymase which is responsible for the fermentation of sugars, such as glucose, into ethanol (ethyl alcohol) and carbon dioxide. Alcoholic fermentation may be represented by the following equation:

$$C_6H_{12}O_6 \xrightarrow{\text{zymase}} 2C_2H_5OH + 2CO_2$$

$$\text{glucose} \qquad\qquad \text{ethanol} \qquad \text{carbon}$$
$$\text{(ethyl alcohol)} \qquad \text{dioxide}$$

If a plentiful supply of oxygen is available, yeast cells will respire aerobically. In this case, yeast enzymes are able to break down sugars more completely, and carbon dioxide and water are produced.

$$C_6H_{12}O_6 + 6O_2 \longrightarrow 6CO_2 + 6H_2O$$

$$\text{glucose} \qquad \text{oxygen} \qquad\qquad \text{carbon} \qquad \text{water}$$
$$\text{dioxide}$$

More energy is obtained from aerobic than from anaerobic respiration. It is important when yeast is being grown commercially that it is supplied with plenty of air so that sufficient energy is available for growth.

The two most important industrial uses of yeast are in breadmaking and for the production of alcohol. The species generally used in these processes is *Saccharomyces cerevisiae*.

PRODUCTION OF ALCOHOLIC BEVERAGES

All alcoholic beverages, such as beers, wines and spirits, are produced by the anaerobic fermentation of a carbohydrate material by yeast. A large range of starting materials can be used; the carbohydrate may be in the form of starch, e.g. in wheat, barley, rice or potatoes, or in the form of sugars, e.g. in fruits, molasses or added sugar (sucrose). In addition, the following substances may be added:

1. *Amylase.* Yeast cells are not able to produce enzymes capable of breaking down starch. Therefore, if starch is used, a substance containing amylase (diastase) must be added. Amylase is an enzyme which catalyses the breakdown of starch into maltose. Malt (germinating barley) has a high amylase content and is used in the brewing of beer.

2. *Available nitrogen.* This is necessary for the synthesis of protein during the growth and multiplication of the yeast cell. This nitrogen may be provided by protein present in the carbohydrate-containing food used, e.g. by the wheat, or it may be added in the form of ammonium salts or nitrates.

3. *Water.* Water is necessary for the growth of the yeast and also to increase the volume of the mixture.

The mixture is enclosed in a container and oxygen is excluded; this ensures that respiration is anaerobic rather than aerobic. It is then held at a warm temperature in order to encourage the yeast cells to grow and multiply. Fermentation is allowed to continue until the desired concentration of alcohol is obtained. The maximum concentration which can be achieved by fermentation is 16%, since if it increases further the yeast cannot grow. The alcohol content of fortified wines, spirits and liqueurs is increased by distillation.

BREADMAKING

The main ingredients used in breadmaking are flour, water, yeast and salt. These are made into a dough and fat, milk and sugar may also be added. The flour provides starch, amylase and protein and is an excellent food for the yeast. The bread dough is allowed to ferment prior to baking and the carbon dioxide produced causes the dough to rise. During baking the carbon dioxide expands causing the loaf to rise further.

A more detailed description of breadmaking is given on page 171. An account of the various enzymes of importance in breadmaking is given on page 130.

Bacteria

Bacteria (sing. bacterium) are a very important group of microorganisms because of both their harmful and their beneficial effects. They are widely distributed in the environment. They are found in air, water and soil, in the intestines of animals, on the moist linings of the mouth, nose and throat, on the surface of the body and on plants.

Bacteria are the smallest single-celled organisms, some being only 0.4 μm (micrometre) in diameter. The cell contains a mass of cytoplasm and some nuclear material (it does not have a distinct nucleus). The cell is enclosed by a cell wall and in some bacteria this is surrounced by a capsule or slime layer. The capsule consists of a mixture of polysaccharides and polypeptides. Figure 15.4 shows a generalised picture of a single bacterium.

FIG. 15.4. A bacterial cell.

Bacteria are classified into four basic groups depending on the shape of the cells:

1. Coccus (pl. cocci)—spherical
2. Bacillus (pl. bacilli)—rod-shaped
3. Vibrio—short, curved rods
4. Spirillum (pl. spirilli)—long, coiled threads

When bacteria are grown on a culture medium in the laboratory the cells may be grouped together. Cocci, for example, may be joined in chains (Streptococci) or arranged in clusters (Staphylococci). The four basic shapes of bacteria are shown in Figure 15.5.

FIG. 15.5. Shapes of bacteria.

Motility

Some bacteria are motile, i.e. capable of movement. These bacteria possess long thread-like structures called flagella (sing. flagellum) which originate from inside the cell membrane. The flagella move in a whip-like manner and help to propel the bacteria through liquid, such as water. Bacteria can be classified further according to the number of flagella they possess and the position of the flagella on the bacterial cell (see Figure 15.6).

FIG. 15.6. Flagella.

Reproduction

Bacteria reproduce by a process known as **binary fission**. The nuclear material reproduces itself and divides into two separate parts and then the rest of the cell divides, producing two daughter cells which are equal in size. This process is shown in Figure 15.7.

Stage 1	Stage 2	Stage 3	Stage 4
nuclear	membrane	formation of	separation
division	formation	cell wall	of cells

FIG. 15.7. Binary fission in bacteria.

Spore formation

Spores are hard resistant bodies which are formed by some types of bacteria when conditions become adverse, i.e. when they are unable to survive in their environment and to obtain the materials necessary for growth. The spore is formed within the bacterial cell and then the rest of the cell disintegrates (see Figure 15.8). Spores can survive adverse conditions for very long periods of time. When conditions become favourable the spore germinates producing a new bacterial cell. Spore formation occurs in only certain types of bacteria. The two groups of bacteria which form spores (*Bacillus* and *Clostridium*) are both rod-shaped.

FIG. 15.8. Spore formation in bacteria.

Bacterial spores are resistant to heat and can survive in food when food is cooked. They are also resistant to cold (e.g. refrigeration) and to many chemical products designed to kill bacteria, such as disinfectants.

The normal cells of bacteria are described as **vegetative cells** to distinguish them from spores.

Toxins

Bacteria produce a variety of substances as a result of their metabolism. Some of these substances are harmful to man and are known as toxins (i.e. poisons). There are two types of toxins:

1. ENDOTOXINS

Endotoxins are produced within the bacterial cell and are not released into the body until the cell dies. Therefore, they tend to have a localised effect and usually cause harm in the region of the body where the bacteria are living. The symptoms of diseases caused by bacteria producing endotoxins usually do not appear until some time after the living bacteria enter the body, since it is some time before the bacterial cells disintegrate. It should be noted that living bacteria must enter the body in order to cause this type of illness.

2. EXOTOXINS

Exotoxins are produced by bacteria and secreted into the surroundings. The toxin may act in the area around the bacteria but often it is carried by the bloodstream to produce its harmful effect in another part of the body. It is not necessary to ingest living bacteria; the illness is caused by the toxin alone. Some types of food poisoning illnesses are caused by eating a food containing an exotoxin which has survived, even though the bacteria which produced it have died. The symptoms of the illness may appear very soon after the exotoxin enters the body, although this is not always the case. Exotoxins tend to be more sensitive to destruction by heat.

Both types of toxins may be enterotoxins, i.e. substances which have a harmful effect on the digestive system. There is some confusion about the use of all three words to describe toxins and some texts give alternative definitions. This confusion may be due to the fact that some bacteria produce both types of toxins. Also in some cases it is not known exactly which type of toxin the bacteria produces.

Bacterial taxonomy

Taxonomy is the science of classification applied to living things and it involves their identification, naming and arrangement. The system of classification devised by Linnaeus (1707–1798), a Swedish botanist, has now been accepted universally as a means of reference. In this system each individual type of organism is called a **species**. Species or organisms having close similarities are arranged in a group known as a **genus** (pl. genera). Genera with similar characteristics are put in the same family, similar families into orders and orders into classes. This sytem uses two Latin names to describe each organism. The generic name refers to its genus and is written with a capital letter and the specific name indicates its species and is written with a small letter. For example, the name *Clostridium perfringens* refers to species of bacteria known as *perfringens* belonging to the genus *Clostridium*. The generic name is often abbreviated to one or two letters, e.g. *B.* for *Bacillus*, *Cl.* for *Clostridium*. Most animals and plants can be classified according to their morphology, i.e. according to their shape, in conjunction with evidence obtained from fossils. However, the classification of bacteria is more difficult, because fossils of bacteria do not exist and it is difficult to distinguish more than four basic shapes with the aid of a microscope. It is possible to classify bacteria using other criteria and some of the more simple means of classification are given in the following list:

1. Motility and possession of flagella
2. Pigment production
3. Spore formation
4. Heat resistance of vegetative cells and spores
5. Selective staining techniques
6. Selective culture techniques
7. Biochemical tests

Selective culture techniques involve the use of a variety of media. Some media contain substances which suppress the growth of most bacteria but allow particular types to grow. Biochemical tests make use of the fact that different species of bacteria use widely differing materials as food and produce different substances as a result of their metabolism.

Selective staining techniques

It is possible to stain either the whole of the bacterial cell or a part of the cell with various stains or dyes. The ability to retain the stain depends on the species of bacteria. The most common stain used is the Gram stain. Bacteria which retain the stain, becoming violet when viewed under the microscope, are Gram positive. Other bacteria which do not retain the stain are Gram negative and appear pink.

Some of the more important genera of Gram positive and Gram negative bacteria known to cause food spoilage and food poisoning are listed below.

GRAM POSITIVE BACTERIA

BACILLUS—Aerobic, spore-forming rods. Often cause problems in the canning industry because the spores are very resistant to heat. *B. anthracis* causes anthrax in man and animals. *B. subtilis (B. mesentericus)* causes a type of spoilage known as ropiness in bread. *B. cereus* may cause food poisoning.

CLOSTRIDIUM—Anaerobic, spore-forming rods. Cause problems in the canning industry due to heat resistance of spores. *Cl. perfringens* causes food poisoning. *Cl. botulinum* causes a rare but lethal form of food poisoning.

CORYNEBACTERIUM—Aerobic rods, do not form spores. Cause food spoilage. *C. diphtheriae* causes diphtheria.

LACTOBACILLUS—Long rods, do not form spores, usually anaerobic. Often cause spoilage of dairy products and processed meat products. Are used in the manufacture of yoghurt and cheese. *L. bulgaricus* is used in yoghurt production. *L. thermophilus* may cause spoilage of milk.

LEUCONOSTOC—Cocci. Often cause spoilage in dairy products and foods with a high sugar content. Produce characteristic slimy growth.

MICROCOCCUS—Can tolerate high levels of salt and grow fairly well at low temperatures. Often cause spoilage of preserved or refrigerated meats. Some species produce characteristic pink or orange-red pigment.

MYCOBACTERIUM—Rods. *M. tuberculosis* causes bovine TB. Unpasteurised milk from infected cattle can transmit the disease to humans.

SARCINA—Cocci, may be aerobic or anaerobic. Cause spoilage of wide range of unrefrigerated foods. Often produce yellow pigments.

STAPHYLOCOCCUS—Large cocci. Found in the nasal cavities of man and certain other animals as well as on the skin. *Staph. aureus* infects wounds and may cause boils and carbuncles. It is also one of the common causes of food poisoning.

STREPTOCOCCUS—Some species occur in the respiratory tract of man and other animals where they may cause diseases such as scarlet fever and tonsillitis. Other species are found in the intestinal tract of man and animals. *Strep. faecalis* is found in animal faeces and is used as an indicator organism for faecal contamination. This organism sometimes causes outbreaks of food poisoning. Some species ferment lactose (milk sugar) and are used in cheese production, e.g. *Strep. lactis*.

GRAM NEGATIVE BACTERIA

ACETOBACTER—Aerobic rods. Cause spoilage of fruits and vegetables. *A. aceti* oxidises ethanol to acetic acid and is used industrially in the production of vinegar from wine.

ACHROMOBACTER—Short rods. Cause low-temperature spoilage of meats, poultry and seafoods.

ALCALIGENES—Rods. Occur widely in nature. Cause spoilage of raw milk and poultry products. *Alcaligenes viscolactis* causes a type of spoilage known as ropiness in milk.

BACTEROIDES—Anaerobic rods, do not form spores and therefore are often overlooked in routine analyses of foods. Found in the intestinal tract of man and animals and may be transferred to meat where they cause spoilage.

BRUCELLA—*Brucella abortus* causes brucellosis in man and animals.

ERWINIA—Motile rods, grow well at low temperatures. Cause spoilage of fruits and vegetables, particularly soft rot of vegetables. Often produce characteristic red pigment.

ESCHERICHIA—Short rods. Main habitat is intestinal tract of man and animals. *E. coli* is used as an indicator organism since large numbers indicate faecal contamination of foods or water.

PROPIONIBACTERIUM—Small rods. Cause spoilage of alcoholic beverages and pickled foods, where they produce propionic acid. Used in the production of Swiss cheeses containing holes or 'eyes'.

PROTEUS—Aerobic motile rods. Cause spoilage of meat and eggs, when these foods are not stored in a refrigerator.

PSEUDOMONAS—Short aerobic rods. Grow well at low temperatures. Cause spoilage of a large range of refrigerated foods, e.g. meats, poultry, eggs, seafoods.

SALMONELLA—Short aerobic rods. Main habitat is the intestinal tract of man and animals. *S. typhi* causes typhoid fever. *S. typhimurium* and many other species cause food poisoning.

SERRATIA—Aerobic rods. Cause spoilage of unrefrigerated foods. Often produce red pigments, e.g. *Serratia marcescens* produces a red colour on mouldy bread.

SHIGELLA—Short, non-motile, aerobic rods. *Shigella sonnei* occurs in polluted waters and the intestinal tract of man. This organism causes bacillary dysentery.

VIBRIO—*V. cholerae* causes the disease cholera which can be contracted by drinking unchlorinated water or eating contaminated food. *V. parahaemolyticus* causes food poisoning.

Factors affecting the growth of microorganisms

All microorganisms require certain environmental conditions for growth and multiplication. There are variations in the growth requirements of different species but it is possible to list six basic requirements and to indicate individual variations under these headings.

1. Time

The rate of multiplication of bacteria varies according to the species and to the conditions of growth. Under optimum conditions, most bacteria reproduce by binary fission once every 20 minutes. For some bacteria the **generation time**, i.e. the time between divisions, may be as short as 12 minutes. If the generation time is 20 minutes, under favourable conditions a single cell may produce several million cells in under seven hours. Table 15.2 shows how this can be calculated.

TABLE 15.2. *Bacterial multiplication,*
assuming a generation time of 20 minutes

Time in minutes	Number of organisms
0	1
20	2
40	4
60 (1 hour)	8
80	16
100	32
120 (2 hours)	64
140	128
160	256
180 (3 hours)	512
200	1024
220	2048
240 (4 hours)	4096
260	8192
280	16,384
300 (5 hours)	32,768
320	65,536
340	131,072
360 (6 hours)	262,144
380	524,288
400	1,048,576
420 (7 hours)	2,097,152

Fortunately, growth does not carry on at such a rapid rate for any great length of time. The life-cycle of a bacterial colony (a large number of bacteria grouped together) has been investigated and it has been found that when bacteria are placed on a fresh medium, there is no multiplication for about 30 minutes. During this **lag phase** the cells are metabolising rapidly, but this activity results in a slight increase in cell size rather than in cell numbers. Following this the cells multiply rapidly for a few hours or even days depending on the organism and the environment. This period of rapid multiplication is called the **log phase**, since the logarithm of the number of organisms varies directly with time. (After x minutes 10 cells produce 100 cells; after a further x minutes 100 cells produce 1000 cells.) The colony now enters a **stationary phase** of growth where the number of cells produced is equal to the number of cells dying. Finally, the growth rate decreases, usually due to shortage of a growth factor such as a vitamin or mineral element. The colony enters the **decline phase**, which is also logarithmic. The four phases of growth are illustrated by the graph shown in Figure 15.9.

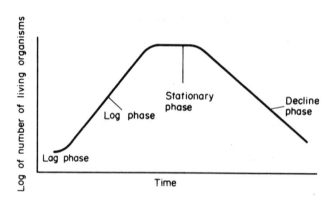

FIG. 15.9. Bacterial growth curve.

2. Food

All microorganisms require nutrients which will supply the following:

(a) energy, usually obtained from a substance containing carbon;
(b) nitrogen for protein synthesis;
(c) vitamins and related growth factors;
(d) minerals.

There are two basic types of nutrition. The organisms may be either heterotrophic or autotrophic.

HETEROTROPHIC NUTRITION

Heterotrophic organisms resemble animals, since they require complex organic substances, such as protein and carbohydrate, for food. All moulds and yeasts and some bacteria, including most pathogens, are heterotrophic. Some can use a wide range of substances in order to obtain their food requirements, while others are more specific and will only grow on certain foods.

Some are able to synthesise vitamins themselves, e.g. bacteria in the intestinal tract, while others must have vitamins supplied by the substrate. It should be noted that the vitamin requirements of bacteria and other microorganisms are not the same as those of humans.

AUTOTROPHIC NUTRITION

Autotrophic organisms resemble plants, since they are able to use simple inorganic substances as food. Many bacteria are autotrophic and there are very few substances that are not biodegradable, i.e. that cannot be broken down by a species of bacteria. Some bacteria can even live on concrete and others can grow in disinfectants such as carbolic acid.

Autotrophic bacteria obtain their energy in two ways:

(a) chemosynthetic bacteria such as the nitrifying bacteria obtain energy by oxidising inorganic compounds. The *Nitrosomonas* species convert ammonium salts to nitrites and the *Nitrobacter* species convert nitrites to nitrates;

(b) photosynthetic bacteria contain pigments closely related to the chlorophyll found in plants and therefore they are able to utilise energy from the sun. This energy is used to synthesise complex organic substances from simple compounds such as water and carbon dioxide.

3. Moisture

Microorganisms, like all other organisms, require water to maintain life. The amount of water available in a food can be described in terms of the water activity (A_w). Pure water has an $A_w = 1.0$. The water activity of most fresh foods is 0.99 but dissolved substances, such as sugar and salt, may lower this considerably. Dried foods have an A_w of 0.6 or less. Bacteria usually require more available moisture than yeasts and moulds. Some species of yeast are osmophilic, i.e. they can grow in an environment supplying very little available moisture. Table 15.3 shows the minimum water activity of some types of microorganisms.

TABLE 15.3. *Minimum water activity of certain types of microorganisms*

Organisms	Minimum A_w
Most spoilage bacteria	0.91
Most spoilage yeasts	0.88
Most spoilage moulds	0.80
Osmophilic yeasts	0.60

4. Temperature

Each microorganism has:

(a) a maximum growth temperature;
(b) a minimum growth temperature;
(c) an optimum growth temperature, i.e. the temperature at which it grows best and multiplies most rapidly.

The optimum temperature is normally closer to the maximum than the minimum temperature.

Microorganisms can be classified into three groups on the basis of their temperature requirements:

(a) **Psychrophiles** (cold-loving organisms) can grow well at temperatures below 20°C; optimum growth range is 10°C to 20°C;

(b) **Mesophiles** (organisms liking moderate temperatures) have an optimum growth temperature between 20°C and 45°C;

(c) **Thermophiles** (organisms liking higher temperatures) can grow well at temperatures above 45°C; optimum growth range is 50°C to 60°C.

This classification is very approximate and sometimes other terms may be used. For example, some organisms may be able to resist the effect of high temperatures even though they are not thermophilic; these are referred to as **thermoduric** (heat-resisting) microorganisms. Similarly, organisms capable of surviving very low temperatures, although they are not psychrophilic are called **psychroduric** (cold-resisting) micro-organisms. Also, the term **psychrotrophs** is sometimes used to cover both psychrophiles and mesophiles, since some mesophiles have a low minimum growth temperature.

Psychrophiles may cause spoilage of refrigerated foods, e.g. members of the genera *Achromobacter* and *Pseudomonas*. The majority of bacteria are mesophilic. Bacteria which are pathogenic to man have an optimum temperature of 37°C (the temperature of the human body). Moulds and yeasts are usually mesophilic or psychrophilic; they do not grow well at higher temperatures. Thermophiles are particularly troublesome in the dairy industry since they may grow at pasteurisation temperatures. Members of the genera *Bacillus* and *Clostridium* produce thermoduric spores and may cause spoilage of canned foods (see page 232).

5. Oxygen

The amount of oxygen available affects the growth of microorganisms. Moulds are aerobic (i.e. require oxygen), while yeasts are either aerobic or anaerobic depending on the conditions. Bacteria are classified into four groups according to their oxygen requirements:

(a) **obligate aerobes** can only grow if there is a plentiful supply of oxygen available;

(b) **facultative aerobes** grow best if there is plenty of oxygen available but can grow anaerobically;

(c) **obligate anaerobes** can only grow if there is no oxygen present;

(d) **facultative anaerobes** grow best if there is no oxygen present but they can also grow aerobically.

Inorganic salts added to food can greatly affect the amount of oxygen available since they act as oxidising or reducing agents, e.g. potassium nitrate, which is used as a meat preservative, increases the amount of oxygen available, since it is an oxidising agent.

6. pH

Most microorganisms grow best if the pH of the food is between 6.6 and 7.5 (i.e. if it is neutral). Bacteria, particularly pathogens, are less acid-tolerant than moulds and yeasts and there are no bacteria which can grow if the pH is below 3.5. Therefore, the spoilage of high acid foods such as fruit is usually caused by yeasts and moulds. Meat and sea-foods are more susceptible to bacterial spoilage since the pH of these foods is nearer to 7.0. Very few foods are alkaline and, therefore, the maximum pH for growth is unimportant. Table 15.4 gives approximate values of the minimum pH for growth of some microorganisms.

TABLE 15.4. *Minimum pH for growth of certain microorganisms*

Organism	Minimum pH
Salmonella typhi	4.5
Escherichia coli	4.4
Yeasts	2.5
Moulds	1.5–2.0

Control of growth of microorganisms

In order to prevent food spoilage, the growth of microorganisms must be prevented. This can be achieved by removing one or more of the conditions necessary for growth or by providing conditions which interfere with microbial metabolism. Many methods of food preservation rely on more than one method of controlling microbial growth. The six most important methods are outlined below.

1. Removal of moisture

In order to prevent the growth of microorganisms in a food the water activity of the food must be reduced to 0.6 or below. In the commercial production of dried foods this is achieved by applying heat and causing the water present in the food to evaporate. The addition of salt or sugar to the food has the same effect. The moisture available to the microorganisms is reduced by osmosis (see Chapter 4). The salt or sugar solutions are more concentrated than the cytoplasm inside the cells of the microorganism. Therefore, water passes out of the cell and the cell becomes dehydrated (see Figure 15.10).

FIG. 15.10. Diagram illustrating the osmotic effect of a salt solution on a bacterial cell.

2. Altering temperature

Microbial growth may be prevented by either decreasing or increasing the temperature.

(A) LOWERING THE TEMPERATURE

There are two types of low-temperature preservation:

(i) *Refrigeration or chilling*. The food is placed at a temperature above the freezing point of water (i.e. above 0°C). The temperature inside a domestic refrigerator should be in the range 0–4°C. Slightly above this range Listeria monocytogenes is able to grow and multiply and this organism can cause a serious form of illness (see page 209). At temperatures in the range 0–4°C the growth of most species of microorganisms is retarded and some may even be killed. However, many microorganisms are still able to grow slowly at these temperatures and bacterial spores survive.

(ii) *Freezing*. The food is frozen and stored at −18°C or below. The freezing process has a killing effect and bacteria continue to die during storage. However, bacteria are only partially eliminated and spores are able to survive. When the food is thawed, the keeping time is shorter than that of fresh food, since the cellular structure of the food has been partially broken down by the freezing process, and bacteria are able to attack the cell contents more easily.

(B) RAISING THE TEMPERATURE

It is possible to destroy both bacterial cells and spores by holding the food at a high temperature for a few hours or longer. The complete destruction of microorganisms by heat is known as **sterilisation**. Cooking may be regarded as a short-term means of food preservation since, if the food is cooked properly, the number of bacteria present will be reduced.

However, if food is to be preserved for longer periods of time, it must be heated in a sealed container, such as a can, to prevent the entry of more microorganisms. Also, for foods other than high acid foods, it is necessary to heat the food to a temperature above 100°C.

When bacteria and bacterial spores are destroyed by heating, the rate of death is logarithmic, i.e. the log of the number of organisms is inversely proportional to time, if the temperature is constant. This may be illustrated by the graph shown in Figure 15.11.

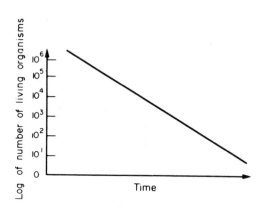

FIG. 15.11. The relationship between the number of organisms and time.

The **Decimal Reduction Time** (DRT) is the time taken to reduce the number of organisms to one-tenth of the original value when heating at a constant temperature. If the DRT is plotted against temperature the relationship is again logarithmic as shown by Figure 15.12.

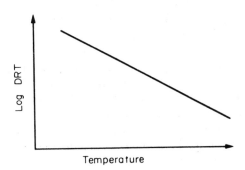

Fig. 15.12. The relationship between decimal reduction time (DRT) and temperature.

The higher the temperature, the shorter the time necessary to reduce the numbers of microorganisms, i.e. the greater the killing effect. Also, using a higher temperature for a shorter time has less effect on the appearance and nutritive value of the food.

3. Exclusion of oxygen

The exclusion of oxygen, e.g. by vacuum packing, prevents the growth of moulds and aerobic bacteria, but yeasts can respire anaerobically and many pathogenic bacteria are anaerobic. Therefore, this may only be used as a means of preservation, if other methods are also used, e.g. destruction by heat in canning.

4. Altering pH

The pH may be lowered so that the food becomes too acidic to allow microorganisms to grow. The most common method is the use of vinegar (acetic acid) in pickling. In the manufacture of yoghurt, bacteria ferment lactose (milk sugar) producing lactic acid. The lactic acid lowers the pH and retards the growth of spoilage organisms.

5. Irradiation

It is possible to kill microorganisms by the use of ionising radiations. On a commercial basis radiation is used mainly for the sterilisation of medical equipment, cosmetics and packaging films. Research has also been carried out on the use of beta and gamma rays for the preservation of food. At the present time the irradiation of food is not permitted in the United Kingdom. However, the government has recently announced that the United Kingdom will fall into line with a proposed EC directive permitting food irradiation and it should become legal by the end of 1990. The use of irradiation as a means of food preservation is discussed in more detail in Chapter 18.

6. Chemicals

A large range of chemicals can be used to check the growth of microorganisms and they can be roughly classified as follows:

(a) **Antiseptics** are chemicals which are used externally on the body. They kill microorganisms but do not harm the skin. If they are taken internally they may be harmful.

(b) **Disinfectants** are chemicals which are used to sterilise equipment in hospitals, in catering establishments and in the home. They may be harmful if used on the body and are only intended for use on inanimate objects. Hypochlorites are often used as disinfectants for articles to be used for food preparation and storage. Other commonly used disinfectants are quaternary ammonium compounds, often referred to as quats. Substances which have disinfectant properties are sometimes referred to as **bactericides**.

(c) **Sanitisers** are mixtures of substances formulated so that they have both disinfectant and detergent properties. They are useful mixtures but, in practice, it is often necessary to make two applications in order to achieve the desired result. In the first application the solution of sanitiser acts mainly as a detergent. It is then rinsed off with water before the second application of sanitiser solution is made, when it acts as a disinfectant.

(d) **Preservatives** are used in food preservation. They do not kill all microorganisms but they retard growth and delay food spoilage (see page 242).

(e) **Antibiotics** and **sulphonamides** are used in medicine. These drugs circulate in the blood-stream and suppress the growth of pathogens in the body.

CHAPTER 16

Food Poisoning

Food poisoning is an illness caused by eating harmful or contaminated food. The most usual symptoms are stomach pains, vomiting and diarrhoea. Food which can cause food poisoning may appear harmless, i.e. the colour, taste and appearance are normal and there is no evidence of spoilage. If food spoilage occurs, the food is unpalatable because the colour, taste and appearance have been changed, although the food may be completely harmless.

There are three types of food poisoning:

1. Chemical
2. Biological
3. Bacterial

Chemical food poisoning

Chemical food poisoning is caused by the presence of toxic chemicals in food. These substances may be agricultural chemicals, which are used intentionally in crop production. The use of weedkillers and insecticides is essential to ensure good yields. However, some of these substances may be dangerous if used indiscriminately, since they may be toxic if they are consumed in large doses. Weedkillers and insecticides are tested very thoroughly before they are placed on the market and farmers are given detailed instructions as to their proper use.

Poisoning may also be caused by the accumulation of certain metals (e.g. lead, mercury and cadmium) in the body. High levels of mercury and cadmium have been found in fish taken from waters polluted by industrial waste. Cases of lead poisoning have arisen as a result of drinking water that has passed through lead pipes.

In addition, food poisoning may be caused by organic mercury compounds, notably methyl mercury. Between 1953 and 1960, 52 people in the Japanese town of Minamata died and about 100 suffered serious brain damage as a result of eating fish containing high levels of methyl mercury. Investigations showed that the source of mercury was effluent from a local chemical factory. The effluent contained inorganic mercury but this was converted into methyl mercury by microorganisms in the mud at the bottom of Minamata Bay. The methyl mercury accumulated in the fish and shellfish living in the bay. Altogether about 900 people showed symptoms of methyl mercury poisoning, as well as many of the seabirds and cats of the area.

197

Outbreaks of organic mercury poisoning have also occurred in Iraq and Guatemala where farmers who had received grain seeds treated with an organic mercury fungicide ate the seeds instead of planting them.

In Spain, during 1981 and 1982, over 350 people died and 20,000 were ill as a result of consuming olive oil which was deliberately contaminated with a chemical.

Biological food poisoning

Biological food poisoning is caused by eating foods containing naturally occurring substances which are harmful. There are many species of poisonous mushrooms, such as *Amanita phalloides* and *A. virosa*, which have caused illness and in some cases death. These mushrooms are very similar in appearance to the edible variety and may easily be eaten by mistake.

Deadly nightshade is a bushy plant which grows throughout Europe and Asia. All parts of the plant contain the drug belladonna, which is used in medicine to relieve illnesses such as asthma, bronchitis and heart disease. However, the drug may be lethal if taken in large doses and children have been poisoned by eating the berries of the plant.

Potatoes are also members of the nightshade family and green potatoes contain a substance called solanine which causes illness or even death if eaten in large quantities. Therefore, green potatoes should always be discarded.

Oxalic acid occurs in the form of its salt, potassium oxalate, in the sap of plants such as rhubarb and spinach. It is also found in very small amounts in the human body. However, in large amounts it can be dangerous and the consumption of large quantities of spinach and rhubarb may be dangerous. In normal circumstances, there is no danger in eating moderate quantities of these foods as part of a well-balanced diet. However, rhubarb leaves should always be avoided, since they contain large amounts of oxalic acid.

Raw red kidney beans contain a toxic substance called haemagglutinin. A number of cases of poisoning have occurred as a result of cooking the beans in a slow cooker at an insufficiently high temperature. Boiling the beans for 10 minutes destroys the toxin. Canned kidney beans are heated sufficiently during processing and are therefore safe.

Scombroid fish, e.g. mackerel and tuna, contain the amino acid histidine. In stale fish this is converted, by bacterial action, into a histamine-containing compound, which is toxic and causes an illness known as scombrotoxic poisoning. It is important, therefore, to eat only fresh fish.

Some moulds produce mycotoxins which cause illness (see page 181).

Bacterial food poisoning

Bacterial food poisoning is the most common cause of food poisoning and stringent hygiene precautions must be taken in order to prevent outbreaks of this type of illness. Since most food poisoning incidents occur as a result of unhygienic practices, this means that they are preventable. There has been a notable increase in the number of recorded incidents of food poisoning since the Second World War. In the 1960s in England and Wales between 4000 and 5000 cases of food poisoning were notified annually. This number increased steadily throughout the 1970s and early 1980s and has since shown a dramatic increase in the latter part of the 1980s. Figures on the number of cases of bacterial food poisoning occurring annually are available from a number of sources. Since the method of collecting the information varies, the figures vary according to the source. However, they all indicate that food poisoning is increasing and that this increase is a cause for concern. Table 16.1 shows the number of laboratory reports of cases of bacterial food poisoning in England and Wales for the years 1977 to 1986.

TABLE 16.1. *Laboratory reports of cases of food poisoning in England and Wales, 1977 to 1986*

Year	Number of cases
1977	9,195
1978	10,572
1979	11,869
1980	10,849
1981	10,665
1982	12.684
1983	15,168
1984	15.312
1985	12,837
1986	15,010

Although there was a decrease in the number of cases in 1985, there was a rapid increase in the years which followed. The number of reported cases in 1988 was about 30,000. In addition, the real situation may be much more alarming than the figures indicate, since it is estimated that about only 10% of all cases are reported. Therefore, the actual number of cases probably exceeds 300,000 per year.

There are several reasons for this increase in the number of cases of food poisoning. Some of the more important reasons are listed below.

1. There has been an increase in the number of meals eaten away from home (in canteens, restaurants, etc.). If a single food in a catering establishment becomes contaminated with food poisoning bacteria, large numbers of people may be affected.

2. Catering establishments now produce more varied menus and this often involves keeping dishes warm until they are required. If food poisoning bacteria enter the food or are already present, they may be given ideal conditions in which to grow.

3. There has been an increase in the number of establishments selling 'take away' meals. These meals are often kept warm on the premises where they are being sold or are cooked earlier and then reheated. They may also be heated up again in the customers' homes. Both situations may provide conditions suitable for the growth of food poisoning bacteria.

4. There has been an increase in factory farming. There is evidence that these intensive farming methods result in more foods being contaminated with food poisoning bacteria, since the animals are reared in close quarters with one another. For example, there has been an increase in the incidence of *Salmonella* in frozen chickens and eggs in recent years.

5. There has been an increase in the use of convenience foods. Manufacturing processes are carried out under hygienic conditions and the whole operation is carefully

monitored. However, mistakes do occur and one source of infection may lead to the contamination of thousands of items. In addition, the use of convenience foods, especially meat products, which are eaten cold or only warmed through, increases the risk of food poisoning.

6. Shopping habits have changed a great deal. Instead of shopping on a daily basis, most housewives shop on a weekly or even monthly basis. This means that food is stored for longer periods of time both in the shop and in the home. Prolonged storage increases the risk of food poisoning unless storage conditions are correct.

7. Many catering establishments employ untrained staff, who may be unaware of the correct hygiene practices to observe in the handling of food. (The use of such staff is a major cause of food poisoning, because of the bad practices they employ.)

8. There are more food poisoning outbreaks during the summer months if the weather is hot. For example, the hot summer of 1983 caused an increase in the number of outbreaks. This is due to the increase in consumption of pre-packed meals, which may be kept at warm temperatures for several hours before they are eaten. Also, in the summer months foods may be stored incorrectly both in shops and in homes and catering establishments, epecially if refrigeration is faulty.

The bacteria most frequently responsible for food poisoning are:

1. Organisms of the *Salmonella* group
2. *Clostridium perfringens*
3. *Staphylococcus aureus*
4. *Bacillus cereus*

Other bacteria which have been responsible for outbreaks of food poisoning, particularly in recent years, are as follows:

1. *Listeria monocytogenes*
2. *Campylobacter jejuni*
3. *Escherichia coli*
4. *Vibrio parahaemolyticus*

Table 16.2 shows the numbers of outbreaks and cases of food poisoning caused by the common food poisoning bacteria in 1985 in England and Wales.

A family outbreak affects two or more people in the same family, whereas a general outbreak involves two or more people in different families.

TABLE 16.2. *Causal agents of bacterial food poisoning in England and Wales, 1985*

Causative agent	General outbreaks	Family outbreaks	Sporadic cases	All cases
Salmonella typhymurium	43	94	3953	4546
Other *Salmonella* sp.	72	116	5688	6626
Clostridium perfringens	56	6	—	1466
Staphylococcus aureus	10	2	1	118
Bacillus cereus and other *Bacillus* sp.	12	3	7	81
Total	193	221	9649	12837

Table 16.3 is a classification of food poisoning according to location of outbreak.

The home is the single most frequently recorded location and it is likely that many of these outbreaks resulted from cross-contamination and inappropriate handling practices in the domestic kitchen. Outbreaks involving meals at restaurants and receptions are the most frequently reported types of general outbreak, accounting for 36% of the total.

TABLE 16.3. *Food poisoning outbreaks classified according to location of outbreak (England and Wales, 1985)*

Location	*Salmonella* sp.	*Clostridium perfringens*	*Staphylococcus aureus*	*Bacillus cereus* and *Bacillus* sp.	Total
Private houses	248	6	2	3	259
Restaurants/receptions	38	17	2	7	64
Hospitals	17	17	1	1	36
Institutions	3	12	2	2	19
Schools	2	4	2	—	8
Shops	4	—	1	—	5
Canteens	6	3	—	1	10
Farms	3	—	—	—	3
Infected abroad	9	—	—	—	9
Other	21	2	1	—	24
Unspecified	21	3	1	1	26
Total	372	64	12	15	463

There are three main types of bacterial food poisoning:

1. The infective type which is caused by eating food containing a large number of living bacteria. After being eaten the bacteria establish themselves in the alimentary canal and when they die they release an endotoxin (e.g. *Salmonella* poisoning).

2. The toxin type which is caused by eating food containing an exotoxin. The toxin is released into the food while the bacteria are growing and multiplying in the food. The bacteria themselves may be dead when the food is eaten (e.g. staphylococcal poisoning).

3. The third type is also caused by a toxin. The toxin is not produced in the food but is released into the alimentary canal after the bacteria have been eaten and while they are growing in the alimentary canal (e.g. *Clostridium perfringens* poisoning).

The incubation period (i.e. the time between the contaminated food being eaten and the occurrence of the first symptoms) is longer for the infective type of food poisoning than the toxin type.

Salmonella

Salmonellae are aerobic bacilli which do not form spores. They cause an infective type of illness and, in healthy persons, about a million living organisms need to be ingested to cause food poisoning. The organism most frequently responsible for outbreak is *S. typhimurium*, but there are about 2000 different types of *Salmonella*, e.g. *S. enteritidis*, *S. agona*. Frequently, the organism is named after the place where it was first recognised as the causative agent of food poisoning. Examples of such organisms are *S. newport* and *S. dublin*.

Illness

Incubation period: 12–36 hours.
Symptoms: abdominal pains, diarrhoea, vomiting, headache, fever.
Duration of illness: 1–8 days (sometimes as long as 14 days).

The people most at risk from *Salmonella* poisoning are the very young, the old and the ill. A number of people die each year as a result of *Salmonella* poisoning. The mortality rate is less than 1%.

Source

Salmonellae are found in the intestines of man and many animals and, consequently, are excreted in the faeces. There are two types of human carriers:

1. Healthy carriers (symptomless excreters). These people carry the organism in their intestines and excrete it in their faeces, but they do not suffer any symptoms of the illness.
2. Convalescent carriers. These are people who continue to excrete the organism after they have recovered from the illness. Some species of *Salmonella* may be excreted for months or even years, whilst others are excreted for only a few weeks.

Animals may suffer from *Salmonella* infections or may be symptomless excreters. Poultry, cattle, pigs, domestic pets (e.g. dogs and tortoises), rats and mice are among animals which are known to be occasional carriers.

Salmonellae are often present in meat and offal, particularly in poultry. Hens' eggs may have Salmonellae on the shell and sometimes the bacteria enter the eggs. Ducks' eggs are frequently contaminated. Raw milk from cows carrying Salmonellae may contain living organisms but they are destroyed during pasteurisation.

Means of spread to food

Salmonellae may be spread to foods by insect pests, vermin and domestic pets. Occasionally, human carriers contaminate foods particularly if they do not wash their hands after using the toilet. Salmonellae in animal feeding stuffs, especially in imported fish meal, can introduce infection into farm animals. Chickens reared under battery conditions are more likely to be infected with *Salmonella* than free-range hens, since the birds are kept close together and cross-infection readily occurs between one bird and another.

One of the most common methods of spread of *Salmonella* is by cross-contamination from raw meat and poultry to cooked foods during handling and preparation in the kitchen.

Foods commonly associated with outbreaks

The foods most frequently responsible for *Salmonella* poisoning are meat and poultry. Cold and reheated chicken and turkey have both been shown to be responsible for outbreaks. Other susceptible foods are eggs and products containing eggs, cream and artificial cream.

Prevention

Salmonellae are readily killed by heat and they do not produce heat-resistant spores or toxins. In order to reduce the risk of *Salmonella* poisoning, food handlers should take the following precautions:

1. Frozen meat and poultry should be thawed thoroughly before cooking.
2. Foods should be cooked thoroughly. Eggs, in particular, should be boiled adequately.
3. The use of finished dishes containing raw egg should be avoided, particularly in food preparation for susceptible groups, such as young children and the elderly.
4. Raw and cooked meats should be stored separately. Raw meat must not be allowed to drip onto cooked meats.
5. Separate knives, chopping boards, meat slicers, etc., should be used for raw and cooked meats and poultry.
6. Foods likely to cause *Salmonella* poisoning should be stored in a refrigerator.

Examples of outbreaks

1. In 1976 there were five outbreaks of *Salmonella seftenberg* poisoning which affected more than 300 people. Four of the outbreaks were in hospitals and one was at an athletics competition, all in the Midlands. The infection was traced to catering-size pork pies produced at a Midlands factory. After a detailed examination of the raw materials, the production line and the finished pies it was found that the source of contamination was the machine used to inject jelly into the pies after cooking. It was found that this machine, because of its construction, was almost impossible to clean. It was assumed that the Salmonellae originated from the gelatin used for making the jelly. The machine was replaced by one of a different design and since then there have been no further outbreaks.

2. In 1986 two workers in a bakery in the North East of England became ill with *Salmonella enteritidis* after handling liquid egg used for glazing confectionery products. The liquid egg came from an importer in the North East who obtained it from a liquid egg processing plant in Belgium. The consignment had been imported as a pasteurised product and had been given no further heat treatment at the bakery. The **Liquid Egg (Pasteurisation) Regulations 1963** require imports of liquid whole egg to be pasteurised before or on arrival in the United Kingdom. Failure to pasteurise the product had been the cause of illness in the bakery workers and the importer seemed to have breached the Regulations.

Clostridium perfringens

Clostridium perfringens is an anaerobic, spore-forming bacillus. The illness caused by this bacterium is due to the eating of food containing a large number of living bacteria which subsequently release a toxin in the alimentary canal.

Illness

Incubation period: 8–22 hours.
Symptoms: nausea, abdominal pains, diarrhoea (vomiting is rare).
Duration of illness: 12–48 hours.

Source

Clostridium perfringens is frequently carried in human and animal intestines. Investigations have shown that about 25% of the human population excrete the bacterium in the faeces. The organism is also found in soil and its spores can survive for long periods in dust and dirt. Flies and bluebottles are often heavily infected with *Clostridium perfringens*.

Means of spread to food

Clostridium perfringens may be brought into the kitchen on raw meat and poultry. About 10% of samples of raw meat and poultry contain the organism. Bacteria from raw meat may be spread to cooked foods by cross-contamination in the kitchen. Food handlers excreting *Clostridium perfringens* can contaminate foods, particularly if they do not wash their hands after using the toilet. Insect pests may also contaminate foods.

Foods commonly associated with outbreaks

The majority of *Clostridium perfringens* outbreaks are caused by cold and reheated meat and poultry, and by dishes such as mince and stews. The anaerobic conditions required for the multiplication of the bacterium are found in foods cooked in bulk, e.g. at the bottom of a casserole or in the centre of a rolled joint. The bacteria are able to survive most cooking processes by forming spores, though the heat resistance of the spores varies depending on the particular strain of *Clostridium perfringens*. Some strains can survive for hours at boiling-point but others can survive for only a few minutes. Spores that survive germinate and start to multiply if the food is kept warm after cooking or if the food is cooled slowly and left unrefrigerated.

Prevention

Since *Clostridium perfringens* form heat-resistant spores it cannot be assumed that the bacteria are killed during cooking. In order to reduce the risk of *Clostridium perfringens* poisoning, food handlers should take the following precautions:

1. Joints of meat weighing more than 3 kg (6.5 lb) should be cut into smaller joints before cooking.

2. Cooked meat and poultry should be cooled rapidly and stored in a refrigerator. It may be necessary to divide large volumes of meat (e.g. mince) into smaller containers to facilitate cooling. Joints of meat should be removed from their cooking liquor immediately after cooking.

3. Raw and cooked meats should be stored separately.

4. Separate preparation areas and equipment (e.g. chopping boards) should be used for raw and cooked meats.

5. Reheating of meat should be avoided if possible. If it is necessary the meat should be heated quickly and thoroughly, and served as soon as possible.

Examples of outbreaks

1. Two outbreaks of *Clostridium perfringens* poisoning occurred in the same school within a year of each other. In the first outbreak, a large number of the children

developed stomach pains and diarrhoea 9 to 12 hours after eating a school dinner which included cold salt beef. Beef joints had been delivered and cooked the previous afternoon. They were cooked in large boilers and left to cool overnight in the cooking liquor. The following day the joints were drained, sliced and eaten cold for lunch. The catering staff were told that cooking the meat the previous day and leaving it to cool slowly overnight was the likely cause of the outbreak. Almost a year later the second outbreak occurred, affecting about 200 children. This time it was caused by rolled joints of beef which were cooked in the afternoon, left overnight in the larder and sliced and eaten cold the next day. *Clostridium perfringens* was found in the meat and in the faeces of the patients. Following the first outbreak the kitchen staff made sure that meat was cooked and eaten on the same day, but in the few months before the second outbreak they had lapsed into their old habits.

2. An outbreak of *Clostridium perfringens* food poisoning occurred involving meals prepared for the 'meals on wheels' service. Minced beef in 2.7 kg (6 lb) frozen packs was incompletely thawed. It was then heated for two hours in chicken stock in a large pan. After heating it was placed in a poorly ventilated vegetable room at a temperature of 21°C for three hours to allow it to cool. The mince was reheated for 20 minutes before being served into foil containers for distribution in electrically-heated cabinets. The cabinets, which were designed to maintain food at a temperature of 63°C, had a highest temperature of 46°C at the beginning of the distribution and this temperature had fallen to 29°C when the last meals were being delivered. This outbreak could have been prevented if the meat had been thawed completely, cooked thoroughly, cooled quickly, stored at a low temperature and then reheated thoroughly and kept above 63°C during delivery.

Staphylococcus aureus

Staphylococci are facultative aerobes and, therefore, they are able to survive without oxygen. They do not form spores. They cause a toxin type of illness and the toxin is heat resistant. Therefore, although the bacteria themselves are easily destroyed by heat (heating for 10 minutes at 66°C is sufficient to kill them), the toxin may survive 100°C, i.e. the temperature of boiling water, for 30 minutes.

Illness

Incubation period: 2–6 hours.
Symptoms: severe vomiting, stomach cramps, diarrhoea—sometimes followed by collapse.
Duration of illness: 6–24 hours.

Source

As many as 70% of the population carry *Staph. aureus* in the naso-pharyngeal region, i.e. the nose and throat. From here the organism is easily transferred to the skin, especially the hands, and to the hair. Also, *Staph. aureus* is the bacterium which usually infects wounds, boils and open sores. The organism is also found in animals, such as cows and goats, and may be present in raw milk.

Means of spread to food

Staph. aureus is spread by food handlers during the cooking and preparation of food. Handling food, rather than using the appropriate utensils, is perhaps the most common means of spread, particularly if the food handler has infected cuts or sores on his hands. Coughing and sneezing near food may cause contamination and hair falling into food or hanging down near food is also potentially dangerous.

Foods commonly associated with outbreaks

Many of the outbreaks of staphylococcal food poisoning are caused by cold meats, such as ham and tongue, and by cold meat pies. The use of nitrates and similar preservatives in these meats has little effect on the growth of *Staph. aureus*. Staphylococcal food poisoning may also be caused by other meat dishes, especially if the meat is used in rechauffé cookery (i.e. if the meat is reheated). Staphylococci have been shown to be present in as many as 38% of raw meat samples tested and cross-contamination from raw to cooked meats may occur.

Foods containing milk or cream, e.g. cakes, trifles, custards, are often responsible for outbreaks. Cheese prepared from raw or inadequately treated milk can also present a problem.

Since *Staph. aureus* may grow anaerobically, the organism may be present in canned foods, if it gains entry after sterilisation, e.g. due to leakage of cooling water. Out-breaks of food poisoning due to canned foods are rare but they can occur.

Prevention

Staphylococci are readily killed by heat but the exotoxin they release into foods is more heat resistant and can withstand up to 30 minutes at boiling-point. In order to reduce the risk of staphylococcal poisoning, food handlers should take the following precautions:

1. A high standard of personal hygiene must be maintained.
2. Foods should be handled as little as possible. Tongs or disposable plastic gloves should be used for cooked meats.
3. Foods likely to cause staphylococcal poisoning should be stored in a refrigerator.

Examples of outbreaks

1. At a wedding reception 40 of the 139 guests became ill about two hours after eating a meal which included cold turkey and ham. Investigations showed that the strains of *Staphylococcus* found in the turkey and ham were identical to those present in the nose and in septic spots on the hands of the person who prepared and cut the turkey and ham on the evening before the reception. Turkeys, chickens, hams, etc., should not be handled, jointed or sliced while still warm, since any staphylococci from the handler which contaminate the meat will have the opportunity to multiply.

2. In 1975 some ham omelettes were prepared for an airline at a mass catering establishment in Alaska. The cook had a staphylococcal infection on the right hand.

Before the omelettes were chilled, they were left for a considerable length of time in a hot kitchen. They were taken on board a 747 Jumbo jet making an intermediate stop on a flight from Tokyo to Paris. Once on board the plane the omelettes were kept for some time at room temperature before being warmed, served and eaten. In total the omelettes were kept at room temperature for 13 hours, which gave plenty of time for the *Staph. aureus* to grow and produce toxin. Out of the 343 passengers on board, 196 developed food poisoning; one member of the crew of 20 was also affected. This outbreak clearly highlights the necessity of correct refrigeration for foods which may be susceptible to infection by *Staph. aureus*.

Bacillus cereus

Bacillus cereus is a spore-forming, aerobic bacillus. It produces an exotoxin which is released into food.

Illness

Incubation period: 1–16 hours.
Symptoms: vomiting, abdominal pains, some diarrhoea.
Duration of illness: 6–24 hours.

Source

Bacillus cereus is found in soil and dust and in water. It is frequently present in cereal foods, particularly in rice and cornflour.

Foods commonly associated with outbreaks

Rice dishes, cornflour sauce and milk puddings have all been responsible for *Bacillus cereus* outbreaks. In Britain the number of outbreaks has increased in recent years, the majority of outbreaks being caused by boiled and fried rice. This increase can be attributed to the greater popularity of rice dishes and to the increase in 'take away' establishments selling meals containing rice. The small numbers of *Bacillus cereus* found in raw rice are harmless, but if rice is cooked in advance and stored in warm conditions large numbers may be present. The heat-resistant spores can survive boiling and will germinate and multiply if cooked rice is kept warm or cooled slowly.

Prevention

In order to reduce the risk of *Bacillus cereus* poisoning, food handlers should take the following precautions:

1. Rice dishes, milk puddings and cornflour sauces should be cooled quickly and stored in a refrigerator.
2. If reheating of the food is necessary, it should be heated up quickly and thoroughly and served as soon as possible.

Example of an outbreak

Five small outbreaks at one Chinese restaurant affected 13 customers who all had fried rice with their meals. All those affected suffered from vomiting one to six hours after the meal and eight of the people also had diarrhoea. *Bacillus cereus* was isolated from the faeces of those affected and also from the fried rice. One sample of rice was found to contain 350 million *Bacillus cereus* per gram. It was common practice in the restaurant kitchen to boil rice intended for frying the day before and to leave it overnight at room temperature to dry off, and also to add old boiled rice left from the previous day to new batches of rice.

Clostridium botulinum

Clostridium botulinum is an anaerobic, spore-forming bacillus. It produces an exotoxin while growing in food. This exotoxin is one of the most lethal poisons known. The illness caused by this organism is called **botulism**.

Illness

Incubation period: 18–36 hours.

Symptoms: the toxin affects the central nervous system. Early symptoms include double vision and difficulty with speech and swallowing.

Duration of illness: the illness reaches its height in one to eight days and death often occurs as a result of paralysis of the respiratory centres; the fatality rate is about 50%. Life may be saved if botulism antitoxin is given in the early stages of the illness.

Source

Clostridium botulinum is found in soil, particularly in marine muds and on the beds of freshwater lakes. It is also found in some fish and on some vegetables.

Foods commonly associated with outbreaks

Since the organism is a strict anaerobe, it is only able to grow and multiply in an oxygen-free environment, such as is found in canned, bottled and vacuum-packed foods. It has also been found in the centre of large sausages and cheeses. In fact, its name is derived from the Latin word for sausage, botulus. *Clostridium botulinum* is not able to grow at a pH of less than 4.5 and, therefore, botulism is not caused by acid foods such as fruits. The spores of some strains can resist boiling for up to six hours but the botulinum toxin is destroyed by heat. Heating to 80°C for 15 minutes is sufficient to destroy the toxin. Commercially prepared foods are now a very rare source of the disease. Outbreaks of botulism in North America have been attributed to home-canned vegetables which were not heated sufficiently to destroy *Clostridium botulinum* spores. Vacuum-packed fish, which was eaten raw, was also responsible for a series of outbreaks in North America.

Examples of outbreaks

Outbreaks of botulism are very rare and there have been only two such incidents in the United Kingdom in the past 30 years.

1. In 1978 a can of salmon was responsible for an outbreak affecting four elderly people in Birmingham. They ate canned salmon with salad for their Sunday tea. During the night they developed severe vomiting and diarrhoea and were taken to hospital where their condition worsened; their vision was blurred and they had difficulty breathing. Botulism was diagnosed and antitoxin was administered on the Monday morning. Two of these people later died as a result of the disease. Examination of the empty can revealed a damaged rim and a small hole which could have allowed the organism to enter. The can was identified as the product of a cannery in Alaska. An emergency investigation of the cannery revealed a number of unsatisfactory practices. These could have led to damage to cans or even contamination of the contents of undamaged cans with botulinum spores, although it could not be shown definitely that the damage and contamination of the Birmingham can occurred at the cannery.

2. In June 1989 a series of incidents of botulism occurred in the North West of England and in Wales. This outbreak of botulism was traced to hazelnut yoghurt manufactured by two Lancashire dairies. Both of the dairies used hazelnut purée supplied by a firm in Folkestone. It is believed that the cans of hazelnut purée had been insufficiently sterilised.

Listeria monocytogenes

Listeria monocytogenes causes **listeriosis**, a serious illness with a fatality rate of 30%. A toxic enzyme produced by the bacteria enters the blood-stream, causing flu-like symptoms, septicaemia or meningitis. Healthy adults are generally resistant to listeriosis but infants, the elderly and people whose immune systems have been suppressed by drugs or disease are all at risk. Pregnant women are also at risk, since the illness may cause miscarriage or stillbirth or it may give rise to meningitis or septicaemia in the newborn baby. The incidence of listeriosis appears to be increasing. It is not as yet a notifiable disease, but laboratory reports to the Communicable Disease Surveillance Centre rose from 31 in 1976 to 122 in 1985. The Department of Health recorded 259 cases of listeriosis in 1987 and 287 in 1988. At first glance these numbers may not seem high, but, because of the danger to vulnerable groups and the relatively high fatality rate, there is much cause for concern.

Listeriosis differs from other types of food poisoning since food may not be the only vehicle of infection. Also, it is not yet known whether large numbers of organisms are necessary to cause the illness. Therefore, it may be considered more like a food-borne illness than a type of food poisoning.

Listeria monocytogenes is a very common organism and is widely distributed in the environment. It is found in soil, water and the intestines of animals and has been found in several foods, including chicken, salads, vegetables and seafood. In one series of tests 60% of chicken carcases, fresh and frozen, were found to be contaminated with *Listeria monocytogenes*. It may also be present in untreated milk and dairy products made from raw milk. In 1989 incidents occurred in which soft cheeses made from untreated milk and imported liver paté were both withdrawn from supermarket shelves after *Listeria monocytogenes* had been detected during routine sampling. Neither of these products would be cooked before they were eaten. The organism is normally destroyed at pasteurising temperatures and is also destroyed by standard cooking procedures. A danger exists in that the organism can grow at low temperatures and may survive in the preparation of foods using cook–chill processes. A survey found *Listeria monocytogenes* in a quarter of pre-cooked chilled supermarket meals which were analysed. *Listeria monocytogenes* can multiply at temperatures below those found in many domestic refrigerators and commercial food cabinets. These findings indicate that the initial cooking process employed in the preparation of these foods should be more thorough and that greater vigilance should be exercised concerning the temperatures of refrigerators. The temperature inside a refrigerator should be below 4°C. In addition, pre-cooked, chilled meals should be reheated thoroughly before consumption.

Campylobacter jejuni

Campylobacter jejuni causes a form of gastroenteritis. The incubation period is two to ten days and the illness consists of flu-like symptoms for the first 24 hours, followed by abdominal pains, fever and diarrhoea which usually lasts from one to five days. It is not normally a serious illness, though some deaths have occurred amongst elderly people.

The illness was first identified in 1977 and since then the number of cases of campylobacter infection has exceeded salmonellosis in every year since 1981. There were 23,463 cases in 1985.

It appears that only small numbers of organisms are needed to cause infection (as few as 500) and there is some debate as to whether campylobacter infection should be regarded as a form of food poisoning or as a food-borne illness.

Campylobacter jejuni is found in the intestines of a variety of animals, including farm animals and domestic pets. It has been found in a variety of foods, particularly raw milk and poultry. Between 1978 and 1985 there were 39 outbreaks caused by raw or incorrectly pasteurised milk. Surveys have shown that between 70% and 80% of frozen chickens are contaminated with *Campylobacter jejuni*. Campylobacter infection can result from eating undercooked, infected poultry, but also from handling contaminated carcases and as a result of cross-contamination from infected poultry to other foods. *Campylobacter jejuni* can survive freezing but is not heat resistant. Milk should be correctly pasteurised and poultry thoroughly cooked to prevent outbreaks. It is also very important that hands are washed after handling raw poultry.

Many cases of campylobacter infection are not food-borne. The bacteria can be spread from person to person and by contact with infected pets, particularly puppies and kittens with diarrhoea.

Escherichia coli

Escherichia coli is a Gram-negative bacillus which can grow both aerobically and anaerobically. It is found in the intestines of man and animals. In most instances this organism is harmless, although its presence in food or water is an indication of faecal contamination. However, there are many different strains of *Escherichia coli* and exposure to an unfamiliar strain may cause gastroenteritis or 'traveller's diarrhoea'. In a survey, more than a third of pre-packed 'corner shop' sandwiches which were examined were found to be contaminated with *Escherichia coli*. This indicates poor standards of hygiene in their preparation. Cooked meals should be safe from contamination, since the organism is destroyed by temperatures above 55°C.

Vibrio parahaemolyticus

This organism has been isolated from fish, shellfish and other seafoods. In Japan, 50% of food poisoning incidents are caused by *Vibrio parahaemolyticus*. Outbreaks in Britain in recent years have been due to seafoods such as imported prawns.

Yersinia enterocolitica

This organism has been found in a variety of foods including milk, vegetables and meat. It causes enteritis (abdominal pains, fever and diarrhoea), mainly in children. Reported cases are particularly high in Norway and Sweden. Like *Listeria*, it can grow at low temperatures and may be of concern in cook–chill products.

Food- and water-borne diseases

Food-borne diseases differ from food poisoning in that the food acts merely as a means of transport for the organism and not as a medium for growth. The incubation period is normally longer and the symptoms are different and more varied. In addition, food-borne diseases may be transmitted by other means; for example, many are transmitted by water. Some virus diseases, such as infectious hepatitis and poliomyelitis, may be transmitted by food but are more usually transmitted by other means.

Dysentery

Dysentery is an infection of the large intestine which may be spread by food or water. There are two types:

1. AMOEBIC DYSENTERY

This is caused by the protozoan *Entamoeba histolytica*. It is rare in Europe but more common in tropical countries. Cases that occur in Britain are usually among people who contract the illness abroad.

2. BACILLARY DYSENTERY

This is caused by bacteria of the genus *Shigella*; most notably *Shigella sonnei*. About 5000 cases occur in England and Wales every year (in 1986 there were 4774). Most outbreaks occur in institutions such as schools. The incubation period for the disease is normally two to four days and the main symptom is acute diarrhoea which may persist for several days. Cross-infection plays a major part in the spread of the disease. Affected people may infect their own hands or, by way of toilet seats, etc., the hands of others. Correct personal hygiene and, particularly, washing the hands after using the toilet are essential if spread of the disease is to be prevented.

Typhoid and paratyphoid fevers

The term enteric fever is used to describe both typhoid and paratyphoid fevers, although there are several differences between the two diseases. Typhoid fever is caused by *Salmonella typhi*, whereas paratyphoid fever is usually caused by *S. paratyphi B*. Both organisms are excreted in the faeces and urine of patients suffering from the diseases or are excreted by healthy carriers. In the past, healthy carriers of *S. typhi* have been responsible for several serious outbreaks of typhoid fever. Outbreaks of both diseases have been caused by water contaminated by sewage.

The typhoid outbreak which occurred in Aberdeen in 1964 was traced to contaminated water used for cooling cans of corned beef. The water had not been chlorinated in order to kill pathogens. *Salmonella typhi* entered one of the cans through a faulty seam, which later sealed on cooling. When the can was opened the bacteria rapidly spread to other foods by cross-contamination and caused a serious outbreak of typhoid fever.

Outbreaks have also been caused by milk, cream and ice cream contaminated by food handlers who were either convalescent or healthy carriers of the organism. Typhoid and paratyphoid bacteria may also be transferred to uncovered food substances by flies and vermin which have been in contact with contaminated excreta.

The incubation period for typhoid fever is usually 7 to 21 days; for paratyphoid fever it is shorter, being between 7 and 10 days. The main symptoms of enteric fever are weakness, fever and diarrhoea. The fatality rate is fairly low, although the illness may still cause death in severe or untreated cases. There were 156 notifications of typhoid fever in England and Wales during 1986; in 120 of these cases the infection had been acquired abroad.

Cholera

Cholera is caused by the bacterium *Vibrio cholerae*. The disease is usually water-borne and is rarely spread by food or from person to person. It does not, therefore, present an important public health problem to countries with high standards of hygiene in the provision of water supplies and in sewage disposal. The chlorination of mains water supplies has been of great importance in the elimination of cholera outbreaks in Britain. However, cases of cholera do occur which have been contracted in other countries. Between 1970 and 1985, 44 imported cases including two deaths, as well as five symptomless excreters, were reported in England and Wales. Most of them were infected in Asia or Africa and only one excreter, the wife who nursed her husband at home, was infected in this country.

The disease has a short incubation period (one to six days), during which the bacteria multiply rapidly in the small intestine. Then violent diarrhoea sets in. This gives rise to severe dehydration, together with a serious loss from the body of alkali and potassium salts. Recovery can be aided by the use of antibiotics but treatment mainly depends on replacing lost water and mineral salts and maintaining the balance of body fluids.

Brucellosis

Brucellosis, or undulant fever, is caused by the bacterium *Brucella abortus*. It was an endemic infection in cattle in the United Kingdom until eradication began in the early 1970s. The disease may be spread from cattle to humans by the consumption of contaminated, untreated milk or by direct physical contact with infected animals. The illness gives rise to prolonged ill health. The main symptoms are the gradual onset of recurrent fever, sweating and pain in the joints and the muscles. The incubation period varies from one to four weeks.

The disease is difficult to recognise, since the symptoms are relatively mild and are often confused with those of other diseases, such as influenza. However, the illness can be diagnosed either bacteriologically or by means of blood tests. The transmission of brucellosis via cows' milk is now rare in Britain, since pasteurisation destroys *Brucella abortus*. In addition, a programme of vaccination of dairy herds was introduced in the early 1970s. Before 1970 laboratory reports indicated that there were at least 400 human cases per year in England and Wales. Most of these cases were due to drinking contaminated raw milk. By 1985 the disease had almost been eliminated. In this year there were laboratory reports of nine cases of brucellosis contracted in England and Wales and a further eleven imported cases.

Brucella melitensis is a similar organism which infects goats and goats' milk, particularly in Mediterranean countries.

Tuberculosis

Tuberculosis is caused by the bacterium *Mycobacterium tuberculosis*. At one time, tuberculosis was very common in Britain, particularly in urban areas, but this is no longer the case. One of the main sources of the organism was untreated cows' milk, but the introduction of pasteurisation eliminated the chances of contracting tuberculosis through drinking milk, since the organism is destroyed by pasteurisation. In addition, all dairy herds in Britain are inspected regularly to ensure that they are tuberculosis-free. The introduction of the BCG vaccine and the immunisation of school children in the late 1950s have helped to prevent the spread of tuberculosis by other means.

Parasitic worms

There are two types of parasitic worms which may be transmitted to humans by food in Britain. There are, of course, many other types of parasitic worms common in other countries.

1. THE TRICHINA WORM (*TRICHINELLA SPIRALIS*)

This is a non-segmented roundworm which infests the small intestine of a variety of hosts, such as man, pigs and rats. The female worm is fertilised within the intestine and burrows its way into the intestinal wall where it lays its larvae. The larvae are carried throughout the body of the host and undergo further development within the muscles. In the case of the pig, if the infected flesh is inadequately cooked and consumed by man, it will cause a disease known as **trichinosis**. Early symptoms of the disease include nausea and fever but later the disease is characterised by muscular aches and pains. In Britain, all carcases in slaughterhouses are inspected by an Environmental Health Officer. If infection by *Trichinella* is suspected, the carcase is placed in cold storage. A period of 20 days at $-15°C$ is normally sufficient to kill the larvae, but progressively longer times may be needed for larger pieces of meat.

The last outbreak of trichinosis reported in England and Wales was in 1955. Infestation in pigs is now very rare and the habit of eating raw meat uncommon, so that the chances of infection in this country are remote. Between 1976 and 1985, 23 cases were reported in England and Wales, all of which acquired the disease abroad.

2. TAPEWORMS

Tapeworms are flat worms consisting of a head and a chain of flat, oblong segments arising from the head-piece. The species most often responsible for disease in man are *Taenia saginata*, which occurs in beef, and *T. solium*, which occurs in pork. Both parasites have a two-stage life-cycle. The larval stage occurs in the intermediate host, i.e. the cow or the pig, and the adult stage occurs in man. Although meat inspectors may sometimes find infected meat, infections by tapeworms are uncommon in Britain. In the years 1976 to 1985 there were 19 cases of *T. solium* infection in England and Wales, all of which were imported. In the same period there were over 700 cases of *T. saginata* infection, most of them imported. This suggests a high standard of meat inspection in Britain and adequate standards of cooking. Also, hygiene standards are such that cattle very rarely eat eggs shed by humans and so the life-cycle is unable to continue. Infection of home-grown beef is therefore uncommon.

CHAPTER 17

Food Hygiene

In order to prevent food poisoning, strict standards of hygiene must be maintained. It is also aesthetically pleasing if food is prepared under hygienic conditions. The main aims of food hygiene are:

1. to prevent food becoming contamined with food poisoning bacteria;
2. to prevent the multiplication of any food poisoning bacteria which do get into food;
3. to destroy any food poisoning bacteria which may be present by thorough cooking.

Some aspects of food hygiene are controlled by law.

Legislation

Legislation controlling food has two principal aims:

1. the protection of the health of the consumer;
2. the prevention of fraud.

The primary piece of legislation in England and Wales is the **Food Act 1984**. This Act is a consolidation of the previous **Food and Drugs Act 1955** and all the amendments to its original form. The main sections relating to hygiene in catering establishments are summarised as follows:

Section 2: It is an offence to sell food that is not of the nature, substance or quality demanded by the purchaser. This Section is used by the enforcement authorities to prevent fraud in the sale of food, but it also applies to the sale of food which is out of condition or stale but which is not unsafe or unfit for human consumption.

Section 8: It is an offence to sell, or have in possession for sale, food which is unfit for human consumption. This Section is used for food which is unfit because it is bad, decomposed, spoilt, contaminated by a foreign substance or contaminated with harmful microorganisms.

Section 9: An authorised officer of a council may seize food which he considers unfit and take it before a Justice of the Peace for condemnation.

Section 31: The 'proper officer of a local authority' (usually the Medical Officer for Environmental Health) has the power to detain food, which he/she suspects might cause food poisoning, in order to enable a further examination to be carried out. This is usually a microbiological examination. If the examination shows the food to be harmful, the authority can take action under Section 8 and Section 9.

The Food Act 1984 also provides for the control of food composition, labelling and hygiene by the issuing of regulations as Statutory Instruments (SI). The main legislation governing food preparation in catering establishments is laid down in the **Food Hygiene (General) Regulations 1970**. The most important of these regulations are summarised in the following list:

Regulation 6: No food business shall be carried on at any insanitary premises or any premises where the condition, situation or construction of the premises is such that food is exposed to the risk of contamination.

Regulation 7: Articles or equipment with which food comes into contact shall be kept clean and shall be constructed so as to:

(a) enable them to be thoroughly cleaned;
(b) prevent absorption;
(c) prevent risk of contamination.

Regulation 9: Food handlers should protect the food from the risk of contamination and should take note of the following:

(a) food should not be positioned so as to involve risk;
(b) food which is unfit for human consumption should be separated from food intended for human consumption;
(c) food in a forecourt or yard must be at least 45 cm (18 in) from the ground unless it is adequately protected;
(d) open food should be adequately covered or screened during delivery or sale;
(e) animal feed should be kept in separate rooms or screened to prevent contamination.

Regulation 10: Food handlers should have regard to personal cleanliness. Anyone handling food should:

(a) make sure that all parts of his/her person and clothing which are liable to contact food are kept clean;
(b) keep any exposed cut or abrasion covered with a waterproof dressing;
(c) refrain from spitting;
(d) refrain from smoking while handling open food or in a room in which there is open food.

Regulation 11: Anyone handling open food (except raw vegetables, liquor or soft drinks) should wear clean, washable overclothing (except waiters/waitresses).

Regulation 13: Anyone handling food who is aware that he/she is suffering from (or is a carrier of) any of the following must inform the Medical Officer for Environmental Health:

typhoid, paratyphoid, other salmonella infections, amoebic or bacillary dysentery, staphylococcal infection likely to cause food poisoning.

Regulation 16: Sanitary conveniences shall be kept clean and shall be constructed so that no offensive odours can penetrate into any food room.

Regulation 17: A clean and adequate water supply shall be provided. The EC Drinking Water Directive 80/778 lays down the standard of water to be used in all food premises.

Regulation 18: Suitable and sufficient washhand basins shall be provided for all food handlers and these shall be conveniently located. Every washhand basin shall be provided with an adequate supply of hot and cold water, an adequate supply of soap or other suitable detergent, nail-brushes and clean towels or other suitable drying facilities. Every such washhand basin shall be kept clean and in good working order. They shall not be used for any other purpose than washing hands.

Regulation 19: Adequate first aid materials shall be provided.

Regulation 20: Accommodation shall be provided for storage of outdoor clothing of food workers.

Regulation 21: Sinks or other washing facilities suitable and sufficient for washing of food and equipment shall be provided in all food premises where open food is handled. For every such sink there shall be an adequate supply of hot and cold water. Cold water only is required where the sink is used:

(a) only for washing fish, fruit or vegetables; or
(b) for washing only drinking vessels or only ice cream formers and servers with a suitable bactericidal agent.

Every such sink shall be kept clean and in good working condition.

Regulation 22: Suitable and sufficient lighting shall be provided.

Regulation 23: Suitable and sufficient ventilation shall be provided.

Regulation 25: The walls, floors, doors, windows, ceiling, woodwork and all other parts of the structure of every food room shall be kept clean and shall be kept in such good order, repair and condition as to:

(a) enable them to be effectively cleaned;
(b) prevent, so far as is reasonably practical, any risk of infestation by rats, mice or insects.

Regulation 26: Adequate provision shall be made for the storage and removal of all waste materials. No accumulation of waste shall be allowed in food rooms.

Regulation 27: This regulation only applies to catering establishments. It provides for temperature control of all meat, fish, gravy, imitation cream, egg products, milk and milk products and all foods containing such foods. These shall be kept at a temperature above 63°C or below 10°C. When such foods are cooked or partly cooked they shall either be served right away or returned to a temperature above 63°C or below 10°C as quickly as possible and stored at the recommended temperatures until required.

Regulation 29: The actual food handler is responsible for complying with these regulations as far as his/her duty to protect food from contamination is concerned. He/she is guilty of an offence if he/she fails to comply with these requirements. The owner or manager of the business is responsible for all those provisions which apply to the structure and condition of food premises and the provision of amenities and equipment and the cleanliness of all such amenities and equipment. He/she is also responsible for ensuring, as far as is reasonably possible, that his/her employees comply with the regulations.

In addition to these general regulations there are other regulations which deal with hygiene standards in the treatment and handling of specific food substances. Milk has a long history of association with food-borne disease and food poisoning in man. Therefore, the conditions under which milk is produced and sold are controlled by a series of regulations. The hygiene requirements of production are laid down in the **Milk and Dairies (General) Regulations 1959**. There are several different types of milk on sale and the different categories are defined in the **Milk (Special Designation) Regulations 1986**. These categories are outlined in the section dealing with the processing of milk in Chapter 18. Similar legislation governing the processing of liquid egg is contained in the **Liquid Egg (Pasteurisation) Regulations 1963** (see page 234). Legislation governing the heat treatment of ice cream is contained in the **Ice Cream (Heat Treatment) Regulations 1959** (see page 234). Other foods which may be vehicles for food poisoning organisms are also controlled. For example, the **Poultry Meat (Hygiene) Regulations 1976** stipulate the conditions required for the handling of poultry.

Prevention of food poisoning

Food poisoning bacteria come from three sources:

1. THE FOOD HANDLERS

Staphylococcus aureus, *Salmonella* and *Clostridium perfringens* may all be carried by personnel involved in food preparation.

2. THE ENVIRONMENT

The spores of *Clostridium perfringens* and *Bacillus cereus* may be found in dust in food-preparation rooms. Also, all types of food-poisoning bacteria may be spread by cross-contamination.

3. THE FOOD

The food itself may contain food-poisoning bacteria when it is brought into the kitchen or the bacteria may enter the food due to faulty handling during preparation.

It follows that measures to prevent food poisoning can be divided into three categories:

1. Personal hygiene.
2. Hygiene in the kitchen.
3. The hygienic handling of food.

Personal hygiene

Personal hygiene is aimed at preventing the spread of food poisoning bacteria from the body or clothing to food. It is the responsibility of the individual and all food handlers should have an elementary knowledge and understanding of its importance.

The following list covers the main points of personal hygiene.

1. WASHING HANDS

Hands should be washed frequently, especially:

(a) before handling food in the kitchen. This is important since bacteria, particularly *Staph. aureus*, may be present on the surface of the skin;

(b) between food-handling operations. This is necessary to prevent cross-contamination of all types of food poisoning bacteria from raw to cooked food;

(c) after using the toilet and before leaving the washroom. This reduces the risk of the transfer of bacteria, such as *Salmonella* and *Clostridium perfringens*, from faeces and door handles to food;

(d) after smoking, coughing and sneezing and after using a handkerchief. This reduces the risk of the transfer of *Staph. aureus* to food.

The use of a soap dispenser for hand washing is more hygienic than the use of cake soap, since it provides less chance of contamination from one person to another. The use of hand creams and antiseptic lotions helps to keep hands smooth and free from bacteria, since cracks and crevices allowed to develop on the skin may harbour harmful bacteria.

Hot-air driers, paper towels or continuous roller towels (which dispense a clean portion to each person) are more hygienic than ordinary cloth towels, since their use reduces the risk of transfer of harmful bacteria from person to person.

Under no circumstances should hand basins be misused for such purposes as washing small pieces of kitchen equipment or vegetables.

2. COUGHING AND SNEEZING

Coughing and sneezing may be responsible for the spread of Staphylococci on to food or working surfaces and should therefore be avoided wherever open food is handled. Handkerchiefs or tissues should be used at all times. Disposable paper tissues are preferable since they can be discarded. In addition, the hands should be washed after using a tissue or handkerchief.

3. SMOKING

It is against the law to smoke in a food-preparation area. Smoking involves contact between the hand and mouth and can be responsible for the spread of *Staph. aureus*. It also encourages coughing.

4. OUTDOOR CLOTHING

Outdoor clothing should be placed in lockers outside food rooms, since it is frequently contaminated by bacteria such as *Staphylococcus* and *Streptococcus*. This contamination is particularly high in congested areas, especially where people make frequent use of public transport.

5. PROTECTIVE CLOTHING

Protective clothing should be worn by all food handlers. It is a statutory requirement that this should be clean and it should cover all parts of the body liable to contaminate food. The clothing must be laundered regularly. Otherwise, if it is worn continuously, it may harbour harmful bacteria. Protective head-wear should be designed so as to retain the hair in position, since hair and dandruff are a potential source of contamination by bacteria, particularly *Staph. aureus*. If hair is long it should be tied back and hair should not be touched or combed in the vicinity of food. The main danger is the transfer of bacteria from the hair to the hands and thence to food.

6. CUTS, GRAZES, BOILS AND SEPTIC SPOTS

Open cuts, grazes, boils and septic lesions frequently harbour Staphylococci and the law requires that these should be covered with a clean, waterproof dressing wherever food is handled. This dressing should be brightly coloured so that, if it is inadvertently removed, it will be readily visible if it falls into food. A well-equipped first-aid box containing these dressings and other equipment, such as bandages and antiseptic, should be kept on the premises.

7. NAILS

Long, dirty nails harbour dirt and bacteria. Therefore, fingernails must be kept clean and short. Nail varnish should not be worn by food handlers, since, if it becomes chipped, it may provide crevices which can harbour bacteria. In addition, chips of nail varnish may enter food and this is neither hygienic nor aesthetically pleasing.

8. JEWELLERY

Personal jewellery may harbour bacteria or may fall into food and, therefore, jewellery, other than wedding rings, should not be worn by food handlers.

9. HEALTH

Any person engaged in handling food who is suffering from diarrhoea, vomiting, septic cuts, boils or discharges from the ear, eye or nose should notify his employer and should not handle food. This is because any of these conditions indicates that the food handler is a potential source of food poisoning organisms.

In addition, if an employee is suffering from or carrying a notifiable illness, as laid down in the **Food Hygiene (General) Regulations 1970** (see page 216), he/she must notify his/her employer who must inform the appropriate medical officer of health.

Hygiene in the kitchen

The rules of hygiene which fall into the category of kitchen hygiene cover the rules applying to the design, layout and maintenance of the kitchen and the equipment it contains.

1. CLEANING THE KITCHEN AND EQUIPMENT

By law all parts of the kitchen and all of the equipment it contains must be kept clean. A large variety of cleaning methods can be used for various purposes and there is a wide range of available cleaning agents. However, most cleaning operations require the use of a solution of a detergent in water and, therefore, it is useful to understand the theory of detergency.

A good detergent should improve the cleansing action of water and, therefore, it should have the following properties:

(a) It should lower the surface tension of the water. Pure water is not a good 'wetting' agent, because it has a high surface tension. Due to hydrogen bonding (see page 42) molecules of water are strongly attracted to one another. For molecules at the centre of a body of water these forces are acting in all directions and there is no net pull in any particular direction. However, for molecules near the surface of the water the net force is a pull inwards. This causes the body of water to tend to assume a shape with the minimum surface area, i.e. a sphere. This explains why water dripping from a tap tends to form spherical droplets. The effect is illustrated in Figure 17.1.

FIG. 17.1. Diagram illustrating the high surface tension of water.

Because of this high surface tension, water will not easily 'wet' a solid surface. However, if a detergent is added, the detergent will go preferentially to the surface of the water and will therefore lower the surface tension. This is illustrated in Figure 17.2.

FIG. 17.2. The action of a detergent in lowering the surface tension of water.

(b) It should be a good emulsifying agent (see page 44) and should hold solid particles in suspension. Most common detergents have molecules which have hydrophilic heads and hydrophobic tails. The action of soap in emulsifying grease has been explained in Chapter 4. The suspension of solid particles of dirt is similar but in this case a double layer of detergent molecules is formed around the particles. This effect is illustrated in Figure 17.3.

Fig. 17.3. The suspension of solid particles by a detergent.

The inner layer of detergent molecules align themselves so that the hydrophilic heads, which are attracted to the particle of dirt, are on the inside of the layer and the hydrophobic tails are sticking outwards. In the outer layer the hydrophobic tails are on the inside and the hydrophilic heads are on the outside in contact with the water. The layers of detergent molecules help to keep the particles in suspension and prevent them clumping together.

Thus an effective detergent helps to disperse grease and dirt, so that they do not form a scum to be redeposited on the articles being washed but can be rinsed away.

(c) It should soften water if the water is hard and prevent the formation of a hard water scum.

(d) It should not damage equipment or harm the skin.

(e) It should be non-toxic.

(f) It should be odourless and tasteless so that it will not taint food.

(g) It should be chemically stable.

(h) It should not be absorbed by the equipment being cleaned and should be easily rinsed off.

(i) It should be cheap and easy to use.

No detergent has all of these desirable properties and cleaning procedures vary. Therefore, different detergents must be selected for different tasks. Table 17.1 outlines a variety of cleaning tasks together with the cleaning agents and procedures which are recommended for tackling them.

WASHING-UP

The most common cleaning process carried out in the kitchen is washing-up. Ideally there should be two washing-up rooms or zones:

(a) the washing-up proper for crockery and cutlery used by customers;
(b) the pan-wash for kitchen utensils, pots, pans, etc.

TABLE 17.1. *Cleaning tasks and recommended cleaning agents and cleaning procedures*

Cleaning task	Cleaning agent and cleaning procedure
Floors	Detergent/bactericide powder (hypochlorite) dissolved in water, applied using mop or mechanical scrubber. Periodic cleaning with abrasive cleaner or caustic solution may be required to remove grease or fat
Walls, paintwork, etc.	Liquid, hard surface cleaner applied by spray or cloth. For heavy duty work—detergent/bactericide dissolved in water
Oven surfaces, canopies	As above, but use heavy duty detergent/bactericide for heavy deposits
Stainless steel hot cupboards, display, shelving	Liquid detergent/bactericide (hypochlorite or quat.). Spray/wipe
Working surfaces	Liquid detergent/bactericide (quat.) spray/wipe or crystal powder shake on and wipe off. Cutting boards may be passed through dishwasher or soaked in solution of detergent/bactericide
Ovens	Spray-on oven cleaner, wipe off. Heavy grease and carbon deposits may be removed with special paint-on jelly or liquid cleaners which need contact time to act
Fryers	Empty oil and fill with water and heavy duty cleaner. Contact time and heating required
Wooden surfaces	Detergent/bactericide (best to alternate between hypochlorite and quat.). Soak and scrub
Refrigerators and freezers	Liquid detergent/bactericide, spray or apply with clean cloth, wipe off
Pots, pans, cooking utensils	Soak in solution of liquid detergent/bactericide
Wiping cloths	Soak in liquid detergent/bactericide, rinse in clean water before use

Pan-washing is a greasy job; it is difficult to get rid of all of the grease from sinks and surroundings. It is, therefore, desirable to keep the two operations separate. In addition, all washing-up should be done away from where food is being prepared and stored in order to prevent cross-contamination.

Washing-up is regarded as a menial task, yet, from the point of view of food hygiene, it is one of the most important operations in the kitchen. There is a real danger that utensils, which come into contact with the mouth and with food may help to spread food poisoning organisms as well as organisms responsible for causing other communicable diseases.

Washing-up can be done by hand or machine. Whichever method is used, the washing-up should be done promptly. The accumulation of dirty utensils should be avoided, not only because they become more difficult to clean the longer they are left, but also because there is a risk that dangerous microorganisms may multiply in food residues. As soon as possible after use the dirty articles should be taken to the washing-up area, sorted into their various categories and sizes and stacked. During this process food residues should be scraped off into refuse containers.

If the washing-up is carried out by hand, a minimum of two sinks should be used. The first sink contains the washing water (at 50–60°C) and detergent and the second sink contains the rinsing water. The temperature of the rinsing water should be between 82°C and 100°C. The dishes should be immersed in this for up to two minutes, depending on the temperature of the water used. A third intermediate sink containing cold water and a suitable disinfectant may also be included. Hypochlorites may be used; they are very efficient disinfectants as long as sufficient contact time is allowed. However, in the case of some metals, it is not possible to sterilise in this way, because of the risk of corrosion. If a chemical is used, all traces of disinfectant must be removed by the rinsing water.

The rinsing process has two functions; it removes all traces of detergent and disinfectant and kills any bacteria which may be present on the equipment. The temperature should be high enough to allow the equipment to be dried in the air, without the necessity of using a cloth. A cloth may harbour harmful microorganisms, which may be transferred from one piece of equipment to another.

2. DESIGN OF EQUIPMENT AND PREMISES

(a) *Equipment and working surfaces*. These should be made of a material which is impervious, easily cleaned and non-reactive to food materials. Stainless steel is used extensively but, for some pieces of equipment, it is too expensive. However, plastics provide a suitable alternative. Galvanised metal is unsuitable in most instances, because it corrodes easily and is difficult to clean. Soft wood is frequently used for shelving and should be covered with a hard, impervious surface, since untreated wood surfaces are easily contaminated and are impossible to clean. Cutting boards should be made from plastic or compressed rubber rather than wood. The only wooden surface which should be allowed to come into contact with food is a hard, wooden chopping block. This should be scrubbed regularly with water containing both a detergent and a disinfectant in order to prevent the accumulation of harmful microorganisms.

The equipment should be designed so that all corners are rounded. This is particularly important in the case of bins and containers, where food particles allowed to collect in corners provide a suitable breeding ground for bacteria and various forms of vermin.

(b) *The premises*. The premises should be designed so that they are easily cleaned. In the case of old buildings, where possible, suitable alterations should be made to facilitate easy cleaning. It is essential that the premises are clean and in good condition and well lighted and ventilated.

(c) *Walls*. Wall-tiling has many advantages. However, tiles are not hard-wearing and may be damaged easily. They also tend to come away from the wall if subjected to intense heat, e.g. behind grills and ovens. In these areas it is preferable to install a metal lining to the wall, as long as the lining is properly sealed to prevent vermin nesting behind it. Elsewhere, at higher levels, walls covered with a good, hard plaster finished with a high-gloss paint form a good surface, which is easy to clean.

(d) *Floors*. Many kitchen floors are covered with quarry tiles. These tiles should be laid as close together as possible, since if wide gaps are left between the tiles, dirt and grease may accumulate. Larger, more modern establishments now use continuous flooring, such as epoxy resin, which can be laid wall to wall; this type of surface is easier to clean than tiling. It is important that coved tiles of at least 2 cm radius be laid at the junction between the floor and the walls.

3. WASTE DISPOSAL

According to the **Food Hygiene (General) Regulations 1970**, 'refuse or filth must not be accumulated or left in a food room unless this is unavoidable'. The law also states that enough space must be provided in a suitable part of the premises for separating unsound food from sound food and for storing waste while it awaits disposal. It is preferable that the waste be stored in a yard outside the food-preparation rooms and that it be stored in suitable bins fitted with lids which prevent vermin from attacking the food. Bins should be emptied and washed out regularly and should be placed on stands about 30 cm (1 ft) above a drained and concreted area, which should be washed down frequently.

4. PEST CONTROL

Rats, mice, flies and cockroaches are the most common kitchen pests. Rats and mice often carry *Salmonella* and other pathogens in their intestines and therefore excrete these organisms in their faeces. In addition, they also carry bacteria on their feet and fur and can contaminate open food and working surfaces. To prevent rodent infestations, food premises should be kept clean and in good repair. Disused drains and holes in walls, floors and ceilings should be blocked. Pipe runs should be sealed at the entrance to buildings and where they pass from one room to another. Store rooms should be regularly cleaned and all stock kept at least 45 cm (18 inches) above the floor and used in rotation. Foods such as flour and cereals should be stored in vermin-proof containers. Poisons, such as warfarin, can be used to kill both rats and mice, though, if an infestation is suspected, expert advice should be sought from a specialist control firm or the local Environment Health Department. Signs of an infestation include gnawing marks, droppings and damage to foodstuffs and containers.

Flies, also, are a health hazard in food premises since they carry pathogens on their bodies and in their excreta. It is virtually impossible to prevent flies from entering buildings, although covering open windows and ventilators with mesh screens does help. Insecticides such as DDT and other chlorinated hydrocarbons should not be used in areas where there is open food. However, pyrethrin-based insecticides can be safely used in food premises. Electrically operated insect killers can also be used. These produce ultra-violet light to attract the insects, and the insects are killed when they touch a metal grid with an electric current running though it.

Cockroaches may also be found in food premises. They live and breed in warm, dark, humid places such as behind ovens and hot-water pipes. They contaminate foods with bacteria from their bodies and excreta, but since they are noctural an infestation may remain unnoticed. They are most likely to be found in premises which are dirty and where food is left out at night. Infestations should be treated with insecticidal sprays or lacquers used under expert advice.

Hygienic handling of food

Hygienic handling, cooking and storage of food is of prime importance if food poisoning is to be prevented.

1. PREPARATION AND HANDLING

It is essential to prevent the contamination of food by bacteria carried by food handlers or by bacteria from raw foods. The direct handling of food should be avoided where possible. Food should be handled with utensils, such as tongs. Food handlers should wear disposable plastic gloves when handling high risk foods, such as cooked meats.

In kitchens it is essential to keep raw and cooked foods separate in order to prevent cross-contamination from the raw to the cooked foods. This means having separate preparation areas for the two types of food, which are often referred to as 'dirty' and 'clean' zones. Raw food has a much higher bacterial load than cooked food and raw meats, in particular, are very likely to contain food poisoning bacteria. Separate equipment should be used for the preparation of raw and cooked foods. Items such as knives and chopping boards can be colour-coded for different uses, e.g. for raw meat, raw vegetables, cooked foods. Equipment such as meat slicers and mincers, which cannot be duplicated, should be thoroughly cleaned after being used for raw meat.

Cloths used in kitchens for wiping and drying harbour bacteria. Disposable paper towels are more hygienic. If cloths are used, they should be washed and disinfected frequently.

2. TEMPERATURE CONTROL

It is essential to control the temperature of food during preparation, processing, cooking and storage in order to prevent the multiplication of pathogenic bacteria. Good temperature control is probably the single most important factor in the prevention of food poisoning. It is thought that a breakdown in temperature control is a major factor in at least 75% of food poisoning outbreaks.

Food handlers must avoid keeping high risk foods, such as meat and poultry, egg and milk dishes, cream cakes and desserts, in the danger zone (5–63°C) for longer than necessary. Consideration should be given to the following processes:

(a) *Preparation.* Food should be kept in preparation areas for the minimum time. Preparation areas should be well ventilated and not too hot. When preparation is finished, foods should be either cooked, refrigerated or frozen.

(b) *Defrosting.* Some frozen foods, such as chickens and joints of meat, must be defrosted before cooking. This should be carried out at a low temperature, i.e. in a refrigerator, or quickly, e.g. in a microwave oven. Care is needed to ensure that food is completely defrosted before cooking. Otherwise, at the end of the cooking time, the centre of the food may not be hot enough to kill bacteria. Small items of meat, such as chops, sausages and burgers can be cooked from frozen, because, during cooking, the heat reaches the centre quickly.

(c) *Cooking.* Foods, particularly meat and poultry, should be cooked thoroughly, so that the centre temperature is 70°C, i.e. high enough to kill most bacteria. This is particularly important for products such as burgers, sausages and rolled joints of meat, where bacteria originally present on the outside of the meat may be transferred to the centre. Stews and gravies should be heated to boiling point (100°C). Centre temperatures can be checked using a probe thermometer. This must be cleaned between being used for different products.

After cooking, foods should be served immediately, kept hot or cooled quickly.

(d) *Warm-holding.* If food is to be kept hot, it should be kept at 70°C or more in preheated hot cabinets or bain-maries.

(e) *Chilling.* Cooked foods should be cooled quickly and within 1.5 hours. They are best cooled at a temperature of 10°C or below. Cooling may be carried out in a well-ventilated cooling room or larder on the north side of the building or in a special cabinet. Blast chillers are now used in many establishments. They use a blast of cold air to cool foods quickly and steadily. Large bulks of food, such as joints, stews, rice, etc., should be divided or spread out to speed the cooling process. Once cold, foods should be stored in a refrigerator.

(f) *Reheating*. Reheating is best avoided but, if it must be carried out, foods should be heated up quickly and heated through thoroughly.

Small portions may be heated in a microwave oven, though care is needed to ensure even cooking and the absence of 'cold spots'. Forced convection ovens are suitable for larger quantities. Stews, gravies, etc., should be heated in pans, brought up quickly to boiling point (100°C) and then simmered for 15 minutes.

3. STORAGE OF FOOD

Foods should be stored in suitable containers, in clean conditions to prevent contamination. A good system of stock rotation is essential, i.e. a 'first in, first out' system.

(A) DRY FOOD STORES

Dried and canned foods should be stored in a cool, dry, well-lit and well-ventilated storage area, in vermin-proof containers. Containers should be stored on racks at least 45 cm (18 in) from the floor to allow for cleaning and circulation of air.

(B) REFRIGERATORS

Refrigerators can be used for the short-term storage of a wide variety of foods. Since most pathogenic bacteria are unable to multiply at refrigeration temperatures (1–4°C), food storage in a refrigerator is reasonably safe. However, the temperature should not exceed 4°C as *Listeria monocytogenes* and *Yersinia enterocolitica* can grow and multiply at temperatures just above this. Many spoilage organisms can grow fairly well at low temperatures and spoilage will eventually occur, even within a refrigerator.

In order for a refrigerator to function efficiently, air must be able to circulate freely around the food. Therefore, refrigerators should not be overloaded.

It is imperative that raw foods should be well separated from cooked foods to prevent cross-contamination by food poisoning bacteria. In catering establishments there should, ideally, be separate refrigerators for raw and cooked foods. If they are stored in the same refrigerator, cooked foods should be above raw foods. With large walk-in refrigerators, different foods should be properly separated so that, for example, raw meat cannot drip on to cooked foods.

Strong smelling foods, such as fish, should be stored in air-tight containers. The use of such containers for other foods prevents dehydration, since moisture evaporates from uncovered food.

Refrigerators with automatic defrosting are recommended, as they keep the ice layer inside the refrigerator to a minimum. For other refrigerators defrosting must be carried out at regular intervals. The operating temperature of refrigerators should be checked with a refrigerator thermometer.

(C) DEEP FREEZE STORAGE

Deep freeze cabinets used for long-term food storage should be maintained at a temperature of $-18°C$ or below. The freezing of food kills some bacteria but spores and some vegetative cells survive. Meat and fish may be stored for up to six months and fruits and vegetables for up to one year. When frozen food is thawed, the bacteria which have survived start to grow and multiply again. Foods should not, therefore, be thawed and refrozen.

However, if foods are partially thawed, as occurs, for example, while shopping or as a result of a power cut, it may be safe to refreeze the food if the central core of the food is still frozen and the food is cold.

Once food is completely thawed, it should be used straight away. It is normally safe to cook raw, thawed food and refreeze it as a cooked dish.

Freezers should be defrosted when necessary (usually about every six months) and operating temperatures should be checked with a freezer thermometer.

CHAPTER 18

Food Preservation

All food was once living tissue and is of organic origin. Some foods, such as meat and fish, are killed before being distributed to the consumer. Other foods, such as fruits and vegetables, may be stored and distributed in the living state. Because of its organic nature, food is susceptible to deterioration or spoilage by saprophytic and parasitic microorganisms.

When food spoilage takes place, two distinct processes are involved.

1. AUTOLYSIS

The word autolysis means self-destruction and is used to describe the cellular break-down caused by enzymes contained within the food itself. This breakdown starts immediately after slaughter or harvest. In many instances a limited amount of enzyme activity may be beneficial; for example, in the ripening of fruit and the tenderisation of meat. However, in most instances it is detrimental.

2. MICROBIAL SPOILAGE

Once the cellular structure becomes disorganised, the food is vulnerable to attack by microorganisms. The main agents of microbial spoilage are bacteria, moulds and yeasts. These organisms break down the complex organic components of the food into simpler compounds and so cause alterations in the flavour, texture, colour and smell of the food. Examples of bacteria which are responsible for food spoilage are given in Chapter 15.

Food preservation

The main aims of food preservation are to prevent autolysis and microbial growth. The growth requirements of microorganisms and the principles of the control of microbial growth have been covered in Chapter 15. Preservation may be short-term or long-term and may be achieved in a variety of ways. Blanching food in order to inactivate enzymes and prevent autolysis may be regarded as a short-term means of preservation. All methods of cooking, including the use of microwaves, will have the same effect and also destroy some of the microorganisms present in the food; therefore they are also short-term methods. In any method of preservation involving the use of heat to destroy microorganisms, it can usually be assumed that most enzymes will be inactivated. Long-term methods of preservation usually involve the removal of more than one of the requirements necessary for growth. Also a method of destruction of microorganisms, e.g. heating, is sometimes involved in the process.

Heat treatment

The two main methods of preservation involving the use of heat are heat sterilisation and pasteurisation.

1. Heat sterilisation

Sterilisation involves the use of heat to bring about the total destruction of all microorganisms and their spores. The sterilised food must be placed in an airtight container to prevent the entry of further spoilage organisms. A steel can coated with a thin layer of tin is the most common type of container. For some products the inside of the can may be coated with lacquer as a further protection against corrosion. Glass bottles and jars are used as containers for some products, particularly jams and preserves. In recent years, flexible plastic containers have been used for a variety of liquid products, particularly milk and cream.

THE CANNING PROCESS

The modern canning process usually involves the following operations:

1. *Cleaning and preparation.* All inedible parts are removed from the food and the food is graded and washed.

2. *Blanching.* Most vegetable foods are blanched, either by being immersed in boiling water or by being exposed to steam. This is often a continuous process in which the food is passed through a tunnel into which the steam is injected. The period of exposure may vary from two to ten minutes. Blanching inactivates enzymes which may affect the stability of the food while it awaits further processing. In addition, the blanching process helps to drive out air bubbles trapped within the food, thus allowing a better 'fill'. If too much air remains in the cans the desired temperature may not be reached during sterilisation and microorganisms may survive inside some of the cans.

3. *Filling and exhausting.* The washed, open cans are filled automatically with a weighed amount of the food. For vegetables, fruits and some other foods the cans are topped up to within 1 cm of the top with liquor. The liquor is normally brine in the case of vegetables and sugar syrup in the case of fruits. After filling, the cans are usually passed to an exhaust box in which they are exposed to hot water or steam so that, when the lid is sealed on, a partial vacuum will form in the can.

4. *Sealing.* Lids are placed on the cans and they are passed to an automatic sealing machine, which bends the edge of the lid and the flange on the can body into a roll. The roll is then flattened forming a hermetic, i.e. airtight, seal.

5. *Sterilisation.* The amount of heat required for adequate sterilisation depends on the following factors:

(a) The size of the can and the nature of its contents. Heat takes longer to penetrate into a large can. Also, heat penetration is faster in convection packs, such as soups, than in conduction packs, such as corned beef.

(b) The pH of the food.

The sterilisation process is designed to eliminate *Clostridium botulinum* and its spores, since this is the most dangerous and most heat-resistant microorganism likely to be present in canned foods. Therefore, foods are classified into groups depending on the heat treatment necessary to eliminate this microorganism.

Foods may be classified into three groups:

(i) High acid foods which have a pH below 3.7. Very few bacteria can survive conditions of such high acidity. Consequently, only a mild heat treatment is necessary to eliminate yeasts and moulds which may be present, since they are less heat resistant than bacteria. For most can sizes heating to 100°C for eight to 16 minutes is sufficient. Bacterial spores may survive but they are unable to germinate and, therefore, cannot cause spoilage.

(ii) Medium acid foods which have a pH between 3.7 and 4.5. Many spoilage bacteria are able to grow in this pH range and, therefore, the heat treatment required is more severe than for high acid foods. However, the pH is still too low to allow the growth of *Clostridium botulinum*.

(iii) Low acid foods which have a pH above 4.5. These foods include meat, fish and most vegetables. In order to ensure complete destruction of bacteria, especially *Clostridium botulinum* spores, it is essential that these products are subjected to a severe heat treatment. The temperature required depends on the time of exposure to heat. The use of a high temperature for a shorter time is preferable, since such a treatment will have less effect on the nutritive value of the product, i.e. vitamin destruction will be minimised. Also, undesirable flavour changes are avoided if a HTST (high temperature short time) process is used.

6. *Cooling.* The can must be cooled slowly by gradually reducing the pressure of the steam used for heating and thus bringing about a gradual reduction in temperature. If the pressure was reduced suddenly, the cans would buckle. The cans are then cooled further using water. Since temporary leakage may occur at this point, it is imperative that the cooling water is clean and sterile. Sterilisation of the water is achieved by chlorination; the usual level of chlorine in the cooling water is between 3 and 5 ppm (parts per million) of chlorine. Cooling is only continued until the cans reach a temperature of 38°C and then the warmth of the can is sufficient to allow the cans to be dried in the air. This avoids rusting and also reduces the danger of microorganisms present in water on the surface being drawn into the can through a temporary leak.

Modern canning processes are completely automated and are run on a continuous system rather than using batch processes.

ASEPTIC CANNING

There are many variations on the standard canning process. One of the most common is the use of aseptic filling, in which the bulked product and the containers are sterilised separately. The containers are then filled aseptically, i.e. under conditions where the entry of microorganisms is prevented, before being sealed. In the case of cans, the cans are filled through a small vent-hole which is then closed with solder.

Aseptic canning is mainly used for liquid foods which are heat sensitive and therefore likely to be overcooked in the standard canning process. Changes in flavour and colour and reduction in nutritive value are minimised if these products are sterilised using a multi-plate heat exchanger, such as is used in the pasteurisation of milk.

SPOILAGE OF CANNED FOODS

The main reasons for spoilage of canned foods are:

1. Insufficient sterilisation, which means that spores of anaerobic bacteria may survive and germinate.
2. Leakage, which is due to either a badly made can or a can which has been improperly sealed.
3. Corrosion of the can, which may be due to attack by the contents, particularly acid foods, or damage due to storage in unsatisfactory conditions, i.e. storage in a warm, humid atmosphere.

There are a large variety of different types of spoilage which may occur but the following are the most common:

1. *Thermophilic gas spoilage.* This is usually caused by anaerobic spore-forming bacteria, such as the genus *Clostridium*. This type of spoilage occurs in cans of low acid foods which have been insufficiently sterilised. Usually, large amounts of hydrogen are produced and this gas causes the cans to swell and sometimes even to burst.
2. *Carbon dioxide gas spoilage.* Non-spore-forming bacteria may enter the can after sterilisation, either through leakage of cooling water or through unsatisfactory sealing. In this case the contents of the can often appear slimy and frothy.
3. *Flat sour spoilage.* Some species of bacteria which produce heat-resistant spores, such as members of the genus *Bacillus*, may survive if the heat treatment is not sufficient. These bacteria may grow anaerobically in low acid foods. They do not produce any marked change in the appearance of the food but they ferment the food producing acid which gives the food a disagreeable taste. Since these organisms do not produce gas, this type of spoilage is not detected until the food is eaten.

STERILISATION OF MILK

According to the **Milk (Special Designation) Regulations 1986**, milk may be sterilised in two ways: either by an in-bottle or continuous flow sterilisation process at 100°C, or by the UHT (ultra heat treatment) process.

1. *The in-bottle and continuous flow sterilisation processes.* In these processes the milk is heat treated to destroy all microbial cells and the majority of their spores. The milk will keep for at least a week (usually longer) without refrigeration. The milk is first homogenised, i.e. the fat globules are reduced in size so that they are evenly distributed throughout the milk and do not form a cream layer on the surface. This is achieved by heating the milk to about 60°C and forcing it through fine holes under high pressure. The milk is then filtered. In the in-bottle process the milk is placed in glass or plastic bottles and the bottles are sealed. According to the **Milk and Dairies (Milk Bottle Caps) (Colour) Regulations 1976**, the caps used to seal bottles of sterilised milk must be blue. After sealing the bottles of milk are heated to sterilisation temperatures. The present

regulations in the United Kingdom state that the milk should be heated to at least 100°C and that it should give a negative turbidity test following sterilisation. A negative turbidity test proves that the heat treatment has been sufficient to denature the water-soluble proteins, i.e. the lactalbumins. The minimum length of time that the milk should be held at 100°C is not stipulated in the regulations. Such a heat treatment is too mild to achieve sterilisation and in practice the milk is heated to between 105°C and 110°C for 20 to 40 minutes.

In the continuous flow process the milk is sterilised in bulk in a multi-plate heat exchanger using similar temperatures and times and it is then aseptically filled into containers which have been sterilised previously. In addition to giving a negative turbidity test, milk which has been sterilised by a continuous flow process must also give a satisfactory colony count.

The main disadvantages of sterilised milk are:

(a) the flavour is altered and the milk has a cooked taste;
(b) the colour of the milk is altered due to caramelisation of sugars and to the Maillard browning reaction which takes place between the sugars and amino acids;
(c) the proteins are denatured and the Biological Value of the milk protein is slightly reduced;
(d) the vitamin content is reduced; thiamin and ascorbic acid are the vitamins which are most affected. However, the loss of ascorbic acid is not of great practical significance since milk is not one of the most important sources of vitamin C.

2. *The UHT process.* In this process the milk is heated to a very high temperature for a very short time. Such a process kills all microorganisms and their spores without producing such a marked effect on the flavour, colour and nutritive value of the milk. According to the **Milk (Special Designation) Regulations 1986**, UHT milk must be heated to a minimum of 132.2°C and held there for a minimum of one second. After processing the milk must produce a satisfactory colony count. Commercial processes are continuous flow processes in which the milk is heated to between 135°C and 150°C for one to three seconds in a multi-plate heat exchanger before being poured under aseptic conditions into sterile containers which are then sealed. This milk is free from microorganisms and should keep unopened for six months or more.

2. Pasteurisation

A food manufacturer regards pasteurisation as a means of extending the shelf-life of a food by using heat to reduce the number of spoilage organisms present. For several products the use of pasteurisation is also advantageous, since the heat treatment eliminates pathogenic bacteria. For example, in the case of milk, the legal requirements are that the pasteurisation process must be sufficient to destroy *Mycobacterium tuberculosis* and *Brucella abortus*.

Under the **Milk (Special Designation) Regulations 1986**, two processes are permitted for the pasteurisation of milk:

1. *The Holder process,* in which the milk is held at temperatures between 62.8°C and 65.6°C for at least 30 minutes and then rapidly cooled to below 10°C.

2. *The HTST (high temperature short time) process*, in which the milk is heated to a temperature of at least 71.7°C and held there for at least 15 seconds and then immediately cooled to below 10°C.

The HTST process is normally preferred since it is a continuous-flow process and, therefore, more efficient. It also has less effect on the nutritive value and flavour of the milk.

Pasteurised milk is tested in order to ensure that it is free from *Mycobacterium tuberculosis*. Since it is not practicable to test for the presence of the pathogen itself, a chemical test is used. It is a legal requirement that the milk must give a negative phosphatase test, indicating that the phosphatase has been inactivated. Phosphatase is an enzyme which is slightly more heat resistant than *M. tubercolosis*. Therefore, any treatment which destroys the enzyme must also the destroy the pathogen.

Liquid milk to be pasteurised is transported from the farm to the dairy in large tanks. These tanks are chilled. According to the **Milk and Dairies (General) Regulations 1959**, the temperature of the milk must be below 10°C. In commercial practice much lower temperatures are used and the temperature is usually below 5°C. Before pasteurisation the milk is filtered and, in some cases, it is homogenised. In the HTST process the milk is then passed through a multi-plate heat exchanger. The process is outlined in Figure 18.1.

Although there have been campaigns to ensure that all milk receives some form of heat treatment, the sale of raw milk is still permitted in the United Kingdom. According to the **Milk (Special Designation) Regulations 1986**, it must be clearly labelled as 'Raw Unpasteurised Milk' and must give a negative methylene blue test. Methylene blue is a dye which is blue in its oxidised form. If large numbers of bacteria are present in the milk, the dye is reduced to its colourless form, giving a positive result.

Both liquid egg and ice cream mix are pasteurised in order to eliminate possible pathogens, especially salmonellae. According to the **Liquid Egg (Pasteurisation) Regulations 1963**, all liquid egg must be pasteurised by being held at a minimum of 64.4°C for at least 2.5 minutes and then immediately cooled to below 3.3°C. Eggs to be used on the premises immediately after cracking or which are held at or below 10°C after cracking and used within 24 hours are exempt from these regulations. The **Ice Cream (Heat Treatment) Regulations 1959** stipulate that where a complete cold mix is reconstituted using wholesome drinking water (and with any of the following additions: sugar, colouring or flavouring materials, fruit, nuts, chocolate or other similar substances), the mixture must be converted to ice cream within one hour of preparation. Otherwise (unless the pH is 4.5 or less) the following must be observed:

1. The mixture should be kept for no longer than one hour at any temperature over 7.2°C before being pasteurised or sterilised.

2. The following times and temperatures may be used for pasteurisation:

 (i) a minimum temperature of 65.6°C for a minimum of 30 minutes;
 (ii) a minimum temperature of 71.1°C for a minimum of 10 minutes;
 (iii) a minimum temperature of 79.5°C for a minimum of 15 seconds.

3. The required process for sterilisation is heating to a minimum of 148.9°C for a minimum of 2 seconds.

4. After pasteurisation or sterilisation the temperature of the mix must be reduced to

Untreated milk

Pasteurised milk

Stage 5   Stage 1   Stage 2   Stage 3
Stage 4

Key:

————————— Incoming milk being pasteurised

— — — — Outgoing milk being cooled

— · — · — Hot water

- - - - - - - - Cooling water

————————— Heat exchange plates

Stage 1 The incoming milk is being heated by milk which has already been pasteurised.

Stage 2 The temperature of the milk is raised to the temperature required for pasteurisation by means of hot water.

Stage 3 The milk is held at 72°C for 15 seconds in order to achieve adequate pasteurisation.

Stage 4 The milk is partially cooled by giving up some of its heat to the cold incoming milk.

Stage 5 The milk is cooled to 10°C or below by cooling water.

Fig. 18.1. Simplified diagram of the HTST pasteuration process.

7.2°C within 1.5 hours and the mix must be held at this temperature until freezing begins.

Once it has been manufactured ice cream must be held at or below −2.2°C until it is sold.

Freezing

The preservation of foods by freezing involves two methods of control of the growth of microorganisms:

1. The growth rate of microorganisms is reduced by the low temperature. Also the rate of undesirable chemical changes is reduced considerably at low temperatures.

2. A large percentage of the water present in the food is converted to ice and is therefore unavailable to microorganisms.

Quick-freezing processes, in which the food passes through the range of maximum ice-crystal formation in the shortest time possible are preferable, since the formation of large ice crystals causes undesirable changes in the texture and appearance of the food. Quick freezing has been defined as that process in which the food passes through this zone ($0°C$ to $-4°C$) in 30 minutes or less. The small ice crystals formed by such a process do not disrupt the texture of the food.

Most foods can be frozen successfully and, in general, frozen food products are superior to canned foods, since the product bears a closer resemblance to the fresh food. Also, the nutritive value of the food is not as seriously affected by the freezing process. In some cases the vitamin content of fresh frozen foods may be higher than that of fresh foods, since foods such as fruits and vegetables often lose ascorbic acid during transportation and storage. Foods containing fat dispersed in a colloidal form, i.e. as an emulsion, may not freeze successfully. The reason for this is that as freezing takes place, the removal of water causes an increase in the concentration of salts in the food which may cause irreversible changes in the colloidal structure.

Before freezing all inedible parts of the food are removed. Most foods, particularly fruits and vegetables, are blanched in order to inactivate enzymes. Blanching also reduces the number of bacteria present by as much as 90%. Before freezing, substances such as ascorbic acid, which reduces browning of some fruits and vegetables, or antioxidants, which prevent undesirable changes in any fat present, may be added to the food.

There are four main methods of freezing:

1. *Plate freezing.* In this method the refrigerant passes through a number of hollow plates. The food is placed between the plates.

2. *Immersion freezing.* In this method the food is placed directly into the refrigerant. The refrigerant used depends on the food being frozen. Brine is sometimes used, especially for fish, whereas invert sugar solutions are often used for fruits and vegetables. In more modern processes liquid nitrogen makes an excellent refrigerant.

3. *Blast freezing.* In this method a blast of very cold air is blown directly on to the food.

4. *Fluidised bed freezing.* This method is very successful for freezing foods which are of small particle size, such as peas. It is an adaptation of blast freezing in which the air is blown upwards through mesh over which the food is passing. The air speed is controlled so that the solid particles of food flow as if they were liquid. In this method the rate of heat exchange from the food to the air may be very rapid and this is desirable for a quick freezing process.

Dehydration

The traditional method of drying foods was simply to lay the foods in the sun. This method is still used for the drying of foods in some countries. Some traditional methods involve the use of other means of control of growth in addition to the removal of moisture. For example, both smoking and salting have been used in the traditional methods used for drying meat and fish.

The modern process of dehydration consists of the removal of moisture from the food by the application of heat usually in the presence of a controlled flow of air. It is important that the temperature used should not be too high, since this will cause undesirable changes in the food. Also, excessive heat may cause 'case hardening', where the outside of the food becomes brittle and hard while moisture is trapped in the centre and is unable to pass through the food by the normal processes of diffusion and capillary action.

Before drying, food undergoes a variety of treatments. In the case of vegetables this includes washing, grading and blanching (to destroy enzymes). Sodium sulphite is usually added to the blanching water; this improves the colour of the product, aids vitamin C retention and destroys many of the microorganisms. Other foods, such as meats, may be cooked prior to dehydration.

There are many types of equipment used for dehydrating foods. Some of the more usual methods of drying are:

1. *Tunnel drying.* In this method the food is placed on conveyor belts or perforated trays and passed through a warm-air tunnel. A more modern development is fluidised bed drying, in which warm air is blown upwards and the particles of food are kept in motion. This method is used particularly for vegetables.

2. *Spray drying.* This method is used for drying fairly liquid foods such as milk and eggs. The food enters the top of a large drying chamber as a fine spray. The spray mixes with warm air, the water evaporates and a fine powder is produced which is removed from the bottom of the chamber.

3. *Roller drying.* In this method the food is applied in paste form as a thin film to the surface of a revolving heated roller or drum. As the drum rotates the food dries and the dried product is removed from the drum by a scraper knife. Products dried by this method include instant breakfast cereals and potatoes.

4. *Freeze drying.* In this method of drying the food is first of all frozen and then subjected to a mild heating process in a vacuum cabinet. The ice crystals which form during the freezing stage sublime when heated under reduced pressure, i.e. they change directly from ice to water vapour without passing through the liquid phase. This results in a product which is porous and very little changed in size and shape from the original food. Since little heat is required there is little heat damage and the colour, flavour and nutrient content affected less than in some other methods of drying. The product, being porous, can be rapidly rehydrated (reconstituted) in cold water. A wide variety of foods can be dried by this method, e.g. meat, shellfish, fruits and vegetables.

Addition of chemical inhibitors

Many methods of preservation, including many of the traditional methods, depend on the addition of antimicrobial substances to foods. Some of these methods are outlined below:

1. *Curing.* The curing of meats such as bacon involves using a brine solution composed of sodium chloride (25%), potassium nitrate (1%) and sodium nitrite (0.1%). The meat may be soaked in the brine or the brine may be injected into the meat by hollow needles. The salt content inhibits microbial growth and the meat develops a characteristic colour and flavour.

Some cured products, e.g. herring and bacon, are also smoked, by exposing them to smoke from a wood fire. The smoke contains antimicrobial substances which reduce spoilage. It also gives the food a characteristic taste.

2. *Preserving with sugar.* Many fruit products, such as jams and crystallised fruits, are

preserved with sugar. Sugar reduces microbial activity due to its dehydrating effect (see page 193).

3. *Addition of acid*. This may be carried out in one of two ways. The food may be pickled, i.e. soaked in an acid solution such as vinegar (acetic acid). This is used for a variety of foods, particularly vegetables. Another method is to inoculate the food with a culture of selected bacteria and to rely on acid produced by the activities of these bacteria. Foods such as yoghurt and sauerkraut (fermented cabbage) are produced in this way.

4. *Other chemical preservatives*. The chemicals which may be added to food in controlled amounts for use as preservatives are discussed in more detail in Chapter 19.

Irradiation

It has been known for many years that various types of radiation can be used to inhibit microbial growth. However, processes for preserving food by means of radiation have only been perfected in the last ten years. At the moment, the use of these processes is banned in the United Kingdom, but legislation is planned which should permit their use by the end of 1990.

In the initial research on the preservation of food by the use of radiation it was found that it was impossible to eliminate all microorganisms without causing undesirable changes in the food itself. Bacterial spores are often very resistant and were found to survive massive doses of radiation. Therefore, the use of irradiation was thought to be restricted to the pasteurisation of refrigerated foods. However, further research has led to the development of a variety of processes which can be used in food preservation.

The two main types of ionising radiation used are:

(a) gamma (γ)-rays from radioactive cobalt-60 or caesium-137;
(b) beams of electrons from radioactive substances produced by linear accelerators.

Gamma rays are highly penetrating radiations capable of passing through large containers of foods. Thus, food can be treated in its final packaging or even in pallet loads. Electron beams have less penetrating power than gamma rays and are suitable only for foods less than 5 cm thick. However, electron beams can be intensified in such a way that high dose rates can be achieved in a very short time, thereby giving the maximum effect. Such treatment is ideal for food which can be transported in a thin layer and at a high speed, such as grain and spices.

Treating food by ionising radiations does not involve any significant change in the temperature of the food. Irradiation, therefore, can be used as a cold process of preservation, killing insects and microorganisms in foods which are sensitive to heat, such as spices, enzyme preparations and frozen foods. It can be used to kill pathogenic bacteria which may be harboured in frozen foods.

MEASUREMENT

Doses of radiation are measured in units known as rads and Grays.

A **rad** is equal to 100 ergs of energy being absorbed by one gram of irradiated matter.

A **Gray** is the SI unit of radiation. One Gray is equal to the energy of one Joule being absorbed by one kilogram of matter.

$$1 \text{ Gray (Gy)} = 100 \text{ rad}$$
$$1 \text{ kiloGray (kGy)} = 1000 \text{ Gray (Gy)}$$

POSSIBLE USES OF RADIATION

Food irradiation treatments can be divided into three types: low, medium and high dose treatments. Table 18.1 gives some examples of these treatments and lists foods which may be treated.

TABLE 18.1. *Possible food irradiation treatments*

Purpose	Dose (kGy)	Products
Low dose (up to 1 kGy)		
Inhibition of sprouting	0.05–0.15	Potatoes, onions, garlic, ginger root
Killing insects and parasites	0.15–0.50	Cereals and pulses, fresh and dried fruits, dried fish and meat, fresh pork
Control or delay of ripening	0.50–1.0	Fresh fruit and vegetables
Medium dose (1–10 kGy)		
Extension of food shelf life	1.5–3.0	Fresh fish, strawberries
Destruction of spoilage and pathogenic microorganisms	2.0–5.0	Fresh and frozen seafood, poultry and meat in raw or frozen state
Improving physical properties of food	2.0–7.0	Grapes (increasing juice yield), dehydrated vegetables (reducing cooking time)
High dose (10–50 kGy)		
Commercial sterilisation (in combination with mild heat)	30–50	Meat, poultry, seafood, prepared foods, sterilised hospital diets
Decontamination of certain food additives and ingredients	10–50	Spices, enzyme preparations, natural gum

Short-term preservation

The following can all be considered as means of short-term preservation of food:

1. *CONVENTIONAL METHODS OF COOKING USING HEAT*, e.g. grilling, roasting, stewing, braising. The heat treatment, if adequate, will reduce the number of microorganisms and kill pathogens, therefore, the useful life of the food will be extended.

2. *THE USE OF MICROWAVES.* Microwaves are very short electromagnetic waves that move with the speed of light and have a wavelength of between 1 mm and 30 cm. They are produced by a magnetron and are able to penetrate foods and cause an increase in temperature. The mechanism for this action is as follows: Water is a polar

molecule (see page 42), this means that water molecules will behave like small magnets. When microwaves are directed at them, they will align themselves in a certain direction in the magnetic field which has been set up. As the current reverses, the direction of the field is changed and the molecules change their direction and turn through 180 degrees. This happens millions of times in a second. This continual movement sets up friction which generates heat.

Microwaves preserve food in two ways:

(a) the internal generation of heat which will reduce the numbers of microorganisms present;
(b) the microwaves themselves also have a lethal effect on microorganisms.

3. *CHILLING.* The temperatures used for chilling vary considerably. The term 'chilled storage' can apply to any reduction in the normal temperature of food. The temperature used depends on the nature of the product and the storage atmosphere. Bananas, for example, are stored best at 15°C, whereas meat is stored at 1 to 2°C.

4. *COOK–CHILL PROCESSES.* These involve a particular application of the chilling process. They are used where food has to be transported long distances from the kitchens where it is prepared to the point where it is served and eaten, e.g. aeroplane meals, school meals, hospital meals. In these situations it would not be satisfactory to cook the food and keep it warm until required. The food is cooked thoroughly and then divided into individual portions. All containers should be dated to ensure efficient stock rotation. They should also be labelled with the contents and required reheating time. The food is chilled in a blast-chiller to between 1°C and 3°C within two hours of cooking and must be kept at this temperature during storage and distribution. When the food is required it is reheated to a centre temperature of at least 70°C. All meals prepared this way must be eaten within five days of preparation and strict standards of hygiene must be maintained throughout.

5. *COOK–FREEZE PROCESSES.* These are similar to cook–chill processes, but the food is frozen rather than merely being chilled. After cooking, the food is blast-frozen to a temperature of -20°C and kept at this temperature until required. Blast-freezing is used because it is a very rapid method of freezing. When needed the food is defrosted and heated to a centre temperature of at least 70°C.

6. *CONTROLLED ATMOSPHERE STORAGE.* This involves controlling the humidity and composition of the atmosphere and is normally used in conjunction with chilling. The optimum humidity depends on the food stored and the temperature of storage. Too high a humidity encourages microbial growth, while too low a humidity results in loss of moisture and, in vegetables, wilting. The composition of the atmosphere affects storage. If the level of carbon dioxide in the air is increased the rate of spoilage is reduced. The optimum concentration of carbon dioxide depends on the food stored. For meat, concentrations of 10% are used, while between 5% and 10% is best for vegetables and 2.5% for eggs.

CHAPTER 19

Food Additives and
Food Labelling

Food additives are substances which are added to food for one or more of the following purposes:

(a) to maintain the nutritional quality of food;
(b) to improve the keeping quality of food;
(c) to make food more attractive;
(d) as an essential aid to food processing.

Food additives should not be used if they disguise faulty processing, deceive the consumer or substantially reduce the nutritional value of the food.

The term 'food additive' is defined legally in the **Food Labelling Regulations 1984** as

> any substance not commonly regarded or used as a food, which is added to or used in or on food at any stage to affect its keeping qualities, texture, consistency, appearance, taste, odour, alkalinity or acidity or to serve any other technological function in relation to food.

Additives may be:

1. *Natural substances*, which have been produced biologically and have been extracted from natural products. For example, lecithin, which is used as an emulsifier, is extracted from soya beans.

2. *Synthetic compounds*, which are 'nature identical'. These have been synthesised either chemically or biologically to match naturally occurring counterparts. For example, L-ascorbic acid (vitamin C), which is used as an antioxidant, can be made synthetically.

3. *Artificial compounds*, which are synthesised chemically and have no naturally occurring counterpart. For example, azodicarbonamide, which is used as a flour improver, does not occur naturally and is synthesised by chemical methods.

Under law, for purposes of control, additives are classified into the following categories:

1. Preservatives	4. Colours
2. Antioxidants	5. Sweeteners
3. Emulsifiers and stabilisers	6. Miscellaneous additives

For each category lists of permitted additives have been drawn up. Of the permitted additives, 280 have been given a number. When the additive has also been approved by the European Community (EC), it has an 'E' in front of it.

Preservatives

Preservatives prevent or reduce the growth of microorganisms in food. There are 35 preservatives which are permitted in the United Kingdom. All of these except one, nisin, are also permitted in the EC. A list of these permitted preservatives and some examples of where they are used in foods is given in Table 19.1. It is useful to note that the serial numbers of the preservatives fall in the range 200 to 290.

The use of chemicals to preserve food is controlled by the **Preservatives in Food Regulations 1979**. Many of the preservatives which are permitted are chemically

TABLE 19.1. *Permitted preservatives and examples of use*

Preservative	Example of use
E200 sorbic acid	Soft drinks, fruit yoghurt, processed cheese slices
E201 sodium sorbate	Frozen pizza, flour confectionery
E202 potassium sorbate	
E203 calcium sorbate	
E210 benzoic acid	Beer, jam, salad cream, soft drinks, fruit-based
E211 sodium benzoate	pie fillings, marinated herring and mackerel
E212 potassium benzoate	
E213 calcium benzoate	
E214 ethyl-4-hydroxybenzoate	
E215 sodium ethyl 4-hydroxybenzoate	
E216 propyl 4-hydroxybenzoate	
E217 sodium propyl 4-hydroxybenzoate	
E218 methyl 4-hydroxybenzoate	
E219 sodium methyl 4-hydroxybenzoate	
E220 sulphur dioxide	Dried fruit, dehydrated vegetables, fruit juices
E221 sodium sulphite	and syrups, sausages, cider, beer and wine, also
E222 sodium hydrogen sulphite	used to prevent browning of raw peeled potatoes
E223 sodium metabisulphite	and to condition biscuit doughs
E224 potassium metabisulphite	
E226 calcium sulphite	
E227 calcium hydrogen sulphite	
E230 biphenyl	Surface treatment of citrus fruit
E231 2-hydroxybiphenyl	
E232 sodium 2-ohenylphenate	
E233 thiabendazole	Surface treatment of bananas
234 nisin	Cheese, clotted cream
E239 hexamine	Marinated herring and mackerel
E249 potassium nitrite	Bacon, ham, cured meats, meat pastes, corned beef
E250 sodium nitrite	
E251 sodium nitrate	
E252 potassium nitrate	
E280 propionic acid	Bread and flour confectionery, Christmas pudding
E281 sodium propionate	
E282 calcium propionate	
E283 potassium propionate	

similar and they can be conveniently placed into groups according to their chemical structure.

Sorbic acid and its salts (E200–E203) are used to inhibit the growth of moulds and yeasts. Sorbic acid is a short-chain unsaturated acid. It is non-toxic and is probably metabolised in the body in the same way as naturally occurring unsaturated fatty acids.

$$CH_3—CH=CH—CH=CH—COOH$$
Sorbic acid

Benzoic acid, C_6H_5COOH, and its derivatives (E210–E219) form a group of widely used preservatives. Benzoic acid occurs naturally in some foods. It is non-toxic. During metabolism it combines with glycine and is excreted as hippuric acid. The derivatives of benzoic acid are metabolised in the same way.

Benzoic acid

Sulphur dioxide and sulphites and metabisulphites (E220–E227) are widely used as preservatives. Sulphur dioxide, SO_2, is a gas which was used traditionally to preserve fruit pulp and wine. Nowadays, it is more common for the salts of sulphur dioxide to be used since they are more convenient. All of these compounds have a drawback in that they impart an unpleasant taste to food and leave an unpleasant aftertaste which can be detected at low concentrations. Therefore, their use is restricted to foods which are boiled or cooked in some way. The heating drives off the sulphur dioxide and the taste of the food is not affected. Another drawback of the use of these compounds is that they cause destruction of thiamin.

Diphenyl and its derivatives (E230–E232) and thiabendazole (E233) are used to prevent the growth of moulds on the peel of citrus fruits and bananas. They are often applied by treating the paper in which the fruits are wrapped with the compounds.

Diphenyl

Nisin (234) is an antibiotic. It is produced by certain strains of *Streptococcus lactis* and it occurs naturally in some cheeses. Nisin is only effective against a limited range of organisms, namely certain species of Gram-positive bacteria. Therefore, its use is limited to certain specialist uses, such as the preservation of cheese, where it prevents spoilage due to gas-forming bacteria. Nisin is not used in medicine. Therefore, the possibility of the development of resistant strains of bacteria does not present a problem. It is a polypeptide and is metabolised in the same manner as other polypeptides in the body.

Hexamine (E239) is manufactured from formaldehyde and ammonia. It has limited use.

Sodium and potassium nitrites and nitrates (E249–E252) are used in the preservation of meats and cheeses. Nitrates are capable of being converted to nitrites either when food spoils or by bacteria in the stomach (especially in tiny babies). Nitrites are able to enter the bloodstream and react with the haemoglobin in the red blood cells. Haemoglobin is responsible for oxygen transport and when the ability to transport oxygen is impaired there may be difficulty in breathing and pallor, dizziness and headaches. Infants are far more susceptible to this condition than adults and nitrites and nitrates are not permitted in foods intended for babies under six months. Nitrates are also capable of reacting with amines present in the stomach to form nitrosamines which are potentially carcinogenic (cancer-producing). However, there is also evidence that intakes of vitamins A, C and E are protective against stomach cancer. In addition, nitrites inhibit the growth of *Clostridium botulinum* bacteria which are responsible for botulism (see page 208). Without the use of nitrites and nitrates it is possible that there would be many more cases of botulism.

Propionic acid, CH_3CH_2COOH, and its salts (E280–E283) are used in bread and other baked goods as mould suppressants. These compounds occur naturally in fermented foods and they are easily metabolised by the body in the same way as any other fatty acid and its salts.

Antioxidants

Antioxidants are used to prevent the oxidative rancidity of fats and oils (see page 64) and to prevent enzymic browning (see page 132). There are 16 permitted antioxidants. All but two of them (diphenylamine and ethoxyquin) are permitted in the EC. The serial numbers of antioxidants are in the range 300 to 322. BHA and BHT are not permitted for use in baby foods. Table 19.2 lists the permitted antioxidants and gives some examples of their uses. The use of antioxidants is controlled by the **Antioxidants in Food Regulations 1978**.

TABLE 19.2. *Permitted antioxidants and examples of use*

Antioxidant	Example of use
E300 L-ascorbic acid E301 sodium L-ascorbate E302 calcium L-ascorbate	Fruit drinks, also used to improve flour and bread dough
E304 L-ascorbyl palmitate	Chicken stock cubes
E306 extracts of natural origin rich in tocopherols	Vegetable oils
E307 synthetic alpha-tocopherol E308 synthetic gamma-tocopherol E309 synthetic delta-tocopherol	Cereal-based baby foods
E310 propyl gallate E311 octyl gallate E312 dodecyl gallate	Vegetable oils, chewing gum
E320 butylated hydroxyanisole (BHA)	Beef stock cubes, cheese spread, margarine, dessert topping
E321 butylated hydroxytoluene (BHT)	Chewing gum, dried potato products
E322 lecithins	Low fat spreads (also used as an emulsifier)
diphenylamine ethoxyquin	Used to prevent 'scald' (a discolorisation on apples and pears)

Emulsifiers and stabilisers

Emulsifiers are used to disperse oils and fats in water in foods or, conversely, to disperse water in oil or fat (see page 44). They also may be used in baked goods to slow down the rate of staling. Stabilisers are used to improve the stability of emulsions and to prevent the breakdown of emulsions into two separate layers. There are over 50 permitted emulsifiers and stabilisers. Most of them have E numbers and are permitted in the EC. Table 19.3 lists the emulsifiers and stabilisers which are permitted for use in the United Kingdom and gives examples of their uses. The use of emulsifiers and stabilisers is controlled by the **Emulsifiers and Stabilisers in Food Regulations 1980**.

TABLE 19.3. *Permitted emulsifiers and stabilisers and examples of use*

Emulsifier or stabiliser	Example of use
E400 alginic acid	Ice cream, soft cheese
E401 sodium alginate	Cake mixes
E402 potassium alginate	
E403 ammonium alginate	
E404 calcium alginate	
E405 propylene glycol alginate	Salad dressings, cottage cheese
E406 agar	Ice cream
E407 carrageenan	Quick setting jelly mixes, milk shakes
E410 locust bean gum (carob gum)	Salad cream
E412 guar gum	Packet soups and meringue mixes
E413 tragacanth	Salad dressings, processed cheese
E414 gum arabic (acacia)	Confectionery
E415 xanthan gum	Sweet pickle, coleslaw
416 karaya gum	Soft cheese, brown sauce
432 Polysorbate 20	Bakery products, confectionery creams
433 Polysorbate 80	
434 Polysorbate 40	
435 Polysorbate 60	
436 Polysorbate 65	
E440 (a) pectin	Jams and preserves
E440 (b) amidated pectin pectin extract	
442 ammonium phosphatides	Cocoa and chocolate products
E460 powdered cellulose	High-fibre bread, grated cheese
E461 methylcellulose	Low fat spreads, whipped toppings
E463 hydroxypropylcellulose	
E464 hydroxypropylmethylcellulose	Edible ices
E465 ethylmethylcellulose	Gateaux
E466 sodium carboxymethylcellulose	Jelly, sterilised whipping cream
E470 sodium, potassium and calcium salts of fatty acids	Cake mixes
E471 mono- and di-glycerides of fatty acids	Flour confectionery, margarine, frozen desserts
E472 (a) acetic acid esters of mono- and di-glycerides of fatty acids	Mousse mixes

TABLE 19.3—*continued*

Emulsifier or stabiliser	Example of use
E472 (b) lactic acid esters of mono- and di-glycerides of fatty acids	Dessert topping
E472 (c) citric acid esters of mono- and di-glycerides of fatty acids	Continental sausages
E472 (e) derivatives of tartaric acid and mono- and di-glycerides of fatty acids	Bread, frozen pizza
E473 sucrose esters of fatty acids	Edible ices
E474 sucroglycerides	
E475 polyglycerol esters of fatty acids	Cake mixes
476 polyglycerol polyricinoleate	Chocolate-flavour coatings for cakes and biscuits
E477 propane-1,2-diol esters of fatty acids	Instant desserts
E481 sodium stearoyl-2-lactylate	Bread, cakes and biscuits
E482 calcium stearoyl-2-lactylate	Gravy granules
E483 stearyl tartrate	Cake mixes
491 sorbitan monostearate	
492 sorbitan tristearate	
493 sorbitan monolaurate	
494 sorbitan mono-oleate	
495 sorbitan monopalmitate	
extract of quillaia	Used in soft drinks to promote foam
derivatives of soya bean oil	Emulsions used to grease bakery tins

Colours

Colours are added to food to make it more attractive or to replace colour lost during processing. Many canned fruits and vegetables have a very unappealing colour if colour is not added to replace that lost during processing. The addition of colours to food is controlled by the **Colouring Matter in Food Regulations 1973**. Only 50 permitted colours may be used. Their serial numbers are in the range 100 to 180 and about two-thirds of them have 'E' numbers and are permitted in the EC.

The commonest food colour is caramel (E150). It is made by heating sugar until it turns brown (see page 53). Many colours are of natural origin and are extracted from plants. For example, curcumin (E100) is a yellow extract obtained from turmeric roots and beta-carotene (E160a) can be extracted from carrots and is a form of vitamin A. There are 15 permitted artificial colours. Some of these are known as the azo dyes. An example is tartrazine (E102).

Table 19.4 lists the permitted colours and some examples of their use.

TABLE 19.4. *Permitted colours and examples of use*

Colour	Example of use
E100 curcumin	Flour confectionery, margarine
E101 riboflavin	Sauces
101(a) riboflavin-5-phosphate	

TABLE 19.4—*continued*

Colour	Example of use
E102 tartrazine	Soft drinks, cake mixes, instant puddings
E104 quinoline yellow	Biscuits, jellies
E110 sunset yellow FCF	
E120 cochineal	Alcoholic drinks, home food colour
E122 carmoisine	Jams, jellies
E123 amaranth	Packet soups, cake and trifle mixes
E124 ponceau 4R	Dessert mixes, jams, jellies
E127 erythrosine	Glacé cherries
128 red 2G	Sausages
E131 patent blue V	Scotch eggs
E132 indigo carmine	Blancmange, sweets
133 brilliant blue FCF	Canned vegetables
E140 chlorophyll	Soups, canned vegetables, confectionery
E141 copper complexes of chlorophyll and chlorophyllins	Parsley sauce, soups
E142 green S	Pastilles
E150 caramel	Beer, soft drinks, sauces, gravy browning and granules
E151 black PN	Brown sauce, chocolate mousse
E153 carbon black	Liquorice
154 brown FK	Kippers
155 brown HT	Chocolate cake
E160 (a) alpha-carotene, beta-carotene, gamma-carotene	Margarine, soft drinks
E160 (b) annatto, bixin, norbixin	Crisps, margarine, cheese
E160 (c) capsanthin, capsorubin	Processed cheese slices
E160 (d) lycopene	
E160 (e) beta-apo-8-carotenal	Cheese slices
E160 (f) ethyl esters of beta-apo-8-carotenoic acid	
E161 (a) flavoxanthin	
E161 (b) lutein	Poultry feed (to deepen colour of egg yolks)
E161 (c) cryptoxanthin	
E161 (d) rubixanthin	
E161 (e) violoxanthin	
E161 (f) rhodoxanthin	
E161 (g) canthaxanthin	Preserves, confectionery, dessert mixes
E162 beetroot red (betanin)	Ice cream, jellies, yoghurt
E163 anthocyanins	Yoghurt, soft drinks
E171 titanium dioxide	Sweets
E173 aluminium	Sugar-coated flour confectionery for cake decoration
E174 silver	
E175 gold	

TABLE 19.4—*continued*

	Colour	Example of use
E180	pigment rubine	Colouring the rind of hard cheese
	methyl violet	
	paprika	Canned vegetables
	saffron, crocin	Rice
	sandalwood, santolin	
	turmeric	Soups

Sweeteners

There are two types of sweetening agents or sweeteners:

(a) intense sweeteners which are many times sweeter than sucrose and are used in small amounts;

(b) bulk sweeteners which have a sweetening power roughly equivalent to that of sucrose and are used in larger quantities.

The use of sweeteners in foods is controlled by the **Sweeteners in Food Regulations 1983**. Only two sweeteners have been given serial numbers and the prefix 'E'. They are mannitol and sorbitol. None of the permitted intense sweeteners have been given serial numbers and they are not approved for use throughout the EC. Table 19.5 lists the permitted sweeteners and gives examples of their use.

TABLE 19.5. *Permitted sweeteners and examples of use*

	Sweetener	Example of use
	*acesulfame potassium	Canned foods, soft drinks, table-top sweeteners
	*aspartame	Soft drinks, yoghurts, dessert and drink mixes, sweetening tablets
	hydrogenated glucose syrup	Sugar-free confectionery
	isomalt	
E421	mannitol	
	*saccharin	Soft drinks, cider, sweetening tablets, table-top sweeteners
	*sodium saccharin	
	*calcium saccharin	
E420	sorbitol, sorbitol syrup	Sugar-free confectionery, jams for diabetics
	*thaumatin	Table-top sweeteners, yoghurt
	xylitol	Sugar-free chewing gum

* indicates that the additive is an intense sweetener.

Aspartame is a dipeptide made up from the amino acids aspartic acid and phenyl-alanine. It is safely metabolised in the body in the same way that any other dipeptide is broken down. However, concern has been expressed about whether aspartame can safely be consumed by people suffering from phenylketonuria (PKU). PKU is a genetic disease and people who suffer from it are unable to metabolise phenylalanine.

Mannitol, sorbitol and xylitol do not require insulin in order to be metabolised and, therefore, they can be safely used by diabetics.

Miscellaneous Food Additives

In addition to the five main categories outlined above there are many other types of additives. The use of these substances is controlled by the **Miscellaneous Additives in Food Regulations 1980**. Under this legislation, over 120 miscellaneous additives have been approved for use in foods. It is not possible in this text to give a comprehensive list of all of these additives and their uses but some examples of the types of substances considered in this category are given below.

(A) FLAVOUR ENHANCERS

These are not flavourings but they are substances which enhance existing flavours and make them seem stronger, although they themselves are practically tasteless. The most widely used flavour enhancer is monosodium glutamate or MSG (621). It is the sodium salt of glutamic acid, an amino acid which is commonly found in proteins (see page 77). Therefore, MSG is readily metabolised in the body. However, it is suspected that the consumption of large amounts of MSG may cause unfavourable reactions in some people. The symptoms are palpitations, chest or neck pain and dizziness. These effects are short-lived and on the whole MSG is not thought to be harmful. MSG occurs naturally in soy sauce, which is made by fermenting soya beans. Commercially, it can be made from seaweed, but it is more usually obtained from sugar beet or wheat.

(B) ACIDS, BUFFERS AND BASES

These substances are added to food in order to adjust or control its pH.

(C) HUMECTANTS

These substances absorb water and, therefore, help to prevent the food from drying out. Glycerol (E422) is added to sweets for this purpose.

(D) FIRMING AND CRISPING AGENTS

These substances are added to foods such as tinned or bottled fruits and vegetables in order to keep them crisp. Calcium chloride (509) is used in this way.

(E) FLOUR IMPROVERS

These substances are used to strengthen doughs, e.g. potassium bromate (924) is added to bread doughs.

(F) FLOUR BLEACHING AGENTS

These substances are added to flour in order to whiten it, e.g. benzoyl peroxide.

Solvents

Many flavourings and colourings are dissolved in other substances before being added to foods. Solvents may also be used to facilitate the addition of other ingredients. The use of solvents is controlled by the **Solvents in Food Regulations 1967** and only nine are permitted. These permitted solvents are listed in Table 19.6.

TABLE 19.6. *Permitted solvents*

Ethyl alcohol (ethanol)
Ethyl acetate (ethyl ethanoate)
Diethyl ether
Glycerol
Glyceryl monoacetate
Glyceryl diacetate
Glyceryl triacetate
Isopropyl alcohol (propan-2-ol)
Propylene glycol (propan-1,2-diol)

Mineral hydrocarbons

Mineral hydrocarbons are mineral oils and waxes of fairly high molecular weight. They are not metabolised and hence have no nutritive value. They interfere with the absorption of vitamins A and D, therefore, their presence in food is not desirable. Their use is controlled by the **Mineral Hydrocarbons in Food Regulations 1966**. The amount of mineral hydrocarbon which may be present in most foods is limited to 0.5% by weight. Their main uses are as follows:

(a) as a coating for dried fruits, such as currants, raisins and sultanas to prevent them sticking together during storage;

(b) as a coating for citrus fruits to replace the natural oils which are lost during cleaning;

(c) as a coating for cheeses to minimise drying our during storage.

Flavourings

Flavouring agents or flavourings are not controlled, although there are plans to control their use in the future. One of the problems of control is that there is a large number of flavourings in use (over 3000). The majority of flavourings are chemical twins of naturally occurring substances that give foods their subtle tastes.

The Controversy Surrounding Food Additives

There is widespread concern over the use of additives in foods. However, the use of additives in foods serve many useful purposes. In some cases it ensures that food is safe to eat and also the preservative effects ensure that perishable foods keep in good condition during transit and increase the variety of foods available throughout the year.

The key to the issue is risk/benefit analysis. The risk of possible ill effects from the presence of additives in foods must be insignificant compared to the benefits gained.

Food Labelling

The labelling of packaged food is controlled by the **Food Labelling Regulations 1984**. These regulations state that the label must show the following:

1. THE NAME OF THE FOOD

This name must be:

(a) the legal name (where a legal name exists). For example, chocolate and honey are legal names;

(b) the customary name (where no legal name exists). For example, pizza and muesli are both customary names;

(c) a descriptive name (where no legal or customary name exists). This name must be sufficiently precise to inform the purchaser of the true nature of the contents and to avoid confusion. 'Malted milk drink' is an example of a descriptive name.

2. A LIST OF INGREDIENTS

Most foods must have a list of ingredients, including water if the water content is more than 5% by weight. The list of ingredients must be arranged in descending order by weight. The heading of the list must be the word 'Ingredients' or must include the word 'ingredients'. The name of the ingredient must be the name which would be used if the ingredient was sold as a food, where this is applicable. An additive must be listed by the principal function it serves, followed by its name and/or serial number.

3. THE NET QUANTITY OF FOOD

This must be clearly shown on most foods and is usually given in terms of weight or volume. Occasionally, the number of units contained in the package may be used, e.g. in the case of some breakfast cereals.

4. A DATE MARK

A date mark is required for most foods, unless the shelf-life is more than 18 months. The date mark indicates the minimum durability of the food. The date mark requirements vary according to the shelf-life of the food. For this purpose foods can be classified into three categories:

(a) perishable foods with a shelf-life of less than six weeks. For these foods the label must show a 'sell by' date (expressed in day/month), which indicates the latest recommended date of sale. An indication of the period from the date of purchase for which the food can be kept if properly stored must be included, together with details of the storage conditions;

(b) foods which have a shelf-life of six weeks to three months. For these foods the label must show a 'best before' date (expressed in day/month) which indicates how long the food can be kept if stored properly, together with details of storage conditions;

(c) foods which have a shelf-life of three to 18 months. For these foods the label must show a 'best before end' date (expressed in month/year).

5. THE MANUFACTURER'S ADDRESS

The name and address of the manufacturer or packer must be included so that the consumer knows who to contact if further information is required or a complaint is to be made. The place of origin of the food should also be included if necessary.

6. INSTRUCTIONS FOR USE

In the case of a dry mix, concentrate or similar food (except custard powder and blancmange powder), the instructions must specify every substance (other than water) required. This must appear next to the name of the food.

NUTRITIONAL CLAIMS

The following nutritional claims are controlled by law:

(a) the claim 'low in polyunsaturated fatty acids' is only permitted if the product contains at least 35% fat and at least 45% of the fat is polyunsaturated, with not more than 25% of the fat saturated;

(b) the claim 'low in cholesterol' is only permitted if the product contains less than 0.005% cholesterol;

(c) claims that a product is a good source of a vitamin or mineral are only permitted if the normal daily portion of that product contains at least one-sixth of the recommended daily amount of that vitamin or mineral.

Percentage contribution of different foods to the nutrient content of the average household diet

	Energy value	Protein	Fat	Carbohydrate	Calcium
Milk, including cream	11.5	16.7	14.6	7.6	43.0
Cheese	2.9	5.6	5.0	—	13.3
Total milk, cream and cheese	14.4	22.3	19.6	7.6	56.4
Meat, carcase	6.0	11.9	10.4	—	0.4
Poultry	1.3	5.6	1.4	—	0.2
Bacon	1.8	2.9	3.4	—	0.1
Other meat, including liver	6.5	10.3	10.0	2.1	2.6
Total meat	15.6	30.8	25.0	2.1	3.3
Fish	1.3	4.7	1.3	0.4	1.6
Eggs	1.8	4.3	2.9	—	1.5
Butter	4.2	0.1	9.8	—	0.2
Margarine	5.9	—	13.9	—	0.3
Other fats	5.2	0.2	12.1	0.1	—
Total fats	15.2	0.2	35.7	0.2	0.5
Sugar and preserves	8.1	—	—	18.1	0.4
Potatoes	5.0	3.6	—	10.1	1.3
Green vegetables	0.2	1.0	—	0.2	1.2
Root vegetables	0.2	0.2	—	0.4	0.9
Other vegetables	3.5	4.6	2.2	4.4	3.2
Total vegetables	8.9	9.3	2.2	15.1	6.7
Fresh fruit	1.2	0.6	—	2.5	1.3
Other fruit	1.8	0.7	0.9	2.9	0.7
Total fruit	2.9	1.2	1.0	5.3	1.8
White bread	8.8	9.6	1.3	15.7	9.5
Other bread	4.8	5.8	1.1	8.0	4.7
Flour	2.9	2.4	0.3	5.5	5.0
Cakes, pastries and biscuits	7.3	3.3	6.3	9.2	4.0
Other cereals	5.8	4.2	1.7	10.2	2.1
Total cereals	29.6	25.2	10.7	48.7	25.3
Beverages and other foods	2.2	2.1	1.6	2.7	2.7

Iron	Vitamin A (retinol equivalents)	Thiamin	Riboflavin	Nicotinic acid equivalents	Vitamin C	Vitamin D
2.5	13.9	10.3	33.4	10.9	5.2	8.0
0.5	3.8	0.5	4.0	3.2	—	1.3
3.0	17.7	10.7	37.4	14.1	5.2	9.3
6.7	0.1	4.7	5.4	12.7	—	—
2.2	—	0.8	1.8	6.7	—	—
0.9	—	3.2	1.2	2.9	—	—
11.2	36.3	5.1	9.7	11.4	1.9	0.9
21.0	36.5	13.6	18.0	33.7	1.9	0.9
1.7	0.1	1.0	1.2	4.0	0.1	14.1
4.3	3.2	1.4	6.2	3.1	—	12.1
0.2	7.0	—	—	—	—	3.0
0.5	10.2	—	—	—	—	45.1
0.1	1.0	—	—	0.1	—	4.1
0.7	18.2	—	—	0.1	—	52.2
0.8	—	—	—	—	1.2	—
5.9	—	8.4	2.7	7.6	21.9	—
1.7	1.6	1.1	1.3	0.9	8.0	—
0.8	14.4	0.6	0.5	0.5	1.5	—
9.1	5.4	6.7	3.7	5.9	18.0	0.1
17.5	21.5	16.7	8.1	14.8	49.5	0.1
1.9	0.7	2.0	0.9	1.2	19.8	—
2.4	0.3	1.6	0.7	0.6	20.4	—
4.2	1.0	3.6	1.6	1.9	40.2	—
10.9	—	13.3	2.4	6.4	—	—
9.6	—	11.5	3.7	3.3	—	—
3.2	—	4.4	0.4	1.7	—	—
5.9	0.5	3.9	2.8	2.1	0.1	2.3
12.3	0.2	16.6	10.9	7.8	0.7	8.4
41.8	0.7	49.6	20.2	21.3	0.8	10.6
5.0	1.1	3.4	7.2	7.1	1.3	0.8

Recommended daily amounts of food energy and nutrients for population groups in the United Kingdom (Department of Health and Social Security, 1979)

Age range[a] years	Occupational category	Energy[b]		Protein[d] g	Thiamin mg	Riboflavin mg
		MJ	kcal			
BOYS						
under 1		(c)	(c)	(e)	0.3	0.4
1		5.0	1200	30	0.5	0.6
2		5.75	1400	35	0.6	0.7
3–4		6.5	1560	39	0.6	0.8
5–6		7.25	1740	43	0.7	0.9
7–8		8.25	1980	49	0.8	1.0
9–11		9.5	2280	57	0.9	1.2
12–14		11.0	2640	66	1.1	1.4
15–17		12.0	2880	72	1.2	1.7
GIRLS						
under 1		(c)	(c)	(e)	0.3	0.4
1		4.5	1100	27	0.4	0.6
2		5.5	1300	32	0.5	0.7
3–4		6.25	1500	37	0.6	0.8
5–6		7.0	1680	42	0.7	0.9
7–8		8.0	1900	47	0.8	1.0
9–11		8.5	2050	51	0.8	1.2
12–14		9.0	2150	53	0.9	1.4
15–17		9.0	2150	53	0.9	1.7
MEN						
18–34	Sedentary	10.5	2510	63	1.0	1.6
	Moderately active	12.0	2900	72	1.2	1.6
	Very active	14.0	3350	84	1.3	1.6
35–64	Sedentary	10.0	2400	60	1.0	1.6
	Moderately active	11.5	2750	69	1.1	1.6
	Very active	14.0	3350	84	1.3	1.6
65–74 }	Assuming a	10.0	2400	60	1.0	1.6
75+ }	sedentary life	9.0	2150	54	0.9	1.6
WOMEN						
18–54	Most occupations	9.0	2150	54	0.9	1.3
	Very active	10.5	2500	62	1.0	1.3
55–74 }	Assuming a	8.0	1900	47	0.8	1.3
75+ }	sedentary life	7.0	1680	42	0.7	1.3
Pregnancy		10.0	2400	60	1.0	1.6
Lactation		11.5	2750	69	1.1	1.8

Nicotinic acid equivalents mg[f]	Total folate[g] μg	Ascorbic acid mg	Vitamin A retinol equivalents μg[h]	Vitamin D[i] cholecalciferol μg	Calcium mg	Iron mg
5	50	20	450	7.5	600	6
7	100	20	300	10	600	7
8	100	20	300	10	600	7
9	100	20	300	10	600	8
10	200	20	300	[i]	600	10
11	200	20	400	[i]	600	10
14	200	25	575	[i]	700	12
16	300	25	725	[i]	700	12
19	300	30	750	[i]	600	12
5	50	20	450	7.5	600	6
7	100	20	300	10	600	7
8	100	20	300	10	600	7
9	100	20	300	10	600	8
10	200	20	300	[i]	600	10
11	200	20	400	[i]	600	10
14	300	25	575	[i]	700	12[k]
16	300	25	725	[i]	700	12[k]
19	300	30	750	[i]	600	12[k]
18	300	30	750	[i]	500	10
18	300	30	750	[i]	500	10
18	300	30	750	[i]	500	10
18	300	30	750	[i]	500	10
18	300	30	750	[i]	500	10
18	300	30	750	[i]	500	10
18	300	30	750	[i]	500	10
18	300	30	750	[i]	500	10
15	300	30	750	[i]	500	12[k]
15	300	30	750		500	12[k]
15	300	30	750	[i]	500	10
15	300	30	750	[i]	500	10
18	500	60	750	10	1200[j]	13
21	400	60	1200	10	1200	15

(footnotes overleaf)

(a) Since the recommendations are average amounts, the figures for each age range represent the amounts recommended at the middle of the range. Within each age range, younger children will need less, and older children more, than the amount recommended.

(b) Megajoules (10^6 joules). Calculated from the relation 1 kilocalorie = 4.184 kilojoules, that is to say, 1 megajoule = 240 kilocalories (1 MJ = 1000 kJ).

(c)

Age range months	BOYS		GIRLS	
	MJ	kcal	MJ	kcal
0–3	2.2	530	2.1	500
3–6	3.0	720	2.8	670
6–9	3.7	880	3.4	810
9–12	4.1	980	3.8	910

(d) Recommended amounts have been calculated as 10% of the recommendations for energy.

(e)

Age range months	BOYS g protein	GIRLS g protein
0–3	13	12.5
3–6	18	17
6–9	22	20
9–12	24.5	23

(f) 1 nicotinic acid equivalent = 1 mg nicotinic acid or 60 mg tryptophan.

(g) No information is available about requirements of children for folate. Graded amounts are recommended between the figure shown for infants under one year, which is based upon the average folate content of mature human nilk, and the 300 μg daily which is suggested for adults.

(h) 1 retinol equivalent = 1 μg retinol of 6 μg β-carotene or 12 μg other biologically active carotenoids.

(i) No dietary sources may be necessary for children and adults who are sufficiently exposed to sunlight, but during the winter children and adolescents should receive 10 μg (400 i.u.) daily by supplementation. Adults with inadequate exposure to sunlight, for example those who are housebound, may also need a supplement of 10 μg daily.

(j) For the last three months of pregnancy only.

(k) This intake may not be sufficient for 10% of girls and women with large menstrual losses.

Reproduced with the permission of the Controller of Her Majesty's Stationery Office.

Further Reading

Braverman's Introduction to the Biochemistry of Foods, Z. Berk (2nd edition, Elsevier, 1976)

Food Science, G. C. Birch, A. G. Cameron and M. Spencer (3rd edition, Pergamon Press, 1986)

Food—the Chemistry of Its Components, T. P. Coultate (The Royal Society of Chemistry, 1984)

Human Nutrition and Dietetics, Sir S. Davidson, R. Passmore, J. F. Brock and A. S. Truswell (7th edition, Churchill Livingstone, 1979)

Food Commodities, B. Davis (Heinemann, 1978)

The Technology of Food Preservation, N. W. Desrosier and J. N. Desrosier (4th edition, AVI Publishing Co., 1977)

Food Science, Nutrition and Health, B. A. Fox and A. G. Cameron (5th edition, Edward Arnold, 1989)

Food Microbiology, W. C. Frazier and D. C. Westhoff (4th edition, McGraw-Hill, 1978)

The New E for Additives, M. Hanssen and J. Marsden (Thorsons, 1987)

Food Poisoning and Food Hygiene, B. C. Hobbs and D. Roberts (5th edition, Edward Arnold, 1987)

Modern Food Microbiology, J. M. Jay (3rd edition, Van Nostrand, Reinhold and Co., 1986)

Food Legislation of the UK, D. J. Jukes (2nd edition, Butterworths, 1987)

Technology of Cereals, N. L. Kent (3rd edition, Pergamon Press, 1983)

Meat Science, R. A. Lawrie (4th edition, Pergamon Press, 1985)

On Food and Cooking, The Science and Lore of the Kitchen, H. McGee (George Allen & Unwin, 1986)

Household Food Consumption and Expenditure: 1984, Ministry of Agriculture, Fisheries and Food (H.M.S.O., 1986)

Manual of Nutrition, Ministry of Agriculture, Fisheries and Food (9th edition, H.M.S.O., 1985)

Principles of Microbiology, T. J. Parry and R. K. Pawsey (2nd edition, Hutchinson Educational, 1984)

McCance and Widdowson's The Composition of Foods, A. A. Paul and D. A. T. Southgate (4th edition, H.M.S.O., 1978)

The Science and Technology of Foods, R. K. Proudlove (Forbes Publications, 1985)

Advanced Human Biology, J. Simkins and J. I. Williams (Unwin Hyman, 1987)

The Prevention of Food Poisoning, J. Trickett (2nd edition, Stanley Thornes, 1986)

Index

Page numbers in *italics* refer to tables